The Well of Ice

An Inishowen Mystery

Andrea Carter

Constable • London

CONSTABLE

First published in Great Britain in 2017 by Constable

This paperback edition published in 2018 by Constable

1 3 5 7 9 10 8 6 4 2

ISBN: 978-1-47212-598-9

Typeset in Bembo by TW Type, Cornwall
Printed and bound in Great Britain by CPI Group (UK) Ltd, Croydon CR0 4YY

Papers used by Constable are from well-managed forests and other responsible sources.

Constable
An imprint of
Little, Brown Book Group
Carmelite House
50 Victoria Embankment
London EC4Y 0DZ

An Hachette UK Company
www.hachette.co.uk

www.littlebrown.co.uk

For my parents Jack and Gloria,
who filled our house with books.

Chapter 1

He hands me a glass of red as the fire crackles gently in the grate and the strains of 'Good King Wenceslas' drift in from the carol singers on the green. The tree looks beautiful, with twinkling white lights and a star glimmering on top.

'It's snowing,' he says. And he smiles as he leans in to . . .

Noise from the street outside jolted me back: voices calling angrily; a rasping cough from a severe case of smoker's phlegm. I turned to the window, mortified, as if my thoughts had been read. Which wasn't likely since I was alone in my office, buried in conveyancing files, exactly where I had been for twelve hours a day the past week, with Leah typing like a demon downstairs.

I stretched out my arms and rubbed my shoulders to relieve the tension in my neck. It was nearly lunchtime and I'd been in the office since seven. The calendar said it was Wednesday 16 December, a week before O'Keeffe & Co. Solicitors closed for Christmas, and we had ten sales to finalise before then. The same thing happened every year. People just had to be in their new houses for Christmas – the world ended on St Stephen's Day.

Not that I was complaining; it was great for business, but a killer on the neck.

In general, things were good. Much of that had to do with my new relationship – if you could call it that – with Molloy. So far we had studiously avoided putting any kind of a label on what had been happening between us these past few months. And we had made a decision to keep things quiet, neither of us ready for the public scrutiny that would inevitably accompany the news that the local sergeant was sleeping with the local solicitor. Or as other people might see it, the prosecution sleeping with the defence.

I had to admit I liked the secrecy of it. I liked his appearance at the back door of my cottage late at night, the way his hand brushed mine when I handed him a legal aid form in court. But if that daydream was anything to go by, I was every inch the sad cliché when it came to Christmas. I'd have to shake that off for a start. The reality was that we hadn't even discussed Christmas, and spending it together might be a step too far if we were trying to keep things quiet. Although there were times when I suspected the only people we were deceiving were ourselves. Glendara is a small town and not much escapes the residents – unless of course they *choose* not to notice something, which happens quite a lot.

The truth was that Molloy was the first good thing to happen to me in a while. Our relationship had made the transition from friendship to whatever-it-was-now the day I'd heard about Luke Kirby's release; Kirby – the man who'd killed my sister. It was Molloy who had told me, and without him I'm not sure how I'd have handled it.

Apart from having to absorb the news myself, I'd had to tell my parents. I didn't want them to find out the way I had, considerably after the fact, or from somebody other than me. Worse, I certainly didn't want them reading about it in the paper. Although with the benefit of hindsight, I could see there had never been much risk of that. There had been no publicity whatsoever, which was why I hadn't heard about it before Molloy told me. No journalists waiting at the gates of the prison, no appalled public outcry that this monster should now be on the loose again, free to walk among ordinary decent citizens, to prey on other vulnerable women. Nothing. My sister's killer had been released quietly, free to return to the UK, which according to Molloy was what he had done and where he intended to remain. Faye's death was old news, yesterday's chip paper, replaced by even more salacious stories of sexual predation, depravity and violence. A murder trial in Dublin had been dominating all available front-page space for weeks.

I understood that Kirby had to be released eventually, of course I did; I'm a lawyer. He had served more than nine years of his ten-year sentence, longer than average for manslaughter, which is exactly what I would have told a client if I'd been asked. But when it's personal, it's different, a realisation that had hit me during the trial. And his release had brought back sickening memories, which had only ever been just below the surface.

I sipped at the coffee on my desk. It was cold and bitter and utterly disgusting, but my throat was dry so I drank it. My throat went dry whenever I thought about Luke Kirby, although I was trying not to let that happen too often any more. It was a precarious peace of mind that I had reached, but a peace nonetheless.

I heard a cry of frustration from downstairs, not the first I'd heard this morning. Leah, like myself, was buried under a mountain of paperwork, probably more so since she was the one who had to type everything up. She didn't have to deal with the phone this morning, at least, but that was merely temporary. We had closed the office to the public for a few hours to clear some of the backlog.

I flipped open my Dictaphone to extract the tape, grabbed the stack of files I'd been working on and headed downstairs, approaching the reception desk with trepidation. Leah looked up at the sound of my footsteps, glaring at me over a mountain of files and stopping me in my tracks. The tape I'd completed remained between my teeth, the files I was carrying close to toppling.

'Please don't give me anything else until I finish this lot,' she pleaded. 'There's no room, apart from anything else.'

She was right. I had no idea how she was going to manage to extricate herself when she needed to, without mixing everything up. I staggered through the door of the waiting room, dumped the files I was carrying on one of the chairs and spat out the tape.

'Okay,' I said slowly, glancing with concern at the list I'd placed on top of the files.

She caught my look and sighed. 'At least go through that lot and let me know what you absolutely need done today. I'll do my best.'

'Agreed,' I said before she could change her mind. I looked at the clock above the reception desk. It was five to one. 'Come on, let's leave this lot for half an hour and get some lunch.'

My right foot slid from under me when I stepped out onto the footpath, and I'd have landed firmly on my backside if it weren't for Leah's quick reflexes. She grabbed hold of my elbow and set me back on my feet with a laugh.

'Cripes. Thanks for that,' I said, reaching for the wall of the office and pulling my hand back the second I touched its icy surface.

I looked down. The pavement was glistening with tiny patches of white. 'We'd better get some salt on there before this afternoon, or we're going to have a load of claims on our hands on top of everything else. It wasn't like that this morning, was it?'

'No, it's definitely getting colder,' Leah agreed. 'Highland Radio is predicting snow for the weekend.'

'Really? A white Christmas, do you reckon?' I breathed in. The air tasted of mint. I had a flashback to my earlier daydream, which I shook off.

She grinned. 'Hopefully.'

I picked my way up the hill with carefully tentative steps. It certainly looked as if snow was a possibility. There was an icy stillness to the air, and the pale sky seemed far too low, as if a false base had been slipped beneath the real thing, lending a claustrophobic, oppressive feel to the day. I had a brief, inexplicable sense of foreboding, but it dissipated as soon as we turned the corner onto the square and were hit with a blast of 'Jingle Bell Rock' from the speakers that had been set up beside the tree.

The huge tree erected in the town square every year by local businesses glowed cheerfully, its multicoloured lights brightening the grey day, its branches covered in a dusting of fake snow, which if Leah were correct might not be needed in a day or two. A few years previously the Glendara Christmas tree had collapsed, brought down by high winds, taking with it two telephone poles and cutting off the electricity to the square for days. The baubles within arm's reach had disappeared quickly, but when an eighty-three-year-old client handed me a cup of

5

tea with a giant angel perched proudly on her mantelpiece, I was baffled. How she'd managed to nab the highest decoration from the tilted tree remained a mystery, but since then sturdy wires had been attached every year to ground the tree in place like a tent. Although there seemed little danger of such high winds this year – it was just very cold.

Town was busy, with cars double-parked all around the square and two tractors facing each other off outside the hardware shop. A gang of kids from the community school lounged on the wall beside the tree, eating chips from steaming greaseproof bags and drinking cans of Coke. They pushed one another and larked about, chasing around the tree like five year olds and stealing each other's food. I couldn't quite understand the attraction of eating outside on a day like today, but I guessed it was good to get out of the school for an hour. I assumed they were in the middle of Christmas exams. The smell of vinegar made my nose tingle and my mouth water as I walked past them.

I was still distracted by the food when I felt a tap on my shoulder.

'Well, solicitor. How are you doing?'

I turned quickly to a broad grin I hadn't seen in a while. The bearer of the grin, Eddie Kearney, was an old client of mine. He'd taken off to Australia to make his fortune but he could only have been gone nine months at the most. Not long to make your fortune.

'Eddie. When did you get back?'

He shook my hand vigorously. 'Sunday night,' he replied. 'I'm just home for a few weeks for the Christmas. See the mother and the sisters and the weans.' He lowered his voice conspiratorially. 'Thought I might have to come home earlier, but I wasn't needed after all that. You heard that mad one pleaded guilty?'

'I did.' Kearney had been a witness in a case that I'd been involved in, rather a reluctant witness if I remembered correctly. But I didn't want to get into that now.

'Are you heading for the Oak?' he asked.

I nodded.

'I'll walk with you so. Calling in to see the sister. Haven't seen her since I got back.'

Eddie's sister Carole was the barmaid in the Oak. He'd worked there himself before he took off to Sydney.

We walked up the street together, Eddie taking up a position between Leah and myself; I sensed it was all he could do not to link arms. He'd lost none of his swagger since he'd been in Australia, but I imagined there was a maturity about him that had been absent before. His hairstyle had certainly improved. Before he'd left Inishowen, Eddie had favoured the straight-up, caught-in-a-strong-gale look and jeans that were so low-slung there were times when I feared for his modesty. Now he was sporting a short back and sides and wearing a tie, and the sun seemed to have cleared up his acne. I wondered if he'd given up the weed, the reason why he had been such a regular client of mine before he left.

A blast of warm air and the original 'Jingle Bells' greeted us when we opened the door of the pub. Eddie stood aside to allow Leah and myself to go ahead of him, something I couldn't have imagined the old Eddie doing. Not because he wouldn't have wanted to be polite but because it simply wouldn't have occurred to him. The old Eddie had no sense; this new one seemed to have acquired some.

The Oak was packed and warm as toast, a roaring turf fire doing the honours. Red and green fairy lights had been strung around the walls and sprigs of holly tucked behind the

7

old black-and-white photographs of the town. Eight bizarrely proportioned hand-knitted reindeer pulled a sleigh suspended above the bar, the one at the front bearing a bright red nose and a rather malevolent-looking grin.

Eddie's sister Carole was standing at the coffee machine behind the counter, her blonde hair tied up in a loose ponytail. She had her back to us when Eddie leaned over the bar and called to her, an excited grin on his face. Though she must have heard him, she didn't respond but finished what she was doing, emptying the coffee grounds and replacing the beans. He called again, impatient for a response, and this time she turned, her expression blank as if she didn't know who he was.

Leah and I exchanged a glance. Hadn't their mother told her he was home? She clearly hadn't expected to see him. But surprised or not, it wasn't the reaction you'd expect from a sister greeting her brother home from the other side of the world. Eddie's grin faded, disappointment on his face. His reaction seemed to bring his sister to her senses and she managed to pull herself together. She smiled broadly as if that had been her intention all along. And then something crossed her face. Fear.

Eddie didn't seem to notice. He looked relieved when Carole gave him an awkward hug, and perched on a bar stool with a pint while Leah and I ordered sandwiches and coffee and left them to chat. We found a table by the window to wait for our food.

Leah frowned. 'Am I imagining things, or was that a bit odd?'

'Maybe they're not that close?'

She nodded. 'Oh aye, there'd be a right age gap between them all right – a good ten years probably. There's a sister in the middle. Still, he has been away for a while.'

My phone vibrated on the table and I picked it up. It was a text from Molloy. One word: *Tonight?*

I must have smiled without realising it, because Leah looked at me curiously. 'Good news?'

I flushed. 'What?'

'The text. You look happy.'

'Oh, it's nothing. I'll answer it later.' I put the phone in my bag and looked around me. The pub was full. We'd nabbed the only free table. 'What's going on? Why is it so busy in here?'

'It's the last cattle mart of the year. Pre-Christmas lunch, I suppose,' Leah said.

'There's none next week?'

She shook her head. I looked around me at the ruddy faces, the checked shirts and the heavy boots, smiling weather-beaten faces with a holiday cheer even though all would be working over Christmas. Carole waved at us from the bar to signal that our food was ready.

When we took our seats again I said, 'I hope the snow doesn't affect the flights from Derry on Friday.'

Leah looked up from her chicken sandwich, eyebrows raised.

'I've decided I'm going to fly to Dublin to close that sale,' I said. 'I'm not too keen on driving with the roads like this. I might not get back.'

I was acting for a couple called the Greys, who were buying an old manor house further up the coast. It would be a three-way completion, which meant that the meeting to close the sale would involve the seller's solicitor, the bank's solicitor and myself. It was the biggest purchase I'd done since I'd come to Donegal, and I was anxious about it. If a document was missing or didn't meet with the approval of the bank's solicitors, then the money wouldn't be forthcoming and the sale wouldn't complete, which meant no keys for my clients before Christmas. And since the seller's solicitor and my clients' bank's solicitor were both in Dublin, I was the one who was expected to travel. I hoped to be able to get down and back in the one day, which wouldn't be possible if I drove – the drive to Dublin took me four hours at the best of times.

'Is all the paperwork done, by the way?' I asked.

Leah nodded and swallowed her mouthful of sandwich. 'The marriage certificate came in this morning, so I've done up all the declarations. It's ready to go.'

'That's great. The Greys are coming in tomorrow morning to sign.' I took a sip of my coffee. 'Have you seen the pictures of the house, by the way? The estate agent's brochure is still on the file. It's a gorgeous spot. Beautiful grounds, just on the water.'

Leah shook her head, concentrating on her food. No interest in discussing work any further at lunchtime.

'They're planning on opening it as a hotel. Maybe something to think about for your wedding?' I smiled.

She stopped chewing and looked up. Now she was interested.

That evening I left the office feeling as if I'd been wrung out like a J-cloth. It was nine o'clock and I'd been in the office for fourteen hours. Although I'd stayed a little longer than necessary because I wanted to ring my parents about Christmas. I wasn't sure what their plans were, but I knew that if they wanted me to spend it with them, I would.

I hadn't been able to get hold of them the last few times I'd rung, but I took this to be a good sign. For years after my sister's death they put their lives on hold, too grief-stricken to do anything other than get through the day, bitter that Kirby had been convicted of manslaughter rather than murder. But recently they had become involved with a support group for parents who had lost children – adult and otherwise – and it seemed to be doing them good. They'd received grief counselling with this group, which meant they had coped far better than I had expected with the news of Kirby's release.

This time when I called, my mother answered on the second ring.

'Ah, Sarah,' she said. 'I was just saying to your father that I must ring you tonight.'

Since I'd come to Donegal, I'd been using a shortened version of my second name, Benedicta, for reasons that seemed to make sense at the time (mainly because I didn't want people to know about my past). As time passed and the story of my sister's death faded from the headlines, it seemed less and less necessary, but I was used to 'Ben' now and I kind of liked it. My mother still used my first name. I used to correct her, but I didn't any more.

'I'm just letting you know I have to be in Dublin for a closing on Friday,' I said. 'I thought we could meet for a late lunch or something?'

'Oh, that's great. We'll get to see you before we go,' she said.

'Go?' I repeated.

'Your father and I have decided we'd like to go away for Christmas this year. So rather impetuously we've gone ahead and booked something.' She sounded a little sheepish.

I was astonished. 'Impetuous' and 'my parents' were not words that would normally have been found in the same sentence. My surprise stopped me from asking the next question before my mother answered it.

'Iceland,' she announced. 'We're going to Iceland.' There was a moment's hesitation before she added, 'You're welcome to come too if you'd like?'

'Oh no. I'll be fine. I'll stay here. Loads of work to catch up on. I think that's a great idea. You'll love Iceland.'

'Are you certain? I'm sure we could book another seat?'

I smiled to myself. The offer was half-hearted at best. 'No, honestly. You deserve a bit of time to yourselves.'

'We're actually going with the group we met through counselling. We thought it might be fun.'

'Sounds great. I might stay with you on Friday then? Since I'm not going to be seeing you next week. I can come back up here on Saturday.'

'Lovely.'

I hung up the phone feeling relieved. I'd had reservations about spending Christmas together just the three of us, especially this year, and it seemed they felt the same. And their absence meant that I could spend it with Molloy. I changed my booking to fly back on Saturday afternoon, with the intention of doing some Christmas shopping before I left.

I dearly love my old Mini, but even I would admit that her heating isn't exactly efficient. It was while I was waiting for her windscreen to thaw out that I realised I hadn't replied to Molloy's text, but when I took my phone out of my bag, it was dead. I decided to call him when I got home. I couldn't face going back to the office for a charger and letting the car freeze up again. But driving out onto the main road, peering through the thawed lower half of the windscreen, I saw that the lights were still on in the Garda station.

Garda Andy McFadden greeted me from behind a sad-looking mini Christmas tree perched on the counter.

'I like the decorations. Very festive,' I said, glancing at the strip of bald blue tinsel taped half-heartedly to the calendar behind him.

He grinned. 'Neither budget nor enthusiasm stretch too far

at the minute.' He shunted a tin of Roses towards me. 'But we do have chocolate.'

McFadden had lost weight over the last few months and his mood had been less than cheerful, so it was good to see him smile. I took a sweet. I like the coffee ones no one else does, which works in my favour.

'You're about the town late. Everything all right?' he asked.

I racked my brains for a reason why I'd be calling into the station at 9 p.m. on a Wednesday evening; stupidly, it hadn't occurred to me that McFadden would be here on his own.

'I wondered if you had statements in that burglary case for next week? I'm bringing some files home with me,' was the best I could come up with. I hoped it hadn't been McFadden who'd told me the statements I was referring to wouldn't be available until after Christmas.

Before he could reply, the door opened bringing a blast of cold air, and Molloy himself appeared wearing a heavy Garda coat and gloves. I felt the dart I always did, while he glanced in my direction with the merest hint of an eyebrow raise.

'Ben's looking for statements in that burglary case,' McFadden said. 'The Buncrana one that's up again on Tuesday.'

'Not ready yet,' he said, pulling off his gloves. 'There's one missing but you'll have the rest of them by lunchtime tomorrow.'

'Okay, thanks,' I said, unsure what to do next. It bothered me sometimes how easily he could dissemble. I wasn't quite so good at it. 'Right, I'd better go.'

'I'll walk you out. I've left something in the car,' Molloy said, pushing open the door of the station and allowing me to go ahead of him. I felt the chill from his coat as I passed by.

On the step outside, I turned. 'Sorry I didn't reply to your text. I've had a crazy day.'

His face softened. 'It's fine. As it turns out, I can't do tonight myself now. I'm sorry.'

'Everything okay?' I asked. Despite his smile, there was something odd in his expression. Something hidden.

He nodded. 'Just work. I'll call you later, or tomorrow.'

He brushed a stray hair from my face and I felt his breath on my cheek. Suddenly the door to the station opened and he pulled back.

McFadden's face appeared. 'Phone for you, Sarge.'

Chapter Two

There was no sign of the threatened snow on Thursday morning when I opened my curtains, but the light was still that pale, eerie grey. I live in Malin, a pretty village a few miles from Glendara accessed by a ten-arched eighteenth-century bridge. The bridge crosses the Ballyboe river as it makes its way to the sea, and leads to a triangular green at the centre of the village, which my cottage overlooks. I watched through the window as three fat robins hopped along one of the benches searching for food. I suspected most of their hopes were pinned on the bakery van delivering to the grocery across the green, if they could avoid their breakfast being swiped by the gulls wheeling and diving above them. The ground would be hard this morning – condensation on the inside of the window indicated another bitterly cold day.

I showered and dressed in a charcoal-grey trouser suit and boots and headed downstairs. Guinness, my enormous black tomcat, was waiting patiently on the step when I opened the back door, and he wove a figure-of-eight through my legs as I walked back to the kitchen. While I fed him and made coffee, I wondered what had kept Molloy so busy the night before. I hadn't seen him since the weekend, which wasn't unusual, but there had been something about his demeanour that made me uneasy. I realised of course that I might never know. Molloy shared only what he wanted to – we had that trait in common.

But there was no time to worry about that now. Since we'd been closed to the public the day before and I'd be in Dublin tomorrow, the office would be busy with back-to-back appointments all day. I left the house at ten to nine.

The waiting room was full when I arrived. I stuck my head in briefly and took in some expected faces and a few surprises, the coughs and splutters of a December waiting room offering me no enticement to hang around. At reception, Leah was on the phone but handed me the first file before I headed upstairs.

My first appointment was with the Greys, the couple whose purchase I was travelling to Dublin to close. I sorted through the file and put the documents in order before buzzing Leah to send them up.

Ian and Abby Grey were an attractive-looking couple, still slim and fit in their late fifties. She was petite, with a small pointed face, brown eyes and a pixie cut of grey-blonde hair, while he reminded me of a middle-aged Paul Newman, complete with chin cleft and smooth jaw. Minus the famous blue eyes – Ian's, like his wife's, were brown.

'Greysbridge is quite a place if the photographs are anything to go by,' I said as I passed them the last of the mortgage documents, marking with an X where they needed to sign. It occurred to me that they were taking on quite a project at this stage of their lives. Their mortgage was small in relation to the purchase price of the house, but it was still a huge undertaking.

'Isn't it?' Abby smiled.

Her accent, like her husband's, was Anglo-Irish. When I'd first met them, I'd wondered if it came from time spent in

England or otherwise, but it hadn't come up and I didn't have the nerve to ask. People can be funny about these things.

'It will be so lovely to have it back in the family again,' she said. 'You should come up and see it.'

'Back in the family?' I said, surprised. 'When you mentioned applying for permission to use it as a small hotel, I just assumed it was a business venture.'

Abby's eyes widened suddenly and flickered towards her husband, as if she was afraid she had said too much.

He didn't seem especially perturbed. 'No, it's true, we do intend running it as a hotel. We've put everything we have into it, so it will have to provide us with *some* kind of a living. We're thinking family occasions, small weddings, that sort of thing, although we'll try and avoid the corporate side of things – we'd like to make it more personal.' He replaced the cap on his fountain pen. 'But Abby's right. The house was owned by my grandfather, although it hasn't been in the family for a couple of generations.' He winced. 'Lost it in rather insalubrious circumstances, I'm afraid. Cards, I believe. Not the family's finest hour.'

I shook my head. 'Funny, it never occurred to me there was a family connection, despite the name. Still, you must be proud you've managed to buy it back.'

He looked at his wife and smiled. 'I think we are, aren't we?'

She nodded eagerly. 'Oh yes. It's such a fine house. It's been allowed to deteriorate rather, so it will be good to bring it back to life. Especially now that our son has agreed to help us run it for a bit.'

Ian placed his hand briefly on his wife's knee and she smiled up at him.

I witnessed their signatures. 'I didn't know you had a son.'

'He's at school in Dublin but he's going to come up as soon

as we move in. Take a year or two off before he starts college.' Abby reached for her bag. 'Is that it?'

'Not quite,' I said. 'There are a few extra declarations that I can't witness.' I took some printed sheets from the file to which Leah had attached yellow Post-its. 'These need to be sworn in front of a commissioner for oaths. So, if you don't mind, I'm going to send you down to Hal McKinney.'

Ian looked amused. 'The undertaker? That sounds ominous.'

I smiled. 'Hal's a commissioner for oaths as well as being an undertaker and a mechanic.' I handed him the sheets. 'Leah will give you an envelope for these downstairs. He's expecting you – just sign them and drop them back when they're done. You won't need to come back up to me.' I stood. 'And that's it. I'll give you a call tomorrow from Dublin to let you know how it's gone, and whether you can pick up the keys.'

Abby crossed her fingers and raised them in a salute.

Leah buzzed just as the door closed behind the Greys.

'Your next appointment has popped out to take a call, but Stan MacLochlainn wants to know if you can see him in the meantime,' she asked. 'He says it will only take five minutes.' She made no attempt to conceal her scepticism, despite Stan's obvious proximity; I could hear his voice.

The last thing I needed today was an extra client, but I knew Stan. He would wait until I saw him even if it took all day, and insist on chatting to Leah in the meantime. I decided to rescue her.

'Okay,' I sighed. 'But tell him I haven't got long.'

With seconds, Stan materialised in the doorway of my office, a vision in purple and pinstripe: aubergine hair styled in a quiff, diamond studs in his nose and ears and a black striped waistcoat with a crocus boutonnière. Despite indications to the contrary, Stan wasn't gay, although I suspected he took firm advantage of any misapprehension about his sexual preferences. He was also a bloody good hairdresser, or so I'd been told. By him.

He was pink and breathless, forehead glistening with perspiration. 'You have to do something,' he announced. 'I know the guards are completely useless, but they might listen to you.'

'I have to do something about what?' I asked.

He came the rest of the way into the room and flopped onto the seat vacated by Abby Grey, leaving the door wide open. 'The noise from the Oak. It's driving me insane.'

I sighed. 'It's a pub, Stan. You knew that when you moved in. It's why the rent was so low. Of course there's going to be noise.'

Stan's hairdressing salon, Illusions Hair Design, was two doors away from the Oak, and the flat he lived in was above the pub itself. I'd acted for Tony Craig, the owner of the Oak, when he'd rented the flat to Stan a year before. Tony also owned the building Stan's salon was in, but he'd been reluctant to rent the flat out because of the noise from the pub. But Stan had convinced him he was fine with it, so Tony had reduced the rent to take account and a clause to that effect had been inserted into the lease.

Stan looked at me now, exasperated. 'It's not during opening hours that I have a problem with it. I'm used to that. I'm a night owl. I'm talking about six o'clock in the morning. What the hell is that all about?'

'Six o'clock in the morning?' I repeated.

He picked up a legal pad from my desk and began to fan himself with it. 'Aye. Two mornings this week, yesterday and this morning again, I've been woken by a dull thumping noise that sounds as if someone is dragging bodies about. What the hell is it? Dracula climbing back into his coffin before daylight comes?'

I tried not to smile. Stan didn't seem to be in the mood.

'It's driving me demented,' he said. 'I'd wear earplugs but then I wouldn't hear the alarm. There shouldn't even *be* anyone in there at six o'clock in the morning, you know.'

'Is it coming from the pub itself?' I asked.

Stan shook his head. 'I can't tell. The first time it happened, I went down – in my dressing gown; God knows who might have seen me – climbed in through the yard at the back and banged on the door. I thought it might be coming from the cellar, but I couldn't see anything. The lights didn't even seem to be on. The noise stopped, but as soon as I left, it started up again.'

I paused. 'Have you thought maybe it might have been a—'

Stan was there before me. 'Lock-in?' He shook his head. 'Nah. I'd know if it was a lock-in. I'd hear voices. And music. There were no voices. Just banging against walls and scraping floors.' He gave me a lopsided look. 'Anyway, who has a lock-in on a Tuesday night?'

I sat back in my chair. 'What do you want me to do?'

He put the pad back down. 'I don't know; write a solicitor's letter, issue proceedings for noise pollution? You tell me.' He waved his hand dismissively, a large amethyst ring glinting in the artificial light. 'Whatever you solicitors normally do in this situation.'

'Stan, you know I act for Tony, so I can't write a solicitor's letter to him or issue legal proceedings against him.'

Stan shook his head. 'I don't want to go to anyone else. That other boy who dealt with the lease charged me a bloody fortune and all he did was read the thing. You did all the drafting.'

I decided not to go into the importance of independent legal advice again. I'd already done that when I'd persuaded him he needed a separate solicitor for the lease.

'I could have a word with Tony if you like? See what's causing it,' I suggested. 'But if I don't get anywhere, you'll have to go to someone else if you want to take it further.'

Stan sighed. 'Aye, fair enough. Anything to make that bloody noise stop. I'm so knackered that I'm going to cut someone's throat instead of their hair by mistake. There's going to be a Sweeney Todd situation in Glendara and it will all be Tony Craig's fault.'

Now I grinned. 'Have you tried speaking to him yourself?'

'I can't find him, can I? I've been trying him these last few days but I keep getting a foreign ringtone.'

When Stan had left, I tried Tony's mobile but was greeted with the long bleep that indicated the phone was in another jurisdiction, so I left a message. It was then that I realised I hadn't seen Tony myself for a few days. Carole had been in the Oak every day this week.

By the time I left the office it was nearly 8 p.m. My flight to Dublin left at 7.30 the next morning, so I took my briefcase and papers with me, calling in to the supermarket to get some milk before driving home. When I emerged, I was surprised to see a light on in Phyllis Kettle's bookshop across the square. After a brief hesitation, I crossed the street.

I pushed open the door, bell tinkling in that old-fashioned way Phyllis has never seen fit to change. The scent of cinnamon and oranges filled the shop, electric icicles hung from the shelves and people stood about chatting in the warm light, sipping from cups of mulled wine and diving into plates of mini mince pies. The bookseller glanced at me from the cash register over a pair of half-moon spectacles, mid sale, a queue in front of her. Now I saw why she was still open. There were eight shopping days till Christmas and Phyllis was nothing if not a businesswoman. I waved at her and she smiled, and I made my way towards the back of the shop.

There is a small recess under the winding staircase that leads to Phyllis's flat, of which I am particularly fond. It has a basket chair and an old-fashioned reading lamp and room to accommodate only one person. Not only is it almost completely cut off from the rest of the shop, but it is on these shelves that I have found some absolute gems, and it is to here that I always gravitate. Unless someone has made it there before me. Today I was lucky.

I was reaching for an old P. G. Wodehouse hardback when something brushed against my legs. I looked down to see a black-and-white Border collie gazing mournfully up at me.

'Hi, Fred. What are you doing here?'

Fred spent most of his time at Phyllis's feet behind the counter; I wondered what had caused him to leave her side. I rubbed his silky head. Despite my tiredness and the realisation that I should be at home packing for the morning, I sank back into the old basket chair and took my time flicking through a stack of books on the ground beside me, while Fred rested his chin on my knee. After a while, I felt myself drifting off. A loud sigh from Fred brought me back and I roused myself. I needed to get home if I was to have any sleep before my flight. Taking a book on gardening for my mother and the P. G. Wodehouse for my father, I made my way to the cash register with the dog in my wake. The shop had cleared, empty plates and cups were scattered here and there around the shelves, and Phyllis looked shattered.

'Did you decide to have a party?' I asked.

The bookseller smiled. 'A wee bit of bribery never does any harm.' She leaned down to scratch behind Fred's ears. 'Poor old soul. He's feeling neglected, still hasn't forgiven me for leaving him for three weeks. Tony took good care of you, though, didn't he?' she said, running her fingers along the dog's nose as he gazed adoringly up at her. 'He was bloody fat when I got back – got all the leftovers from the pub.'

Phyllis had just returned from Borneo, which was where I suspected the rather spectacular outfit she was wearing – a royal-blue ankle-length dress with large red print – had come from. Phyllis isn't a small woman, but no one could describe her dress sense as cautious.

She straightened herself with a groan. 'Do you want me to wrap these?'

'Yes please, Phyllis. Separately if you would. They're for my parents.'

'Going home for Christmas?' She eyed me curiously as she rooted out scissors and Sellotape.

'Doesn't look like it, no. I thought I would be, but my parents are off to Iceland.'

Her face lit up. 'Oh, great choice. Reykjavik is wonderful. And the hot springs are amazing.' Her eyes narrowed. 'You weren't tempted to go with them?'

I shook my head.

Her lip curled in amusement. 'Something more enticing in Glendara, by any chance?'

And in that one question, I realised that all my suspicions were correct. Molloy and I weren't fooling anyone, at least not Phyllis.

I changed the subject, not quite ready for one of Phyllis's interrogations. 'Is Tony away himself, by the way?'

She frowned. 'I don't think so. Why?'

'You said he took care of Fred while you were on holidays, but I haven't seen him around for a while. It's always Carole in the pub these days.'

Phyllis grinned. 'That can't be good for business. I'm sure he'll turn up. What kind of a publican would leave his pub at Christmas?'

'True.'

She finished wrapping the books, then I handed her a note and she opened the cash register. While she was searching for change, she broke off suddenly and looked up.

'If you're going to be here, do you fancy coming to mine for Christmas dinner? I've decided to have a few people over. First time I'll have been in Glendara for Christmas for a while – I usually like to be gone this time of year, but I can't leave poor old Fred again.'

When I hesitated, she grinned mischievously. 'Only if you're going to be on your own, of course. I'd hate to see you pulling the wishbone by yourself . . .'

Chapter Three

It was pitch black when I left the house the next morning, and bitterly cold. A light sprinkling of snow had fallen overnight, a day earlier than expected, gathering in the eaves and by the sides of the road. I suspected it was a mere precursor of something more significant to come. I took my time driving down the peninsula. The road across the mountain to Quigley's Point is tough going at the best of times, full of unexpected bends, but lethal in any kind of icy conditions, especially in the dark. The heating in the Mini had just about kicked in by the time I reached the Foyle, where it began to snow again, making me wonder if the plane would even take off; I didn't fancy having to drive the whole way to Dublin in this weather. On the other hand – I stole a glance at the clock on the dashboard – if the flight left on time, I was going to miss it; the speed at which I was forced to drive meant I would be half an hour late to the airport.

As it turned out, the flight left an hour later than scheduled, but my meeting wasn't until twelve so I had plenty of time. Although I'd have preferred the extra hour in bed instead of in Derry airport's draughty departure area.

The flight from Dublin to Derry is by way of a thirty-two-seater turbo-prop plane, not one for the faint-hearted. I like it. It reminds me of a bus service — it's rare that I don't run into someone I know, and this morning was no different. As we waited for the call to board, I noticed Carole from the Oak sitting a couple of seats away from me. She briefly caught my eye and studiously avoided my gaze from then on. I was happy not to force the issue. I generally like to be alone with my newspaper both on and off the plane, and had never been a great fan of Carole's anyway.

Unfortunately, on the plane, we were seated together.

'Oh, hi,' I said, keeping up the pretence that we'd only just seen one another. 'Cold morning.'

'Aye, it's baltic.'

I shoved my briefcase beneath the seat in front. 'I wasn't sure we'd be able to take off.'

'I wouldn't know. It's my first time. I usually take the bus,' she said in a tone that implied no small degree of resentment towards those who didn't usually take the bus.

'I've done that too,' I said. 'It's a good service. But if you have to be in Dublin early, you really do have to fly.'

I don't know why I felt the need to justify myself. The reality was that I couldn't afford the time away from the office that driving would entail. But — and I sighed inwardly at this — it wasn't the first time I'd been on the back foot with Carole; she could be harsh in her judgements of people she didn't know, and not slow in offering her opinion.

I took my seat and was surprised to find myself squashed into a tighter space than usual. Though petite, Carole had managed to take over both armrests, and her elbows encroached even further as she shook out her magazine. With difficulty, I snapped my seat belt shut.

'You heading down for business, then?' she asked. Despite her obvious resentment, her tone was inquisitive.

I nodded. 'Yes. You?'

I wasn't surprised she sidestepped the question. With Carole, information was generally a one-way street. She sniffed. 'How long is the flight?'

I checked my watch. 'We should be landing about half past nine, all going well.'

She didn't respond, just stared straight ahead and chewed the nail of her index finger, before picking up her magazine again. This time I noticed a set of wooden rosary beads on her lap. She caught my glance and quickly gathered them up to shove into the pocket of her coat.

'Is Tony on holidays, by the way?' I asked.

Carole peered at me over her magazine, the headline on the cover *Mother marries daughter's killer. Pregnant with twins at fifty-five!*

'Why?' she asked.

'I haven't seen him around for a while. With Christmas coming up, I thought it would be his busiest time.'

'He's got me,' she said defensively.

I backed off. 'Of course.'

Carole shrugged and returned to biting her nails and reading her magazine, which she continued to do for the remainder of the flight.

We landed at half past nine on the dot. The weather in Dublin was no different from Derry – a flurry of snow greeted us as we made our way into the terminal building, a crocodile of hunched and for the most part suited individuals carrying briefcases and coats above their heads, trying their best not to get soaked.

Liam McLaughlin, the estate agent from Glendara, was sitting in the waiting area when we walked through.

He grinned when he saw me and tapped his watch. 'What time do you call this? You're over an hour late.'

'Hardly my fault.' I paused to chat to him and lost Carole at the same time. Two birds with the one stone.

Liam nodded to her as she passed and she gave him a smile.

'How'd you manage that?' I asked, nudging him. 'I've been sitting beside her the whole way down and she hasn't smiled at me once.'

'It's my irresistible charm,' he said with a smirk. 'What are you down for?'

'Sale closing.'

'Without me?' He faked indignation.

'Not all the conveyancing I do is with you, Liam. What has you in Dublin anyway?'

'Ach, an auld course. One of those continuing education yokes. Dull as fuck . . . Stayed for a few pints last night so thought I'd treat myself to a flight rather than driving up and down.'

'Good plan. Especially in this weather.' I glanced through the windows of the terminal. Slush covered the runway and the sky looked full and dark.

'Are we going to get those two farm sales done next week?' Liam asked.

'I hope so. Give Leah a shout when you get back to Glendara and she'll tell you if there's any hold-up with the cheques.'

'Will do,' he said as he headed off towards the boarding gate with a wave.

I took a taxi into town, catching a glimpse of Carole dragging a large suitcase from the baggage carousel on my way through the airport. I wondered where she was off to with so much luggage. If she was going to be away for a while, I supposed Tony must have reappeared to run the pub. The Oak had various part-timers who stepped in now and then, but none who could have taken charge. I decided to give him a call again later about Stan.

The sale closing went smoothly, apart from a slight hiccup when a property search in the Registry of Deeds couldn't be located but turned up just in time, and an uncomfortable moment when the solicitor for the bank and I recognised one another from a time I was sure neither of us had any desire to remember. By unexpressed mutual agreement it wasn't referred to and the moment passed. Law in Ireland is small; these things happen.

I telephoned the Greys to deliver the good news on my way out of the enormous cube of green glass that housed the seller's solicitor's office, and when I finished the call my head was split-ting. I hadn't had anything to eat since five; I needed coffee and something sweet. When I looked around, I saw that I wasn't far from where I'd worked years before, and I remembered a place I used to go, a little Italian that did great pizzas and pastries. I wondered if it was still there.

The pavement was slushy and unpleasant as I picked my way carefully along the Luas tracks. Pedestrians passed with the equivalent of snow tyres on their shoes, a fad that hadn't yet reached Donegal. And then I spotted it, the Italian, in a little square between the Luas and the Liffey.

I ordered a cappuccino and a Danish at the counter and chose a table by the window, tucking my briefcase and bag beneath my seat. Someone had left a paper on the table and I picked it up, the headline on the front page catching my eye. *Rural Garda stations set to close!* The image below was shocking – dozens of naked, bleeding people. Then I read the caption underneath the picture: *Hundreds take part in 'bloody' protest against bullfighting in Madrid.* I smiled. The headline and picture didn't match. I sipped my coffee and read the piece on Garda stations – . . . *rural Ireland is gradually being closed down. What will be next? Our post offices, our doctor's surgeries?* – until my phone vibrated in my bag and I took it out to answer it. Molloy.

As usual, he dispensed with opening pleasantries. 'You're in Dublin.'

'You got my message, then.'

'I did. Sorry I didn't get back to you last night . . .' His voice began to fade in and out. 'I'm going to lose you . . . I'm on the Muff road.'

The road between Derry and Quigley's Point is a notorious black spot for mobile phone coverage, probably because of its proximity to the border between Northern Ireland and the Republic. I'd often lost the connection there during an important exchange.

'Text me,' I said in a loud whisper.

'When are you back?' he asked, his voice muffled by static.

'Tomorrow. I'm staying with my parents tonight,' I said, but I had no idea whether he heard me or not – the connection was gone.

I tried to ring back, but the call went straight through to voicemail and I didn't leave a message. We seemed to be finding it difficult to communicate at the moment, and I couldn't blame it all on static.

I flicked to the article connected to the bloody photograph: *Thousands of Spaniards have taken to the streets to demand an end to the centuries-old tradition of bullfighting in the city. Protesters covered themselves in red paint and carried banners with captions such as 'Bullfighting, a national shame', and 'The torture of animals is not entertainment'. There were a number of arrests.*

When I left the café, the sky was heavy with the next fall of snow. Walking back towards the Luas, I tried Tony Craig's mobile again. Again it rang out, but this time the ringtone was local, so he was back in the jurisdiction. I sent him a text asking him to give me a call when he had the chance.

A tram approached and I stood at the edge of the tracks to let it pass, taking the opportunity to put my phone back in my bag. When I looked up to cross, a man was watching me from the other side. He gazed at me evenly, without expression. For a second I was suspended in time, a freeze frame in a film, disbelieving. Then the sickening reality hit and my throat tightened. The man I was looking at was Luke Kirby.

I couldn't move my limbs. Since I'd heard he was out, I had imagined the moment when I might see him: what I would say, what I would do (most of the time I had a gun or a knife in these imaginings). Now it was here and I was frozen, unable to do anything but shake.

Kirby crossed the tracks, palms raised cowboy-style. Mocking. A numbing sensation crept up my neck and into my face, like poison working its way around my body. He stopped about ten feet away, hands still in that exaggerated gesture of conciliation. He didn't speak, just continued to look at me in that self-assured manner he always had, waiting for me to say something. I couldn't even look at him.

'Sarah,' he said eventually.

That voice: silky, English, educated. Speaking my name, a name I no longer used because of him. I had nothing to say to him. It was too late. Nothing I could say would change a damn thing. Tears pricked my eyes as I turned to walk away.

He spoke to my back. 'Looking good, babe.'

I spun on my heel and he smiled, showing a set of perfect white teeth. I tasted bile in my mouth and realised with horror that it was perfectly possible that I might retch, right here on the street in front of him. I stumbled away, unsure of where I was going or what I was doing, knowing only that I needed to keep moving. He didn't follow. Somehow, after everything, he was in control, watching me walk away.

I don't know how long I walked, but when I finally took in my surroundings I was at O'Connell Bridge and I badly needed a drink. I made my way down Westmoreland Street and turned in at Fleet Street, darkened now with a line of buses waiting to depart. I fought my way through the huddled groups on the footpath and called into Bowes, a pub I used to go to when I was at college. Dark wood, warm and comforting, like the Oak. I ordered a whiskey with ice and sat in one of the booths to drink it. The whiskey burned my throat but relieved some of the numbness I was feeling.

I'd hoped that prison might have broken Kirby, taken away some of the arrogance that had so attracted me in the first place, but it seemed to have had no more effect on him than nine years in a solicitor's office. Less. Fewer grey hairs. He'd looked fit, had probably had to bulk up; men who kill women are known to have a hard time in prison. His Oxford-educated accent wouldn't have helped. The thought gave me comfort. I hoped he'd been cornered in the showers; I hoped he . . . And then: what the hell was he doing in Dublin? Molloy had said he had returned to the UK. The notion that he was out of the jurisdiction had given me more comfort than I'd realised.

I drained my glass and when I checked my watch it was half past two. I had told my parents I would be with them about four. I couldn't mention my encounter with Luke, not when they were finally doing so well. But how the hell was I going to conceal this dread I was feeling in the pit of my stomach? While I figured it out, I ordered another drink.

I managed to limit the whiskeys to two and was soon in a taxi to Chapelizod. Thankfully my parents were so full of excitement about their trip to Iceland, they didn't notice that I was quieter than usual.

'Are you sure you'll be okay on your own for Christmas?' my mother asked me for the umpteenth time as she handed me a plateful of turkey and ham. 'You could still come with your father and me, you know. I'm sure the others wouldn't mind.'

'I'll be fine, Mum.' I smiled for the first time since my encounter in town. The notion of an adult daughter travelling with her parents made me think of an Agatha Christie novel.

My mother shot me a quizzical look. 'So who will you spend Christmas with?'

'A friend of mine has asked me for dinner,' I said, grateful, not for the first time, for Phyllis.

Chapter Four

A walk in the Phoenix Park the following day cleared my head after a broken night's sleep. The ground had frozen overnight and the place looked like a Christmas card – all deer and patchy snow and kids with toboggans – making it difficult for me to hold onto my bleak mood from the day before. I left my parents' house around two, glad that I hadn't told them about my encounter with Luke. I didn't see what could be gained by it; they already knew he was out, and seemed to be coping. Better than I was, if I was honest. It was good to see them excited about something for the first time since Faye's death.

I went straight to the airport, having changed my mind about doing some Christmas shopping in town. I told myself it wasn't because I feared another encounter – that would be too much of a coincidence. But I really wanted to get back to Inishowen, not least because I wanted to talk things through with Molloy.

The flight was quiet, with no more than six or seven people on board, and the weather was calm and dry, which meant no delay this time. I picked up my car at Derry airport and drove straight to Glendara. It seemed that no more snow had fallen, and what little remained was scattered like spilled salt on the grass verges and in the fields, making them appear a paler shade of green than usual. All very pretty, but the roads were lethal. I took one bend slightly too fast and skidded straight across the centre line, scaring the life out of two sheep who were frighteningly close to the hedge. Luckily there was no traffic and I was able to right the car with no damage done, but it didn't help the state of my nerves, already in fairly ragged shape.

I felt the tension ease as I drove into town and realised how happy I was to be back. Originally a refuge, a place to escape, Inishowen had become my home almost without my noticing. I wondered how much of that was to do with Molloy.

I pulled in opposite Stoop's newsagent's with the intention of buying Saturday's papers before heading back to Malin, assuming there were any left – it was already after five. As I took the key from the ignition, my phone rang. It was Maeve, my friend and the local vet.

'You're back.'

'How do you know?'

'I can see you.'

I looked around the darkening square but there was no sign of Maeve's familiar figure. Then just as I was about to get out of the Mini, a jeep pulled up beside me and she grinned at me from the driver's seat. I climbed out and opened her passenger door. She was red-cheeked and damp, and the sweet smell of manure wafted in my direction from her heavily stained boiler suit.

'Are you still working?' I asked.

'Just finished, thank the Lord. I haven't been able to feel my hands for about two hours.' She removed them from the steering wheel and shook them out.

'Fancy a coffee?' I asked.

She gave me a wry look. 'I'd kill for a hot port, to be honest, but I have to drive home later. And,' she glanced at her watch, 'Stan was supposed to be cutting my hair ten minutes ago, so I'd better get back to the clinic and change out of this gear. He'll have a fit if I enter his inner sanctum looking like this.'

'Fair enough.'

'Are you heading home now?' she asked.

I nodded. 'After I grab the papers.'

'Okay. I might give you a shout once I've been shorn.'

'Don't let Stan hear you saying that!'

The irony of Pat the Stoop, the newsagent, being a strapping six-foot former GAA player always struck me, but then I suppose that's the way with nicknames. Pat McLaughlin alone would never have been enough to distinguish him from the hundreds of other McLaughlins in the area. I had a filing cabinet each for Dohertys and McLaughlins, most of whom were not related. Pat was about to close up when I pushed open the door.

Stoop's is a long, narrow shop with stone flags and floor-to-ceiling white shelves offering periodicals on everything from surfing to embroidery. Other than a regular lick of paint, I suspect it hasn't changed in forty years. Never the brightest of retail outlets, with some lights turned off it was like a cave; it was brighter on the street. But the *Irish Times* wasn't yet packed away, so I nabbed one from the stand and brought it to the counter.

Pat was stacking boxes of Christmas cards. 'Ben. How are you?'

Unlike his grandfather, who had acquired the nickname originally, the newsagent was a straight-backed man with a high colour and rheumy eyes. I'd often wondered if that was why he kept his shop so dark.

'Good,' I said. 'Busy day?'

'Aye, not too bad,' he replied as he took the fiver I offered him. 'But just you wait till next week, when it's too late to go into Derry and they'll all be in here looking for their wrapping paper and Sellotape. That'll be the really busy time for us. Especially if the snow comes back.'

'You're probably right.'

'I am,' he said with certainty. 'Do you know?' He leaned forward conspiratorially as he handed me the change. 'I've sold selection boxes on Easter Saturday and Easter eggs on Christmas Eve. Desperate people.' He winked. 'There's always someone who leaves it just that wee bit too late.'

My cottage was in darkness when I arrived back in Malin, and there was no sign of Guinness despite my calling him a couple of times. I called Molloy too, but got his voicemail so left him a message.

The house was freezing, having been empty for two days, so I dumped my briefcase and bag on the kitchen table and went straight to the sitting room, where I found a fire log in the box by the fireplace and lit it, tossing a couple of bits of turf on top. Then I returned to the kitchen, took a lasagne from the freezer and stuck it in the microwave – easy options all round. Finally, feeling a little sorry for myself, I opened a bottle of wine.

I spent the evening by the fire with the papers. Alone. There was no sign of Molloy, Maeve or Guinness all evening. So much for looking forward to getting home. At eleven o'clock, I put some food out for Guinness in case he came back during the night, and went to bed having decided to take advantage of my solitude and go for an icy dip at Lagg beach in the morning. It would give me the shake I needed.

★ ★ ★

The next morning, Sunday, I woke early to the sound of rain lashing against the window. There had been a thaw during the night, but the weather had turned really nasty. I opened the curtains to the sight of skeletal trees on the green thrashing about like angry stags, and quickly changed my mind about going for a swim. Icy sea swimming might be helpful to my mental health, but I wasn't prepared to risk my neck to do it. I took myself to a hot shower instead.

A bedraggled-looking Guinness was waiting for me on the doorstep when I went down.

'Where have you been?' I asked, but he wasn't exactly forthcoming.

He looked so pathetic that I let him into the back kitchen, where I fed him and put down an old towel for him to sit by the radiator. He appeared distinctly unimpressed when I closed the kitchen door on him, leaving him to dry out.

As I waited for the coffee to brew, I checked my phone. No messages. Where the hell was Molloy?

When I'd finished breakfast, I decided to drive to Glendara to track him down. I didn't usually go to his place – we had got into the habit of him coming to my cottage instead – but I thought in the circumstances I would make an exception. I needed to talk to him about Kirby.

The Mini was shunted all over the road as I drove in along the coast, and the sea looked threatening, angry in shades of grey and green. I hoped there were few boats out today. I thought of wives and mothers waiting for the return of a fishing trawler, five days before Christmas.

It was early, not yet nine o'clock, when I approached Glendara. The town would usually be quiet at this time on a Sunday morning, the only people about being early mass-goers. But today there were cars parked all along the road on the way in, as if for a wake or a funeral. Had there been a death, I wondered, one I hadn't heard about? It would explain Molloy's absence; guards were often needed to police traffic at a wake. But as I passed the fire station, I saw that its doors were wide open and the fire engine was gone.

About five hundred yards from town, the road was blocked off; the squad car parked across the centre line created a temporary barricade. There was no one in it. Where was everybody? Despite all the parked cars, there wasn't a soul about. After a brief hesitation, I turned the Mini around, found a space to park and walked the rest of the way into town, pulling up the hood of my coat. It was still raining, although less heavily now, and the wind had died down.

A smell of smoke like a damp bonfire hung in the air. I reached Phyllis's bookshop and saw that her lights were on, but when I pushed at the door, the shop was closed and there were no lights in her flat above. If I were a detective, I would think that she had left in a hurry.

I came to the corner and the air was acrid. A group of about thirty people was clustered at the far side of the square; a motley collection with coats and hats and umbrellas. They were watching something. I caught a glimpse of yellow tape, and as I walked closer, smoke. Not billowing, but rising in wispy lines above the crowd, like steam from the spout of some giant kettle.

Then I saw the words on the tape: *Please do not cross.* I took in the two fire engines, hoses, men in high-vis yellow jackets and helmets, and felt the stab of fear that comes with the sight of an emergency vehicle. But there was a lack of urgency about the scene, as if I had arrived late, as if I were witnessing the aftermath rather than the main event.

I made my way to the front of the crowd and found myself looking at a blackened, soaked building belching out small puffs of bluish smoke. Whatever it had been, it was unrecognisable now. Three walls remained, the floorboards splintered and broken, timbers protruding between the floors at strange angles. It looked like a child's toy that had been kicked to pieces. Charred debris was scattered over the footpath and onto the road. My mind raced as I tried to work out what the building used to be. I knew this square well, but the scene was so shocking that I was disoriented. Whose house had it been?

I examined the buildings on either side, the shops at ground level: Liam McLaughlin's estate agent's a few doors down, Stoop's newsagent's on the other side of the road, Illusions Hair Design two doors to the right. Suddenly I knew what I was looking at. An empty vodka bottle with optic still attached rolled towards my feet, confirming it. My heart sank. It was the Oak. The Oak pub had burned down.

The smoke stung my nostrils like chlorine, the foul air a noxious taste on my tongue. A voice behind made me turn. It was Phyllis. She looked awful, her face smudged black and her hair sticking up in tufts, as if she'd been helping put out the fire herself. Her eyes were brimming.

'Oh Ben, it's so awful. It's completely destroyed.'

'What on earth happened?'

'I don't know. It happened during the night. Poor Tony.' She switched her gaze to a tall figure in a waterproof jacket, his face deathly white, talking to one of the firemen.

'Was there anyone in there?' I asked, horrified, realising as I looked at the wreckage again that of course Stan's flat was gone too. The walls separating the pub from the buildings on either side were intact, but everything else was destroyed. It was amazing that the fire hadn't spread, that the fire service had managed to isolate it, especially with the wind.

'Doesn't seem so.' Phyllis shook her head, running her hand through her hair and making it stick up even more. 'That's one thing to be thankful for, I suppose. Stan must have been out. Apparently the fire started about four o'clock this morning. God knows how.'

'How long have you been here?' I asked. 'You look shattered.'

She smiled, a watery smile. 'Since six. I heard the sirens. Wanted to see if I could help. But there was nothing I could do, just watch helplessly like everybody else while it burned. And try to talk to Tony.'

We stood watching the scene for a few minutes in shocked silence. At one point, I spotted Molloy and he caught my eye but didn't react.

'Do you fancy a cup of tea?' Phyllis asked suddenly. 'I'm parched and I don't think there's anything useful we can do here for the moment. We can come back out in half an hour.'

'Okay,' I said gratefully.

I followed Phyllis as she made her way back across the square and towards her shop. She took a deep breath before turning the key, as if giving silent thanks for own hearth, and we walked through the bookshop and climbed the winding staircase that led to her flat. Fred greeted her with great excitement and she fondled his ears affectionately.

'You want your walk, don't you? Well, I can't let you out at the moment, I'm afraid. Too many burning embers. But I'll bring you out on a lead after we've had our cup of tea.'

She filled the kettle in her kitchen, switched it on and dumped some tea leaves into a huge earthenware teapot. 'Earl Grey and Barry's do you? It's my new house blend.'

'Great.'

I slumped at the table while I waited for my tea. 'How on earth did it happen? I presume it started in the pub rather than the flat?'

She shook her head. 'No idea. I presume so. Maybe it was an electrical fault? Or someone left something burning? You know they needed two fire brigades to put it out? Buncrana is there as well.'

'Who locked up last night, I wonder?'

'Tony says it was Carole. He was trying to get hold of her when I saw him first.' Phyllis looked grim. 'I think for a while he was terrified she was still in there. But the firemen are certain the whole place was empty, flat, pub and cellar.'

Cellar, I thought, remembering Stan's complaint about the noise. Could that have had anything to do with the fire? From what I had seen, the cellar seemed to be completely burned out.

Phyllis handed me a steaming cup, breaking my train of thought. The tea was refreshing, washing away the itch of smoke at the back of my throat.

Half an hour later, we left Phyllis's flat and returned to the square. It had stopped raining now, and other than a few small heaps of smouldering debris, the fire was out. One fire brigade remained, with two firemen working through the wreckage. That ominous stench was still in the air.

With the exception of a few stragglers, the crowd had dispersed, but Tony remained where we had left him, in front of his ruined pub like the chief mourner at a wake. He was hunched, hands buried in his pockets, speaking to Eddie Kearney. Eddie was holding his hands up defensively and appeared close to tears. Before we reached them, Eddie turned and left, draping his arm around a slight dark-haired girl who was waiting for him.

'God, Tony, I'm so sorry,' I said as the publican turned to greet us.

He looked haggard, his long face pale in the morning light, his skin merging with his neat grey beard, the usual flicker of humour absent from his grey eyes.

'How did this happen?' he said helplessly. 'I wasn't even *in* the pub last night. I had Carole and Eddie running the place for me.'

My eyes were drawn to Eddie's departing figure, his arm still around the girl.

Tony followed my gaze. 'I knew it would be too busy for Carole on her own, the Saturday before Christmas, so I asked him to work a few shifts. He was happy enough to do it.' He shook his head, distraught. 'But God knows – did they leave something switched on? A heater or a kettle or something?'

'You think that's how it happened?' I asked.

'Eddie swears they didn't, but these things don't happen by themselves.' He frowned. 'And by the sound of him, he left early, snuck off to Culdaff to listen to some band or other. Left Carole to lock up on her own.'

'Did you get hold of Carole?' Phyllis asked.

Tony shook his head, his face troubled. 'She's not answering her phone. It's going straight through to voicemail.'

'Maybe she's still asleep. If she had a late night?'

He nodded stiffly.

'I presume the fire service will be able to tell you what caused it?' I asked.

He sighed. 'I hope so. And then I need to speak to my insurance company.'

43

'What can we do?' Phyllis asked, placing her hand gently on Tony's arm. 'You know everyone is going to want to help.'

He looked up gratefully. 'Thanks, Phyllis, but I don't think there's anything anyone can do. Unless you can track down Stan MacLochlainn. He's another one who's not answering his phone.' He shook his head. 'The guards have been trying to get him too. I'm told he's away to Dungloe to see his mother.'

He looked up at the smouldering wreckage of his pub. 'I just thank God he wasn't here.'

Chapter Five

Realising there was little I could do to help, I took myself back to Malin after my conversation with Tony and Phyllis. As I drove back along the coast road, I thought again about Stan's complaint the previous week. Could the noise have had anything to do with the fire? And where had Tony Craig been for the previous few days? He'd made no mention during our chat of being away, and it hadn't seemed the appropriate time to ask.

I was rummaging in the fridge trying to find something for lunch, realising that I needed to buy groceries if the best I could do was a stale sandwich from the Oak, when there was a knock on the back door. Guinness, who'd been watching me with interest, leapt down from the windowsill while I went to answer it.

Molloy looked almost as wrecked as Tony and Phyllis had earlier. He closed the door behind him and wrapped his arms around me, burying his head in my shoulder though he had to bend forward to do it. His uniform smelled of smoke.

'Long night?' I said, into his hair.

'You could say that.' His voice was hoarse.

We pulled apart and he followed me into the kitchen. 'Do you want some food?' I asked.

He shook his head. 'No thanks.'

'Just as well.' I chucked the sandwich I'd left on the table into the bin.

'A coffee would be great, though.'

'Coming up.'

He pulled out a chair and sat at the table while I stuck the kettle on and took two mugs from the cupboard.

'Any developments on the fire?' I asked. 'Do they know what caused it?'

He didn't reply.

'Something electrical? Stray spark from the hearth or something?' I took the coffee pot from the cupboard above the sink and spooned some grains into it.

'It was deliberate.'

I spun around. 'What?'

'The fire was started deliberately. Petrol, according to the fire service. They found the remains of a can at the back of the building. Garda forensics will have to do a full report, but they seemed to be pretty sure.'

I exhaled loudly. 'Does Tony know?'

'He does now.'

'Lord. Who on earth would do that?'

'God only knows. But it looks as though it's going to be a criminal investigation. Last thing we need this close to Christmas.'

'What about Carole? Did you find her? Tony said he couldn't get hold of her.' I poured boiling water into the pot and added the plunger.

He shook his head. 'That's the other thing. Carole is missing.

No one has seen her since last night. Not even her husband. She hasn't been home.'

I crossed my arms. 'Seriously?'

Molloy sounded weary. 'Her husband said she sometimes sleeps in the spare room when she works late. Then he'll get up with the children in the morning and she can lie on. He said he only realised she wasn't home when he heard about the fire on the radio and went in to tell her.'

'Where could she be?' I asked.

'He says he has no idea. He's worried sick, of course, convinced she might have been in the fire, but the fire service are certain there was no one in there.'

I poured coffee into mugs. 'She was on the same flight to Dublin as me on Friday morning, if that means anything. But she must have come back fairly quickly if she was working in the Oak last night.'

Immediately Molloy was on the alert. 'Really? Any idea where she was going? Or why?'

I shook my head. 'Carole's never been the most forthcoming. About her own business anyway,' I added.

I handed him a mug. 'But she did have some luggage with her. A fairly big suitcase. I saw her collect it at the carousel when I left the airport in Dublin. And she wasn't on the flight back yesterday afternoon; I'd have seen her – there were only six people on it. Maybe she came back the same day, Friday.'

'But then why would she have had luggage with her?' Molloy asked.

'I don't know. That's why I was surprised that she was working last night. I assumed she was going away for a while.'

'I'll talk to George. See what he knows about it.' He took a drink and briefly closed his eyes. 'God, I need this.'

'George is the husband?'

Molloy nodded. 'George Harkin. He's a music teacher at the school. Plays a bit in the pubs too. They live in Culdaff.'

'You mentioned kids,' I said. 'How old are they?'

'Four and two,' he said softly.

'Seems odd she would leave them. Especially this close to Christmas.'

'Yes, it does.' Molloy emptied his mug in one long draught and stood up with a sigh. 'Anyway, I'd better go and see what George knows. Thanks for the coffee. That'll keep me going for another bit.'

'Will I see you later?' I asked.

'Possibly. Depends on how the rest of the day goes.'

My expression must have given something away, because suddenly he looked concerned. He touched my arm. 'Everything okay?'

'Fine,' I said. 'I'll talk to you later.' And I pushed him out the door.

After lunch – I found two eggs that were only just out of date, so I scrambled them with some crackers – I needed a walk to clear my head. But when I drove around the green in Malin, I found myself turning east towards Culdaff rather than north-west towards Lagg, my usual walking spot. The power of suggestion, I suppose, Molloy having mentioned that Carole and George Harkin lived there.

Culdaff is a small seaside village with a triangular green, a few pubs, a restaurant, and two lovely old stone bridges. With a sheltered harbour at Bunagee and a beautiful golden beach, it's popular with summer visitors, but I like it in the winter when there are fewer people about. After the ten-minute drive from

Malin, I turned left at the green and drove out along the shore, leaving the Mini in the car park by the beach and wrapping myself up well in scarf and hat before getting out to walk. A vicious east wind stung my face and my scarf blew wildly about my head as I made my way over the marram grass and through the dunes. I was surprised by how many people were on the beach: couples arm in arm, kids with balls, and dogs rolling about, emerging filthy and panting from the dunes. Families out for a stroll after their Sunday lunch, needing a blast of sea air, undeterred by the weather.

I watched two small boys playing at the edge of the water and thought about how Carole's husband must be feeling, trying to keep his children distracted while hiding how worried he was. My heart went out to him, though I'd never met him. Until now I hadn't even known Carole was married, had never given it any thought. I'd simply known her as Carole Kearney, Eddie's sister.

Was her disappearance connected with the fire? I was shocked by Molloy's pronouncement that the Oak had been deliberately torched. Tony Craig was a decent sort of publican, the kind who would refuse you the last drink you didn't need and then drive you home. I couldn't imagine anyone wanting to do him harm. The only complaint I'd ever heard about him had come from Stan last week. Molloy hadn't mentioned Stan, I realised suddenly. I wondered if he'd returned to Glendara yet.

As I battled the biting wind, Luke Kirby was in my thoughts too, although he'd been pushed to the chorus line today, which was no bad thing. I was beginning to wonder if I should mention him to Molloy at all. He had enough on his plate.

About halfway down the beach, I looked at my watch. It was four o'clock and dusk; the hills in the distance purple, the line between land and sky a blur. I needed to pick up my pace if I wanted to make it back to the road before dark. I turned in left with Bunagee pier on my right and followed the shoreline to the small inlet, passing the mudflats and making my way up onto the road just in time. With the street lights I'd be able to complete the circuit and reach the car in safety, but the temperature was dropping and I was very cold. I pulled my gloves from the pocket of my coat and put them on, grateful that they happened to be there.

A black Mercedes passed on the road, then slowed down, stopped and reversed until it was alongside. The driver's window rolled down and Liam McLaughlin's head and elbow appeared.

'You look as if you could do with a good strong hot whiskey.'

I replied with difficulty. 'You're not wrong there. I can't feel my face.'

'Do you want a lift back to your car?'

'Absolutely.'

Liam pushed open the passenger door from the inside and I walked around the car and climbed in.

'I presume you've heard the news,' he said as he pulled away from the kerb.

'The Oak?' I nodded. 'I was in town this morning and saw it. Awful.'

'I hear it was started deliberately.'

It never ceases to amaze me how quickly news travels in Inishowen, but I made no comment, unsure if Molloy would want me discussing it at this stage. Liam didn't seem to notice. His mind was on something else, his gaze fixed on the road ahead as if he was on some kind of mission. I asked him what he was doing in Culdaff.

'I'm heading out to George Harkin's house,' he said. 'You heard Carole didn't come home last night?'

50

I nodded. 'Is George a friend of yours?'

'We used to fish together.'

'You *fished*? On a trawler?'

I realised I sounded like a right city slicker, but it was too late. Unusually, Liam let me away with it.

'Most people around here would have done it at one time or another. George stuck it longer than I did. I wasn't really cut out for it.' He shot me a crooked smile. 'I did the cooking.'

'I thought George Harkin was a teacher?'

'He is now. The fishing was a long time ago, when we were young fellas with no sense. All we wanted was a few pounds in our pockets to go out at the weekend. Anyway, I thought I'd call and see how he's doing. See if there's anything I can do.'

'I'm sure he's worried sick.'

Liam nodded. 'Poor wee ones must be missing their mother. I don't know what George has told them.'

We passed the football pitches on our left, floodlit, with some hardy souls in shorts kicking a ball about.

I paused. 'Liam, have you any idea why Carole was in Dublin on Friday?'

He looked at me askance for a second before his expression cleared. 'Oh Jesus, that's right. She was on the same flight as you down from Derry, wasn't she? I'd forgotten that. The one that was late. I've never seen her on that flight before. I wonder what she was doing?'

'She wasn't very forthcoming when I was talking to her. But whatever it was, she obviously came back up again, because she was working in the Oak last night, according to Tony.'

He looked thoughtful. 'That's right, she was. I was in there for a quick pint myself before I went home.'

'How did she seem?'

51

'Wee bit distracted, now you mention it. I had to call the pint twice.'

We arrived at the car park and Liam pulled in beside the Mini, dwarfing it with the Merc. He pulled a face. 'When are you going to get yourself a decent grown-up car?'

I feigned indignation. 'How dare you. That *is* a decent car.'

He winked. 'Hardly fitting for the local solicitor.'

Meeting Liam reminded me of all the work that remained to be done at the office. So much of my energy the previous week had been concentrated on the Greys that other work had been left to the wayside. The office was due to close on Wednesday, the day before Christmas Eve, which gave us three days to get everything done. It was going to be tight. Watching Liam drive away, I knew I should go in for a few hours, but I couldn't summon either the energy or the enthusiasm. I decided to go home and head in early in the morning instead. Light the fire and curl up with the latest Kathy Reichs, that was my plan.

It was not to be.

I expected to see Guinness sitting on the doorstep demanding his dinner when I parked the car, but there was no sign. Then, walking up the path, I heard a faint mewling in the shrubbery. It was dark, so I turned on the torch on my phone. I heard the mewling again, but still couldn't see anything. Convinced that it was Guinness, I poked about under the shrubs, trying to follow the sound and getting soaked in the process. Eventually I found him curled up under a laurel bush, looking absolutely filthy. I reached in and touched his head. He looked out at me, his eyes showing pain, seeming unable to move. With difficulty, I managed to gather him up in my arms and bring him into the house. I found an old blanket and placed him gently down on it, and immediately he struggled to his feet, disoriented as if drunk. Suddenly he lurched forward and began to retch, but nothing came up.

I grabbed my mobile from my bag and rang Maeve.

She heard the panic in my voice straight away. 'What's wrong?'

'It's Guinness, he's sick. I think he's eaten something. He's weak and retching but nothing's coming up.'

'Okay,' she said calmly. 'I'm in the clinic. Can you bring him in here? I might need to pump his stomach.'

'I'll be there in ten minutes.'

I placed the cat and blanket in a cardboard box on the passenger seat, and drove into Glendara as fast as I could without causing him any more distress than necessary. It was strange to have him lying beside me, unresisting. Usually if I had to take him anywhere in the car he leapt about like a lunatic, causing havoc. He steadfastly refused to get into a cat basket.

I'd had Guinness since he was a tiny kitten. On my way to a Bar Association meeting in Letterkenny, I'd caught sight of a little black shadow in the centre of a main road with cars whizzing by on both sides. I'd driven on for a couple of minutes before convincing myself that I'd seen the shadow move, at which point I'd executed an illegal U-turn and driven back to where I'd seen it. Once there, I'd risked my neck to run into the middle of the road and scoop a frightened little kitten into my arms. He had been hit by a car and was bleeding with a broken leg. He was so terrified that he scrambled onto my shoulder, where he stayed, clinging on to my neck, while I drove around frantically trying to find a vet. It occurred to me now that perhaps that was why he hated cars so much. When finally I'd succeeded, I'd left him at the clinic and driven on to my meeting in my bloodstained shirt, happy with my good deed but confident that was the last I would see of him. I certainly didn't want a cat – I could barely take care of myself at that point. But a few weeks later I had a call to inform me that despite recovering beautifully from his injuries, no home had been found, and of course I adopted him. I'd had him now for five years. Guinness was temperamental and spoilt, but I knew I would miss him dreadfully if anything happened to him.

I pulled into Maeve's clinic and lifted the box from the passenger seat as gently as I could. The cat was listless now, depressed and barely moving. Maeve met me at the door and took the box from me, and I followed her to the small animals examination room at the back of the clinic, where she lifted him out of his box and placed him gently on the table. I watched as she examined him, looking into his mouth, feeling his stomach and checking under his tail while he lay limply to one side.

'You're right,' she said. 'It looks as if he's eaten some kind of poison. I'd guess antifreeze.'

'Where would he get that?' I asked. 'And why in God's name would he want to eat it?'

'Antifreeze is sweet and cats drink it because they like the taste of it. If it is that, let's hope we've got him early.'

My heart sank. 'Could he die?'

'Antifreeze acts quickly and usually it's not noticed till too late, by which stage the cat is in acute renal failure.' Maeve's brow was furrowed until she caught my expression. 'Don't worry, I'd say we've got him in time. But you're going to have to leave him with me.'

She pulled on some gloves.

'What are you going to do?'

She gave me a half-smile. 'I'm going to put him on a drip with fluids and vodka.'

'Vodka?'

'Medical ethanol or vodka. We don't have ethanol in the clinic, but vodka works just as well. He'll need to stay on the drip for three days, until all the antifreeze is cleared from his system.'

I touched Guinness on the little white patch on the top of his head. He looked utterly miserable.

'Don't worry,' Maeve said again. 'If we've got him within three hours – and I suspect we have or he'd be in a much worse way – then the prognosis is good.'

'Okay,' I said slowly.

'Now go on and leave me to it,' she said. 'I'll give you a call later on.'

I walked reluctantly towards the door. 'Thanks, Maeve.'

'Oh, and you'll need to do a proper search around your house to make sure there isn't anything left of what he ate,' she called after me. 'Check to see if there is any meat or fish lying around that would have tempted him, and get rid of it.'

'In case he finds it again?'

She nodded. 'Cats are pretty smart, it's unlikely he'd go back for seconds, but just in case.'

'Okay.' I turned to go, then turned back. 'Oh, what do I owe you?'

She waved me away. 'Don't be an ass.'

Chapter Six

The following morning I called Maeve first thing and she told me Guinness was looking a lot brighter. Relieved, I did a thorough search of the garden to see if I could find what he had eaten. It was bitterly cold, but dry, so I could see what I was doing without getting drenched, but I found nothing that a cat would have been tempted to eat. After half an hour poking about in the frosty grass, I gave up, came back inside and put the kettle on for tea.

I opened the fridge for milk but found only an empty carton – tea would have to wait till I got to the office, and I really needed to buy some groceries. I threw the carton in the bin. As I did so, I caught sight of the sandwich I'd chucked out the day before and fished it out. The cellophane was torn and a large chunk was missing. It had to have been Guinness. The sandwich was salmon – he'd have been unable to resist. I remembered I'd left it on the table when I'd gone to answer the door. He must have taken a chunk and disappeared with it before Molloy and I returned to the kitchen.

Was that why he'd been sick? Was there something wrong with it? I held it up to my nose and sniffed. It wasn't gone off, just stale. I'd got it as a takeaway from the Oak on Thursday and hadn't eaten it, leaving it in the fridge with the intention of going back to it at some stage.

I took an old knife from the drawer, cut off a piece and put it into a plastic bag, not sure what I intended doing with it but certain I should preserve it. Then I threw the rest in the bin, along with the knife, and washed my hands thoroughly. I wasn't about to take any chances.

It seemed pretty far-fetched that there would be something wrong with the sandwich, but I couldn't think of anything else. There was nothing in the garden.

I got to the office about half past nine. Leah was there before me, piling up files on the desk and glugging from a huge mug of coffee. After a brief shocked exchange about the fire in the Oak, it was back to work.

'Right,' she said, separating the files into two stacks and pointing to the first. 'These are the files where we need to receive cheques today if we're to complete before Christmas. Insurance and life assurance are all sorted, I'm told, so hopefully there'll be no hold-up.'

I counted them. 'Okay – seven. We can manage that, just about. I'll go through them now and make sure everything's ready to go. I'll be finished in court by lunchtime tomorrow, so we should be able to close a couple of sales in the afternoon. I'll draft searches now and you can email them . . .'

I broke off as the door opened and Liam strode in. 'Morning, all.'

'Morning, Liam – perfect timing.' Three of the files were sales that Liam had negotiated. I held them up. 'Do you want to come up with me and we'll go through these?'

He nodded and followed me upstairs. It didn't take long. Ten minutes later we'd done what was needed and Liam sat back in his chair, ready to chew the fat.

'So how did you get on with George Harkin yesterday?' I asked.

'Ach, God love him – the man doesn't know what to do with himself. He's very worried.'

'Did you ask him about Carole going to Dublin?'

His brow furrowed. 'I did. Strange, that. He knew she was going – she wanted to get a few things for Christmas that she couldn't get in Derry – but he thought she was taking the bus. Until I told him, he didn't know any better. She came back up that night, late he said, around midnight, but she didn't mention taking the flight.'

Liam must have got to George before Molloy, I thought. 'Did he drop her to the bus station?'

Liam shook his head. 'She drove herself into Derry and back again.' He crossed his arms. 'Now why do you think she would lie about something like that?'

'No idea.'

'I guess we should tell Molloy.' Liam scratched his chin. 'I presume he's involved in looking for her? Especially after the fire.'

'I've already told him she was on the flight on Friday morning,' I said. 'I'll tell him what George said, but I'd say he's spoken to him himself by now.'

Liam narrowed his eyes. 'That's right. You and the sergeant are tight these days, aren't you?'

I coloured and changed the subject. 'Did you know Eddie, Carole's brother, is home from Australia?'

Liam grinned. 'Aye, followed the girlfriend, I hear. Didn't want her out of his sight for too long.'

'I wonder if he knows anything?'

'Doubtful. Wouldn't be the sharpest tool in the box, that young fella. That girlfriend of his could buy and sell him.' Liam stood up to go. 'Anyway, I suppose it's too early for a full-scale search. Hopefully she'll just turn up. Are you still on for the usual bunfight on Wednesday night?'

For the past few years, Liam and I and some of the other businesses in the town had forgone a work Christmas party in favour of a night out on the last day before the holidays. It was usually a good night, but it always started in the Oak.

'Do you think we should, in the circumstances?' I asked.

'Ach, I'm sure Tony will understand. It's still Christmas. People aren't going to go on the dry because the Oak has burned down. He might even be persuaded to join us. I'm sure he needs a bit of cheering up.'

I thought that was a bit unlikely but I said, 'Fair enough. Where will we go?'

'Golf club?'

My face fell. 'What about somewhere in Culdaff?'

'All right,' he said easily. 'Sure why not? We could catch some music.'

My first appointment, straight after Liam, was with Ian Grey who was in to pay his bill. He sat in the chair Liam had vacated while he signed a cheque and handed it across the desk.

I thanked him. 'I wish all my clients were so prompt. When do you plan on moving in?'

'Oh, not for a few months yet. We've a fair bit of work to do on it. Late spring, we hope. We'll keep renting where we are for the moment.'

'You're in a lovely spot where you are.'

'I know,' he replied. 'We'll be sorry to leave. Abby will miss her job, I think.'

The Greys were renting an old thatched cottage on the road to Culdaff, the type of place that would usually have been impossible to get for a long-term letting, but they'd arrived in the autumn after selling their family home in Dublin and been lucky. Abby had been a psychologist, but now she worked in a riding stables by the beach. I wasn't sure what Ian did. When I had asked him for his occupation for the deed of transfer of Greysbridge, he'd simply said, 'Self-employed.' He hadn't seemed prepared to be any more specific.

I wrote out a receipt. 'You're not going too far, though. Greysbridge is what? Thirty miles from here?'

He nodded. 'About that. As a matter of fact, we came up here as a kind of experiment. To see if we could live in Donegal, see if we wanted to try and buy back the house.'

I handed him the receipt. 'You obviously decided you could.'

'We've grown to love it here.' He smiled. 'Despite being jack-eens. Though with Donegal roots in my case, of course,' he added.

'You've lived in Dublin all your lives?'

'Apart from a short stint in London. This has been our first time living outside a city.'

I grinned. 'Must be quite a culture shock.'

'It is. I'd never even seen Greysbridge until I saw mention of it in the paper. I was always aware of this large house in Donegal being the family seat until it was lost in the 1930s, but I only had the vaguest notion of where it was.'

'Well it's great you've got it back. And now you're going to restore it.'

He stood up with a wry smile. 'Hopefully we haven't bitten

off more than we can chew.' He shook my hand. 'Thank you for everything.'

'You're welcome. I hope it goes really well for you.'

At the door, he turned back. 'Awful about the fire in the pub, wasn't it?'

I nodded.

'The barmaid there, Carole – she does some work for us, you know?'

I looked up. 'Really?'

'Yes. Cleaning, ironing, that sort of thing. I asked her if she might like to come and work for us at the hotel once we open for the summer next year. She seems keen, although it might be a bit of a trek for her.'

I was surprised. 'She must be busy. I thought she had a full-time job at the Oak.'

He shrugged. 'She said she needed the money and it sounded as though she could manage both. I must give her a call. She'll be very upset about what happened to the pub.'

I hesitated. 'You haven't heard she's missing, then?'

He frowned. 'Missing?'

'Yes. No one has seen her since the night of the fire. She never went home, apparently.'

His eyes widened in shock.

'Hadn't you heard?' I said. 'I thought the town grapevine would be all over it.'

'No.' His lips parted as if he was about to say something, then he seemed to change his mind. He looked at the ground thoughtfully. 'I suppose we've been so preoccupied with buying the house.'

'I don't suppose you know where she might be?' I asked. 'I know her husband is very anxious.'

He shook his head. 'Haven't the foggiest.'

★　★　★

He was still shaking his head in disbelief when I followed him downstairs to see him out. I went back into reception to give Leah his cheque.

'Stan's back,' she said as I handed it over. 'I've just seen him.'

'I hope Tony managed to get hold of him before he saw what remains of his flat. Where did you see him?'

'I nipped out to get stamps while you were with Ian Grey, and he was on the street outside the post office having a right old go at Tony. Arms flying everywhere.'

I sighed. 'Understandable, I suppose, although it doesn't appear to be Tony's fault. He's suffered as much as Stan.'

'Anyway, he spotted me and said he'd be calling in later.'

'Who? Tony or Stan?'

'Stan.'

At one o'clock I drove down to the veterinary clinic to check on Guinness. Maeve wasn't there, but her nurse directed me to an area out the back that had a number of cages with recuperating cats and dogs. I found Guinness in the one at the end, lying on a blue blanket and attached to a drip. He was stretched out on his front, fast asleep. I watched him for a minute or so but he looked so peaceful that I left again, feeling relieved.

I drove on out to Malin for lunch, remembering to collect some groceries on the way. At the house, I made myself a cheese sandwich and coffee, and as I ate, I thought again about the sandwich in the bin. Maeve seemed to be convinced that it was antifreeze that Guinness had consumed. So if the salmon was the culprit, had it been laced? It seemed crazy. I tried to recall where the sandwich had been since I bought it – my bag, my office, the car, my house. Anyone could have interfered with it. I shivered, then wondered if I was being paranoid, my imagination running wild after my encounter with Luke in Dublin.

When my phone buzzed, I jumped, feeling foolish, especially when it was a text from Molloy saying he'd be over later. I pushed all disturbing thoughts from my mind and replied saying I'd cook. There was a Godello in the wine rack I'd been waiting to try.

As I walked from the car park to the office that afternoon, I saw Tony Craig talking to a young woman outside Phyllis's shop. I'd never seen her before, but I was curious; it looked to be rather a tense exchange. Tony's day seemed to be revolving around tense conversations on the street.

Stan was waiting for me back at the office, leaning on the reception desk and bending Leah's ear. He looked unusually crumpled – there was a definite air of the morning after about him.

'I told you there was something funny going on in the Oak, didn't I?' he declared before we'd even made it up the stairs.

'Yes, Stan, you did.'

When he sat down heavily on the chair nearest the window, I realised he'd left the door open again and stood up to close it, but his eyes widened in alarm.

'Do you mind if we leave it open? I have a bit of a cough. It's probably all this upheaval.'

'Of course.' I sat back down. 'So do you think the noise had something to do with the fire?'

'It's a hell of a coincidence if not, don't you think?' The jewel in his nose flashed under the lights, mirroring his tetchy mood.

'What has Tony said?'

63

Stan looked exasperated. 'Ach, all he's interested in is the insurance. Fat lot of good insurance is going to do *me*. I was only renting. All I'm left with are the clothes on my back.'

The clothes on his back consisted of a pair of violet pinstripe trousers and matching shirt, which made him look a little as if he was wearing pyjamas. I wondered if he'd been wearing them since Saturday.

'I'm sorry. It can't be easy for you. But you'll get something for contents, won't you?'

His eyes flashed. 'How's that going to get me my home back?'

'No,' I said soothingly. 'You're right. It won't.'

He leaned back in the chair and sighed. 'Ach, maybe it was time to move on anyway, buy myself a nice wee house somewhere. Maybe I've been long enough in Glendara.'

'You'd really think about leaving? What about your business?'

'I can set up anywhere. Maybe Tony Craig's done me a favour.'

'You'd be missed.'

He shrugged.

'Do you have somewhere to stay?' I asked.

'One of the girls is putting me up.' He scowled again, as if the reality of his situation had just hit him anew. 'But we can't open the salon until we're told it's safe. Christmas bloody week. What a handling. Do you know how many appointments I've had to cancel?'

Once Stan had left, I drove to Buncrana to close two of the seven sales we had to deal with that week. The seller's solicitor was the same in both cases and all went according to plan, so I was back in the office by six, glad to see that Leah had gone home; I was beginning to feel guilty about her long hours. Although she had, of course, left me copious notes on the remaining files, and papers for court the next day.

Flicking through the court file, I estimated I had a good chance of being finished by lunchtime; the list was short and nothing was listed for hearing, so I could close the remaining sales in the afternoon. I called each of the buyers' solicitors – as expected, all were still in their offices – and arranged times for the following day. Two would be in court in the morning anyway, so we could meet after that. Once that was done, I sat back and took a deep breath. We were on the home strait. I made myself a coffee, did another hour's work, left the files on my desk and went home.

The house was cold when I got in. I usually set the heating to come on about six, but it had turned off again by the time I got home, so I lit the fire before opening the Godello. I poured myself a glass as I began to cook: pasta with seafood – not particularly seasonal, but there'd be enough turkey and ham around to poison the whole town by the end of the week. Also, I didn't want to lose my fish nerve after the incident with the sandwich.

There was a knock at the back door at eight. I opened it to Molloy with a bottle of red, and I felt a comfortable unfurling, an easing of tension when I saw him.

'Where's the cat?' he asked as he followed me into the kitchen.

I poured him a glass from the open bottle and told him about Guinness's rough night.

When I'd finished, he frowned. 'So what was it then? If you couldn't find anything in the garden?'

There was a time when I found Molloy's concern for me irritating. It was when it seemed to come with nothing else, when he had been seeing his ex and I needed to give him a wide berth. It didn't help that the ex, Laura Callan, was the pathologist who gave evidence at Luke Kirby's trial. A rather unfortunate coincidence. Now, I liked his care for me but I was wary of relying on him too much. I had been burned before by trusting the wrong man.

'The only thing I could find was this,' I said as I took the plastic bag with the piece of sandwich from the cupboard I'd left it in earlier.

He examined it. 'Are you sure this is what he ate?'

'Not completely. But there was a chunk missing from it and Guinness is the most likely culprit. Especially since it's salmon.'

'Where was it?'

'In my fridge.'

Molloy raised his eyebrows.

I laughed. 'He may be smart, but he's not that smart. It was on the table when you called on Sunday. I'd taken it out of the fridge to throw it out. I presume Guinness got it then.'

'Where did *you* get it?'

'The Oak.'

He frowned again as he took a sip from his glass, leaning back against the worktop as I began to chop some garlic. Now that he was finally here, listening to what I had to say, I didn't want to give voice to the fear that had been lurking at the back of my mind. The two incidents were connected in my head only because of their proximity in time. Anything else was irrational.

'What is it you're not telling me?' Molloy asked.

I bit my lip.

He took the knife from my hand and placed it on the worktop, held my shoulders and looked into my eyes. 'Go on, spill.'

I told him about my encounter with Luke Kirby.

A shadow crossed his face. 'He's supposed to be in the UK.'

'I know.'

'Are you okay?'

'I am now. I was pretty shaken at the time, but all this stuff with the Oak and Carole pushed it into the background. Until this . . .' I pointed to the sandwich.

'I can't imagine how awful it must have been to see him again,' Molloy said. 'But is Luke Kirby really likely to come up here and poison your sandwich?'

'I know,' I admitted. 'It seems a bit far-fetched. But there was that call he made to the office, remember? He threatened to come and see me.'

'True.' Molloy took another sip of his wine. 'But he hasn't. And after my enquiry in September, I think it's unlikely he'd be in this part of the country without someone letting me know. I'll give his probation officer a call in the morning if you like, though. It should be easy enough to check.'

'That would be great. And the salmon . . .' I paused. 'Is there any way you could get that tested?'

'I can't see anything being done before Christmas, and I suspect it's unlikely to go to the top of the queue if I admit the crime was cat poisoning.' He smiled. 'But I'll figure something out.'

'Thanks.' I turned back to the garlic, then felt Molloy's arms around me and a pleasurable shiver as he buried his face in my neck. It was just the distraction I needed. Although dinner ended up being a lot later than planned.

Chapter Seven

On Tuesday morning I awoke to an empty bed. Molloy had said he'd be leaving early to prepare for court, and he wasn't one for romantic notes, so I wasn't particularly surprised. But I felt better for having told him about Luke, and I knew he'd be as good as his word about talking to Kirby's probation officer.

I walked up to court from the office about a quarter past ten. It was still bitterly cold, and the footpath was precarious, glistening and silvery as if tiny fragments of broken glass had been strewn across it. Leah was insistent that there would be 'proper snow' in the next couple of days, and I suspected she was right.

Town was busy for a Tuesday, with almost a Saturday-afternoon bustle about the square. Multicoloured lamps strung from telegraph poles lifted the bluish winter light, and there were carol singers outside the bank. I recognised Hal McKinney, the undertaker, who possessed a rather startling tenor voice. Then I passed the spot where the Oak used to be; the site had been blocked off, tarpaulin covering the worst of it. It was like a bomb site; an open wound in the town's face; a jarring note in the midst of all the lights and decorations.

I hadn't realised I had stopped until Phyllis appeared beside me, a carton of milk clutched to her bosom.

'Looks awful, doesn't it?'

I nodded. 'It sure does.'

'Breaks my heart every time I walk past it. God knows what it's doing to Tony. I've seen him here a few times, just staring at it as if he still can't quite believe what's happened.'

'I'm sure he can't.'

'Looks as if Stan's got the go-ahead, though.' Phyllis nodded towards Illusions Hair Design. There was a sign in the window saying: *Reopening for business at 11 a.m.*

'Have you spoken to him? Tony, I mean?' I asked.

'Aye. He was here with some insurance assessor yesterday morning. They move quickly enough, don't they?'

'I hope so, for Tony's sake. I presume he'll want to rebuild as soon as possible.' I paused. 'I saw him talking to a young woman yesterday. Bleached blonde. That wasn't the assessor, was it?'

Phyllis looked at me with sudden distaste. 'That was his daughter, Susanne. As if he hasn't enough to deal with . . .'

'She's been away, hasn't she?' I said.

Tony was a widower; his wife had died a few years before from cancer, and he had four adult children. With the exception of Susanne, I'd met them all over the years.

Phyllis snorted. 'Not for long enough. He's had to go and fetch her. From Spain.'

'Fetch her?' The expression didn't fit. I thought the girl had looked about twenty-five.

'God knows what it is this time. She's always been trouble, that one,' Phyllis said. 'Remember you asked me if he was away? Well, that's where he was. He didn't tell anyone he was gone until he was back.' She shook her head. 'That one.

Booze, drugs, you name it. Into everything since the time she was a wee one.'

'Really?' I checked my watch. It was twenty-five past ten.

'God knows what happened to her; the other kids are decent sorts. I'll lay a bet she's never supported herself, that Tony's been sending her money. Always tied up with some man or other. No use to man or beast.'

While Phyllis tut-tutted, I realised I should still speak to Tony about the noise. It could be relevant to the fire. In the meantime, I needed to get to court.

Phyllis was still muttering. 'Gorgeous, of course. That's what allowed her to get away with so much. Those doe eyes. At least she *was* gorgeous. Maybe it's time for her to get a job and support herself.'

I spotted Molloy crossing the street with an armful of files.

'I'd better go,' I said quickly.

Phyllis followed my gaze. 'Fair enough. Duty calls. By the way, have you thought any more about my "orphans' lunch" on Christmas Day?'

I grinned. So that's what we were calling it. 'Sorry, Phyllis. I'll give you a shout later and let you know, if that's all right?'

'Sure, no bother. You can let me know the day before if you like. I'm not going anywhere. And . . .' she added with a grin, glancing after Molloy's departing figure, 'you can even bring a date.'

I caught up with Molloy and matched his stride as we walked towards the courthouse. Not an easy thing to do normally, but progress was slower than usual with the icy footpath. Before I could raise the subject of Christmas, he said, 'There have been developments.'

'Developments in what?' I asked.

'Carole Harkin's disappearance. It seems she sent a text message to her husband last night saying that she was sorry she hadn't been in touch, but that something had happened that she needed to sort out. That she'd be back before Christmas and explain it all then.'

'Oh well. I suppose that's good news. How's he taking it?'

'Seems happy to have heard from her. It seems an odd thing for a woman with two small children to do a few days before Christmas, head off like that in the middle of the night without a word to anyone, but he seems to accept it. Maybe she's done it before.'

'Did you ask him if he has any idea where she's gone? Or what it's about?'

'Yes,' Molloy said slowly in a do-you-think-I'm-completely-stupid voice.

I smiled. 'Sorry.'

'He says he doesn't, but I think it's possible he knows exactly where she is and that's why he's not worried. I've told him we need to talk to her about the fire, and that if she doesn't reappear in the next day or two we'll have to issue a warrant for her arrest.'

'Will you do that?'

He opened the gate to the courthouse and stood aside to allow me to walk in ahead. The path had been salted, making progress easier than it had been on the street.

'Probably not. But she can't be unavailable to us indefinitely. Especially now that we know the fire was started deliberately.'

'Are you sure of that? Is the fire report back?'

He nodded. 'I'm waiting for the final Garda forensics, but yes it's definite. Of course, with all that alcohol, it went up like a box of matches.'

71

We stopped at the entrance to the courthouse and stood to one side, our voices lowered as people walked past us up the steps.

'But who on earth would want to set fire to the Oak? And why?' I asked.

'Usual reasons for arson are insurance claims, revenge, covering up a crime . . .'

'You mean Tony himself?' I said in disbelief, my voice barely a whisper.

'I agree it seems pretty unlikely.' He sighed. 'But we've made zero progress so far in working out how, who or why. And it doesn't help that the last person to leave the premises has done a disappearing trick.'

'Amazing it didn't spread, isn't it?'

'That's the advantage of having a fire brigade here in town. They were able to get to it within minutes. And it would be a priority to protect the buildings on either side.'

Molloy's phone rang. He looked at it and said, 'I have to take this.'

'Who raised the alarm?' I asked quickly.

'Stoop,' he said. He gave me a wry look. 'Looks as if his insomnia may have saved lives.'

I left him to it and went inside. As usual, the courtroom was freezing, with solicitors and guards huddled around the radiators like schoolkids in a prefab. It never lets us down, that courthouse; it is consistently boiling in summer and icy in winter. You could bet your last euro on it.

Court was brief. No cases were listed for hearing, and everyone including the judge was anxious to get back to whatever work needed to be finished before the holidays. The session was over by half past twelve. I rang Tony as I was leaving the court and left him another message.

Five minutes later, I collided with the man himself, coming out of the door of my office.

'Tony,' I said. 'I've just left you a message.'

The publican seemed to have aged ten years in the past few days. The lines from his nose to his mouth and around his eyes had deepened, making his long, mournful face seem even longer.

'I'm sorry,' he said. 'I know you've been trying to get hold of me.'

'Don't worry,' I said. 'I know it's been rough. Have you time for a chat now?'

He nodded. 'As a matter of fact, that's what I was hoping for.'

He followed me back in and I left him chatting to Leah at reception while I ducked into the kitchen and made three coffees. I left one on Leah's desk and gave another to Tony before bringing him upstairs into my office.

'So how are things, really?' I asked after I'd taken a deep slug of my drink.

He closed his eyes. 'They've been better.'

'Phyllis said you had the insurance assessor out. Will they pay up quickly, do you think?'

'God knows.' He sighed. 'Started deliberately and the employee in charge does a disappearing trick. I'm not holding out much hope.'

'Well let's hope she comes back sooner rather than later.'

He shrugged. 'George seems to think she will, so it looks as if I'll just have to wait. She's not answering *my* calls anyway – they're just going straight through to voicemail.'

'I suspect you're not the only one trying to get in touch with her.'

'No, I suppose you're right. Not much I can do before Christmas anyway.' He gave me a sad smile. 'My first one off in twenty years.'

I took another sip of my coffee. 'I hear your daughter's home. At least you'll get to spend some time with her.'

His smile faded. 'I wish that was something I could be happy about. She's in some kind of trouble but she won't tell me what it is. Last week she rang and asked me to go and get her, from Madrid of all places. I knew she was travelling with her friend but I didn't even know where she was until she called me.' He gave me a rueful look. 'I know you'll think I'm a fool. Stupid old father – drops everything and comes running as soon as the daughter claps her hands, but . . .'

'She's your daughter,' I offered.

'She's my daughter,' he agreed, his mouth set in an uncompromising line. He paused. 'The thing is, I wondered if you might have any work for her? Not now, obviously, but after Christmas maybe. It doesn't have to be anything too much – some photocopying or filing, that kind of thing. You wouldn't have to pay her. I'd do that.'

I gave him a sympathetic smile. 'To keep her in Inishowen?'

'Something like that.' He sighed. 'The problem is, she's been going out every night since she's been home, and I don't want her to spend her time here drinking. I'd have given her work in the pub, but . . .' He spread his hands helplessly.

'Yes.'

'I'd ask Phyllis, but they'd clash. Phyllis thinks I'm too easy on her. I could see her delivering a few home truths.' He looked down. 'I know it's a big favour I'm asking.'

'Do you mind me asking – how old is she?'

He looked embarrassed. 'She's twenty-six.'

'Has she any qualifications?'

'She started a degree in arts, but she didn't finish it.' He grimaced, knowing he wasn't exactly selling her to me.

'I don't know, Tony. We're a small operation here. And confidentiality is a huge consideration. It's why I don't really take kids in on work experience.'

I didn't mean it to come out the way it did, but it hit home – I could see it in his face. Susanne was no kid. A woman of twenty-six should be able to stand on her own two feet without her father asking for a job for her. I felt a stab of guilt and I softened.

'Tell you what, let's get through Christmas and I'll see how I'm fixed in January. You never know, she may have found something herself by then.'

He looked relieved. 'Thanks. I know all she needs is a bit of a leg-up.'

I imagined Phyllis snorting: *That girl has had so many legs-up . . .*

Tony stood up to leave with a groan. Even his limbs seemed to have aged in the past few days. At the door, he turned.

'I almost forgot. What did *you* want to speak to *me* about?'

I'd nearly forgotten myself. 'Oh yes. Stan MacLochlainn came to see me last week. He wanted me to talk to you about noise coming from the pub.'

'Noise?'

I nodded. 'He thought it might have been coming from the cellar.'

'When?'

'In the early hours of the morning, Wednesday and Thursday.'

'What kind of noise?'

'He thought it sounded like someone moving furniture. A thumping noise, he said.'

Tony looked baffled. 'Is he sure?'

'Seemed to be. He went to the back door and was pretty sure it wasn't coming from the pub itself. Any ideas?'

'None whatsoever. I wasn't here on Thursday or Friday, and Saturday was the fire, but we cleared out early on Monday, Tuesday and Wednesday. Trying to keep our bibs clean for Christmas.' He shook his head sadly. 'Fat lot of good that did us.'

By the time I made it downstairs, Leah had her coat on and was ready for lunch.

'Where to?' I asked, never a question we usually had to ask ourselves. I was beginning to realise the huge hole in our social lives that the Oak would leave.

'The café?' she suggested. 'It'll be chips rather than sand-wiches, but sure, we need a bit of insulation with this cold weather.'

Tim's chipper was clearly benefiting from the absence of the Oak. We fought our way to the counter through a throng of kids who didn't look happy to have their territory invaded on their last day of school by women in suits. Maeve appeared just as we were trying to find somewhere to sit with our bags of greasy food.

'No decent coffee anywhere in town,' she sighed as she made her way up to order. 'I'm going to be getting the shakes.'

'Let's take this back to the office,' I suggested to Leah. 'We can have coffee there. It won't be up to the Oak's standards, but at least it'll be fresh.' I called over the heads of two teenage boys hitting each other with empty burger cartons. 'You coming, Maeve?'

She nodded, and waved at us to go ahead.

'What did Tony Craig want earlier?' Leah asked as we made

our way back across the square. I saw her glance wistfully at the place where the Oak had been; it was impossible not to.

'He wanted to see if we could give his daughter some work.'

Leah's eyes widened. 'Susanne?'

I nodded. 'Just something part-time like filing or photocopying. Do you know her?'

'She was a friend of my sister's. I thought I saw her on the street yesterday all right.'

Leah had three sisters, all younger. I wasn't surprised there was one about Tony's daughter's age. There seemed to be one to fit most people.

'*Was* being the operative word,' she added. 'Susanne Craig went completely off the rails after school.'

'So I believe. Drugs?'

'Drink, drugs and everything in between. What did you say to Tony about the job?'

'I stalled. Said we'd wait and see how we're fixed after Christmas. I'd like to do him a favour with everything he's going through, but . . .'

'Sinéad might still be friends with her on Facebook. Do you want me to see what I can find out about her?'

'Definitely.'

Maeve followed us over after a few minutes. I cleared the magazines and papers from the coffee table in the waiting room and we spread our food there, dividing ourselves between the couch and the chairs while Leah went to the little kitchen at the back to make a pot of coffee.

'How's Guinness doing?' I asked.

'Much better,' Maeve said. 'He should be able to come off the drip this evening and you can take him home.'

'Ah, brilliant. Thank you so much. I got a horrible fright when I found him like that. I was sure I was going to lose him.'

'No bother,' she said with a grin before biting into a burger. 'Glad to be of service. I'm fond of the little guy myself. When are you closing, by the way?'

'Tomorrow,' I said. 'Assuming we get everything done.'

Leah gave me a look as she brought out the coffee, followed by a laugh. 'Well I'm out of here, even if you're not. Anything that's not done by tomorrow can wait till after Christmas.'

I grinned. 'She's right. Nothing's going to happen on Christmas Eve. You working over Christmas as usual?'

Maeve nodded. 'Unfortunately. What are you doing on the day, now that you're not going to Dublin? You're welcome to come to us, of course, but there's no guarantee I'll be there myself.'

'Thanks, but would you believe Phyllis has asked me over? She says she's having an orphans' lunch.'

'God, that sounds great! I'd grab that invitation with both hands. The food will be fabulous.'

'I think I will,' I said. 'What about tomorrow night? Are you going to join us for drinks? Liam was suggesting the golf club, but I managed to persuade him that Culdaff was a better option.'

'Good idea,' Maeve said. 'I'm not on call tomorrow so I'll see how the others in the clinic are fixed. We can organise a taxi so no one has to drive.' She pushed her hair out of her eyes.

'I like the new haircut, by the way,' Leah commented.

Maeve smiled. 'Stan always does a grand job. Although he was a pain in the neck to listen to: moaned and complained the whole time about how he wasn't getting enough sleep.'

Chapter Eight

When I was about to get into my car that evening, it hit me: there were only two more days till Christmas and I'd done little or no Christmas shopping. I usually bought something for Maeve's boys, and Leah too, neither of which I had done, since my plan to shop in Dublin had changed. I didn't want to even think about Molloy. The prospect of buying him a present made me squirm in embarrassment. It would be an acknowledgement of something I suspected neither of us was ready for yet. But what if he gave me something and I didn't him? Such a clichéd dilemma.

Whatever way I looked at it, a trip to Derry was required. I knew it would be thoroughly unpleasant to have to make the trip so soon before Christmas, but I wasn't going to find what I needed in Glendara. It was either now or on Christmas Eve, when despite my best intentions I knew damn well I would have a hangover.

So I rang Maeve to tell her I'd collect Guinness later than planned, and instead of turning the car towards Malin and the refuge of my cottage, I drove to Quigley's Point and down along the coast road into the city, the line of red lights ahead telling me what I already knew – that I was an idiot who should have done her Christmas shopping weeks ago.

★ ★ ★

Turning right before a Foyle Bridge strewn with blue lights, I parked on the top floor of the Foyleside Shopping Centre, the Mini allowing me to park in a spot that wasn't strictly speaking a parking space. I took the lift down to the shopping floors, found an ATM and joined a queue that snaked around the base of the escalator.

The shopping centre was packed. Shakin' Stevens' 'Merry Christmas Everyone' was blaring from the sound system and the shops were full of black velvet and glitter. A huge Santa's Grotto had been constructed on the ground floor and a line of families waited beneath the Christmas tree with its flashing coloured lights. There were people everywhere laden down with bags and boxes and wrapping paper, couples squabbling, parents shouting at their kids. Christmas spirit in abundance.

My gaze switched to the queue ahead and I counted five more people before I reached the ATM. I thought I recognised a young couple a few places in front of me. At first I couldn't be sure, but then the man looked back, recognising me at the same time I did him. It was Eddie Kearney with the girl I'd seen him with after the fire. He gave me a wave and whispered something to the girl, who glanced back in my direction. When they finished at the ATM, they came back to talk to me.

Eddie did the introductions. 'This is my girlfriend Róisín. Miss O'Keeffe is the local solicitor, Ro.'

He was proud of his companion and I could see why. The girl was pretty; petite, slim and dark with long black lashes that made a stark contrast to Eddie's coarse fair ones. A black laptop bag was strapped over her shoulder. She smiled shyly.

'Did you two meet in Australia?' I asked.

Eddie laughed. 'Aye, we did, though Ro's from the Derry

80

road. I had to go all the way out to Sydney to meet an Inishowen woman.'

It sounded like a line he'd used more than once. His girl-friend was familiar but I couldn't place her.

'Did you work in town at some stage?' I asked. I was sure she hadn't been a client or I wouldn't have risked it.

She nodded. 'Aye. I'm a hairdresser. I worked for Stan MacLochlainn.' She spoke softly.

I smiled. 'And did the two of you really never meet? Even though you were working a few doors away from each other?'

Eddie looked sheepish and I felt mean, as if I'd taken all the drama out of his story. Apparently he still had the ability to make me feel that he was a child I'd just chastised.

'Aye, well, we met. But we only started going out together in Australia.'

I tried to compensate. 'Well it was good you were able to get home together.'

Eddie grinned. Apparently he still bounced back quickly too. 'She says I followed her. She went off travelling, but when she said she'd be home for Christmas, I said I might as well come too.'

I reflected that even if Eddie *was* punching above his weight, it was unfortunate that he thought so. Before I could say any-thing, we were interrupted by a charity collector shaking a box for the hospice. I produced a few coins and Eddie shoved a note into the box with a flourish.

When the collector moved away, I turned to Róisín. 'How is Stan doing after losing his flat?'

Eddie butted in before she could reply. 'Ach, sure, he's doing all right – moved in with Ro's family, being spoilt rotten. Landed on his feet there.'

So Róisín was the girl who was putting him up, I thought.

She smiled. 'My ma is mad about him.'

I hesitated before asking my next question. 'Any word on your sister, Eddie?'

Eddie shook his head and frowned, a note of annoyance entering his voice for the first time. 'I'll tell you one thing for nothing. She needs to get back here sharpish. I don't know what she's up to, worrying everyone like that. My other sister Emma is stuck minding her wee ones.'

At that point, one of the ATMs became free and Eddie and Róisín moved away. As I shoved my card in, I wondered at Eddie's lack of concern for his sister. It made me think that maybe Molloy was right in his theory that this was something Carole had done before. I considered people's usual reasons for going off the radar. One was alcohol; disappearing on a three-day binge was not unknown. Did Carole have a drink problem? Could she have started the fire by accident, then taken off in shame? But what about the petrol? Starting a fire with petrol was no accident. And I hadn't ever seen Carole drunk, though she worked surrounded by the stuff.

As I placed the sterling notes into my wallet and moved away from the cash machine, my phone rang. It was Molloy.

'Any news on Carole?' I asked before he had a chance to say anything else.

He seemed taken aback. 'No. Why? Do you know something?'

I recalibrated 'No. I just ran into Eddie, the brother, that's all. Sorry. What's up?'

But Molloy wasn't letting go that easily. 'What did he say?'

'Nothing really. He just seemed annoyed rather than worried. I thought it was a little odd.'

I heard Molloy heave a sigh of frustration. 'I wish we knew where the hell she is. We're no further with the fire investigation, mainly because there's a bloody great hole where Carole Harkin's statement should be. I'm going to have to seek a warrant for her arrest soon.'

'Was that why you rang?' I asked.

'No.' Molloy cleared his throat as he always did when he was uncomfortable about something. 'Did Phyllis Kettle ask you to her place for Christmas dinner?'

'Yes, why?'

'Because she's just asked me too. It's a bit strange. We're not exactly close. She spun me some tale about an orphans' lunch . . .' He trailed off as if he could tell I was grinning. 'What?'

'She knows about us,' I said. 'That's the only explanation. She must have guessed.'

'How? Have you told anyone? I thought we'd decided not to.'

'Not a soul, not even Maeve. But if Phyllis is having us both over for Christmas dinner, it means she's worked it out. We've been busted.'

There was silence on the other end of the phone. I felt a sudden pang as it occurred to me that maybe keeping our relationship a secret had been more Molloy's idea than mine and I simply hadn't noticed.

'She said something about having heard I was on duty that night so I wouldn't be able to go too far. That I might be at a loose end,' Molloy said eventually.

I hadn't even known Molloy was on duty on Christmas Day. It just hadn't come up. I felt uncomfortable, so I said nothing.

'Ben? Are you still there?'

'That's Phyllis,' I said. 'She wouldn't say it directly.'

There was a pause at Molloy's end, followed by an apprehensive laugh. 'Well it looks as if we'll be spending our first Christmas together then, doesn't it?'

I collected Guinness on my way back through town. He seemed much better, though not quite back to his old self, so I left him to sleep on a blanket in the warm back kitchen with lots of water; Maeve had told me to keep giving him fluids.

The next morning, he shot out between my legs like a bullet from a gun, and five minutes later was scratching at the back door demanding to be let back in. While I tried to have a coffee, he took a flying leap onto my knee, circling and clawing at my lap looking for a comfortable position, knocking the cup out of my hand. It was confirmed: the cat was back to his infuriating old self.

Eddie Kearney was waiting for me when I arrived at the office. Seeing him huddled on the doorstep with his hands buried in the pockets of his coat, collar hiding much of his face, reminded me of his past visits, usually clutching a bunch of new charge sheets. There was a time when it seemed that McFadden's favourite pastime had been nicking Eddie Kearney for possession of various quantities of weed. Judging from Eddie's nervous glance when I appeared, he was having similar flashbacks.

'Everything okay?' I asked.

The heavy-lidded look of the habitual dope smoker was back. I hoped it was simply lack of sleep.

'Aye. I just thought I should have a word with you after I ran into you in Derry. Ro agreed.'

I unlocked the door. 'Okay. Come on in and have a chat. I have five minutes before my first appointment.'

In my office, Eddie flopped on the seat and unbuttoned his coat. He was flushed. 'It's about Carole.'

I looked up. 'Is she back?'

He shook his head. 'I think she's been on to George again, but no sign of her yet.'

'So what is it?'

He shifted uncomfortably in his seat. 'It's just . . .'

'Go on,' I said.

He took a deep breath. 'For a while now she's been asking me for money. I've been sending it over to her from Australia.'

'And you need it back?' I wondered if that was why Carole had seemed less than happy to see her brother when he'd appeared in the pub on Wednesday.

'No.' Eddie swallowed nervously. 'Well, aye, of course I do at some stage. But I'm worried about her, especially with her running off. I know I sounded like I was pissed off with her, but what if she has a problem, gambling or something? I don't know whether to say anything to George or not.'

'George doesn't know about the money?'

'No.'

'How much is it, if you don't mind me asking?'

Eddie's freckled brow furrowed. 'It's a right wee amount when you add it up. She gave me some story about not getting enough shifts at the pub, but George said she's been working all the hours God sends, that he hardly ever sees her. That made me think I should talk to you. I mean, what would she need all that money for? It's not as if George isn't working. Sure, teachers make a fortune.'

I remembered what Ian Grey had said about Carole working for them. 'Did you get a chance to talk to her about it?'

He laughed uneasily. 'Aye, but she nearly took the head off me. Turned dog on me entirely. As if I was asking for it back, which I wasn't. I wanted to help her.'

It occurred to me that the person Eddie should be discussing this with was Molloy. 'You know the guards need to talk to her about the fire in the Oak?'

He nodded. 'Tony Craig is spittin'. She needs to come back soon or she'll be in trouble.'

'And you've no idea where she might be?'

'None. I left her in the pub on Saturday night and haven't seen her since. I asked if she wanted to come out to Culdaff with myself and Ro that night, but she said she wanted to get home. But she never went home, did she?'

Tony had been right: Eddie had left Carole to lock up by herself. Culdaff was a favourite destination after the pubs in Glendara closed.

'Does she have any friends who might know where she is?' I asked. 'Or why she needed money? Your other sister maybe?'

He shook his head. 'George has asked any of them who might know. But I doubt she'd have told anyone about the money. Especially Emma.'

At six o'clock, I breathed a huge sigh of relief. Christmas holidays at last. The office wouldn't reopen until after the New Year and we had managed to close all our sales.

I turned the key in the lock and looked at Leah. 'Drink?'

'Absolutely!'

The evening was bitterly cold and I know we were both thinking the same thing: that it felt sad and strange not to be walking around the corner to the welcoming fire of the Oak. Instead we took a taxi from the square and headed out to Culdaff.

The driver glanced at us through the rear-view mirror. 'I've been meaning to talk to you about a speeding summons I got.'

'Sorry,' I grinned. 'As of five minutes ago, I'm off the clock.'

'Starting the holidays?'

I nodded. 'Have you been busy?'

The driver winked. 'Ach now – taxi drivers are like priests, see everything and say nothing.'

I stared at my reflection in the window as we drove, leaving Leah to chat. The taxi dropped us outside the pub, under an inky blue sky filled with stars, frost already forming on the green. When I was paying the fare, my phone rang. I was surprised to see it was Phyllis. I'd phoned her earlier to accept her invitation for Christmas and wasn't expecting to hear from her again. I handed Leah some money for drinks and took the call in the porch.

Phyllis sounded stressed.

'Is everything all right?' I asked.

'Aye. Sorry. The shop is packed. It's not that I'm not grateful for the business, but why on earth do people leave it till the last minute?' She lowered her voice. 'And if one more person asks me for *Fifty Shades of Grey*, I'm going to scream. Apart from anything else, the bloody book is four years old.'

I laughed and stood aside to allow a crowd of people into the pub.

'Anyway, the reason I rang was, would you mind taking Fred for a walk on Christmas morning? I'll be up to my tonsils cooking and he'll be dying to get out.'

'Of course, I'd love to.'

A taxi pulled up and more people climbed out, laughing and talking. One of them was Tony Craig's daughter Susanne, the girl I'd seen on the street; my prospective employee. I wondered if she knew that. She gave no sign of recognition as she passed.

She pulled open the door to the pub, forcing me to raise my voice to be heard over the noise. 'If the weather's okay, I could

87

head up to Sliabh Sneacht. Be a nice way to spend Christmas morning.'

I didn't catch what Phyllis said in reply. I put a finger in one ear. 'Sorry, Phyllis. I'm outside a pub in Culdaff. What did you say?'

'I said, you'll need to be careful going up Sliabh Sneacht if it snows. It was looking very much like it earlier, and it's freezing tonight. Every time the door of the shop opens, there's a blast of cold air that would split you in two.'

'Okay.'

'Anyway, if you could take the poor old fella for some kind of a walk, that would be great.' There was a smile in her voice. 'Maybe the sergeant will go with you.'

With Liam, his assistant Mary, and Maeve and her veterinary nurse, we were lucky enough to commandeer a large table at the back of the pub. The place was jammed with people who had finished work for Christmas, many who would usually be in the Oak. About eight o'clock, the door opened to a rush of cold air and a man strode in carrying what looked like a guitar case. Chunky and square-faced, with an angular beard and black hair, he went straight to the bar. Liam crossed the pub to greet him, and I watched while they shook hands and had a brief chat.

When Liam returned to the table, he leaned across. 'That's George Harkin.'

'Carole's husband?'

He nodded. 'He's playing here tonight. Said he was booked months ago, and decided he'd still do it. Reckoned he had to get out of the house or he'd crack up.'

'Carole's still not back then?' I asked.

Liam shook his head. 'No, but he doesn't seem overly

concerned any more. Just irritated. Said he'd had another text. He seems to be expecting her tomorrow. Said she never stays away more than a couple of days.'

So, Molloy was right, I thought. I gave Liam a sidelong look. 'She does this regularly?'

Liam scratched his forehead. 'Well, he didn't say regularly, but I don't think it's the first time.'

'And where does she go?'

Liam shrugged. 'I have no idea. Maybe she just needs some space?'

'Funny time to leave, though, don't you think? In the middle of the night after a shift at the pub? A pub that then goes on fire.'

'You'll get no argument here.'

We watched George set up. He carried in amps, plugged in what turned out to be a banjo and set up the microphone, then sat on a high stool tuning the instrument.

Liam leaned forward again. 'Wait till you hear him. He's good.'

George *was* good. He had a clipped, rather nasal singing voice, a bit like an Irish Hank Williams, but seemed to be able to manage anything: folk, bluegrass, jazz. The punters lapped it up. I found it difficult to take my eyes off him, I couldn't put my finger on why. He wasn't immediately attractive, but he had something, that was for sure. He took a break after an hour, saying he'd be back in ten minutes, and I continued to watch him while he ordered a Guinness and sat at the bar. His situation seemed so strange: his wife missing for days while he had a pint and played music in his local pub. Every so often he had a brief exchange with someone at the bar – Susanne Craig at one point, Liam at another – but for the most part he remained alone, hunched over his pint, flipping a beer mat.

Then the door opened and a couple walked in wearing heavy coats and hats. It was getting colder – you could feel the draught from where we were sitting, a good twenty feet away. They nabbed a table by the window that had been recently vacated, and when they removed their hats, I saw that it was Abby and Ian Grey. They shrugged off their coats and Abby gave me a wave and a smile.

Ian went up to the bar leaving Abby alone at the table, gazing into the distance with a wistfulness I hadn't seen before. He stood beside George for a few minutes, waiting for his drinks. Then he said something to George, and George turned slowly to look at him, an expression of contempt on his face. He raised his hand and brought it down on the bar with a bang before saying something under his breath. Ian turned away, shocked, to bring the drinks down to his wife.

Chapter Nine

Christmas Eve passed under the fog of the predicted hang-over. The night before had finished up at about 2 a.m. with Liam behaving in his usual paternal fashion, organising taxis for everyone. I was a little disappointed. Tempted as I was (due to sheer nosiness) to try to orchestrate some sort of an intro-duction to George, there just hadn't been a proper opportunity or excuse. We went for food around ten, and by the time we returned to the pub, George had left, his place taken by a troupe of traditional musicians who kept the session going late into the night.

I spent much of the following afternoon curled up on the couch by the fire with Guinness, watching *It's a Wonderful Life* and *Miracle on 34th Street* back to back, thankful that I'd forced myself to take that trip into Derry on Tuesday. The only time I left the house was to drop presents out to Maeve for her boys. Her house was empty when I got there so I left them at the back door, texting her to tell her what I had done, happy to be relieved of any human interaction. Molloy was working so I didn't see him either, but he promised to call over first thing so we could go to Phyllis's together.

★ ★ ★

Christmas morning dawned beautiful and frosty and a good night's sleep meant that I was ready to appreciate it. When I glanced out of my bedroom window, it still looked as though snow was a possibility, though it had been threatening so for a week now since the first fall. I was beginning to think the weather forecasters were crying wolf.

By eleven o'clock, Molloy and I had completed the track that began the walk to Sliabh Sneacht, and started on the route across the heather to the summit, following the red markers. The sky was white and it was bitterly cold even on the lower slopes, which were usually blustery and soft. Fred charged off while we took our time trying to avoid patches of bog, the white tip on his tail a beacon ahead as he stopped and started whenever a scent required further investigation. Every so often he would come flying back, careering around us like a puppy before permitting one or other of us to rub his ears and heading off again.

It had been a good morning so far. I'd woken to the church bells ringing for Christmas Day and Molloy had appeared at my house at nine in red jacket and scarf with the ingredients for a proper fry-up. He wasn't on duty until six that evening, so the day stretched pleasurably ahead. I'd made coffee while he cooked, and when we'd finished eating he surprised me with a present. An antique letter-opener in the shape of a silver dagger, inlaid with green stones, in a leather case. I wasn't sure what I'd expected but it wasn't that. But it was beautiful and quirky, I loved it and he seemed pleased. I presented him with a good bottle of whiskey. Not particularly imaginative or romantic but he seemed to like it too.

As we walked higher up the scrubby hills, the wind became stronger and more biting and the ground rockier underfoot.

Our route was broken here and there by a large boulder or a patch of green moss where it was wet underfoot. My calves ached, my hands froze on the rare occasions I took them from the pockets of my coat, and my face was so cold I could barely speak, but I couldn't remember a Christmas morning when I had felt so content.

Turning to gaze at the view and catch our breath, we saw the twin mounds of King and Queen Mintiagh overlooking the sea, Lagg and the Isle of Doagh to the right, Inch and Buncrana to the left, and the smaller hill, Sneacht Beg. Ahead was a route over scree and jagged rocks, bracken and scrubby grass.

'Dalradian quartzite,' Molloy said under his breath.

'Sorry?'

'The rock. It's sandstone that has been changed to quartz by heat. It's metamorphic rock.'

'Oh,' I said, surprised.

He grinned. 'I took a geology course as part of my science degree. A very long time ago.'

Watching his long stride when we set off again, I realised, not for the first time, how little I actually knew about him. Molloy was from Cork, so I'd never met his family or friends. I knew him only in the bubble that was Inishowen. The truth was, I was in no rush for that to change. What he knew about me was limited to what I chose to tell him, too.

We rounded a hill and the summit was in sight, with patches of white: Sliabh Sneacht – Snow Mountain. We climbed the last section in silence while Fred careered ahead of us over the jagged rocks, touched the rocky cairn at the top at the same time and then, laughing, slowly circled the monument while we caught our breath. When we stopped, it was deathly silent, the air crisp and cold. Cairns of various shapes and sizes dotted here and there gave the place the look of a moon surface. I pulled out my phone to take some pictures.

Molloy stopped suddenly and I walked over to join him. He was looking down at a square hole filled with brackish water, a large stone flag partly covering it.

I stood beside him. 'What's that?'

'I think it must be Tobar na Súl,' he said. 'The Well of the Eyes.'

I gazed down.

'It's a holy well,' he said. 'People with sight problems used to come here to drink the water or bathe their eyes. They believed it had healing properties.'

I knew that Sliabh Sneacht had traditionally been a place of pilgrimage in Inishowen, but I hadn't heard of the well.

'The Well of Eyes,' I said. 'Sounds like a horror film.'

Molloy remained gazing into the black water while I took some more pictures. As I moved away, I placed my foot directly into a freezing puddle. Fate punishing me for my mockery. Molloy laughed as I grimaced and extracted it with difficulty.

I shook off some of the mud. 'The Well of Ice would be more like it.' I looked at my watch. 'Shall we start to head down?'

'Sure.' Molloy seemed reluctant to leave.

I looked at him curiously. 'What's wrong?'

He took a deep breath, hands buried in the pockets of his jacket. 'I spoke to Luke Kirby's probation officer.'

I felt my stomach sink.

He looked up. 'I wasn't sure if today was the right day to mention it but I knew you'd be wondering.'

He was right, I had been wondering, but with everything else I'd put it to the back of my mind and been happy to leave it there.

'Well?' I asked.

'She knew he was back in Dublin for a few days – he had a meeting with her, as a matter of fact. But she's pretty certain he's gone back to the UK now. Her view is that he is genuinely rehabilitated, says he has expressed remorse for what happened.'

'Right.'

'You don't sound convinced.'

'I'm not.' I didn't want to get into this now, but if I had to, I wasn't going to pretend how I felt. 'I don't think Luke Kirby is capable of being rehabilitated. I'm sure he's still sticking to his position that he killed Faye accidentally, that it was a case of rough sex gone wrong. He'll never admit that it was intentional. He knows he got away with it.'

Molloy was silent for a few seconds before replying. 'I understand why you feel that way, of course I do. But as far as the authorities are concerned, he's served his time. Maybe it's time to leave it alone and trust the probation officers to do their job.'

I bridled. 'Like we did first time around? When he got off with manslaughter when he should have been convicted of murder?'

I knew I sounded like my parents. I'd never told Molloy that they blamed his ex for the fact that Kirby was convicted of manslaughter rather than murder, or that there were times when I blamed her myself. Under cross-examination, Laura Callan had admitted that she couldn't be sure the sex hadn't been consensual, that Faye hadn't willingly taken cocaine with Luke Kirby that night. She couldn't be sure that Faye hadn't willingly engaged in 'extreme risk-taking behaviour'.

Molloy didn't respond. What could he say? He looked at me, eyes full of compassion, and I knew that everything he was saying was true. I needed to let things go, for my parents' sake as much as my own; that ship had sailed.

I shook my head, snapping out of it. 'I'm sorry. I shouldn't be taking it out on you. I'd never have been able to handle his release if it hadn't been for you. I just wish I hadn't run into him last week. It's brought it all back up again for me.'

Molloy nodded. 'That was bad luck, but hopefully that's all it was.'

He reached out for me and pulled me towards him, holding me close, his warmth calming me down. It was only when we drew apart that I realised I hadn't seen Fred for a while or heard his excited bark as he discovered a new scent. I said as much to Molloy, who turned and whistled, but there was no response. I called and looked around. The view was clear. We should have been able to see him.

'He's not here,' I said. 'Maybe we should go back down a bit.'

We walked a few yards and scanned the view again, but there wasn't a soul or a canine about.

'Let's try going around to the left,' Molloy suggested. 'He's probably gone chasing after a rabbit or something.'

'I hope he hasn't found any sheep.'

Molloy shook his head. 'There aren't any that I can see. And anyway, he used to be a farm dog, didn't he?' He smiled. 'He'll probably just try and herd them.'

'I suppose.'

We made our way back down, taking a different path to the one we'd taken up. This route was rougher – I nearly landed on my backside a few times tripping over uneven rocks. It was wetter too, full of boggy patches with icy shards on the surface. Twice I heard a crunch before finding my foot fully immersed in a bog hole, freezing water seeping into my boots. Both boots were soaking wet now.

Suddenly our path was bisected by a narrow rough track

running from right to left; we chose the left. But five minutes later there was still no sign of the dog and I was starting to feel worried and guilty. Molloy and I had been so distracted by our disagreement that we hadn't noticed Fred's absence. What was I going to say to Phyllis if we couldn't find him?

'Where the hell is he?' I said as Molloy whistled for him again.

Suddenly we heard a bark echoing over the hill. I heaved a sigh of relief and we followed the sound, skirting further to the left. I called out, and the bark came again.

'It's coming from near that mound over there,' Molloy said, pointing towards a hidden dip.

Suddenly Fred came into view, sniffing at something at the base of a pile of rocks. A flock of crows flew up, unconcerned at the dog's presence but clearly unhappy with ours. Fred looked up but stayed where he was, our appearance not enough to distract him from whatever it was he found so engrossing.

'What's that pile of stones?' I asked. 'There's something on top of it. Something red—'

Molloy cut across me, breaking into a run. 'What the hell has he got?'

Fred looked up and trotted over to meet us, tongue lolling out of the side of his mouth, breath coming in little puffs of white mist, startled when Molloy ran past him.

The first thing I saw was hair; dark blonde hair. Then legs, hands and feet. Molloy reached the woman before I did, crouching down beside her. She was face down, arms and legs at strange angles, dressed in jeans and a blue puffed jacket. The jacket had ridden up at the back and I caught a glimpse of a red and orange top. My eyes widened in horror – I knew that top. My gaze travelled down her legs. A few yards away

I'd thought I was mistaken; now I could see I was not. The woman was barefoot, the soles of her feet so white they were almost blue.

'Is she . . .' I began, although I knew the answer. If she'd been alive she'd have been freezing. Her feet looked so painful.

Molloy nodded. 'No pulse. She's been dead a while.'

Wet hair covered her face. Molloy gently pulled back a lock to reveal part of her forehead, one closed eye, skin mottled with dirt. I'd known it already, but now there was no doubt. It was Carole Harkin.

Molloy pointed to a mark on her neck, a groove more obvious towards the front. A ligature mark. 'Looks as though she's been strangled.'

'Jesus.'

He checked her pockets but they were empty, then stood up. 'You need to leave.'

'What? Where do you expect me to go?'

He shook his head. 'You can't be here. We don't know if whoever did this is still around.'

'Well if that's the case, I'm damn sure I'm not going all the way back to the car on my own.'

Molloy fell silent; there was little he could say to that. He glanced around him.

'Look at the rocks.'

I saw now that the pile of rocks seemed to have been recently stacked. And with a clenching in my gut, I realised that the colour I'd seen in the distance was a pair of red Christmas socks, secured in place by a rock.

'It looks like a flag,' I said quietly.

Molloy nodded. 'Whoever did this wanted her to be found. Although if we hadn't come up here this morning . . .'

'How long has she been here?'

He looked down. 'I'm no expert, but I'd say not that long. The body is still intact, though the cold would have helped to preserve it, so it could be a few days. No predator activity. But we'll need the pathologist to confirm all of that.'

I looked around. This was a desolate, wild place, a place for walkers, those who enjoyed the outdoors.

'How did she get here?' I asked. 'There was no other car where we parked.'

'She didn't have a car with her when she disappeared,' Molloy said. 'George said she usually got a taxi in and out to work.'

'So someone *brought* her up here.' I shivered. I couldn't take my eyes off her feet, had to resist all my instincts to put her socks back on.

'Look,' Molloy said, pointing. 'There's a bit of a trail.'

I followed his hand. There was indeed a faint trail leading back over the hill, the heather indented and matted by something other than the wind. It was possible that Carole could have come that way; Carole and whoever she had been with.

'Should we follow it?' I asked.

Fred gave a sudden excited bark as if he understood what I was saying. He'd been running around in circles, waiting to see what we would do next, well behaved until now, staying back when instructed to do so by Molloy.

'Let me call it in first,' Molloy replied. 'We can't leave her.'

'Of course.'

He took out his phone and walked away to make the call while I stood uncomfortably beside Carole's body, rubbing Fred's ears and chatting to him to dispel the eerie silence. I was relieved when he returned.

'Buncrana will be here in ten. McFadden in five. At least he'll be parked in five. God knows how long it'll take him to get up here.'

'McFadden's on duty on Christmas Day too?'

Molloy gave me a wry look. 'Only till twelve.'

I looked at my watch. Five to twelve. Lucky McFadden.

'He'll stay with the body while I follow that trail. Buncrana will secure the scene when they get here.' Molloy rooted in his pocket for his keys. 'You can go back to Phyllis's with Fred when McFadden gets here. Take my car; I can get back with McFadden whenever that is.'

I shook my head. 'I'll come with you.'

'Absolutely not,' Molloy said firmly. 'We have no idea where that path leads, or to whom.'

'All the more reason to have a dog with you. With us,' I said as Fred gazed up at us with his soft eyes, looking the absolute antithesis of a guard dog.

McFadden reached us in half an hour, a superhuman effort made obvious by the red-faced heavy breathing he was doing when he arrived. His weight loss clearly hadn't improved his fitness. Molloy ordered him to stay put until the Buncrana guards arrived, and he stood obediently beside the body, looking as if this was precisely how he would have chosen to spend his Christmas Day lunchtime.

I had another shot at persuading Molloy to let me go with him, but he insisted I stay with McFadden. I waited until he was out of sight before surreptitiously releasing Fred from his lead. He took off up the hill as I'd known he would.

'I'd better follow him,' I said to a startled McFadden as I set off at a run after the dog.

★ ★ ★

When I rounded the hill, I could see Molloy in the distance, his red jacket making him easy to spot. He was following the trail towards a small copse of trees. I made my way in his direction as quietly as I could, but a bark from Fred made him turn, and he waited for me. He wasn't happy that I'd followed him, but he didn't send me back.

We followed the trail into the copse, Fred leading the way. The trees were dark and coniferous, a damp and gloomy canopy with needles brushing our faces and roots like writhing snakes underfoot. Broken branches implied that someone had come through recently, though it seemed there must be a more established route.

After a few minutes, we came to a clearing. Molloy, ahead of me, stopped dead and Fred did the same. When I emerged to join them, they were standing in front of a tiny semi-derelict cottage with a blue door, or a door that had once been blue. Now it was faded, the colour long since stripped of its vibrancy, any patches of paint that remained curled like dead winter leaves. It had a roof of corrugated iron and small, mean-looking windows. Walls that had once been whitewashed now had tea-coloured lines running from the windowsills like old blood.

The blue door was ajar.

Chapter Ten

Molloy motioned for me to stay back with Fred, and I did so, holding tightly to the dog's collar while Molloy made his way cautiously inside. A few minutes later, he reappeared in the doorway.

'There's no one here.'

'Can I have a look?'

'No – you stay here. I think this place may be connected with what happened to Carole.'

'Why? What have you found?'

'Just wait here, will you? And tie himself up in case he follows me in.'

I put Fred's lead back on and tied him to one of the trees, ignoring his reproachful look, while Molloy went back into the cottage. I peered after him into the tiny hallway, careful not to put my feet inside. From the little I could see, it was clear that cold and damp had taken its toll on the place: wallpaper hung in strips off the walls and old brown linoleum bubbled on the floor. There was a smell of mould and old turf fire.

There were three doors leading off the hall. Molloy disappeared through the first. Frustrated, I walked around the perimeter of the house, peering in through the windows. The first was covered on the inside with cheap adhesive plastic. I guessed it must be the bathroom. There was a section at the bottom where the adhesive had come away, and I looked in to see an old pink toilet, washbasin and bath, all equally stained. There was rubble on the floor.

I moved to the next window, which looked on what must originally have been a bedroom, though there was no bed from what I could see. Instead I saw a pink dresser and two armchairs. The chairs were covered in a filthy patterned fabric with tears from which brown horsehair sprouted. There was a picture on the wall – a framed picture of the Madonna and child – tilted to one side. A grubby lace curtain hung from the lower half of the window.

I moved to the other side of the house, to what had once been a kitchen. A beige solid-fuel cooker dominated the room, with black scorch marks around the oven and grate, a flue pipe disappearing into the wall. A huge old kettle rested on one of the rings, rusted and blackened. The walls had the same peeling, mildewed wallpaper as the hall, and the floors the same brown linoleum, a half-moon-shaped burn beneath the cooker. A second religious picture hung to the right, obscured partly by what looked like a washing line. Something was hanging from the line, and I rubbed the glass to get a clearer view. Two items, brown and beige, soft-looking like animal skin. A pair of boots, facing one another, toes touching. I recalled Carole's poor cold feet and I could hear my own breath.

A face appeared at the window and I nearly jumped out of my skin. It was Molloy. He came outside.

'Were those Carole's boots?' I asked.

'It certainly looks like it.'

I shuddered. There was something unforgivably cruel about

leaving the woman barefoot to the elements, while her boots were left in this mocking pigeon-toed display.

I was almost too afraid to ask. 'What else did you see in there?'

Molloy hesitated. 'I think the cooker has been recently lit; there's a smell of smoke in the kitchen but I don't want to look inside the grate until the crime-scene lads get here. There's no other sign of occupation that I can see.'

I stared at the house. It made me shiver. 'What a creepy place.'

'Yes,' Molloy agreed.

'I wouldn't fancy having to spend a night here. Do you think Carole did?'

'It's possible.'

Fred barked suddenly, frustrated at being left out of things.

'Anyway,' Molloy said. 'Let's get ourselves out of here. It may very well be a crime scene.'

Once out of the trees, Molloy made another call, this time to give directions to the cottage. When he'd finished, he turned to me. 'Right, they're with the body, securing the scene. *Now* you really do have to get out of here and let the authorities do their job.'

This time I didn't argue. The cottage and the little wood had given me the creeps. Molloy walked me back to where we had found Carole. The place was swarming with people, the area cordoned off and a white tent erected over the body. McFadden was deep in conversation with a guard I didn't know. Molloy approached them and came back with McFadden. His face was grim.

'Andy is going to take you back to Malin. I need to go and see George Harkin.'

I nodded. I didn't envy him his task.

'Don't say anything to Phyllis,' he added. 'At least until I've told George. I'll text you.'

Saying nothing to Phyllis wasn't easy. She knew the instant I appeared at her door that something was up, although I did provide her with some hefty clues, returning without Molloy and with a pallor she could tell wasn't solely because of the cold. Fred was a mess too, his legs and front wet with mud and his coat strewn with pine needles.

The scent of mulled wine hit me as soon as we climbed the stairs, and Phyllis shoved an enormous goblet with floating chunks of apple and orange into my hand while she took Fred into the kitchen to rub him down and give him something to eat. It allowed me a couple of minutes by her fire to gather my thoughts, for which I was grateful. I tried to distract myself, usually not too difficult in Phyllis's eclectic sitting room. I looked around the walls: a shield with crocodiles and crossed black spears, a family of ebony hippos, a carving of a man with a beard and kind eyes. Then my gaze fell on the open door to the kitchen and Phyllis's red range, and it was impossible not to think of the cottage again. I took a deep drink. The wine was a comfort but the smell of food made me queasy. I wasn't sure how long I would be able to hold off telling her what had happened.

'He seems to have enjoyed his walk,' she said, drying her hands on an old towel when she came back into the room.

I nodded and took another sip of my wine.

Phyllis ladled out a glass for herself from the cauldron on the hearth and eyed me curiously. 'Is there something you're not telling me? Did something happen up there?'

I shook my head and looked at my phone.

'Why is the sergeant not with you?'

'He had something he needed to do. He'll be along later.'

My phone buzzed with a text from Molloy. He had spoken to George, the news was out and I could tell Phyllis. He told me not to give any details and asked if I would pass on his apologies for his absence.

Phyllis sank into her armchair in shock, taking a long draught from her glass. 'Oh my good Lord. How awful. Who on earth would want to do that to Carole?'

I shook my head. 'I have no idea.'

'What was she doing up *there*?'

'I don't know,' I said. 'I don't know how long she'd been there.'

Phyllis paled. 'Tony's coming later with Susanne. We'll have to tell him.'

'I'd be surprised if he hasn't heard,' I said. 'The road up to Sliabh Sneacht is crawling with Garda cars and flashing lights. I'll be amazed if it isn't all around the town by now.'

Phyllis shook her head in disbelief. 'Christmas Day. Her poor family.'

We sat staring into the fire until the clicking of Fred's paws as he trotted back into the room roused us. He placed his head on Phyllis's knee and she fondled his ears affectionately before standing up to take my glass and refill it along with her own.

'How well did you know Carole?' she asked as she lowered herself back down into her chair. For the first time, I noticed her shoes: red Cinderella-style with a strap and a rose on the side that matched her rather startling crimson dress. At any other time, they would have been worthy of comment. Now they just made me think of Carole's poor feet.

'Not well,' I said. 'I didn't even know she was married until she disappeared. Why?'

Phyllis dropped her gaze. 'I'm trying to imagine why someone would want to kill her.'

'And?'

She shifted uncomfortably. 'I know it's too early to speculate, but I always thought she was a bit hidden, if you know what I mean?'

I nodded. 'I do, but I thought that was just part of the barmaid's code. Hear no evil, see no evil, speak no evil, like a taxi driver.'

'I'm not so sure. I think she may have been quite a secretive person.'

'Do you mean she *had* secrets?'

Phyllis shrugged.

'I assume she *heard* lots of secrets,' I said. 'I mean, you would, wouldn't you, if you were working in a bar with people in their cups . . .'

Phyllis shot me a sly look. 'A bit like a solicitor, you mean?'

'A bit,' I conceded. 'Although people aren't generally drunk when they come to me. Not generally.'

'Do you think it's possible that she heard something she wasn't meant to?' Phyllis asked.

'You mean something that got her killed? In Glendara?'

'Maybe.' The doorbell went and Phyllis stood, a grim expression on her face. 'That'll be Tony and Susanne.'

She disappeared downstairs with Fred trailing after her, the dog negotiating the spiral staircase with surprising agility for a creature on four legs. I stared into the fire, continuing Phyllis's line of thought. I'd shown disbelief, but then I remembered Stan and the noises in the Oak. What if there *had* been something going on and Carole had discovered it? Eddie had said his sister needed money. What if she had been blackmailing someone?

A few minutes later Phyllis reappeared, alone except for Fred. She sank back into her chair with a groan. 'That was Garda McFadden looking for the sergeant. He thought he might be here.'

It occurred to me that Molloy might have gone back to the cottage after speaking to George, might even have taken him there if he'd admitted to knowing his wife's whereabouts.

'Phyllis, do you know a cottage around the foot of Sliabh Sneacht?' I asked.

She narrowed her eyes to think. 'No.' Then her eyes widened. 'Oh hang on, is it in a wood? A wee copse of pine-trees?'

I nodded.

'It's tiny – only one bedroom, I'd guess. Empty a long time? Would be completely derelict by now, I'd say?'

'That's the one,' I said.

'That house used to belong to Peter Stoop, Pat the news-agent's brother. He's been dead a long time now. He was a bit of an oddball, Pete, religious nut, kept sheep on that hill . . .' She broke off suddenly. 'Why are you asking me about that?'

I avoided her eye. 'We came across it on our walk. It seemed a spooky sort of place.'

'I'd say it is. He came to a rather gruesome end, old Pete Stoop, dead a good few weeks before anyone found him. Terrible really, but the truth was that he drove everyone away. In the end, no one would go near him, he was so unpleasant.' Phyllis gazed into the fire.

'So he died alone?'

'It was assumed so. He was dead so long that no one could tell *how* he'd died.' She pulled a face. 'It was a hot summer that year . . .'

'Jesus.'

'No one wanted to live there after that.'

'I'm not surprised. Who owns it now?'

'Stoop himself, I'd say. The newsagent, that is. It's not much use to him up there but I'd say it wouldn't be too easy to sell either.' She looked at her watch. 'Now where are the others? That turkey is going to be done in about fifteen minutes. I know it's far from being a normal Christmas Day, but people still have to eat. And I've prepared enough food to feed an army.'

A third glass of wine, the doorbell rang again and this time it *was* Tony and his daughter. Phyllis had told me Susanne was the only member of Tony's family to be home for Christmas, which was why she'd invited them to her orphans' lunch. But their grim expressions when they walked in made it clear we'd been relieved of passing on the news of Carole's death at least.

Tony was carrying two bottles of champagne. He looked shocked, almost on the verge of tears. 'I bought these before I heard. Seems fairly crass, but I didn't know what else to do with them.'

'Oh to hell with it,' Phyllis said, taking them from him and heading out to the kitchen. 'I don't think anybody would argue that we all need a drink.' She called through the doorway, 'Will everyone have a glass?'

There were sounds of agreement all round. While Phyllis was gone, Tony introduced his daughter, Susanne, the young woman I'd seen him arguing with on the street, and whom I'd seen later in the bar in Culdaff. Bleached blonde with a pierced nose, and remarkably fit-looking for someone who'd suffered from addictions, she shook my hand without a flicker of a smile.

For all the bookseller's efforts to inject some Christmas cheer, dinner was a subdued affair. As Maeve had predicted, she had gone to a lot of trouble with the food. There was a turkey with all the trimmings for the traditional taste, but she'd also included some more exotic flourishes she'd picked up on her travels, like coconut and chickpea curry, and prawns in garlic. An eclectic mix. Which was just as well, since as we sat down to eat, Susanne announced she was a vegan. It seemed to come as news to her father, but it didn't faze Phyllis, who pointed to three or four dishes she could eat.

But Molloy's empty chair ensured that there was no ignoring the grim reality of the day's events, and for all of us Christmas pudding seemed a step too far; dessert remained untouched when we left the table and returned to the fire. Even Phyllis seemed to have lost her appetite at that point.

Fred flopped out on the hearth while we attempted to find other avenues of conversation, by unspoken agreement having decided to take a break from Carole's death. Phyllis asked Susanne about her veganism. I'd noticed a warning look from Tony when his daughter had tried to broach the subject at the table, the same look he gave her whenever she refilled her glass, but now the angry disciple appeared, with her views on animal testing and industrial farming. In the normal course of events I'd have been interested in what she had to say, but today I was distracted, although grateful for her chatter since it allowed me to sink into my own thoughts.

At some point I glanced at Tony, shadows flickering across his face as he gazed into the fire with unseeing eyes, and I realised that he wasn't listening to his daughter either. He looked worried and sad, hardly surprising when you considered that in the past six days his pub had been burned to the ground and his employee murdered.

During a lull in Susanne's monologue, Phyllis spoke, a glass of brandy balanced precariously on the arm of her chair. I thought she'd been the only one listening, but it seemed she'd just been putting on a better act.

She sighed. 'I can't stop thinking about George and the boys. Christmas will be forever ruined for them. They must be heartbroken.'

'I thought you said George and Carole couldn't stand the sight of one another,' Susanne said acidly, throwing a glance at her father.

Tony reddened. 'No I did not. And now is not the time to bring up something like that.'

There was an uncomfortable pause. I stole a glance around the room; Phyllis looked curious, Tony embarrassed, and Susanne had shrunk back in her chair as if she regretted her sharp words.

'Although to be fair,' Phyllis leaned forward eventually, 'it is the first place the guards are going to look. That's what usually happens when a woman is killed, isn't it – they look to the husband or partner first?'

A draught from the kitchen caused one of the candles to gutter, making us all jump. Phyllis went to shut the door, taking the opportunity to refill everyone's glass before she sat back down.

'So?' She looked at Tony again when she had settled herself.

Tony stared into the fire, his thoughts far away.

But Phyllis wasn't about to let him off her hook. 'Come

on,' she said impatiently. 'What do you know? Did Carole and George have a good marriage?'

Tony shrugged but didn't look at her. 'I suppose. I mean, how can you tell really? None of us knows what goes on behind closed doors, do we?'

Chapter Eleven

I left Phyllis's place about ten. When she opened the door to the street we were greeted by an eerie silence. The long-threatened snow had fallen. We'd been so distracted that none of us had noticed. It was still snowing, in fact, the street lights casting an orange glow, the night sky a wash of purple through the flakes.

'So, we have a white Christmas after all,' Phyllis said with a sigh as she huddled on the step, blanket wrapped around her like a shawl, still wearing her red shoes. 'Seems to have lost its appeal now, doesn't it?'

I nodded, pulling my scarf over my head to keep it dry. 'It's been a strange day all right.'

I found a taxi, one of two lonely-looking cars in the square, and although the chat on the way home was entirely about the discovery on Sliabh Sneacht, my presence didn't seem to figure, so I could avoid admitting I knew more than the driver. I suspected I had Molloy to thank for that. It hadn't been easy to depart Phyllis's fire – Tony and Susanne had shown no signs of wanting to leave. Their relationship struck me as tense; I assumed an evening together at home held little attraction for either of them. But I felt guilty for abandoning Guinness all day, not that he would care given that I'd left him plenty of food. I assumed he'd learned his lesson when it came to stealing other people's.

I was in the door five minutes when there was a knock. Molloy looked done in, snowflakes on his jacket and in his hair. I made him a sandwich while he lit the fire, and before joining him I opened a bottle of brandy that one of my clients had given me for Christmas. I didn't need another drink but Molloy looked as if he could do with some company.

'So?' I asked, curling up on the armchair with my legs folded beneath me. 'Any answers?'

He took a sip from his glass and shook his head. 'Hopefully we'll have some after the post-mortem.' He looked suddenly uncomfortable. 'Actually, you're not going to like this, but Laura is the pathologist.'

I looked away. Not only had Molloy's ex given evidence at Kirby's trial, but earlier this year she had wanted Molloy back. He'd told me that his feelings for me had been too strong, but the mention of her still made me uneasy.

'I thought she was a forensic pathologist now?' I asked. 'A forensic pathologist isn't necessary in this case, is it?'

Molloy shook his head. 'It's because it's Christmas and she was the only one available. She came up from Dublin this afternoon. They've moved the body to Letterkenny – she's doing the post-mortem there. And she's staying there,' he added, slightly unnecessarily, I thought.

I gave him a weak smile. 'I didn't think she'd be staying with you. Is that why you're here? To tell me that?'

I felt badly that Molloy should have to protect my feelings in this way. He had enough on his plate. Then I thought about how Carole Harkin's family must be feeling this evening and

I felt worse. Anything Laura Callan could do to find out what had happened would be worth tolerating her presence for.

Molloy shook his head. 'I didn't get to spend much of Christmas with you. And I needed a drink and didn't want to drink alone.' He raised his glass with the ghost of a smile.

I knew how that felt. A purring Guinness wandered in from the kitchen and went straight to Molloy, who bent down to give him an affectionate rub. I smiled at them and stared into the fire for a minute or two.

'How was George?' I said eventually

The cat leapt up on Molloy's knee and found a comfortable spot.

'Shocked, devastated. As you'd expect. I don't envy him the task of breaking the news to his kids.' He sighed. 'How do you tell two children that their mother is gone? Someday he'll have to decide which version of the truth to tell them.'

I thought about that expression, 'version of the truth'. That was the point, wasn't it? Everybody's version of the truth was different. It was something as a lawyer I'd had to consider more than once.

'And the rest of her family?'

Molloy took another sip as he stroked the cat's head. The sandwich I'd made him lay untouched on the coffee table despite his claim that he'd eaten nothing all day. 'I've interviewed George, I've interviewed her siblings, Eddie and Emma, and I've interviewed her mother, and none of them seems to have the slightest idea who might have wanted to hurt her or where she's been since Saturday night.'

He frowned suddenly. 'We had to bring George up to formally identify the body before we took her to Letterkenny. I thought his response to where she was found was a little odd.'

'Why?'

'I can't put my finger on it. He seemed shocked that she was dead but unsurprised by where she was found.'

'As if he knew she'd been up there? In the cottage maybe?'

'I don't know. He said not, but it didn't seem to shake him the way I thought it would. The location to me was one of the strangest things about all of this.'

'According to Phyllis, that cottage used to belong to Pete Stoop,' I said. 'Pat the newsagent's brother.'

Molloy nodded. 'Yes. We've discovered that. It's been empty for about fifteen years, since Pete died.'

I pictured the cottage with its mildewed walls. You'd have to be truly desperate to stay there. Had Carole been that desperate? 'Do you think that's where she'd been since Saturday night?'

Molloy shook his head. 'I don't know.'

'Where is George now?' I asked.

Molloy sighed. 'Oh Ben, please stop the questions.' He looked weary, eyes with dark crescents underneath. He put his glass on the table beside him and ran his fingers through his hair. 'I'm sorry. I just need some time to think. And you know I can't tell you everything.'

I felt stung. 'I know that, but I *was* there with you today, remember?' I wondered again if there was something else going on, something other than work.

'I remember. Although you really shouldn't have been. At least not after we found Carole.'

I took a sip of my drink and stared into the fire. There was a brief uneasy silence.

Molloy spoke again after a minute or so, his voice softer. 'George and the boys are staying with Carole's sister Emma. I think the mother is with them too, and Eddie. Their father died a few years back.' He yawned.

'What's your thinking about George?' I said, knowing I was pushing it.

Molloy looked up sharply. 'Why? Do you know something?'

I shook my head. 'I've never met him, though I watched him playing music in Culdaff on Wednesday night. It was something Tony said tonight. Or rather something his daughter said he'd said. About George and Carole's relationship not being particularly happy.'

'Anything specific?'

'No. He pulled back from it straight away, didn't seem to think it was appropriate.'

'Well that's something we'll be looking at anyway. But first we need to establish when she died. At the moment, all we have is sometime between early Sunday morning, when she was last seen at the pub, and this morning when we found her. Five days. George says he can't tell if she took a bag, but he did confirm that when we found her she was wearing the clothes she was wearing when she disappeared.'

'Apart from her boots and socks.' I shuddered. 'So if she was killed soon after she disappeared, her body could have been lying in that spot for days.'

'Assuming that's where she was killed, of course. She may have been killed somewhere else.'

'Like the cottage.'

'Like the cottage,' he agreed. 'Anyway, the post-mortem should establish time and place of death and then we can start to look at alibis.'

'What about the text messages George said he received?'

'We've taken his phone, so that's being looked at. No sign of

Carole's, of course. The tech bureau are checking out the cottage; maybe we'll find it there, although I doubt it.'

He stood up to throw an extra log on the fire. Before he did so, he leaned over me, held my chin in his hand and looked into my eyes.

'And now, can we please talk about something else?'

Molloy was gone before I awoke. I didn't even hear him leave. What actually woke me was my phone ringing on my bedside locker. I reached my arm out into the cold to answer it. It was Maeve, or rather Maeve's sons, calling under duress to thank me for their Christmas presents. As soon as they'd done their duty, they made their escape and the phone was handed back to their mother.

'How the hell do you manage to find yourself in the middle of these things?' she exclaimed.

'You've heard, then?'

She lowered her voice to a loud whisper, the boys obviously still within earshot. '"Solicitor finds body on Christmas morning". Unlikely that's going to go below the town radar.'

I didn't say I was rather under the impression that it had, until now. 'I wasn't on my own.'

'God, it's so shocking. Poor Carole.'

'I know. It's awful.'

'Hang on, you're not counting Fred, are you?' Maeve's tone changed. She'd just registered what I'd said about not being alone. 'I did hear you had Phyllis's dog with you.'

It always amazes me how many versions of the same story can circulate in a small town. Such an odd detail to keep. I took a deep breath, decided it was now or never. 'And Molloy.'

'Why would you have Molloy with you on Christmas

morning . . .' Maeve paused, followed by a sharp intake of breath. 'Really?' she asked. 'You and Molloy?'

I felt myself flush even though Maeve couldn't see me. 'Sort of.'

'Jesus. Someone asked me that a few weeks ago and I said it was nonsense. Shows how much I know.'

I resisted asking whom. There were more important matters afoot.

Maeve's tone was sober again. 'I'm going to go and see Carole's family later. See if there's anything I can do.'

'Really?'

'Aye. I've known them a long time. Her father kept a few sheep, I was his vet. A dapper little man, a nice man. I thought I'd drop in with some food. It's all so awful – I feel I should do something.'

'Do you want some company?' I asked.

I knew Maeve must have questioned my motives – I'd never been Carole's greatest fan and knew her sister only in passing – but she chose not to voice it. I told myself I knew Eddie reasonably well, professionally at any rate.

'Okay. I'm heading there about two o'clock if that suits. I'll call by and pick you up if you like?'

'That would be great . . . Oh, and Maeve?'

'Yes?' she said slowly.

'Any chance you'd drop me into town afterwards to collect the Mini? I left it in the square last night.'

At two o'clock, Maeve's jeep was outside my house. She didn't bother coming in, just beeped from the road, and I didn't blame her. It was still snowing and getting heavier all the time. It looked as if Leah had been right. We were going to have a longer run this time round.

119

'What's that?' I asked as Maeve shifted some veterinary equipment from the passenger seat to make room for me: a box of small bottles with some loose syringes sticking upwards.

'Blood testing kit, with used needles. You don't want one of those up your backside, I can tell you that for a start.'

She indicated left, took a sharp turn onto the Culdaff road and then glanced over at me. 'So do they know who did it? Some random nutcase?'

'It's an odd place for a random nutcase to rock up, isn't it? Halfway up Sliabh Sneacht? It's hardly some dark alleyway in Caracas.'

'What was *Carole* doing there?'

'Good question.' I told Maeve about the cottage. Now that it was being checked over by the Garda technical bureau, the whole town would know of its connection to Carole's death. I didn't mention the boots.

She frowned. 'Oh God. Old Pete Stoop's cottage. I'm amazed that place is still standing.'

'Only barely. It's a creepy old place.'

'It sure is.' She spoke with such feeling that she obviously knew it. Maeve had grown up in Inishowen, and as a vet she knew most of the back roads and smallholdings. 'So was Carole *staying* there then?'

'I don't know.'

After Molloy's tetchiness the night before, I was afraid to reveal more than I should, so I gazed out at the bleached fields with their scrubby bushes and skeletal trees, the falling snow altering the landscape, making it look strange and unfamiliar.

When I spoke again, I changed direction. 'Phyllis said Pete Stoop died alone. No family.'

Maeve shook her head. 'No. He had a son, Dominic. Took

off to Chicago or somewhere and never came back. That's probably what Phyllis meant. I think that's what finally broke the
old divil. With wife and son both gone, he was left with just
his sheep.'

'The wife left too?'

'She died before the son went. Some kind of heart trouble.
Rough on the old boy. Although some say he brought it all on
himself, drove his son away and his wife into an early grave. I
never liked how he treated his animals either – emaciated sheep,
an old dog that I'm sure got more kicking than affection. I was
only newly qualified, but I was tempted to report him, had a
row with him about it – told him to improve things or I *would*
report him. The next thing I knew, he was dead.'

'And the son had left by that stage?'

'Long gone. Left shortly after the mother died,' she said as she
took a sharp right onto the road that led to the beach, the sea
visible now as a silvery grey line on the horizon. 'It's the third
house along this road, I think. So how was Christmas dinner
chez Phyllis?'

'Bit less joyful than expected, as you might imagine.'

'Who was there?'

'Just Tony Craig and his daughter. Molloy was supposed to
come but he was otherwise detained.'

She looked at me with interest. 'The wild one?'

There was no possibility she was referring to Molloy. I
nodded. 'Although she didn't seem very wild yesterday. Intense,
driven, a bit obsessed maybe, but not wild.'

'I think that's the problem,' Maeve said. 'She has an addictive
personality, takes everything that little bit too far. Her mother
used to say that her levels were set all wrong. She'd meet a man
and want to marry him the next week, that kind of thing.' She

121

shot me a sidelong glance with a flicker of amusement. 'A lot of men, I believe.'

'Well the things she's motivated by now all seem pretty worthy: clean earth, animal welfare, that kind of thing. Hard to argue with. Although I'm not sure I'd be disagreeing with her unless I had to.'

Maeve raised her eyebrows. 'Oh? Well maybe she's sorted herself out. That'll be a relief to Tony; they've had a very fraught relationship. She had an awful time with drugs when she was younger.'

'So I hear.'

'Pity she doesn't appreciate how lucky she is to have a father like Tony. I think he'd do anything for her – for any of his kids – especially since they lost their mother.' She slowed down and indicated right. 'Do you think the pub will be rebuilt, by the way?'

'I hope so,' I replied. 'Glendara without the Oak doesn't bear thinking about. I suppose it depends on the insurance. Although it's possible that Tony won't have the heart to start again now, with what's happened to Carole.'

Chapter Twelve

When Maeve said we were looking for the third house along the road, I somehow imagined she was referring to a bungalow. I got that one wrong. She swung the jeep in between two huge pillars and drove up to a large red-brick house with a fountain in front, an expansive garden and a view of the sea. A life-sized Santa and sleigh and a snowman and woman stood on the snow-covered lawn.

'This is Emma's house?' I asked with surprise. 'Carole's sister?'

Maeve nodded. 'The husband inherited money and they were able to build on Emma and Carole's father's land – nice combination if you can manage it.'

She pulled in beside a battered old Ford, one of a number of other vehicles in front of the house. I climbed out of the jeep and glanced into the Ford's back seat: a banjo case – George's, I assumed.

A huge unlit Christmas tree was visible through one of the windows as I rang the bell. Maeve's arms were full; she'd brought a casserole and some loaves of bread. At the last minute I'd grabbed a set of cheese and crackers that someone had given me for Christmas; it seemed more appropriate than a bottle of wine.

The door was answered by a darker version of Carole, in black jeans and green polo-neck sweater, heavy make-up concealing bloodshot eyes.

Maeve gave her a one-armed hug, still clutching her offerings. 'Emma, you know Ben,' she said, nodding in my direction.

'I'm so sorry about Carole,' I said, with earth-shattering inadequacy.

'Thank you. You're good to call, girls. Come on in.'

We followed Emma through a wide hall into a state-of-the-art kitchen, where she tried to find space for our offerings on an overloaded worktop. Food in a crisis, I thought. At a time when people least feel like eating, those who want to help bring food. I remembered it happening when Faye died, and now I was guilty of doing it myself.

'There's tea and sandwiches in the sitting room,' she said as if reading my thoughts. 'People have been so good.'

Crystal chandeliers and a huge silver mirror overlooked a room full of people drinking tea and eating cake, avoiding one another's eyes. There was almost no conversation. It seemed the standard 'sorry for your troubles' didn't work so well when someone had been strangled and left on a hill outside town. I scanned the room for Carole's children but couldn't see them, and I was glad. The atmosphere in the room was oppressive. I nodded at a few familiar faces – a smile seemed inappropriate.

Watched by everyone, grateful to have something to distract them, I expect, Emma guided Maeve and me to a large bay window that overlooked the garden. George was there, on an overstuffed white sofa with silver cushions, sitting between Eddie and Róisín, looking bewildered. Eddie stood up at our approach, nudging George, who looked startled for a second before doing the same.

Emma introduced me to George and I expressed my condolences in my usual stilted way while he shook my hand mechanically, as if he wasn't sure who I was or what I was doing, his long musician's fingers weak in their grip. But while Emma introduced Eddie to Maeve, he asked my name again. I repeated it and something cleared in his expression.

'You were the one who found her,' he said, his voice reverberating like a loudspeaker in the silent room.

'Yes,' I said quietly. 'I was.' It seemed trite to mention that I hadn't been alone at the time.

I was peripherally aware of Emma's eyes boring into me, and when I met her glance, she looked at me as if something unclean had found its way into her home. I realised I should have told her at the outset. She reached for George's hand but he pulled it back while I struggled for something to say, and I was grateful when Eddie, with surprising gentleness, took George, who had returned to his previously catatonic state, and led him out of the room.

I stood there helplessly until Maeve spoke. 'Is your mother here?' she asked Emma quietly. 'I'd like to express my sympathies to her if that's okay.'

With an effort, Emma switched her gaze away from me. 'Of course, she's in the small sitting room off the hall. The kids are with her watching television, but I'll take them out and get them a drink. I'll take you in there now.'

Not wishing to cause any more grief than I had already, I said I'd wait outside in the jeep, and there was no objection to that. As I left, Róisín gave me a sympathetic smile. She hadn't moved from her position on the couch since we'd come in.

★ ★ ★

Once outside, I stood in the snow beside the jeep, slapping my hands against my sides to warm them up; I'd forgotten to get the keys from Maeve and I wasn't about to go back in looking for them. It was bitterly cold, but at least the fall had stopped. When I'd passed through the hall I'd caught a brief glimpse of two small boys being taken upstairs. The elder, a pretty child with striking blue eyes, gazed up at me and smiled as he was carried away, adding to my guilt.

I looked up suddenly as the front door opened, sooner than I had expected. But it wasn't Maeve, it was Eddie. He came down the steps and walked over to me with a conciliatory smile.

'You were good to come.'

I smiled weakly. 'I'm not so sure. I don't seem to have helped – I've just upset people.'

He shook his head. 'It's not your fault that you found her. Someone had to. George knows that too. I think you just gave him a land. That's why I came out; he wanted to say sorry.'

'God, no . . .' I was mortified. My main motive for coming here today had been curiosity, and I felt appalled at my own lack of sensitivity.

'He wanted to know if he could come and see you, professionally.'

It was then that I realised how much of a mistake my visit had been. George Harkin was bound to be a suspect in his wife's murder. I couldn't take him on as a client when I was the one who had found the body. There would be a huge conflict of interest.

I stalled. 'Did he say why?'

Eddie shook his head. 'I think he just needs someone to talk

126

to. He's in bits. He doesn't have any family of his own and he won't talk to any of us. I've said you're a good listener.'

I thought of the times in the past when I had treated Eddie as if I were a headmistress scolding a naughty child, and wondered at his recommendation.

'Thanks, Eddie. But I'm not a counsellor. I wonder if he should see someone like that?'

Eddie shook his head. 'I think he needs some advice. He was talking about going to see you before Carole was found, but he never got around to it.'

'The office is closed until next week,' I said, knowing it sounded feeble.

Eddie knew it too, and so I found myself giving him my mobile number and suggesting he get George to give me a call when he was feeling up to it. As he walked away, I saw Maeve approach and wondered what the hell I had just agreed to.

Driving back out through the gates, we passed Liam McLaughlin on the way in. He wound down his window, his face grim.

'Shocking, isn't it?' he said, as his breath misted in the gloomy air.

'Awful,' Maeve agreed. 'You heading in?'

'Not for long. I was here earlier – I'm just dropping something off. They've enough gawpers without me adding to it.'

'I know what you mean. Show your support and then go is my motto,' Maeve said.

I could feel my cheeks reddening though I wasn't part of the conversation. The two drivers' windows were next to one another and in the passenger seat I was out of the loop.

'Fancy a quick one in Culdaff before heading back?' Liam said.

Maeve shook her head. 'I've just had a call to go to Moville, so *I* can't anyway.' She nodded in my direction. 'And I have to drop this one back to Glendara to collect her car.'

'I'll take her, sure,' Liam said, making me feel like a child being passed from one parent to the other. 'Drop her at the pub in Culdaff, and I'll meet her there in ten minutes.'

It was only as we were driving off that Maeve said, 'That okay?'

Maeve dropped me and sped off in the direction of Moville, having performed her usual trick of removing rings and other jewellery while driving and placing them on the dashboard.

Sitting with a coffee by the fire in the Bunagee Bar, I felt a sudden draught as the door opened and Liam appeared. He offered me another coffee, which I declined, before heading up to order himself a drink.

'That poor family,' he muttered, shaking his head when he'd settled himself on his stool.

'I know.'

'George is beating himself up that he didn't make more of it with the guards when she first disappeared. He was so sure she'd be back.'

'Why *was* that, do you know?' I asked.

'He was getting those texts from her saying she would be. And she'd done it before. He said she'd take off for a day or two, but she always came back.' He took a long draught of his Coke and wiped his mouth.

'He sounds very understanding.'

'Said she was someone who needed her space. With him being a teacher, she was alone a lot with the kids during the day, so maybe he felt he owed her?'

'But he played in pubs at night too, didn't he? How did they manage that with Carole's job in the Oak?'

'I think Emma was always willing to step in. She only works part-time. No kids of her own.'

I felt again the wave of shame I'd felt at the house. 'Did he say where Carole went when she took off those times?'

Liam shook his head. 'I don't think he knew. I don't know if he asked.'

I couldn't imagine a marriage where that was considered normal behaviour. But then what did I know? I'd never been married. So I hesitated before asking my next question. 'Did he ever wonder if there was another man?'

'If he did, he never said anything to me about it. Not really one to confide in people, though, is George.'

'Or ask too many questions apparently,' I said.

Liam shrugged. I wasn't surprised. Liam's attitude has always been of the horses-for-courses variety. Nothing ever seems to surprise him about human behaviour.

'I wonder what she was doing in Dublin last week,' I said.

'It's funny you should ask that,' Liam said slowly. 'I was talking to Stan MacLochlainn before she was found and he said he saw her on Friday night at the bus station in Derry. With a man.'

'Who was the man? Did Stan know him?'

Liam shook his head. 'I don't think so. I think he was just having a gossip. You know Stan. But she must have come back up on the bus. Why would she have done that if she flew down? Surely it would be as cheap to get a return flight.'

Despite everything, I couldn't help but smile. It was typical of Liam to focus on the finance.

'Does George know about that?' I asked.

Liam looked uncomfortable. 'I don't think so. It wasn't as

129

if Stan said he saw her doing anything inappropriate. She may have been just talking to this guy. Although it does seem a bit more significant now, all right.'

The light was on in the Garda station when Liam dropped me to collect the Mini, so I called in. Molloy and McFadden were both in the reception area, looking as if they'd had a day they had no wish to repeat. I sensed a tension between them; McFadden was pulling files from a steel filing cabinet and slamming the drawers shut in a display of temper I'd never seen before. Surprisingly, Molloy didn't react.

'Have you a minute?' I asked him.

He nodded.

'Everything okay?' I asked as I followed him into the little interview room at the back.

'We've had the NBCI here along with the super from Letterkenny.'

I knew that the National Bureau of Criminal Investigation had been established as a response to an increase in serious and organised crime in Ireland, and that they were brought in when needed to provide support and specialised expertise to the local Gardaí. I also knew that neither Molloy nor McFadden would relish the invasion of their patch. Still, I'd have thought that would be more Molloy's concern than McFadden's.

'Something up?' Molloy asked, closing the door of the interview room behind us.

'Has Stan MacLochlainn been to see you?' I asked.

Molloy nodded. 'Is this about the man Carole was seen with in Derry?'

'You know then. Liam's just mentioned it to me.'

'Yes, we know. We've asked the family but none of them

seem to have any idea who it might have been. Stan wasn't hugely helpful either. He'd had a few drinks at the time so he admits his memory isn't what it should be. He was in some bar and had snuck out to get some cigarettes when he saw her.'

'Don't they sell cigarettes in the bars in Derry?'

Molloy raised his eyes to heaven. 'That's what I said, but he insists that's what he was doing. Maybe he was having a smoke. Anyway, he says he caught a glimpse of Carole, with a man he thought had his arm around her, but he couldn't be sure.'

Sunday brought more snow and was a day for the fire. Guinness joined me for most of it, moving very little from the couch. Every so often he stretched, yawned widely and went back to sleep. I wasn't much different. I hoped Molloy would appear, since I knew he was off, but at six he sent me a text to say that something had come up and he wouldn't make it.

A phone call to my parents in Iceland produced only voice-mail, so I sent my mother a text. There was no reply. I hoped that was a good sign; that the news of another untimely death in Inishowen hadn't yet reached them.

At eight o'clock, I had a call. George Harkin wanted to see me the following day.

Chapter Thirteen

I drove into Glendara to meet George on Monday after-noon. There was a strange feeling around town. The benign, lazy atmosphere that usually prevailed in the days between Christmas and New Year was absent, replaced by an uneasy chill. Much of the snow had been cleared, leaving slushy roads and footpaths. The lights seemed duller, the tree that little bit more bedraggled and the expressions on the faces I met were devoid of any Christmas cheer. The absence of the Oak didn't help; the pub would usually have been the hub of social activity during the holidays, with people meeting for coffee and Christmas treats or a sneaky pint in the afternoon. A couple of other places in town had taken up the slack, but it wasn't the same without the roaring wood fire and cosy dark timbers of the Oak. I couldn't shake the feeling that the town had been attacked at its heart. I hoped Tony would be able to rebuild, to somehow re-create the atmosphere of the original. Although I knew the fate of its barmaid would always hang over it now.

The office was freezing – the heat had been off since Wednesday – so I dragged an electric heater into reception. I decided to see George in the waiting area; not having the formality of a desk between us might serve to emphasise that I could not take him on as a client.

I made us both a coffee when he arrived, more for warmth than anything else, and we sat beside one another as if at some kind of support meeting. A quick glance told me that he looked better. Still shaken, but less shell-shocked than on Saturday and more in touch with reality. He gripped the mug with both hands, elbows resting on his knees.

'I thought she was in contact with some other guy. That's what I thought,' he said. There was a catch in his voice.

For the first time I noticed an earring, a small stud in the upper part of his ear.

'Why did you think that?'

'I saw texts.'

I made a mental note to ask Molloy if Carole's phone had ever been found. Whether he would tell me or not was another matter.

'Did you ask her about them?' I asked.

George shook his head. 'It sounds crazy now, but at the time I just decided to ignore the whole thing – I thought if I let her have her freedom, it might go away. We were used to spending time apart anyway. We get along better that way.' There was a sudden shocked look on his face, as if he realised the implications of what he'd said and that the tense was no longer apt.

'Did you tell the guards about the texts?' I asked.

He shook his head again. 'I've been afraid to. I didn't tell them when she was missing, and now this has happened. Maybe it's my fault. Maybe they could have done something if they'd known.'

There was no point my offering any false comfort on that

score. The truth was that he was probably right. But then it's easy to be wise after the event.

'They'll see me as a suspect if they think she was playing away, that I knew and didn't tell them.' His voice broke. 'I couldn't bear it if they took me away from the boys . . . even for a night.'

I leaned forward. 'I hate to have to tell you, but they'll probably see you as a suspect anyway, no matter what you do. The husband is always the first person they look at. You're far better off being honest with them now if you have nothing to hide.'

He looked up. 'You know she was seen in Derry . . . with someone?'

I dropped my gaze. I wasn't sure how much I was supposed to know. 'Who told you that?'

'The sergeant asked me if I had any idea who it might have been.'

'And what did you say?'

He shook his head. 'Not a notion. It's the truth. I don't know who she was texting and I don't know who she was with. I wish to God I did.'

I remembered what Molloy had said about George's response to where Carole had been found. 'Have you any idea why she might have been up there on Sliabh Sneacht?' I asked gently.

A peculiar expression crossed his face. He didn't reply immediately.

'George?'

He frowned. 'It's not so much where she was found; it's the cottage. The sergeant took me to the wee cottage.'

'Pete Stoop's old place?'

'Aye.' He looked at me, his eyes so dark the pupil merged with the iris. 'Carole used to go out with Dominic, Pete's son. No one around here would know that; she never told anyone.

He was trouble, hot-headed, got himself into all kinds of violent stuff. He ended up doing time for it. They met in England, years ago when they were younger, long before she met me.'

'I thought he went to Chicago?'

He shrugged. 'Maybe he did, but Carole met him in England. She's never been to America.' Again his face clouded, as if suddenly realising the places Carole would never go, the things she would never do.

'Do you think that could have been who she was in contact with?' I asked.

He shook his head. 'I don't know. I always thought she still carried a torch for him – she stayed in touch with him a long time after they split up.' He gave a sad smile. 'The bad boy.'

'So he could have been the man she was with in Derry?'

He shrugged again. 'Maybe.'

'What about the texts?'

He smiled weakly. 'All I know is they were from a "John".'

'And you don't know a John?'

George looked at me as if I needed help. There was even the ghost of a smile. 'We know about twenty Johns, so there was no way she'd have the name in her contacts with nothing else. It must have been a cover. And the way she was behaving, all secretive, I knew there was something up.'

He stared hard at the wall as if the answers he sought were there, looking suddenly lost, out of his depth. I felt out of my depth myself. I'd been asking him too much without letting him know I couldn't represent him, and I realised that wasn't fair. It was time to be straight with him.

'Eddie said you wanted to come and see me last week? Before Carole was found?'

He nodded. 'I wanted to know what my rights might be

when it came to the boys, in case we split up.' He rubbed at his beard. 'Seems awful now that I was thinking like that, while she was lying up there . . . or worse.'

I placed my hand on his arm. 'You were just being a good father. Don't feel bad about that.' I paused. 'How are they doing?'

'They're wee kids – I don't think they really understand. They were back to running around like lunatics yesterday.'

I smiled.

George stared into what remained of his coffee. 'They're very attached to Emma and their grandmother. Most of their mothering came from Emma anyway.'

He fell silent, not realising or not caring how disquieting that sounded in the aftermath of his wife's murder. I took a second to gather my thoughts.

'So you've no idea what happened to Carole on Saturday night after she finished work?'

He hung his head. 'None. Do you think this John person had something to do with it?'

'I don't know. Did you get to read any of the texts?'

'No – she wasn't too happy when she found me with her phone; said I wouldn't like it if she was reading my texts. So I said nothing.' His brow furrowed and he ran his hand through his hair. 'I keep going back over the past few weeks, wondering if she was meeting him.'

'Do you think she was?'

For a few seconds he didn't reply. Then he looked up suddenly, placed his mug on the table and sat back with his arms crossed. His tone hardened. 'Do you know, she was working for that Grey fellow and I didn't know anything about it? What kind of a muppet am I, not knowing what my own wife was up to?'

I wondered if George suspected that Ian Grey was the other man. It would explain the exchange in the pub in Culdaff.

'*And* she took the plane down to Dublin when she pretended to me that she'd taken the bus. Why did she keep lying to me?'

I remembered Carole's luggage. 'Did she take anything to Dublin with her, as if she was planning to be away for a few days?'

He shook his head. 'I don't know; she left early so I didn't see her. There could be clothes missing and I just wouldn't know.'

I nodded. Unless it was something obvious like a toothbrush, it would be impossible to tell from someone else's belongings. And you can always buy a toothbrush.

He looked at me again, his anger dissipated. 'What do you think I should do?'

I felt suddenly uncomfortable. 'The thing is, George, I can't represent you. I know it's a weird situation, but . . .' I didn't relish bringing it up again, but I had no choice. 'Since I was one of the people who found Carole, I may have to give evidence, so there's bound to be a conflict.'

He gave me a sad smile. 'In case I'm charged.'

I decided to sidestep that one. 'If you want my opinion – and it's not a legal one – I think you should talk to Sergeant Molloy. The more information the guards have, the more likely they are to find out who did this. But if you want to speak to another solicitor before you go to the station, then do that. It's probably advisable.'

He uncrossed his arms and held his hands out. 'What could I possibly have to hide? I've lost my wife, the mother of my kids. I just want the bastard caught.'

★   ★   ★

At George's request I went with him to the Garda station, where he told Molloy everything that he had told me. Molloy was kind; he took notes and said he'd contact George in the morning to make a formal statement. But he asked one question at the end that seemed to unnerve him.

'What were you doing on the night of Saturday the nineteenth? Were you at home with the boys?'

A shadow crossed George's face. He swallowed. 'Is that when . . . ?'

Molloy shook his head. 'I'm not saying that, George. We just need to know. It's the last time Carole was seen.'

George looked at the floor. 'I was playing music.'

'Where?'

'In the Bunagee Bar in Culdaff.'

The admission that he'd been playing music at the very time when his wife was in trouble seemed to take the last bit of fight out of George, and he left the station with his shoulders hunched as if he'd just seen the last of his world come crashing down.

As the door closed behind him, Molloy stood at the counter with his arms crossed. 'Are you representing him?'

'I don't think I can since I found the body. I've told him that.'

'I think that's sensible. You can't have any kind of professional role in this.'

I had to stop my hackles from rising; I knew he was right, but it sounded like a warning. Who I chose to represent was my decision, not Molloy's. But I decided not to say that.

'Does he need it, do you think?' I asked instead. 'Representation.'

'Maybe. It's too early to say. But he should have a solicitor with him tomorrow when he makes his statement.'

'I've told him that. Did you find Carole's phone, by the way?

To see if he was telling the truth about those text messages she was getting?'

Molloy shook his head. 'No. But he was certainly getting texts from her, telling him that she was all right. We've seen that from his phone.'

'Can you retrieve Carole's texts from the phone company?'

'Unfortunately not. Phone companies are under no obligation to retain data, and for the most part they wipe it immediately. In this case, that's exactly what they did. Carole's phone has been off since Christmas Eve.' He went back behind the counter, picked up his own mobile, checked it and put it back down. He looked distracted.

'No fire report yet?' I asked.

Molloy shook his head. He picked up a sheet from the desk and was about to say something when his mobile rang. Brow furrowed, he made the five-minute sign to me and took the phone into the interview room at the back.

I waited for him, elbows resting on the counter, watching through the glass door as he paced left and right. The minutes ticked by and I couldn't help myself from glancing at the desk, at the sheet he had just handled. I caught sight of the heading: *Post-mortem results – Carole Harkin.*

I glanced at the door, reached over the counter, turned the page so it was facing me and snuck a quick look: . . . *death by asphyxiation. Victim was strangled, probably with a belt.*

An image crept into my mind. Had Carole been strangled with her own belt? Had whoever killed her removed her boots, socks and belt? I checked the door again, then glanced back at the sheet.

No signs of sexual assault.

Oddly relieved and becoming bolder, I turned the page. *Rigor mortis passed . . . Initial presumption that she had been dead for more than thirty-six hours, further complicated by cold temperatures that delay the onset of rigor and preserve the body . . .*

Molloy's voice made me turn. My heart was beating loudly but the interview room door was still closed. His voice was raised, his Cork accent more apparent than usual. He sounded angry.

I risked another look: *Lividity in the backs of her legs and posterior indicates victim was in a seated position for some time after death.*

I knew that lividity was pooled blood. I knew too that lividity shifted position if the body was moved within the hours after death. I worked back. We'd found Carole on Friday, Christmas morning, which meant she'd been dead by Wednesday evening at the latest, but it could have been longer than that. When we'd found her, she was on her stomach, so she had to have been moved, and some considerable time after she died. So was she killed in the cottage and then moved to the hill?

Hearing a goodbye from the interview room, I quickly replaced the page and pulled back, but not before I caught the signature: *Laura Callan, pathologist.*

The door opened and Molloy reappeared. He looked stressed.

'Everything okay?' I asked.

'Fine.'

The shutters were up. I could knock on them all I wanted, but they wouldn't reopen until Molloy himself pulled the cord. George Harkin's words came back to me: *the way she was behaving, all secretive, I knew there was something up.*

'Okay,' I said. 'Shall I go?'

Molloy exhaled and put his phone back on the desk. 'No. I'm sorry. Difficult day.'

I took advantage of the softening. 'Have you any idea *when*

Carole died yet?'

He gathered up the post-mortem report and placed it in a file. 'The estimate is that she was dead at least four days when we found her. Fibres from the armchair in the cottage discovered on the body indicate that she was killed in the cottage and moved to the hill. They can't be sure how long she was on the hill, but given how well preserved the body was, it's unlikely she was exposed to the elements for very long.'

'So she could have died shortly after the fire on Saturday night?'

'Within a period of thirty-six hours, they reckon.'

I digested this. 'So most of the time we thought she was missing, she was dead? Lying in that awful cottage. And then she was taken out to the hill and left there?'

'It looks like that. Yes.'

'Why? Surely that was a risky thing to do?'

'We can only assume that the killer *wanted* her found,' Molloy said. 'It could have been weeks before she was found in that cottage. Remember Pete Stoop.'

I shuddered. 'God. That would have been a grim discovery. I wonder why he would want her found, though? Assuming it *was* a he?'

He placed the file in the filing cabinet and pushed the drawer shut. 'It most probably was a man. Carole was slight, but it would have been difficult for a woman to carry her alone as a dead weight.'

'Was there anything in the cottage?'

'No DNA, unfortunately. Whoever it was was careful to burn everything he touched.'

'The old solid-fuel cooker?'

Molloy nodded.

'Someone knew what they were doing.'

'And . . .' Molloy paused. 'They found traces of petrol on Carole's hands.'

'Oh. So she might have been the one who started the fire?'

'Yes. We'll be looking at alibis from Saturday night, Sunday morning. We need to know where Carole went after the pub closed and who she was with. And whether she went voluntarily or otherwise.' He crossed his arms. 'Anyway, most of this will be released.'

Molloy was making sure I was under no illusions that he was giving me special treatment, which made me feel guilty about sneaking a look at the post–mortem results. But he was right: the important question now was what had happened to Carole after the pub had closed on Saturday night.

My phone buzzed with a text from Leah as I left the station. She'd had a chat with her sister, done some checking up on Susanne Craig ('snooping' was the way she put it, with a smiley face emoji), and would be in town the following day if I wanted to meet at the office. I suspected she also wanted to hear about my Christmas morning. So I texted back saying I'd meet her at eleven, glad of the distraction.

When I got to the square, I saw that the bank had reopened. My exchange with Leah reminded me that there were some cheques in the office I hadn't had a chance to lodge before Christmas, so I went to fetch them.

Back at the bank, I collided with Tony Craig in the doorway, dropping my cheques. He apologised profusely but didn't help me pick them up, which wasn't like him; just stood there and watched while I did it, looking hassled and stressed.

When I'd straightened myself, I asked how he was doing,

though it hardly seemed necessary. The answer was right there in front of me in his unkempt hair and bloodshot eyes.

'I'm worried sick that the insurance company won't pay out to rebuild the Oak,' he said. 'Especially if they think one of my employees had something to do with it.'

'Carole?' I wondered if he knew they'd found traces of petrol on her hands.

He nodded. 'I know that's what they think. But they won't give me an answer one way or the other.' He lowered his voice. 'Some people are saying that I did it myself, for the insurance.'

'Ah no. I don't think people really think that, Tony. It's just talk. And the insurance company are probably waiting for the final report.'

He looked defeated. 'I don't blame them. I'd probably think it myself. I feel guilty even mentioning it when Carole's poor family are going through this. I mean, what's money when it comes to losing a loved one, a wife, a mother?'

'It's still your livelihood, Tony. And the people of Glendara would be broken-hearted if the town was to lose the Oak permanently. I know I would be.'

He gave me a weak smile. 'It's kind of you to say so.'

'Any idea when the report *will* be ready?'

He shook his head. 'Not yet. The time of year doesn't help. The insurance office has been closed for the past few days, but I'm hoping to get something tomorrow.'

'I hope you do. Anyway, I'd better get on or I'll miss the bank.'

I'd noticed that the security guard was sliding the locks at the bottom of the door. It was almost closing time. He stepped aside to allow someone out and I was surprised to see it was McFadden, dressed in jeans and a heavy jacket. I smiled at him but he walked past as if he didn't see me, his face like thunder. He looked haggard, his weight loss more obvious somehow out of uniform.

'There's a man with even worse problems than I have,' Tony said under his breath.

'What do you mean?' I asked.

But Tony knew he'd said too much. He shook his head. 'Ach, trying to solve everything that's happened this last week can't be easy. Small-town guards just don't have the resources. We're lucky to have a station open at all.'

There was a meaningful cough from the security guard. I took a step towards the door.

'Have you given any more thought to what I asked you last week, by the way?' Tony asked.

'About Susanne?'

'Aye.'

'I'm sorry, Tony, but I haven't really had a chance,' I said. 'I promise I'll let you know by the end of the week. Is she sure she wants to work in a solicitor's office, though? She might find it pretty dull.'

The publican sighed. 'Dull will do her no harm. We could all do with a bit of dull for a while,' he said as he gazed after McFadden's departing figure.

Chapter Fourteen

When finally I turned to go into the bank, I heard a shout from across the street. Phyllis was waving at me from the doorway of her shop, dressed entirely in the precise shade of yellow a child would paint a summer sun, providing a stark and uplifting contrast to the hard grey of the afternoon.

I couldn't hear what she was saying. She cupped her two hands over her mouth and shouted again, and this time I heard her. 'Coffee?'

I nodded and pointed towards the bank, diving in as the security guard gave a loud martyred sigh.

Ten minutes later I was perched on a stool in Phyllis's shop, a steaming cup in my hands, a plate of home-made ginger biscuits on the counter between us. It wasn't difficult to work out how the bookseller was the size she was. Food played a major part in any encounter with Phyllis and was regarded as essential fuel for a chat. And as she regularly pointed out, much pleasure had gone into the acquisition of her considerable bulk. Phyllis viewed her size like laughter lines on a face, the sign of a life well lived.

'So,' she said, biting into one of her own biscuits with relish, ignoring Fred's imploring expression at her feet. I reserved my sympathy; he'd get one eventually, he always did. 'Any news?'

I knew Phyllis well enough to know this wasn't a general enquiry. Despite Molloy saying that all would be made public, I wasn't sure how much he would want me to reveal at this stage, so I decided to keep it vague.

'I think the guards need to work out what happened to Carole on the night of the fire. I don't suppose you were in the Oak that night?'

Phyllis shook her head. 'I'm not keen on the place at weekends. Too many people.' She corrected herself. 'Too many young people, out to get as paralytic as possible as fast as possible. Some of those kids would drink it out of an auld wet sock.'

I suppressed a smile, but I knew what she meant.

'I did take Fred out for his night-time constitutional, though,' she added. 'A quick stroll around the square then out as far as the Derry road. Plastic bag in tow in case you were wondering.'

'What time was that?' I asked.

'About half past twelve, midnight, that is. We came back about one-ish. Turfing-out time.'

'So the Oak was still open?'

She nodded. 'Not serving, though, I don't think. The lights were still on and people were leaving. I saw Carole's brother and his girlfriend, that girl who used to work for Stan.'

'Róisín.'

'That's right, Róisín McCann.' She swallowed the last of her biscuit and helped herself to another. 'I know her mother. She was a right whizz with a computer, that wee girl. I don't know why she went into hairdressing. Anyway, I saw the two of them getting into one of those minibuses that take people out after the pub. Eddie was still drinking a pint from a plastic glass. The bus was packed.' She shook her head. 'Why you'd want to go out further, after a night in the pub is beyond me.'

'You're getting old, Phyllis,' I said with a smile.

'Probably. Although I'd have no problem having an extra drink by the fire at one o'clock in the morning, you know that. It's the idea of heading up the road and then trying to get home again afterwards – that's what I wouldn't be keen on. I'm definitely too old for that.'

'Eddie's family live in Culdaff, though,' I said. 'If that's where they were going. He could have got home easily enough afterwards.'

I remembered that George had said he was playing music in the Bunagee Bar in Culdaff that night. I wondered if they had gone to see him play.

'What about the girlfriend, though? The McCanns live the other direction entirely – they're out towards Derry,' Phyllis said.

'Maybe she was staying with Eddie?'

'Not if Eddie's mother had anything to do with it,' Phyllis smiled. 'Not if they weren't married.'

'Really?' I said, surprised that that was still an issue. Eddie must have been twenty-five at least. 'Even if they slept in separate beds? '

Phyllis raised her eyebrows.

'Maybe they stayed with Emma? Carole and Eddie's sister? She has a big house.'

'She's worse. The women in that family are like something out of the fifties.'

I had a sudden flashback to Carole on the flight to Dublin with the rosary beads in her lap.

'What about Carole?' I asked. 'Did you see her that night?'

147

Phyllis shook her head, dunking her biscuit in her mug. 'I presume she was inside the pub clearing up.' She shuddered. 'God, I wonder if she had any inkling that it would be her last time. Those poor wee boys. I can't stop thinking about them.'

'I know.'

'Although if they get enough mothering elsewhere, they might be okay.'

I noticed that Phyllis used the same word that George had: 'mothering'.

She shook her head. 'I still think she must have known something. Something someone didn't want her to know.'

'Like what?'

'I have absolutely no idea. I just can't think of any other reason why someone would want to do away with her.'

Not for the first time, I wondered if Phyllis might have a point. If Carole needed more money than she could earn or borrow, was it possible she had been blackmailing someone to get it? As I drained the last of my coffee, I noticed the paper that Phyllis had left by the cash register. The headline screamed: *Barmaid's body found in the snow on Christmas morning.* It didn't look real somehow, more like a piece of horror fiction.

The following morning was bright and crisp, and I realised when I awoke that I badly needed some fresh air. The snow was gone and I hadn't been out for a walk since that fateful hike on Christmas morning, so it was time to blow away the cobwebs. I might even go for a dip. I threw together a towel and swimming togs before making a quick coffee and standing at the kitchen sink to drink it.

There was a loud knock at the front door, which made me jump. I went to open it, mug in hand. Charlie, my neighbour from next door, stood on the step, his little corgi Ash, who Guinness loved to taunt, at his feet.

'I think you might have to move your wee car.' Charlie's tone was light, but he wasn't smiling.

'Why?' I was confused. I always parked my car directly in front of my house and was sure I had done so the night before.

He beckoned. 'Come and have a look.'

With trepidation, I followed him out to the green. The sight that greeted me was bizarre. The Mini was parked in front of my house all right, but horizontally across the road, blocking it completely, as if someone had picked the car up and turned it ninety degrees. Two men in work gear stood glaring at it, their own vehicles backed up behind, engines running.

'They wanted to lift her but I wouldn't let them,' Charlie said.

I ran in and collected my keys. When I came out again, the men were back in their cars. They watched as I manoeuvred the car laboriously into its usual position alongside the footpath – there's no power steering on an old Mini. I climbed back out and waved an apology as the two cars sped off.

Charlie stood, hands in pockets, looking amused as I locked the car door. 'How did you manage to leave it like that?'

Ash gazed up at me, his grey face and soft brown eyes echoing his master. I couldn't produce an answer for either of them.

'Thanks for letting me know, Charlie.'

I returned to the house shaken, baffled and mortified at the same time. Had I forgotten to put the handbrake on? But then how had the car turned the way it had; how had it ended up in that strange position?

By the time I'd finished my coffee, I still needed to get out of the house but I'd changed my mind about the swim. Ten minutes later, I found myself driving through Glendara and towards the mountain road to Sliabh Sneacht.

I parked the car in the same spot Molloy and I had parked on Christmas morning, four days before. I had plenty of time; I wasn't due to meet Leah until eleven, and it was only nine now, so I dragged on my coat and hat and climbed out of the car. Unlike Christmas Day, I wasn't alone – a battered blue Fiat Punto was parked diagonally alongside, as if someone had dumped it. No Garda cars; they had obviously gathered all they needed in the past few days.

I walked along the track and began the trail, sorry not to have Fred with me this time. I wasn't entirely sure why I was here. But whether it was underlying guilt at never warming to the woman, or finding her body on Christmas morning, I knew I wouldn't be happy until I discovered what had really happened to Carole. I thought that if I returned to the place where she had been found, something might occur to me.

I'd gone only a few hundred yards when I spotted two figures walking towards me, making their way carefully across the heather – the owners of the Fiat Punto, I assumed. It was only when we were almost level that I recognised them as Susanne Craig and Róisín, Eddie Kearney's girlfriend. I realised how alike they had looked from a distance, both petite, one with black hair, the other bleached blonde. They were engrossed in conversation, heads bowed as they watched their footing, and they didn't notice me as they neared. They didn't break from their chat at all and I suspect would have walked right past me without a greeting had I not forced the issue with quite a loud hello. When I spoke, they looked up, recognition showing on both faces.

'Beautiful day, isn't it?' I said.

Róisín nodded, while Susanne looked around her as if noticing her surroundings for the first time.

'You'd never think something so awful could have happened in such a beautiful spot,' I added.

'One of the few unspoilt parts of Donegal,' Susanne said. 'Bungalow fucking blight, most of the county.'

I met her gaze evenly. 'There are still plenty of beautiful parts of Inishowen.'

She looked away as if she couldn't be bothered having a discussion with someone who was so ill-informed, and I pictured her in my office railing at clients whose mortgages were financing the bungalow blight.

I dismissed the image and turned to Róisín. 'How are Carole's family doing?'

'They're surviving,' she said quietly. 'The wee boys don't really know what's going on, which is just as well. But they've released the body so at least we can have the wake.'

'Oh, that's something, I suppose.'

She nodded. 'Emma and Eddie are pleased. The wake will be tonight and tomorrow at Emma's, and then the funeral is on Thursday.' She gave a timid smile. 'No kissing under the tree this year.'

With a jolt, I remembered that Thursday was New Year's Eve, the night when the people of Glendara poured out of the pubs at midnight to ring in the new year under the tree.

'How is Eddie?' I asked.

She sighed. 'He blames himself. He thinks he shouldn't have left Carole to lock up by herself, that we shouldn't have gone out to Culdaff. But she insisted, wanted us to go and see George, said he'd be glad of the support. Practically shoved us out the door, didn't she, Sue?'

Susanne nodded. She looked down, kicking at a clump of heather with her boot.

'Why do you think she did that?' I asked.

Róisín lowered her gaze. 'I thought at the time she just wanted Eddie to have some fun while he was home, but I wonder now if she was waiting for someone. Although I haven't said that to Eddie. It'll only make him feel worse.'

'Who would she have been waiting for?' I asked.

'I don't know,' she said sadly. 'What I do know is that she kept looking at her watch. Eddie thinks she's been afraid of something since we've been back, but he's only being wise after the event; he doesn't know. None of us do.'

'When are you due to go back to Australia?'

'Oh, she's not going back,' Susanne interjected, the first time she'd spoken since her bungalow comment.

A look was exchanged between them; I wondered what it meant.

'Are you staying here, then?' I asked. 'In Glendara?'

I wondered what Eddie would feel about Róisín not returning to Australia with him. He seemed pretty besotted. Although it occurred to me that he might decide to stay on too, to support his mother and remaining sister.

Róisín nodded. 'I never really intended staying in Australia. I was only there on a working holiday. I'm back working for Stan again.'

'Maybe I'll come in for a trim.' I smiled.

'Good idea,' she said, then looked self-conscious when I laughed.

As I left them to make their way back to their car, I wondered at their choosing a place for a walk where a murdered woman had been found so recently. But then at least there were two of them – I was walking here too, and I was alone. The notion made me glance anxiously over my shoulder.

I made my way over the heather, doing my best to retrace our steps from Christmas morning, wishing again that I had Fred with me. The wooden markers made it easy enough, and within half an hour I'd come to the spot where Fred had found Carole's body. The little pile of stones was still there. It was eerie seeing it again, remembering the bright socks, trying to imagine what had happened to her. In my present state of mind, the red moss beneath my feet reminded me of pooling blood.

After a few minutes, I went on, following the route we had taken to the cottage and reaching the copse within a few minutes now that I knew where it was. I realised that it would have been perfectly possible for a man with strength to carry a body this distance, particularly someone as slight as Carole and particularly downhill.

My heart raced as I made my way through the trees; even the branches appeared threatening. It was hard not to imagine what it must have been like for Carole if she had been brought here against her will. I wondered if she had ever come here with Dominic, then remembered she had known him only in England. From what George had said, she had never even told anyone they were a couple. Appearances were important to Carole; I had witnessed her pass judgement on others more than once, sometimes unkindly. She wouldn't have wanted to leave herself open to that same judgement. I wondered suddenly why she had told George.

The cottage was just as we had found it, its front door still ajar. But this time I went inside, making my way into the tiny hallway to the still-present odour of damp and old turf fire.

I went into each of the rooms in turn – bedroom, bathroom and kitchen – rooms I'd only been able to peer at through the windows on Christmas Day. Some of the furniture had been removed, for analysis I assumed, although from what Molloy had said, they had found nothing of note. Finally I stood in the kitchen, with its peeling wallpaper, its scorched and bubbled floor, and wondered how three people had ever lived here. The washing line with its pegged boots had been removed, but the memory of Christmas morning returned with a vengeance and the ground seemed to sway beneath my feet, as if the entire house were tilted to one side. There was a malevolence here that made me shiver.

And something about the boots and socks that bothered me. Something that didn't fit. But it remained just out of reach.

It was time to leave.

Although it was morning, and too early in the day for the light to be failing, the bright winter sky had clouded over when I came outside, and once in the trees I lost my way quickly, veering off the path Molloy and I had followed. Uneasily I wondered if the malevolence I had felt at the cottage was connected with what had happened to Carole, or if it was something further back. What exactly had Dominic Stoop done to wind up in prison?

Fighting off sharp, burned-looking branches to find my way back onto a better path, I saw something glint on the ground a few yards in front of me and made my way towards it. Silver, I thought at first, but when I reached it, my breath caught. It was a belt, a woman's brown Western-style belt with a decorative silver buckle. Could it be the belt with which Carole had been strangled? If so, why had the guards not found it? Or the killer taken it?

However it had ended up here, one thing was certain. I needed to take it with me. I searched in my pockets for a handkerchief, but the best I could come up with was a used tissue. I was sure Molloy would tell me off for that, but it was better than picking the belt up with my bare hands. I hoped. I crouched down and scooped it up, hands trembling a little, then, holding it straight out in front of me and trying to avoid any more contact than necessary, made my way back down the hill. Hoping not to meet anyone else; wondering how I would explain myself if I did.

I didn't. I drove back into town with my precious cargo and headed straight for the Garda station. Molloy, alone when I walked in, took it from me in stunned silence when I told him where I had found it. He wasn't thrilled about my tissue, but he used a clean cloth to place the belt carefully in a plastic evidence bag, then took a DNA sample from me. I knew it was needed so that my DNA could be eliminated in case any had transferred from the tissue to the belt, but he still explained it to me as if I were a child.

He leaned over me to take a swab from inside my cheek, his face so close to mine that I inhaled his scent. We'd had so little time alone together lately that I flushed. He looked into my eyes, and I made a joke to cover my embarrassment.

'This means my DNA will be on file, doesn't it? I'd better not commit any more crimes so . . .'

He raised one eyebrow but didn't respond. He placed the swab in a glass tube, sealed and marked it and put the tube into another evidence bag. Then he shook his head in frustration.

'How the hell was this not found?'

155

Chapter Fifteen

I was late, so Leah was in the office before me. She had turned on the heating, made herself a coffee and was sitting at her computer when I arrived. If it hadn't been for the oversized penguin jumper she was wearing, you'd have thought it was an ordinary working day.

She looked up as I closed the door behind me. 'Jesus, you've had an eventful Christmas, haven't you?'

'I hope yours was quieter.' I nodded at her mug. 'Do you want another?'

She shook her head. 'It's just made. I picked up some milk on the way and stuck it in the fridge. And there's some of my mother's Christmas cake if you can face it.'

'I might have some later . . . Bit early for me still. Thanks, Leah.'

I headed out the back to make myself a coffee. When I returned, the familiar blue masthead on her screen showed that Leah had logged onto Facebook. While not a user of the site myself – I've always been afraid of what I might reveal if I signed up to it – I do see its attraction. And I hoped it would be useful now. I perched on the reception desk beside her while I sipped my coffee.

'So, what have you found out about our prospective employee? Is she the trouble with a capital T I keep hearing she is?'

'Just give me two wee seconds.' Leah tapped some keys, then angled the computer towards me so I could see the screen. 'Remember I told you she was a Facebook friend of my sister's? That they were in the same year in school?'

I nodded.

'Well, it took a bit of persuasion, but Sinéad agreed to give me her password so I could log onto her page, which means I now have access to her friends' pages.' She grinned. 'Bribery always works with my sisters. Especially around Christmas.'

I looked at the page. Sinéad's profile picture showed her somewhere hot, wearing a bikini and a broad smile and holding a cocktail. Leah clicked on her sister's 'Friends' and a series of images and names appeared. She moved the cursor down, selected an image of a monkey, clicked on the image and Susanne Craig's Facebook page popped up. On closer view, the monkey picture was not a happy one. It had been taken from an anti-vivisection site, and the creature was the picture of misery, splayed on an iron frame, hooked up to wires and needles. I swallowed. It was one of those images of animal suffering that gets you in the gut and stays with you long after you've seen it.

'I thought she was supposed to be a party girl?' Sinéad's page looked more like what I would have expected for Susanne, at least until I'd met her on Christmas Day.

'She certainly used to be,' Leah agreed. 'Drugs, drink, dodgy boyfriends, the lot. But looking at this, she seems to have gone to the other extreme. Everything she posts is about listening to your conscience.'

'Amnesty International, that kind of thing?'

Leah's brow furrowed. 'Not so much human rights; more

environmental issues and animal rights. Particularly animal rights. She's a vegetarian, according to her profile . . .'

'Vegan,' I said.

'Sorry?' Leah turned to look at me in surprise.

I smiled. 'She's a vegan. I had Christmas lunch with her.'

'Jesus, you have been busy. Where did that happen?'

'Phyllis's. I'll tell you about it later. Anyway, what kind of *work* has she done? I suppose we need to know her employment history if we're to think about giving her a job. She seems a bit old for work experience.'

Leah ran down through her page. 'It's not very clear. She describes herself as "a citizen of the world".' She raised her eyes to heaven. 'And she's not on LinkedIn or any of those worky networking sites. The weird thing is that after posting nearly every day for ages, she disappears completely from view online about three months ago. Nothing since then, not a dicky bird.'

'I think she may have got herself into some kind of strife. I don't know what. Phyllis said Tony had to go to Spain to bring her back. Has your sister had any direct contact with her, or is it just Facebook stuff?'

'Just Facebook, I think. I don't think they even communicate on Facebook, just have access to each other's posts. They were friends when they were kids, but that's a long time ago.'

I leaned back and took another sip of my coffee. 'So what do you think of giving her some work?'

Leah shrugged. 'You could suggest a couple of days a week as a trial, see if she's any use and if we have enough for her to do. Then if it doesn't work, we have a way out.'

'Maybe,' I said doubtfully. I wasn't keen. 'I'd be doing Tony a favour really. We don't need anyone, to be honest.'

Leah raised her eyebrows, and I had a flashback of her buried behind a mountain of files the week before Christmas. But Christmas week was exceptional – there was a distinct possibility that by March we'd be painting each other's nails.

'Okay, okay,' I said, my hands up. 'I'm concerned about the confidentiality end of things, though.'

Leah grinned. 'There's always the attic.'

'Oh God, could we do that to her?'

The attic hadn't been cleared out since I bought the place. It was crammed with junk that had belonged to the man who owned it before I did. He had fancied himself as something of an artist, and the attic was full of his paintings and sketches. I'd been tempted to throw the whole lot out, but so far I'd stalled, hoping to find the time or the enthusiasm to go through it and see if there was anything of value. Leah was right. It might be a job for Susanne, which would keep her away from anything confidential.

'I'll give it some thought,' I said. 'So who else can we spy on?' I asked, leaning in with interest.

'Ach now.' Leah settled back in her seat with her mug in her hands. 'I think that now we have that sorted, you'll have to tell me about your Christmas. What on earth happened to poor Carole?'

I told her as much as I knew. I trust Leah, but she is also bound by office confidentiality. A bibs-and-braces approach, if you like. It makes it easier for me to discuss things I wouldn't with anyone else, and I expect it makes things easier for her. There is no grey area.

'God, what a thing to happen at Christmas,' she said. 'Those poor kids.'

'I know,' I said. Then something hit me. 'Actually, I wonder if Carole had a Facebook page? Would we be able to see it if she had?'

'Depends on her privacy settings,' she said. 'Although she was over thirty-five, and often the over thirty-fives aren't too smart about that kind of thing. We might be able to see more than she would have wanted us to.' She turned back to the computer.

Just as she was about to type in Carole's name and move off Susanne Craig's page, something caught my eye to the right of the screen. It was a thumbnail picture of a man singing. 'Hang on a second. Isn't that George Harkin, Carole's husband?'

Leah looked. 'Aye, it is,' she said. 'It looks as if he and Susanne are friends.'

'Facebook friends?'

She nodded. 'George would have taught Susanne in school. He taught my sister music too.'

'Is it not a bit odd to be friends with your teacher?' I asked.

Leah shrugged. 'Maybe. I'm not sure I'd want to be friends with any of mine. But he's her ex-teacher. And it would be a good seven or eight years since he taught her.'

'Can you click on his page?' I asked.

She did so, and a larger image appeared. It had been taken in a pub by the look of it; it might even have been the Oak. Beneath the image it said: *To see what George shares with friends, send him a friend request.*

'He's been careful with his privacy settings so I can't access his page fully because Sinéad isn't a friend of his,' Leah said. 'But I *can* see some stuff. It seems to be mostly about music. Maybe that's why they've stayed in contact? Maybe Susanne is interested in music?'

'Maybe,' I said, although I still thought it was a bit odd. 'What about Carole?' I asked. 'Did she have a page?'

Leah scrolled down through George's friends. 'She doesn't seem to have.' She threw me a look. 'If she did, she wasn't friends with her husband.'

I watched as she did a search using Carole's name – there were a number of Carole Harkins, but none was the right one. She tried again using Carole Kearney, but had no luck with that either.

I sat back. 'So Susanne and George know each other,' I said thoughtfully.

I remembered seeing her talking to him in the pub in Culdaff before Christmas, and racked my brain to see if I could remember anything unusual about it, but I couldn't. It was the exchange with Ian Grey that I remembered.

'It might be just online,' Leah said. 'Susanne sent him a friendship request and he accepted it.'

'I still think that's odd for a teacher and pupil.'

'Ex,' she said again.

'Okay, ex. Let's see if he's friends with Róisín. Can you check that?'

Leah turned her chair to look at me, surprised. 'Róisín McCann? Why?'

I nodded. 'She's Eddie Kearney's girlfriend.'

'Really? She's going out with Eddie Kearney?'

'Yes. Why?'

Leah shrugged. 'I just wouldn't have put them together. The druggie and the swot.'

'You make it sound like an American high-school movie,' I laughed. 'I met herself and Susanne on Sliabh Sneacht this morning. They seem to be friends.'

'Oh aye, they'd have been great muckers in school. Róisín McCann was a lot quieter than Susanne, though. Susanne was wild enough for the two of them.' She did a search, then shook her head. 'No, Róisín doesn't have a Facebook page. Although that doesn't surprise me.'

'Why not?' I said. 'Don't most people your sister's age have one?'

'Róisín was a real computer whizz in school. One time she hacked into the school's system and generated a series of emails to parents telling them that the school was to close for a week because of burst pipes. There was chaos.'

'Wow. Was she expelled?'

'Suspended,' Leah grinned. 'The school didn't know how to fix it so they had to get her back in to do it for them. She'd encrypted everything. A bit embarrassing all round. I'd say she keeps her online activity fairly hidden.'

'I'll bet.' I stood up and rubbed my neck. 'Okay. Thanks for that, Leah.'

'No bother.' She glanced up. 'So are we done? Is that all you need?'

'Yep. You can go back to enjoying your Christmas holidays.'

She sighed as she switched off the computer. 'To be honest, I'm bored stiff. Wouldn't have thought I'd be saying that last week!'

Before she put on her coat, I noticed that she couldn't help tidying up a few things on her desk, and as I pulled on my own coat and scarf she picked up a sheet of dictation, one that hadn't been reached when we closed for holidays. She showed it to me, pointing to one item on the list with a grim smile. 'I presume I can cross that one out?'

It was a letter to Tony Craig. It took me a second to recollect what it was, and suddenly I remembered what I needed to do.

I said goodbye to Leah at the county council offices, where she had parked her car, then made my way back towards the square. Averting my eyes from the painful gap where the Oak used to be, I pushed open the door of Illusions Hair Design. I'd never been to Stan's salon before, preferring the anonymity of Derry, so I felt a little apprehensive.

The sweet scent of shampoo mixed with the more chemical smell of ammonia greeted me immediately, the room I entered small but highly decorated: black wallpaper with red poppies covering one wall, while the others were white. There were two sinks in the centre of the room and three circular mirrors along one wall, Hollywood-style lights surrounding each. Two women were engrossed in magazines under dryers, while another was having some complicated dyeing procedure administered by Róisín, who looked up and gave me a smile. The heating must have been on full blast, since all the windows were open. I wondered if they were still trying to clear an underlying smell of smoke.

Stan himself had his back to me and the drone of the hairdryers meant he hadn't heard me come in. I watched while he moved from client to client like a priest offering benediction, clearly in his element. Finally, he turned, spotted me, and came over. I smiled. He was wearing black combats and a violet T-shirt with *I am a Glendara girl!* emblazoned across it.

'Are you lost?' he asked.

I ignored the dig. 'I was wondering if I could make an appointment for a trim? Tomorrow, if possible?'

He gave me the quick once-over. 'We can do you now, darling. It looks like it might be urgent.'

I flashed him a fake smile. 'No, it's grand. Tomorrow will do if you have the space. I think I can last till then.'

He pursed his lips. 'If you say so. I'm not sure I would.'

He sashayed over to the desk, where Abby Grey was waiting to pay. I hadn't noticed her till now.

'Four o'clock do you?' Stan asked when he'd checked the book.

'Great.'

'I'll look forward to it. I like a challenge,' he grinned.

Abby shot me a sympathetic look.

I was standing on the footpath rooting in my bag for my keys when she emerged, coat and scarf in hand.

'I suppose that's Stan's revenge for my never having come to him before,' I said.

'Yes,' she smiled, pulling on her coat. 'He does seem to expect absolute loyalty. He's worth it, though.'

'I like your cut,' I said, and it was the truth. Stan had managed to maintain Abby's pixie style without making it seem too young for her.

'Actually, it was Róisín who did this,' she said. 'I know it sounds pretty shallow, but it always gives me a bit of a boost having my hair done. I get it blow-dried about once a week. It's been a rough old Christmas.'

'Yes.'

She glanced towards the Oak. 'The town looks so dreadful with that big hole in the middle of it. Stan's not too happy about it.' She wrapped her scarf around her neck and knotted it loosely. 'He was never awfully keen on Tony to begin with, and now this.'

'Really?' I tried to keep the surprise out of my voice, but failed.

Abby flushed. 'Oh, maybe I got the wrong end of the stick,' she said hurriedly.

'I thought they rubbed along okay? I mean, I never thought they were bosom buddies, but . . .'

But it was no good. Abby Grey wasn't going to say anything further. She was the out-of-towner who had said too much.

'Oh, don't mind me,' she said quickly. 'I was probably putting two and two together and getting five. I'm sure it was just the noise he was complaining about.'

'He mentioned that?'

She bit her lip. 'Just that he couldn't sleep. I was in before Christmas and he said something about it.'

She couldn't get away from me quickly enough. Even her body language was in retreat. I changed the subject. 'Are you going to Carole's funeral?'

She looked relieved. 'Oh yes, we will, of course. She did some work for us, you know?'

'Yes, Ian told me.'

'I was fond of her.'

There was something about the way she spoke with her lips almost closed that made it sound as if she meant the opposite. It made me recall what Phyllis had said about Carole knowing things. There was no better way to discover things about people than to clean for them.

'Ian said she might have been going to work for you in the hotel?' I said.

'Oh yes,' she replied, her eyes gleaming, and then she was suddenly silent.

Abby Grey was not a good liar. It was clear that she had had no idea that her husband had offered Carole a job.

Chapter Sixteen

The following morning my phone buzzed on my bedside locker first thing. It was a text from Maeve.

Fancy heading into the sales in Derry? Finally have a day off and could do with a bit of light relief.

I knew what she meant. A morning's potter around the shops and lunch out sounded good, in the midst of all this darkness. I typed a response.

Only if we're back by four. I have an appointment for what Stan considers an emergency haircut.

My phone buzzed again.

You're on. And from what I've seen of you lately, he's probably right. She signed off with a winking face emoji.

I put a pillow behind my head and lay in bed trying to block out the sound of Guinness mewing on the doorstep downstairs. I knew if I left him long enough he'd appear at my bedroom window, making his way up the tree outside and leaping across to the sill, but I needed to organise my thoughts. Today was Carole's wake. Róisín had said it would be in Emma's house, probably because it was big enough to handle the numbers they would expect. I tried to decide if I should give it a miss after the reception I'd received the last time I'd been there.

A scratching at the window interrupted my thoughts; the cat had given up waiting. I climbed out of bed, flung on a bathrobe and let him in. Downstairs, I made porridge, chucking in some banana, honey and cinnamon, and finished off with a big pot of coffee, while Guinness got his usual dried food and water. I wasn't taking any chances with his diet since the incident with the salmon. By the time I threw the dishes into the sink, I had decided to avoid the wake and go to the funeral in the morning instead.

The radio forecast said icy weather, but when I looked at the sky as I left the house, I had a horrible feeling that snow might be on its way again. I really wasn't sure I could face a third bout. But they were right about the ice – when I went out to the car, the windscreen was frozen.

While I was defrosting with the kettle, Charlie and Ash appeared at their gate.

'Another cold one.'

'Sure is, Charlie.'

He walked over, the little dog trailing after him, both of them standing to watch while I continued my task.

'No more bother with that handbrake?' he said, lips curling in amusement.

'No, Charlie.'

'Still closed for the holidays?'

I nodded and splashed water over my feet at the same time. So much for women being able to multitask. Charlie took a step back, clearly not trusting my aim. As did Ash.

'Any news on Tony Craig's pub?' he asked. 'Two weeks on Saturday since it burned.'

'I don't think so.'

'Pity.' He smiled. 'Wild man to tell a long story is Tony.'

'He hasn't been doing too much of that lately, unfortunately.'

'Aye. Decent man all the same. Many's the time he's driven me home after one too many.' He winked at me. 'Sure, we've all done it.'

A wave of embarrassment spread up my neck and into my face as it dawned on me. Charlie thought I had driven home drunk.

I took extra care on the roads on the way in. Driving through Glendara, I spotted Molloy and McFadden standing in front of what remained of the Oak, deep in conversation. I pulled in. They turned simultaneously as I climbed out of the car. McFadden smiled and Molloy's expression softened. I was glad about both, although McFadden looked pale, with dark circles under his eyes. Molloy handed him the keys of the squad car and told him he'd meet him back at the station, and McFadden took them without a word.

'What's going on?' I asked as we watched him drive off.

'We've to go to Letterkenny to meet with the super this afternoon.'

'Why? Has something happened?'

'The Garda forensics report is back. There was another inspection after we found Carole's body.' He paused. 'They found traces of explosives in the cellar.'

'You're kidding.' I turned to face him. 'Is that what caused the fire?'

He shook his head. 'If it had, the whole town would have blown up. All those bottles of spirits. No, the traces were minute. Whatever explosives were there were removed before the fire started. But it's a shockingly dangerous thing to do, keep explosives in a pub cellar.'

I whistled. 'Beneath where people congregate.' I was horrified that I even had to ask the next question. 'Do you think it was Tony?'

'It was his pub.'

'But why? What would he want with explosives? And why would he keep them *there*?'

'I have absolutely no idea,' Molloy said.

I hadn't mentioned Stan's noise complaint to Molloy, since I felt bound by solicitor–client confidentiality, and I felt uncomfortably duplicitous about it now. I decided to ask Stan to tell him.

'The concern is,' Molloy continued, 'where are they now? And what is their intended use? You don't just buy explosives on the off chance you might need them at some stage. They're meant for something specific.'

He stared at the blackened walls of the Oak as if waiting for them to give up their secrets. Watching him, I had a feeling he was distracted by something else. So I asked.

He sighed, as if giving up all pretence of keeping anything from me. 'That belt you found?'

I nodded and held my breath.

'They've identified DNA on it. Other than yours and Carole's.'

I exhaled. 'Carole's was on it. So it was the murder weapon?'

'It looks that way.' He paused and ran his hands through his hair. 'But they've also found DNA belonging to Dominic McLaughlin. Dominic Stoop.'

'Pete the Stoop's son?' I said, stunned. 'Son of the man who lived in that cottage?'

He nodded.

'So he's back? Was he the man Carole was seen with in Derry?'

Molloy shook his head. 'He couldn't have been.'

'Why not?'

Molloy closed his eyes for a second before speaking, then enunciated each word as if he couldn't believe what he was saying. 'Dominic McLaughlin died in prison in the UK three months ago.'

'You're kidding.'

'Nope. He'd just begun a new sentence.'

'Are they sure?'

'It's a prison, Ben. They're sure.'

He broke off suddenly when Liam walked by. Eschewing his usual chat, the estate agent must have sensed a tense conversation. He passed us with just a nod, hands buried in the pockets of his coat. Molloy nodded back.

I lowered my voice. 'Could it have been someone else pretending to be him? Serving his sentence? I mean, DNA is indisputable, isn't it?'

Molloy sighed. 'I'm not going down that road. We have to trust that the UK prison service know who they have in their cells. All *we* need to know is that the DNA on the belt matches a prisoner from Glendara by the name of Dominic McLaughlin. Who died three months ago.'

'Could it be family DNA? His father's, even? Could it have transferred from something in the cottage?' I was grasping at straws, I knew. I didn't really understand how long DNA lasted, how it transferred.

'No,' Molloy said firmly. 'It's definitely his. They took it from hair caught on the buckle. A few tiny follicles, but enough for them to get a sample from. We know it's McLaughlin's because we have his DNA on record here. He committed offences in this state too, served time here.' He shook his head in disbelief. 'But he's *dead*.'

'Was there anything in the cottage – DNA-wise?'

'A faint trace of material from a blanket found in the ashes in the cooker, but any DNA was destroyed.'

I was reluctant to make my next suggestion. 'What about a twin – don't identical twins have the same DNA?'

'I'm choosing to ignore that.' Molloy sounded exhausted. 'And I'm going to go and have a word with Dominic McLaughlin's uncle.'

With that, he walked off towards the newsagent's.

I resisted following him into Stoop's and drove on into Derry to meet Maeve, taking the road slowly and keeping an eye out for black ice. I had a feeling that despite his dismissal of my twin theory, Molloy would ask Stoop anyway. He was nothing if not thorough, even if he regarded the idea as ridiculous. But our conversation had left me feeling agitated. I knew Molloy was stressed, but it was beginning to feel as if our relationship had been suspended by recent events; our exchanges of late limited to the fire and Carole's death. He'd cancelled on me a few times without giving me a reason, and there was that call he had taken in the station, the one he had been so secretive about. Was there something he wasn't telling me?

When I reached the city, I decided to put all of that to one side for a few hours. I parked in the multistorey car park in the Foyleside Shopping Centre on the same level where I'd parked the last time, a couple of days before Christmas, when Carole had been merely missing. It seemed a long time ago now.

As I made my way towards the shopping area, my phone buzzed with a text from my mother. She said how much she and my father were enjoying Iceland and that she'd speak to me when they got home. It was clearly a holding text; she didn't want to engage, didn't want me to reply, just wished me to know they were all right. I *had* been a little concerned, since she hadn't answered any of my calls or texts, and I still wasn't completely reassured, but I was glad to hear from her and sent off a brief reply. Despite my resolution, it made me think about the texts George had received while Carole was missing. The likelihood now was that she had been killed shortly after she disappeared, so who had sent them? Were they designed to stop people looking for her? Had she only been found when the killer wanted her to be? There was something distinctly Machiavellian about that possibility.

When I emerged from the shopping centre, the icy wind hit me like a punch and I wrapped my scarf around my head as I walked towards the wall and made my way under the arch at the junction with Artillery Street.

I had arranged to meet Maeve in a little café on Ferryquay Street, and a welcome blast of warm, bready air greeted me when I pushed open the door. I quickly spotted Maeve sitting at a table at the back wall. She was almost completely hidden behind a magazine, with a fruit scone and a massive black coffee in front of her. I planted myself by the table and she peered at me over the top of the magazine.

I grinned. 'I was going to ask you if you wanted anything, but I see you're all set.'

She closed her eyes. 'God, this is bliss. No kids, no cows, no sheep. City life for a whole two hours.'

'I can leave you if you want. Let you have your afternoon's peace.'

Her eyes opened again and flashed. 'Don't you dare. A spot of gossip will be the cherry on the cake.'

'Or the fruit scone.'

'Exactly.' She took a bite from the one in front of her.

I returned to the counter and came back with an only marginally smaller cappuccino and a pain au chocolat. Maeve had found a coffee shop that dealt in huge helpings; Phyllis would approve.

'Are you going to the funeral in the morning?' she asked, putting down the magazine when I joined her at the table.

The place was busy, a comfortable buzz of conversation and background radio allowing us to chat easily.

I nodded. 'Thought I'd give the wake a miss after the last visit. I don't want to upset them any further.'

'Fair enough. Any news on the investigation? Now that you're so close to the local police.' She narrowed her eyes, then broke off as if something had just occurred to her. 'That's odd.'

'What?'

'I've remembered who asked me if there was anything going on between you and Molloy.'

'Who?'

'Carole,' she said slowly. 'I remember thinking it was a bit odd at the time; it came out of the blue.'

'Why would she ask that?' I said.

'No idea,' Maeve replied. 'I know she was a bit of a nosy parker about other people's business, but she'd never showed any interest in you before.' She grinned as she spread some jam on the remaining half of her scone. 'To be honest, I never thought she liked you very much.'

'Probably true.'

She took a bite. 'So are they any further in finding out what happened to her?'

'They need to work out what happened after the pub closed on the night of the fire. That's when she was last seen.'

Maeve frowned. 'A few years back, you and I would both have been there on a Saturday night. Who *would* have been out, I wonder? I might ask around discreetly.'

I raised my eyebrows. 'You're the one who's always telling me not to get involved in this kind of thing – to mind my own business.'

'I know. Usually I'd think that, but I've known that family for so long, I wish I could do something to help. I really did like her dad; he was one of my first clients.'

I stirred my coffee. 'Is it true they're really religious? Phyllis mentioned something about it.'

Maeve laughed. 'The mother is, and she's passed that on to her daughters. I think the father could take or leave it.'

'Did you know that Carole used to go out with Dominic Stoop?'

She looked up in surprise. 'You're kidding? Peter Stoop's son? When?'

'Oh, years ago, I think. They were both living in England. The Donegal diaspora, I guess. But that's why it's so strange that her body was found close to the Stoops' old cottage.'

I didn't mention the fact that she was probably killed there.

Maeve gazed at the wall, where a vast selection of fruit teas was displayed. 'God, I really hated going up there. Never knew what I was going to find. I don't know why Pete even bothered to keep any stock – it's not as if he made money out of them; they were always in such terrible shape that no one wanted to buy them.' She shook her head. 'If I told him off about it, he'd plead poverty and say he'd try to do better. Until the next time.'

'Did you know Dominic?' I asked.

She shook her head. 'Not really. He was a bit of a shadow. Never said very much. Frightened of the father, I thought, although the animals were in better shape while he was there. He left as soon as he was old enough to get away. I'd have done the same in his shoes.'

'Did he have any brothers and sisters?' I asked.

She shook her head. 'An only child. Unusual enough back then. Just as well – I don't know how the three of them fitted in that tiny cottage.'

'And the father died after the son left?'

'Within months, I think.'

'Did Dominic come back for the funeral?'

Maeve shook her head. 'When he left, he left. Never to be seen again as far as I know. Although to be sure, you'd have to ask his uncle.'

'Pat?'

She nodded. 'If you can get him to talk about the black sheep of the family, that is. So Carole went out with Dominic, did she? She was in England for years. Lost touch with her family for a while, I believe. Then she came back, met George and never left again.' She brushed some crumbs from her jumper. 'Always thought they were a funny match.'

'George and Carole? Why?'

Maeve shrugged. 'Carole being so religious and George the muso with the earring, I suppose.'

I smiled. 'But he ended up teaching. Teaching's fairly conservative.'

'I suppose it's hard to be all free-spirited and broke when you have kids. And he's popular – I'll say that for him.'

There was an edge there that I couldn't ignore. 'What do you mean?'

'Maybe now's not the time,' she said uneasily. 'He's just lost Carole. It seems a bit mean-spirited to talk about him like this.'

'But what if it's relevant to what happened to Carole?'

Her eyes widened. 'You don't think . . . ?'

I shook my head. 'Not necessarily, but you can never tell. What do you know?'

'Well, I don't *know* anything as such. But I've heard rumours.' She looked uncomfortable. 'And I did see something once, up at Knockamany Bends.'

'Go on,' I urged.

She lowered her voice. 'One night I was coming from a call to Malin Head and I cut back by the road to the beach. I wouldn't normally do that, but I'd had a calf die on me that I wasn't expecting and I needed to clear my head. Wanted to stand and look at the sea for a few minutes. George's car was there, parked. I thought it was a bit odd. Anyway, when I saw it, I changed my mind about getting out of the jeep, so I turned around to go home. The headlights of the jeep flashed on his windscreen as I was turning.'

'Go on.'

'George was inside. And there was someone with him.'

'A girl?' I asked.

'Girl or woman, I couldn't be sure. But I can tell you one thing. It definitely wasn't Carole.'

Chapter Seventeen

We drained our troughs of coffee and made our way back out onto the street. At the City Wall, we stood to one side to allow a couple to pass by, the woman draped around the man while he strode along with his hands in his pockets seeming oblivious to her attentions. As I watched them, it occurred to me that it was possible that Carole had told George about Dominic to make him jealous. It seemed like the kind of thing she would do. Carole was someone for whom attention from men was important; I had seen her deliver a man's coffee to his table while leaving a woman at the same table to fetch hers from the bar. It wouldn't have been easy for her having a husband whose attention was easily diverted.

Back in the Foyleside, Maeve and I stood at the top of the escalator whilst we made a decision to split up and meet again for lunch, struggling to stand still amongst the waves of shoppers.

'Got to get you back in time for your emergency haircut,' Maeve grinned, pulling her bag onto her shoulder.

'Speaking of which,' I said. 'Did you ever have an inkling that Stan disliked Tony?'

I thought she would dismiss the notion as I had, but to my surprise, she stopped to think.

'Abby Grey said something about it,' I prompted.

Maeve's eyes widened as if she'd just remembered something. 'Oh, I know what that was. It was the afternoon before the fire. I was in getting my hair cut – remember I ran into you in the square? Abby and myself were the only ones left in the salon and Stan was with Róisín at the back where they keep the coats. The radio was on but it went dead for a few seconds – I don't think he realised we could hear them.'

'What did you hear?' I asked.

Maeve gave me a wry look. 'Something like "Everyone thinks Craig is so perfect but they'll soon find out he's not." I didn't think much of it at the time, just thought they'd had a run-in about the noise. He'd been giving out yards before that.' She frowned. 'You don't think it was Stan who started the fire, do you?'

'Seems unlikely, since his flat was destroyed too.' I remembered that Stan was supposed to have been in Dungloe with his mother that night.

As I travelled down the escalator, I remembered too the row that Leah had witnessed between Stan and Tony in the square. But then Stan *had* just lost his home at that point and Tony had lost his pub. Tempers were bound to be running high.

On the ground floor, sales were everywhere. Clothes hung carelessly off hangers, were piled untidily on shelves; the same sparkle and glitter that had enjoyed pride of place a week ago now in bargain baskets, time in the spotlight short-lived. Now that I was here, I found I had no appetite for shopping, so I sat on one of the benches to work through what was really occupying my thoughts.

Stan said he'd seen Carole on Friday night, the day before she disappeared, here in Derry and in the company of some man. They'd been close to the bus station, he'd said, according to Liam. The shopping centre was only a short distance from the station. Maybe it was worth a wander down, if only to get a sense of what was there?

I exited onto Orchard Street and turned right. The footpath was glistening and I was glad I was wearing flat boots with a good grip. I walked down the steep hill past the old Orchard cinema, and turned left at the library, from where I could see the walls of the bus station. Buses arrived at and departed from an entrance on the other side, close to the Foyle, but the pedestrian access was here – I could see it from where I was standing. I watched as people emerged from the gap carrying rucksacks and cases, and realised I had no idea exactly what Stan had seen or where he'd been. I needed an excuse to ask him. Then I remembered I'd wanted him to tell Molloy about his noise complaint.

I dialled the salon.

Stan answered straight away. I could hear the salon noise in the background: female chatter, hairdryers, a radio. He didn't sound thrilled to hear my voice. 'You're ringing to cancel.'

'No.'

'Late, then.'

'No, I'll be there.' I paused. 'Have you told the guards about the noise you heard in the Oak?'

'Why?'

'Because I think you should. Even though it was a few days before the fire, it could still be relevant, could even be relevant to what happened to Carole. Tony might not think of it, and you were the one who heard it.'

He sighed. 'Okay, I'll give the sergeant a call later. Was that it? I have some highlights to get back to.'

'One other thing. You saw Carole in Derry the Friday night before the fire, didn't you?'

'Who told you that?' He sounded wary and impatient at the same time, not a great combination if I wanted information.

'Liam. We were talking about it because we both met her that morning.' I didn't mention that it was on the flight rather than the bus. I didn't want to get Liam into trouble. 'Liam told me you saw her with a man, and I was wondering if maybe I'd seen him too. Can you remember what he looked like?'

'You know I've told the guards all of this?' he said impatiently.

'Please, Stan. I've been torturing myself about it, wondering if I might have seen something that could help.'

I was amazed that appealing to his sympathy worked. He gave a martyred sigh, but he answered.

'I couldn't be sure with the street lights. It was dark. But tall, with brown hair, I would say. Handsome.'

'*Where* did you see her exactly?'

'On the street outside the station. It was only for a few seconds. She headed up towards the Strand Road.' There was a pause. 'I think . . . now don't hold me to this, but I think she went through a door beside the casino. I didn't tell the sergeant because I couldn't be sure. Didn't want to find myself giving evidence about it and getting tripped up by some smart-arsed barrister.'

'With the man?'

'I think so. It was dark,' he said again.

'What time was this?'

'About twelve.'

'And where were you?'

180

He finally snapped, but I'd been expecting it. 'What is this? I thought you just wanted to know if you'd seen the same man.'

'Sorry. I was just wondering how well you could see her.'

'I'm sure it was *her*, if that's what you're wondering. I worked in the same square as Carole Harkin. I didn't know the man. And to answer your question, not that it's any of your business, I was in the Barclay Arms across from the station with some friends, and I was standing outside it at the time. Now if the interrogation is over, I have clients to attend to. I'll see you at four o'clock as arranged.'

'Thanks, Stan.'

He snorted and hung up.

I could see the Barclay Arms from where I was standing. It didn't seem like Stan's kind of place. It was a rough-looking joint: blokes standing outside with plastic glasses even though it was the middle of the day, not prepared to be parted from their drinks for the length of time it took to smoke a cigarette.

I decided not to go in; not a difficult decision to make when I was catcalled across the street: 'Like what you see, darling? Ach, why don't you come and have a wee drink for yourself?' I crossed over and walked quickly in the direction that Stan said Carole had gone with this man. I glanced across at the station. Stan was right: his view would not have been clear, particularly at night. The Guildhall stood in front of me, majestic with its red and yellow brickwork and fine clock tower.

A figure came into focus, jauntily, as if recognising me: McFadden. He stopped with a broad grin.

'I thought you were in Letterkenny?' I said.

'Small detour.'

'I see.' Unused to seeing McFadden out of his usual context, I was stuck for small talk. It seemed he was the same.

'You in for the sales?' he asked.

'Something like that.'

And with that, we were out. He gave me a friendly wave and headed off, his mood obviously improved from the last few times I'd seen him.

I continued on towards the beginning of the Strand Road. It was early dusk and the light was eerie, smoky and cold. I passed a row of shops and suddenly I was standing outside the Hampton Beach Casino. *Billiards! Poker! Blackjack!* the sign screamed, the windows plastered with images of pound signs and slot machines. To the left was a red door, to the left of the door a row of doorbells; it was a house divided into flats. When I turned back, I could still see the pub. Suddenly the door opened and a woman came out pushing a buggy, shooting me a suspicious look as I stood aside to let her pass.

I walked on quickly up the street to gather my thoughts, but returned a few minutes later. I looked at the names on the door-bells – none were legible, the print far too faded. Should I ring one of them? Was I brave enough? My hand had almost reached the first bell when my phone rang. It was Molloy. I answered it.

'Are you all right?' he asked.

'Yep. Why?'

'You sound a bit breathless.'

I came straight out with it. 'I'm in Derry, close to where Carole was seen with that man. Stan said he thought she went into a door beside the casino.'

'What?' Molloy snapped. 'And . . . ?'

'I'm standing at a door beside the casino.'

Molloy cut across me. 'Get the hell away from there, now.'

I decided not to argue. I was feeling a little exposed standing on this doorstep. 'Okay, okay, I'm going.'

'What's the address?' he asked abruptly.

I gave it to him.

'Right. Now leave Derry and come back to Glendara immediately, do you hear me? Let me deal with this. It may be nothing, but let me deal with it.'

'Yes, yes. I will. I'm leaving now.'

Molloy hung up, and for once I did what I was told, walking considerably faster on the way back than I had on the way down. Molloy had spooked me with his tone. It was getting darker *and* I was late to meet Maeve.

There were fewer people about as I made my way back. I couldn't deny I'd have liked a bit more company. I felt wired, my heart beating fast. When I reached the Barclay Arms, I heaved a sigh of relief – it was brighter here, busier – but as I passed the pub, someone shouted in my face and made me jump. There was a burst of laughter behind me as I pushed down a wave of fear and quickened my pace. I turned right at the library and marched up the hill towards the shopping centre, my breath coming quick and fast. I felt someone tap me on the shoulder, but when I spun around, there was no one there. I heard footsteps behind me and cried out before a young guy in a tracksuit ran past, giving me the same look as the woman at the red door. My mind was playing tricks on me. Finally I turned into the shopping centre and stood for a minute to catch my breath, feeling foolish, but relieved to be back in the bright lights.

Maeve was waiting for me at the top of the escalator. 'Where have you been?' she asked, her expression changing from irritation to concern when she saw my face. 'Jesus, are you all right? You look as if you've seen a ghost.'

'I'm fine. Just didn't notice the time. Then I had to run so I wouldn't be too late. Sorry. What do you think? A quick bite to eat and then home?'

'I might stay a bit longer. There's a pair of boots I've been stalking,' she grinned. 'And I've no emergency haircut to get back to, remember?'

We went to the self-service restaurant at the top of the stairs, where we grabbed ourselves a couple of sandwiches and more coffee – it occurred to me that maybe it was all the coffee that was making me so jittery – then made our way to the cashier. I was ahead of Maeve when I reached into my bag to pay.

The woman at the cash register was patient. 'Take your time, love. There's no rush.'

I rummaged about again, then looked at Maeve. 'My wallet's gone.'

She frowned. 'Are you sure?'

'Certain. I think it must have been stolen on the Strand Road.'

'What were you doing down there?'

'I'll tell you later. But it's gone. I'm sure of it.'

Maeve offered a twenty to the cashier. 'That should cover both.'

'Thanks, Maeve,' I said, as the cashier gave me a sympathetic look.

I looked across at Maeve.

'What's going on, Ben?' she asked.

Chapter Eighteen

I didn't tell Maeve what I'd been doing down the Strand Road. If it turned out to be significant, she'd hear about it soon enough. In the meantime, I didn't want to spoil her one shopping day in Derry; it was enough that she knew I had been pickpocketed. When we had eaten – or rather, when Maeve had eaten; my sandwich remained pretty much untouched – I made my way back to the car.

I left Derry to drive back to Glendara in sleeting rain, strangely glad of the appalling weather since it took up all my concentration and stopped me thinking about what had happened. So much so, in fact, that it was only when I reached Quigley's Point that I remembered I hadn't cancelled my missing cards. I pulled into the Point Inn, a bar-restaurant-hotel on the Foyle, and parked in the car park. It was quiet, which was unsurprising the day before New Year's Eve, and a huge, brightly lit Christmas tree stood outside the main entrance. I did a search for the emergency credit-card line – grateful that my phone hadn't been taken along with the wallet – and dialled the number.

As I waited for an answer, a movement at the front of the hotel made me glance up. The main door was open and someone was coming out; a man, his face partly concealed by an upturned collar. As he turned to walk down the steps, head bowed, hands rammed deep into the pockets of his coat, the light caught his profile. It was George Harkin. I found myself hunching down in my seat like some 1950s PI. I watched as he walked towards the old Ford I'd seen outside Carole's sister's house, climbed in and drove off. I wondered why he wasn't at the wake, but then maybe he had needed a break, to get out for an hour or two.

Finally, the helpline was answered and I cancelled my cards. I put the phone back in my bag, started the car and drove back towards the entrance. As I was waiting for an opportunity to pull out onto the main road, a taxi pulled in. I recognised the driver as the one who had driven us to Culdaff on the night of the Christmas drinks, and he gave me a wave as he passed me. I watched in my overhead mirror as he drove to the entrance of the hotel and waited until a woman emerged carrying a large bag. She opened the passenger door and climbed in. It was Susanne Craig.

Fifteen minutes later, I pulled into the square in Glendara, relieved to be back. It even looked as though I would be on time for my appointment with Stan, until I remembered that I had no wallet. Maeve had given me the coins I needed to get out of the car park in Derry, but I had refused a further loan. With relief, I saw that the bank was still open. I checked with the cashier that my cards had been cancelled and new ones ordered, and withdrew enough cash to get me through the next few days. Then I crossed to Stan's salon, anticipating a tongue-lashing; I was now ten minutes late.

I was saved. The salon was quiet, with only two clients and

one stylist – Róisín, Eddie's girlfriend. I was surprised to see her; like George, I'd expected she would be at the wake.

She came over looking apologetic. 'I'm so sorry, but Stan's had to step out. He said to give you another appointment, but I could do it for you if you don't mind waiting. I'll only be another five minutes.'

She gestured towards one of the mirrors, where a woman sat with a magazine. The woman waved; she was one of my clients.

'That's fine. I'm happy to wait.'

'Are you sure?' Róisín smiled. 'I won't be offended if you'd prefer to wait for Stan.'

'Not at all,' I said. 'I'm sure you'll do a great job.'

She made me a coffee and I sat in the little waiting area with its table strewn with magazines. One caught my eye and it gave me a wrench. It was the same one Carole had been reading on the flight to Dublin.

'Is that okay?' Róisín asked as she tied a pink-striped smock at the back of my neck a few minutes later. 'Not too tight?'

'No. It's fine.' I leaned back into the sink and she began to wet my hair. 'It's nice and warm in here today.'

'That's because the windows are closed. Stan insists on keeping them open; he'd open the door to the street if he could. It's madness; we have to keep the heating going full blast to make up for it.' She clicked her teeth as she massaged some shampoo into my hair. 'He does the same at our house. It drives my mother nuts.'

'Did you do hairdressing in Sydney?' I asked.

'Only thing I'm qualified to do. I wasn't there very long, though. I'm not that adventurous. Going to Australia was the most exciting thing I've done. First time out of the country.'

'That's quite a first trip.'

'I suppose. I didn't go on my own, though – I went with a crowd. And we went travelling after.'

'Eddie didn't go with you?'

'Eddie was working. But when he heard I'd be back in Glendara for Christmas . . .'

I smiled. 'He decided he'd be here too?'

'Something like that.' I sensed her embarrassment.

'Stan must be glad to have you back. Although I should imagine it's strange living with your boss.'

Róisín laughed. She had a tinkly, shy kind of laugh; it was the first time I'd heard it. 'Stan's all right, once you learn how to tune him out. He was going to stay in a B and B but my mother wouldn't have it. I don't mind.' She applied some conditioner. 'She's so busy looking after him, she's not hassling me. Calls him her surrogate son, even though there's only ten years between them.'

'That smells nice,' I said.

'Apple,' Róisín said. 'Cruelty-free.'

I wondered if that was Susanne Craig's influence. It would be hard to be anything other than environmentally aware if you were regularly in Susanne's orbit, I thought.

'It's not difficult once you put a bit of thought into it. We can all do our bit.' Róisín wrapped my hair in a towel and rubbed my head vigorously before moving me to one of the mirrors.

As I took my seat, I mentioned Carole's funeral the following day.

'Aye, it's going to be a rough old day for George and the boys,' Róisín said, pulling the tangles from my hair with a comb. 'They're lucky they have Emma.'

'Did George teach you at school, by the way?' I asked as she began snipping at the ends of my hair.

'He did. He was one of the "cool" teachers. Of course, it helped that he taught a subject people liked, rather than maths or something.' She met my gaze in the mirror, put down the scissors and leaned on the back of my chair. 'Who on earth would have done that to Carole?'

'I don't know.'

'It's making all the girls nervous. No one wants to go out at night on their own any more.'

'I'm sure they don't.'

She picked up the comb and scissors again. 'The whole thing's so fucked up.' She caught my eye in the mirror. 'Sorry,' she said sheepishly.

'No, you're right. It is.' I took a sip of my coffee. It was cold. 'You were in the pub with Eddie that Saturday night, weren't you?'

'Aye, Susanne and myself were both there. Eddie was behind the bar with Carole. Susanne's da asked him to help out and Eddie thought it would be a great way to get to see everyone again, so he jumped at it.'

'Did you see anyone in particular talking to Carole, anyone strange come into the pub?'

She shook her head. 'But she was in a funny mood. Grouchy with Eddie, kept nagging him to clean glasses and take out the bottles, that sort of thing.' She grinned. 'But then he *was* doing more chatting than work.'

Now *that* sounded like the Eddie of old.

'But then at closing time she seemed to be dying to get rid of us, just when I'd have thought she'd want Eddie's help to clean up. Insisted that we head out to Culdaff to see George.'

189

'Didn't she want to go herself?' I asked.

Róisín shook her head. 'She didn't seem to. I offered to help the two of them clear up so she could come with us, but she said she was wrecked and wanted to head home to bed.'

'So you went on out to Culdaff with Eddie to see George play?'

'Aye, and Susanne came with us.'

I had a flashback of Susanne emerging from the Point Inn. Could Susanne have been the girl that Maeve had seen him with that night in the car?

At ten o'clock, there was a knock on the back door. I'd been waiting to hear from Molloy all day, but had resisted calling him. Now I threw Guinness off my lap and hurried to open it.

Molloy raised his eyebrows. 'New haircut?'

'A Stan MacLochlainn special. At least it was supposed to be a Stan special. It turned out to be a Róisín one.'

'It's good. Suits you.'

I smiled. That was positively effusive in Molloy's book. He followed me into the kitchen, where I gestured to the wine rack. 'Red?'

'Great.'

I took a corkscrew from the drawer while Molloy grabbed two glasses, and we headed back to the fire, where Guinness had stretched out again on the sofa. I pushed him over and we both sat down, the cat leaping back up onto Molloy's knee and circling repeatedly until he found himself a comfortable spot.

'Well? Did you take a look at the place in Derry?' I asked.

'The PSNI did. This afternoon.'

'And?'

'Nothing. The landlord was co-operative, but all the flats are rented for cash. Tenants changing all the time. He gave the PSNI a list, but there's no one on it of any significance. We've given the PSNI Carole's photograph, so they'll circulate it amongst the tenants and in the casino.'

'Oh.' I wasn't sure what I had been expecting, but I was disappointed.

'What exactly did Stan say to you?' Molloy asked.

'Just that he thought he saw Carole go through a door beside the casino.'

'And why the hell didn't he tell us that?' Molloy shook his head in frustration.

'He said it was dark so he couldn't be sure. Maybe he didn't want to chance getting someone into trouble.'

'All he told us was that she was with a man. Brown hair, tall. Hugely helpful.'

I hesitated. 'Does that description fit Dominic Stoop?'

Molloy nodded. 'Dominic Stoop and half the rest of the male population. But Dominic Stoop is dead, Ben.'

'I know, I know. I accept it's pretty unlikely that the UK prison authorities would have got it wrong.'

I could tell there was something else bothering him. But I'd learned not to press him. He stroked Guinness's fur.

'We've found out something else about the same Dominic Stoop.'

I held my breath.

'He was married. To Carole Kearney.'

I sank back into the couch. 'Divorced?'

Molloy shook his head. 'Nope. Still married to her when he died three months ago.'

'But she's married to George.'

'It would appear not, not legally anyway.'

I whistled. 'When did they marry? Carole and Dominic?'

'Seventeen or eighteen years ago. He was in his early twenties, she must have been about nineteen.'

'Did they have any kids?'

'Not that we can tell.'

I whistled. 'I presume George didn't know she was already married when she married him?'

'I haven't spoken to him yet,' Molloy said. 'I thought I'd wait till after the funeral.'

That seemed the kindest course of action. Then it hit me. What if it was Carole herself who was being blackmailed? What if that was why she needed the money? While I considered this, Molloy picked the cat up and placed him to one side, then stood up and wandered restlessly towards the window, glass of wine in hand.

'God, she was rightly trapped, wasn't she?' I said. 'Until Dominic died and solved her problem. Pity you're not investigating *his* death. You'd have at least one prime suspect.'

Molloy pushed the edge of the curtain to one side and peered out. 'Which is more than we have for Carole.'

'Why was Dominic Stoop in prison?' I asked. 'All I've been told is that he was trouble. Hot-headed and violent.'

Molloy let the curtain fall and turned to face me again, taking a sip from his glass. 'I suppose you'd call him an eco-terrorist. He campaigned against experimentation on animals, intensive farming, hunting; set bombs in two pharmaceutical plants, one in Kerry and one in Manchester, fatally injuring one person and maiming two. He was in and out of prison all his life.'

'Maeve said his father was cruel to his animals.'

Molloy shrugged. 'Maybe that's where it started. But he

certainly went the wrong way about it. He was hugely into animal rights but he didn't seem to care how many people he hurt.'

'I wonder what he and Carole had in common? He doesn't sound like her type.'

'Maybe she was different when she was younger.' He gave me an odd look. 'Most of us were.'

'Yes.'

He seemed lost in thought for a second, then shook his head. 'Anyway, I don't see how any of this helps in trying to find out what happened to her.'

'What about the trace of explosives found in the Oak? That's a bit of a coincidence, isn't it? If Dominic was convicted of explosives offences?'

Molloy sighed. 'And it would be hugely significant if it weren't for the fact that Dominic Stoop died in prison three months before the Oak burned down. Which is the problem we keep coming back to.'

I was glad that Molloy stayed the night. I dismissed the unease I'd felt earlier in the day and relaxed into his presence, and he seemed to sense it, wrapping his arms protectively around me when we settled down to sleep. But I lay awake for some time, turning scenes over in my mind. I sensed Molloy's restlessness too, although he didn't speak.

I fell into an uneasy sleep, to be woken a short time later completely unable to move. My brain was awake and alert, but I was frozen, lying on my stomach with my arm trapped beneath me. I tried to turn over but couldn't, tried to lift my head and failed, tried so hard to open my eyes that my head hurt. I sensed Molloy beside me and I tried to move my leg to get his attention, but I was paralysed. The onset of panic made me cry out, but no sound came. I was trapped within my own body.

Suddenly I felt Molloy's touch. He held my arm and shook me awake. My eyes opened, overwhelming relief followed immediately by a pounding headache.

Chapter Nineteen

Molloy was gone when I awoke. This time he'd left a note.

Hope you're okay after your nightmare. Come over tonight? I'll cook.

What had happened the night before hadn't been a nightmare. It was a bout of sleep paralysis, which hits me occasionally when there's something bothering me, often something in my subconscious I can't put my finger on. I was glad Molloy had been there; glad he'd recognised and responded to my distress even if he hadn't known the cause.

I reread his text: an invitation to dinner at his house. Molloy lived in the sergeant's house in Glendara. One of the reasons we met at mine was that we'd be less likely to be outed if someone came looking for him. Though I suspected that ship had sailed, this was a new development. While I was trying to figure out what it meant, my phone rang. It was Leah.

'You're up early for the holidays,' I said.

'I'm saving my lie-in for tomorrow when I'll need it.'

Of course, it was New Year's Eve. Molloy's text made more sense now. The days of this holiday seemed to be merging into each other.

'I thought I might go to Carole's funeral,' Leah said. 'It is this morning, isn't it?'

'Yes. Half eleven, I think. Are you sure?'

'I think I should. Let's face it, she's given me my lunch almost every day for the past year. It mightn't have been with a smile, but I feel I should pay my respects. And also I've found something I want to show you, if you have time after the service.'

I sat up in bed. 'What's that?'

She answered my question with another question. 'Have you said anything to Tony about giving Susanne a job yet?'

'No, why?'

'Good. There's something I think you should see first. We can look at it on my phone.'

'Why don't I meet you at the church ten minutes early? About twenty past?'

'Grand. See you then.'

I was unable to sleep after that, so by the time I'd showered, breakfasted and fed Guinness, I was at a bit of a loose end. I had an hour and a half before the funeral. Standing at the back door with coffee in hand, I saw that the morning was cold and dry, which meant a chance to go for my oft-postponed swim. The last one of the year.

I drove to my usual spot, Five Fingers Strand, or Lagg, depending on whether you were a visitor or a local. The shore was beautiful and deserted, just the way I like it. The five jagged rocks protruding from the sea below Knockamany Bends glinted in the winter sunshine, dramatic and serene, as I made my way onto the beach. Luckily the tide was in, so I undressed at high speed and ran into the sea before I could change my mind, managing about five strokes in the freezing water before I stumbled back out, teeth chattering as I dressed again as quickly as I could.

I decided to walk a little way along the beach to get the

blood flowing again, but as often happened, once I'd started, I found myself marching the full length of the shore. It was cold and bright, sand dunes majestic and brooding on my left, little oystercatchers picking at the seaweed to my right, a brooding Glashedy Island visible in the distance.

I turned left at the end of the beach and made my way across the stretch of wet sand towards the road to complete the loop. Once there, I climbed over the wall and lowered myself onto the grass verge, where a man in coat and scarf was locking his car. When he turned, I saw that it was Ian Grey.

'Great minds,' he smiled.

'Good day to blow away the cobwebs. You're a bit far from home, though, aren't you? Wouldn't Culdaff be your closest beach?'

He nodded. 'I love Culdaff and I walk there all the time. But sometimes the wide-open space here clears my head.'

I looked at my feet. 'I know what you mean. I thought I'd get a bit of fresh air before facing the funeral later.'

'Yes. It will be a tough one.'

His voice sounded odd, and when I looked up again, I saw that his eyes were full. I was surprised; although Carole had worked for him, I wouldn't have thought they were especially close. But maybe I was wrong.

'You were fond of her?' I said.

'If I'm honest, I didn't really know her very well. I mean, she worked for us, but . . .' He shook his head, struggling to get the words out. 'It's not that. Oh, ignore me.'

'Are you okay?' I asked.

He smiled weakly. 'Probably not. But it's a little hard to explain.' He zipped up his coat. 'Anyway, I'd better get going if I'm going to be back for the funeral.'

* * *

An hour later, a crowd had gathered outside the church but the hearse had not yet arrived. Leah and I sat in her car. The choice of vehicle wasn't difficult; hers was considerably larger than the Mini, with a heating system that actually worked. I waited while she searched through her phone.

'Ah, here it is.' She passed it over to me. 'It's something I didn't notice the first time we looked at Susanne's Facebook page, but I was messing around last night and I spotted it. Have a look at her "likes" section. Bottom left of the page.'

I scrolled down and over to the left.

She pointed. 'See the link to a website called animaloutrage. com. Click on that.'

I did what she said and a site opened, littered with images of animals in various states of distress – fox hunting, battery hens, zoos, aquariums, animal testing labs – and various sound bites: *Time for change – time for revolution! Humans are selfish, concerned only with ourselves! Human filth, destroying the planet with greed! Destroying it for other species. It's time to dispose of those who do not value our planet, who do not value its flora and fauna.*

I scrolled through a list of the group's 'achievements': an attack on a mink farm in the UK; a raid on an animal testing laboratory in Canada; rabbits freed from a rabbit farm in Spain; businesses torched; a Spanish minister whose support for bull-fighting was well known kidnapped; trucks overturned; bombs planted. Industrial sabotage, anarchism and violence over a period of many years. This was no well-meaning, liberal site with an environmental agenda. This was a radical organisation advocating violence against those who did not support its aims.

I sat back. 'So this is the kind of eco stuff she's into?'

Leah nodded. 'It's all fairly extreme.'

I scrolled back to the menu at the top. There was a gallery option, which I clicked on. There were further distressing images of animal experimentation and industrial farming, but also protests: long-haired, pierced individuals being forcibly removed by police; a man with protuberant eyes, face wet with fury, making a speech. The name underneath made me read it twice – Dominic McLaughlin. I swiped through the remaining pictures and he appeared in many others: marching, demonstrating, being arrested, stirring up the crowd.

I showed Leah. 'Do you know him?'

She took the phone and shook her head. 'Dominic McLaughlin?'

'I think that might be Dominic Stoop,' I said. 'I know he was involved in this kind of thing.'

Leah's eyes widened. 'Stoop the newsagent's nephew? I heard he's a complete header.'

I nodded. '*Was* a complete header. He's dead.'

'Really? I never heard that.' She looked again at the picture. 'I didn't know he was into this kind of stuff. I just heard he was in prison; I kind of assumed it was drugs. People don't really talk about him.'

'He was convicted of explosives offences. Linked to eco-terrorism. And it looks as though Susanne Craig is into the same kind of thing. I wonder how seriously?'

Leah shrugged. 'Just because she has it on her Facebook page doesn't mean she's doing anything illegal. It could be the extreme end of what she's into. Plenty of people are armchair socialists but the last thing they'd do is start a revolution.' She grinned. 'And if someone else did it in their vicinity, they'd run a mile in the other direction.'

'True,' I said. 'Although it's a bit of a coincidence if this is

Dominic McLaughlin from Glendara.' I stopped to think. 'He would have been gone from here by the time she was growing up, wouldn't he?'

'I'd say so. I never met him and I'm older than she is. Unless she met him somewhere else.'

'True. She might have been impressed by the fact that they were from the same town.'

I scrolled through some of the pictures again and spotted one of the bloody bullfighting protest in Madrid. Could this have been the trouble Susanne was in when she called her father from Spain? Had she got herself arrested because of her involvement? I clicked on the contacts page on the site but there was no real information, just an email address: jessie@co.org.

Leah's voice interrupted my thoughts. 'It looks as if the hearse has arrived.'

We left the car and joined the crowd moving slowly into the pretty old church, George, Eddie and Tony Craig amongst the pall-bearers. With no small difficulty, we found a space for two at the back of the church; it seemed that everyone who'd ever been in the Oak was in the church this morning. When I glanced back, I caught a glimpse of Molloy and McFadden in the doorway and remembered that I hadn't responded to Molloy's invitation for tonight. I gave him a small wave.

As the service began, I looked around me. A row of teenagers in the uniform of Glendara Community School had taken over three rows in the centre of the church; I expected a guard of honour once the service was over. Hal McKinney was at the top of the aisle, hands clasped in front of him in his funeral director's pose, and I saw Susanne Craig, Liam, Phyllis, Maeve and the Greys as well as Stoop the newsagent. Even my neighbour

Charlie was here – he winked at me conspiratorially from across the aisle, probably assuming I had a hip flask rammed in my pocket.

It occurred to me as I scanned the church that I had never seen Carole with any female friends, women she might have confided in. I wondered why that was. Phyllis had described her as secretive. It turned out she was right about that. Carole had had a secret marriage. But who was the man she was seen with in Derry? Ian Grey was considerably older than her, but I remembered his unexpected show of emotion at the beach.

The service was short and traditional, with a few religious readings and prayers. There was no music, which seemed odd for the funeral of a musician's wife, but I assumed George had been unable to face putting something together. I was surprised, then, to see the priest nod to him at the end of the prayers and watch him make his way up to the lectern.

He stood for a few seconds looking at the congregation before he began, scanning the pews as if searching for someone. I risked a glance at Leah, and she raised her eyebrows. Whether he found what it was he was looking for I don't know, but eventually he began.

It was a halting, hesitant speech, the words delivered staccato as if he was determined to get them out. He began by thanking people who had been kind to the family since Carole's death and inviting everyone back to the bar in Culdaff after the service. And then he cleared his throat.

'Marriage is not easy. And mine was no easier than most.' He attempted a smile. 'She was a wee bit flighty at the start.'

I smiled to myself, wondering how Carole's religious family would take that.

'But then there were the boys. We wouldn't have managed

without help. But I relied on others I shouldn't have.' He bowed his head. 'I am sure there are things that she regrets too, though she can't speak now.'

His voice broke at this point, but he pulled himself together. He took a deep breath and took a last look at the congregation.

'I tried and I failed her. And I am sorry for that.'

Chapter Twenty

Leah headed home after the graveyard but I decided to call briefly into the bar in Culdaff with Maeve. Molloy and McFadden seemed to have disappeared, so I sent Molloy a text to say that I'd love to come for dinner and that I'd see him later. I felt a pleasurable flutter at the prospect.

Two older women on the way into the pub ahead of us made no attempt to lower their voices. One of them shook her head in disgust.

'All about him, of course. Typical man.'

'I don't think he even used the wee girl's name, did he?'

A clicking of teeth in disapproval. 'I don't think he did, you know.'

The bar was full and the heat was a welcome relief from the icy wind when we'd first arrived, but quickly became stifling. Two turf fires blazed at either end, but with the body heat of so many people, they just weren't needed. A table with sandwiches had been set up at the back wall, and people crowded around it; some with cups of tea while others were on to the pints already, starting the New Year's drinking early. Although there was something jarring about the

Christmas decorations and lights that remained around the walls of the pub.

Maeve and I made our way over to Phyllis, who had found a spot by a window, which she had surreptitiously opened. She was chatting to Tony, who shunted over to allow us in.

'Who'd have thought we'd be spending New Year's Eve at a funeral?' Phyllis was saying.

'Or Christmas Day finding a body,' I added.

Phyllis shook her head. 'I'll never forget you coming back with Fred. The shock of it, and the shock you must have had finding her like that. Although thank God you did. She could have been there for days or weeks if you hadn't.'

I remembered Molloy's view that the stones had been placed deliberately to assist in finding the body, and suddenly I had a flashback to the Christmas work night out. I remembered taking the call from Phyllis asking me to bring Fred for a walk, and my suggestion of Sliabh Sneacht. Had someone heard me? Had someone meant *me* to find her – someone who had been there that night? According to the pathologist, Carole had been dead for a few days at that point. Was her killer getting impatient for her to be discovered? He could hardly just drive into town and dump her in the square.

I tried to remember who had been here that night. I had taken the call in the porch; anyone who passed could have heard me. Before I could work it out, there was a tap on my shoulder.

It was Stoop the newsagent, with a pint of Guinness in his hand. 'Do you have a minute?'

'Of course.'

He glared meaningfully at the others, who looked at each other, amused, and moved away.

When we were alone I asked, 'What do you want to talk to me about, Pat?'

'I'm sorry to bother you here, but I know your office is closed.'

'Just until Monday,' I said.

'I'm not sure I can wait until then.' His head was bowed; he wasn't meeting my eye. 'It's these things that people are saying about Dominic, my nephew. That he might have killed Carole.'

'*Are* people saying that?' I was surprised. I didn't think the fact of the DNA on the belt had been released.

He shook his head dismissively. 'It's because of where she was found. It's crazy talk; the man is dead three months.'

'Yes. So I believe. I'm sorry.'

Stoop lowered his voice. 'I admit Dominic was dangerous. Some say it came from his father; Pete was a cruel man, no denying that. But Dominic wouldn't have killed a woman in cold blood. People are saying he faked his own death somehow and hid in that cottage.'

I wondered how much of this was Stoop's paranoia. I certainly hadn't heard this talk.

'I *know* he's dead – I was at his funeral,' he continued, his voice even lower.

'I see.' Somehow I had assumed a family split.

Stoop gazed down into his pint. He'd been drinking it slowly; the head looked old and yellow. 'I didn't tell anyone at the time that he was dead. I should have; there wouldn't be this talk now if I had. I didn't want people to know he'd died in prison, especially my children – his cousins. I thought I'd tell them eventually, when the time was right, but I just never got around to it.' He looked sad. 'He was cremated; just me and a few prison officers. I don't know what happened to his ashes. I just told them to do whatever they thought best.'

205

'I didn't realise you'd stayed in touch.'

'I didn't like to talk about him. But when all's said and done, he was still my nephew.'

'Did you know . . . ?' I stopped, unsure whether to continue. Stoop rubbed his nose. I glanced in George Harkin's direction and he caught my meaning.

He lowered his voice to a whisper. 'That Dominic was married to Carole? Aye, I did. God knows what they'd be saying if they knew that. I'm not sure why he told me – he warned me to keep it quiet. They didn't even tell the prison. She left England and didn't give the prison any contact details, and he didn't enlighten them.' He looked down. 'I didn't even tell *her* he was dead. Maybe I should have, but George has a bit of a temper on him and I didn't want to cause her any trouble.'

'Did Dominic know she'd married again?' I asked.

'He chose to let it go, wanted her to have some wee bit of happiness, and I respected his wishes. Dominic had one love only: his cause. He couldn't see anything beyond that. It was like some kind of mania. He didn't even care . . .' Stoop stopped suddenly, as if he feared he had said too much.

'He didn't care about what?' I asked.

He looked away. 'I was just going to say that he didn't care about anything else.'

'Not even Carole?'

He shook his head sadly. 'I don't think so.'

'So what is it you want *me* to do?' I asked.

'I want you to administer his estate,' he said firmly. 'It'll stop the crazy talk. I've never done anything about it, but maybe it's time I did. If there's one thing people around here understand, it's property. Land.'

'Did he leave a will?'

He shook his head. 'I wouldn't say so.' He gave a sad smile. 'He wasn't what you'd call a conformer. The only thing he'd have owned would be the cottage. He had nothing else. Always lived from hand to mouth, running with that wild hippy crowd of his.'

'And he had no brothers or sisters?'

'He was an only child.'

My mind raced ahead as I tried to work out the chain of inheritance. If Carole had died after Dominic, as his legal spouse she would inherit everything, assuming they had no children. Which meant that their marriage and Carole's subsequent biga-mous one would be exposed if I administered Dominic's estate, since Carole's own beneficiaries would have to be informed. I wondered if Stoop knew this. Maybe he didn't care now that Dominic and Carole were both dead.

I was about to ask him when I realised he was no longer looking at me. He was distracted by something at the back of the pub, where raised voices could be heard over the general chat. I turned and followed his gaze. George and Ian Grey were involved in yet another altercation, and Ian was backing away, his hands raised in surrender. People close by stared into their drinks, embarrassed.

'Just as well the wee boys aren't here.' Phyllis appeared at my shoulder as Stoop drifted away saying he'd give me a call, having clearly decided the practicalities could wait now that he'd made the first move.

'Where are they?' I asked. I remembered seeing them at the funeral, two little boys in coats and scarves, clutching toy cars designed to distract them from the reality of the occasion.

'Emma's taken them home. I think she's coming back later.'

Ian strode past us and out of the pub, Abby in his wake. I took the opportunity to go to the bathroom, and when I came out again, they were both in the porch. They didn't see me, and I'm ashamed to say that I stood behind the large Christmas tree in the hall and listened to what they were saying.

Ian was pacing up and down, clearly stressed, while Abby hissed at him furiously. 'How could you try to open all of this up again? It was bad enough with Carole.'

'I told you. I didn't say anything to Carole. I wouldn't have until you were happy about it.'

'I don't believe you,' she snapped. 'I thought you were wrong to do it then. But now? What possible good could it do? How could you even *think* of it?'

Ian slumped down onto a small bench and I took a sudden step back, afraid that he might see me. But he was too upset. He seemed helpless and sad but he wasn't backing down. 'I was only doing what I thought was right. I couldn't have known what was going to happen.'

'But *now*? Why *now*?'

'You know why. He should have been here. It's his right.' He waved towards the pub in disgust. 'Anyway, that ignorant man wouldn't even listen to me, so there's nothing lost. Our secret is still safe.'

Abby gave him one last furious look and stormed out. Ian sighed deeply before dragging himself to his feet and following her.

I returned inside with the same thought I'd had in the church. Could Ian Grey have been the man Stan saw with Carole in Derry? He'd said he hadn't recognised him, but it might be worth asking again. I scanned the pub for the hairdresser. It was only then that I realised I hadn't seen him in the church, or in the graveyard either. Was it possible he hadn't bothered to come? It seemed unlikely.

Spotting Róisín and Eddie in the corner, I tapped her on the shoulder as discreetly as I could. She turned with a smile.

'Have you seen Stan?' I asked in a low voice.

She looked around her. 'Isn't he here?'

I shook my head. 'I didn't see him at the church either.'

She frowned. 'Come to think of it, neither did I. I came with Eddie straight from the house, but I haven't seen Stan since he left the salon yesterday afternoon before your appointment.'

'Where was he going?'

'He said he was going to visit his mother and he'd be back this morning.' She shook her head. 'He wouldn't have missed Carole's funeral.'

'That's what I thought.' I went back to the porch and rang Stan's number, but it went straight through to voicemail.

I decided it was time to leave. The pub was beginning to clear and I wanted to go home before heading to Molloy's. I went over to Phyllis and Maeve to say goodbye before taking my leave of George.

'What are you doing tonight?' Phyllis asked.

I looked at her, confused. 'Why?'

She smiled. 'New Year's Eve. I know it doesn't seem much like it. Tony's having a few people round to his house. He's just left, but he asked me to mention it. I think he misses hosting New Year's Eve at the Oak.' She raised her eyes to heaven. 'And Susanne has a new boyfriend she wants him to meet. I don't think he has the energy to face it on his own. He thought a bit of a gathering might cheer people up.'

'It's a nice idea,' I said. 'But I have plans for dinner, I'm afraid.'

Phyllis nudged Maeve. 'No need to ask who with—'

She broke off as Ian Grey burst back into the pub, breathless, as if he'd been running.

'It's Stan,' he said. 'He's hurt on the beach.'

Róisín and Eddie were the first to react, racing out of the pub after him, followed by a crowd that included Maeve, Phyllis and myself. We ran along the shore road and made our way down to the beach over the dunes. It was early dusk and the sea was a strange shade of blue and purple, like a bruise. Stan was lying on his back on the sand in an area below the playground, with Abby leaning over him. Blood was oozing from a cut on his forehead.

'I'll call an ambulance,' Phyllis said, her phone in her hand.

'I've already done it,' Abby said. 'The one from Glendara hospital will be here in half an hour – it's up at Malin.'

A voice sounded from the car park above, making us all jump. 'Is everything all right?

'There's someone hurt down here,' Phyllis shouted back.

We heard the rustling of someone clambering down through the marram grass and a man appeared beside us, a concerned look on his face. It was the taxi driver from Glendara who had driven myself and Leah to our work night out and picked Susanne up from the Point Inn.

He took one look at Stan and exclaimed, 'Oh Jesus. He doesn't look too healthy. I can take him to the hospital in Glendara if you like?'

Maeve, the closest thing to a medic we had, shook her head. 'We shouldn't move him; we can't take the risk with a bang on the head. We'll have to wait for the ambulance.'

I kneeled down beside him. The sand was freezing. 'What happened, Stan?' I asked.

His voice was slurred, as if he had been drinking. 'I fell. Should have been looking where I was going.' He attempted a smile, but there was fear in his eyes. 'God knows what I look like.'

It was clear that whatever had happened to Stan, he hadn't just fallen. There was no way that the sand he was lying on could have done such damage to his head. But it wasn't the time for questions; it was far more important to get him to hospital.

Despite the half-hour estimate, the ambulance arrived in ten minutes and Róisín went with him. Watching the red lights disappear along the shore road, I found myself standing beside the taxi driver, who had waited with us in case the ambulance didn't arrive.

'That's a nice wee girl,' he said.

'Róisín? Yes, she is.'

He lowered his voice. 'I gave her a lift back into Glendara the night of the fire. Dropped her in with her friend.'

In light of what he had said about taxi drivers being like priests, I was surprised he was sharing this with me. 'Back to her house?' I asked.

He glanced around, but the rest of the crowd were already making their way towards the pub. 'No, back to the Oak. When I heard it had burned down, I did wonder if there had been a lock-in – a careless cigarette or something; you know what the young ones are like. So I was glad to hear it was deliberate.' He flushed. 'Well not glad exactly, but you know what I mean.'

'Did you tell the guards about dropping the girls back?'

He shook his head, a little sheepishly I thought. I got the feeling that telling me was getting something off his chest.

'I didn't want to get them into any bother. I mean, it wasn't as if I saw them go into the pub. I just left them off outside.'

'Eddie wasn't with them? Carole's brother?'

He shook his head again. 'No, it was just the two wee girls.'

Chapter Twenty-One

I rang Molloy to tell him what had happened, afraid that if Stan didn't want to report it then no one else would. I told him that Stan wasn't admitting to his injuries having been caused by anything other than a fall, although that seemed unlikely.

'I'll go and talk to him,' Molloy said. 'Has he been taken to the hospital in Glendara?'

'I think so.'

'I'll give you a call later on,' he said before he rang off.

I drove back to Malin taking the longer road along the coast for no reason other than that I wanted to think. Had the Greys scared off whoever had attacked Stan? Assuming he *had* been attacked, which seemed pretty certain. What would have happened if they hadn't?

I stopped at the coast road and was waiting at the junction to turn right towards Malin when a large blue BMW passed by. I caught a glimpse of its blonde female driver and it gave me a shock. It was Laura Callan, the pathologist; I was sure of it. Why was she still in Donegal? The post-mortem on Carole was long since completed. And what was she doing here, in this part of the peninsula, if she had been working and staying in Letterkenny? A thrum of unease started somewhere in my gut.

When I arrived back in Malin, I was happy to see Guinness waiting for me on the doorstep. I let him in, made a pot of strong coffee and sat down to drink it while he curled up on my knee. I ran a few things by him but he wasn't particularly helpful. Then my phone rang. It was my mother calling to wish me a happy new year, in case I was busy later on. She and my father had returned from their trip the day before. After she had told me all about it, I asked if they had any plans for New Year's Eve.

'A reunion dinner of the Iceland crew,' my mother said.

'Haven't you seen enough of them?' I joked.

'Yes, but they're such good fun. You could do with a bit of that yourself, you know. Faye wouldn't want you to—'

I didn't let her continue. 'Yes, I know.'

Though I knew she was right, it seemed strange to hear her speak like that. It had taken ten years for either of my parents to smile properly after my sister's death. I knew I should be grateful. My phone vibrated in my hand with a call waiting. Molloy.

'I have to go, Mum. There's someone else trying to call me.'

'Okay, Sarah – I'll talk to you tomorrow. Happy New Year again.'

'You too, Mum.'

I pressed the end call button and took Molloy's. For some reason, I stood up, Guinness leaping off my knee in disgust.

'I'm at the hospital. Stan's unconscious.'

I sank back down into my chair again. 'But he was okay earlier. Well, maybe not okay, but he could walk, he could talk.'

'Some head injuries are like that, take a while to take effect.

213

He was conscious for about an hour at the hospital then slipped into some kind of coma. They have no idea how long it will last.'

'Did you get to speak to him?'

I heard the hospital PA system in the background. 'Briefly. He admitted he'd been hit on the head, but couldn't say by whom. Seems the Greys scared off whoever it was.'

'Did you get a chance to speak to them?'

Molloy sounded weary. 'They said they were walking onto the beach when they heard a scuffle and someone running. Then they came upon Stan, who insisted he had fallen.'

'That's what he said to me. Why would he lie? Initially, at any rate?'

'Looks as if he was afraid of something. Of someone.'

I shuddered. 'Who would have wanted to hurt Stan?'

'I have no idea. Do you?' There was a sudden edge to his voice. 'Since you're the one people seem to be talking to.'

I ignored the edge and told Molloy about the noise in the Oak. Since Stan had mentioned it to everyone else he'd met, I told myself there wasn't a confidentiality issue any longer.

Molloy inhaled. 'Really? What kind of noise?'

'He said it sounded like people moving furniture. The thing is, he said he went down once to have a look and the noise stopped.'

The background sounds changed and I heard traffic. Molloy had taken the call outside.

'And you think maybe someone saw him? Or perhaps he caught a glimpse of something someone didn't want him to see?'

'If he did, he didn't tell me about it.'

Molloy sighed in frustration. I couldn't blame him. 'I don't suppose you could have told me this before now?'

'I'm sorry. It was a few days before the fire. And I thought Stan would have mentioned it. There is one other thing . . .'

'Go on.'

'Róisín and Susanne came back to the pub the Saturday night of the fire. At least they were dropped outside it. The taxi driver who brought them back thought there might have been a lock-in.'

'How the hell do you find out these things?' Molloy said in exasperation.

I had the grace to look embarrassed, though Molloy couldn't see it. I shrugged. 'People tell me stuff. Maybe it's because I'm a solicitor.'

'I wish they'd tell *me* stuff.'

I smiled. 'Maybe it's because you're a guard that they don't.'

I thought about this when I ended the call. Why didn't people talk to Molloy? Was it just because he was a guard? There's always been an instinctive Irish mistrust for authority, but I wondered if it was more than that. My phone buzzed in my hand with a text from Maeve.

I'm going to Tony's later. Are you sure you and the sergeant don't fancy strutting the red carpet? Coming out to the world.

I rang her back since she obviously hadn't heard about the latest development. She was shocked, and wondered aloud if Tony would go ahead with his drinks party.

'He'll go one of two ways,' she said. 'Cancel it out of respect for Carole and Stan, or go ahead with a vengeance because we all need a bit of cheering up. Are you still having dinner with your sergeant?'

'No. He's had to cancel, with this attack on Stan.'

'Will you come, then? To Tony's? If he goes ahead with it?'

'You're on.'

'Great. I'll ring him and check.'

215

She rang back in five minutes. 'He's going ahead. Bit later than planned. Nine o'clock at his place. He's going to see Stan at the hospital first.'

Glendara Community Hospital was shrouded in icy fog, dark silhouetted figures putting me in mind of a scene from Jack the Ripper's London. I parked in the car park and sat there for a while, listening to the sound of my own breathing and trying to work out why I'd come. Stan was unconscious so wouldn't be able to speak to me, but I wanted to see him all the same; he'd looked so vulnerable when we'd found him on the beach. And if I was honest, I also hoped I might run into Tony.

I locked the car and the fog swallowed me immediately as I negotiated my way through the car park towards the hospital entrance. The glow from the lamps was pale and ineffective, diffused light no match for the dense fog, and a couple of times I collided with a parked car I hadn't realised was there. The air was still, as if the figures I'd seen on the way in had been absorbed into the mist, the only movement my own. I felt like a ghost. A tall, hunched figure appeared on my right. My heart-beat sped up; my instinct was to run, dash for the door of the hospital, but I didn't. I kept my steady pace until I heard a voice.

'Ben.'

I heaved an audible sigh of relief. It was Tony Craig.

'Are you okay?' he asked, concerned.

'I'm fine. It's just a little eerie. I couldn't see your face.'

'It's freezing fog. The roads are going to be lethal tonight. I'm wondering if I should cancel my drinks.'

My eyes focused. 'It's up to you, but I'd be happy to come and raise a glass to a better year than this one.'

'Fair enough. I'm sure you won't be the only one. I have to

meet another of Susanne's boyfriends, and I could do with a crowd around me when I do that.' He gave a weak smile.

'Phyllis said.'

'Although she tells me this one's got a bit of class, not one of her usual scruffs, as she put it.'

We walked together towards the hospital entrance. 'Are you going to see Stan?' I asked, although I already knew he was.

He nodded. 'I expect they'll move him to Letterkenny, but it may not be safe to take him yet. I thought I'd just . . .' He trailed off, lost for words.

'I know what you mean. Although they may not let us in since we're not family.'

We approached the desk behind a huge fake tree and spoke to the receptionist, who made a call upstairs.

'You can see him,' she said as she hung up the phone. 'But only for a few minutes. He won't respond but he may be able to hear you. He's on the first floor in St Martha's Ward. The nurse up there will take you in to him.'

To reach Stan's room, we passed through a small anteroom filled with medical equipment, where a nurse gave us plastic aprons and masks before showing us in and closing the door quietly behind us.

Stan looked pale but himself, his breathing barely audible over the beeping of the machines. He was hooked up to an oxygen mask and a drip but he seemed peaceful; the fear was gone. In fact, he looked more at ease than I had ever seen him. Stan MacLochlainn spent most of his life putting on a performance, I realised; the loud, acid-tongued drama queen was a caricature he had created for himself. I wondered if any of us knew the real Stan.

Tony approached the bed first, brow furrowed as if trying to work something out. He looked confused for a second, and then his eyes widened and he moved suddenly to the end of the bed. I took his place by Stan's side; there was nowhere else to stand, the other side too full of equipment and wires.

I heard a sharp intake of breath and my heart jumped. I looked at Stan, thinking for a second that he was coming around, until I realised that the noise was coming from the end of the bed. Tony was gripping Stan's chart, his face deathly pale.

'Tony?' I asked. 'Are you all right?'

He dropped the chart on the floor with a loud clatter. 'I have to go . . . I have to . . .' He turned and walked out the door, leaving it to slam shut behind him.

I made my way to the end of the bed, picked up the chart and scanned it quickly, before the nurse came in to ask about the noise. It was full of charts and figures, none of which meant anything to me. Then I glanced at the top, where Stan's name and date of birth should be. The name on the chart was Stephen Stanley.

Chapter Twenty-Two

Tony had gone to a huge amount of trouble in decorating his house for the party, with lights and holly and a sprig of mistletoe over each doorway. It was almost as if he was trying to re-create the Oak as it was the week before it burned down. He'd even managed to get some hand-knitted reindeer like the ones over the bar.

'Mrs McKinney knits them,' he said when Maeve asked. 'Hal's mother. They're a bit bonkers, as is she to be honest, but I like them. When she said she had a spare set she hadn't managed to sell before Christmas, I thought why not? Maybe they'll bring us a bit of luck.'

'They didn't bring the Oak much luck,' Phyllis muttered, looking rather startling in a full-length blue kaftan and headdress.

Tony shrugged. 'No, but if we can't spend New Year's Eve in the Oak, then at least we can have a bit of the Oak here on New Year's Eve.'

'I'll drink to that,' Maeve said, glass of Bacardi in hand.

She was wearing a green silk dress and high heels, a rarity for her. Everyone had made an effort, I noticed. I was glad I'd changed from my funeral suit into a red vintage skirt I'd bought online. I watched as Tony moved about the party, pouring drinks and offering snacks; he was playing the cheerful host, but I had a sense he was wearing a mask that could easily crack. His face had taken on the cadaverous look of a crumbling Rembrandt visage.

When he went to the kitchen to get more drinks, I followed him. I pushed open the door to see him standing at the door of the fridge, tray of ice in hand as if he'd forgotten what he was supposed to do with it. He half turned when he heard my steps and his face fell; he looked cornered. He straightened himself, put the tray on the draining board and hung his head.

'I know what you're going to ask.'

'What's that?'

'You're going to ask me about the hospital earlier.'

I placed my glass on the island in the middle of the kitchen. 'Well I *was* wondering. You were there one minute and gone the next.'

He turned. 'I know. I'm sorry. I should have stayed. But I needed to gather my thoughts.'

'Was it anything to do with the name on the chart? Why was Stan using the name Stephen Stanley?'

Tony groaned, as if in pain. 'Stephen Stanley,' he said. 'I never thought I'd hear that name again. I really thought he'd emigrated. I'm sure that's what I'd heard. Or maybe it was just wishful thinking on my part, an easy way out.'

'Tell me,' I urged.

Tony walked over to the kitchen door and closed it, blocking out the noise from the living room. When he came back, he poured himself a whiskey, refilled my glass of wine and sank down onto one of the kitchen stools, glass gripped between his two hands. I joined him.

'I don't know if I've ever mentioned it, but I went to boarding

220

school,' he began. 'Not very common around here in those days, but my father was away a lot and my mother worked. Also not very common. I went to a boys' school over the west of Donegal. I did well, was popular and eventually became a prefect. When I was in my final year, a new boy arrived, halfway through the term.' He stopped as if unable to continue.

'Stephen Stanley,' I prompted.

'Stephen Stanley. A pudgy boy, with a stammer. Just ripe for bullying. Low-hanging fruit, as they say – easy prey. And he *was* bullied, mercilessly. Stephen the Stutter. Spitting Stephen. It was unfortunate that both his names began with S. Anyway, I tried to help him, but it was impossible. He was five years younger than me and I couldn't be around him all the time. Hardly at all, in fact. But there was one time when I found him being hung upside down by his underpants in the sports room and I knew I'd have to do something about it. I tried to get some of the other prefects involved so I wouldn't have to go to the teachers, but they weren't interested. They said he just needed to toughen up. So I did something I regret.'

'Go on.'

His frown grew deeper as he remembered. 'I went to the head. Stephen had pleaded with me not to, said he'd just get more grief, but I really thought he was going to be seriously hurt if it continued.'

'And . . .'

Tony clicked his teeth in disgust. 'The head was useless. I don't know what I expected him to do. Maybe I just wanted the worry off my own shoulders. He called in the boys I'd named, told them off and left it at that. Left me out of it completely so they thought Stephen was the one who'd told on them. Unforgivable in that school.'

'Unforgivable in any school at that time, I'd say. What happened?'

'Stephen went missing. For a full day and night.'

'He ran away?'

'That's what was generally assumed. It's what I thought anyway.' He put his head in his hands. 'I didn't even bother looking for him.'

'He hadn't run away?'

Tony shook his head. 'He'd been locked in a cupboard in the games room. One that was rarely used. For a full day and night. A proper search was launched the next day and one of the other prefects found him . . . he'd passed out in panic. Hadn't even screamed. Had wet himself.'

'The poor kid.'

Tony looked at me. 'That's not all. The reason Stephen Stanley had been sent to boarding school in the first place was because his mother was sick. Really sick. She had cancer – it was terminal. And the reason there was such a huge search for him the day after he went missing was because she had taken a turn for the worse.' He swallowed and ran his fingers through his hair. 'She died while he was locked in that cupboard. He never got to say goodbye to her.'

I was stunned into silence. 'God. How awful.'

'I told him afterwards, at the funeral as a matter of fact, that it had been me who'd told the head about the bullying. I said I was sorry, that he had been right and I shouldn't have done it. I couldn't have it on my conscience.' He shook his head. 'But I don't know if it did him any good, telling him. I probably should have kept it to myself. It wasn't going to bring his mother back or give him a chance to say goodbye to her.'

'And you had no idea that Stan MacLochlainn was Stephen

Stanley?' I asked. 'He never told you in the year or two he's been here?'

'No,' Tony said. 'And I didn't recognise him. The last time I saw him, he was thirteen. He left the school after that. He was really overweight when I knew him. He's unrecognisable now from that pudgy thirteen year old. There was a school reunion about fifteen years ago and I'm sure someone told me he'd gone to Australia.'

'Maybe he left and came back,' I said. 'How did he react when you told him it was you who'd told the head about the bullying?'

Tony shook his head as if the memory was painful to him. 'He said that I should have left him alone, that he'd have been able to take care of himself. He told me that someday I'd understand what it meant to lose everything. To not be able to say goodbye.'

I pictured a thirteen-year-old Stan trapped in a locked cupboard while his mother passed away, and my heart went out to him. Then something hit me. Hadn't Stan said that he had been to see his mother in Dungloe on the night of the fire? Hadn't Róisín told me that that was where he had gone yesterday, too, when I'd been looking for him at the funeral?

I said as much to Tony and he paled again. He looked away. 'He mentioned his mother to me a few times too. I wonder now if he was testing me, seeing if I'd remember that she was dead. But I didn't. He's been here for eighteen months and I never realised who he was. Living in my flat, renting my business premises.'

'I wonder why he came here in the first place?' I said.

Before Tony could reply, there was a knock on the door and Phyllis stuck her head in. 'Susanne's here with her new man.'

★ ★ ★

I let Tony go to be introduced to Susanne's boyfriend while I stayed perched at the island in his kitchen, thinking about what he had just told me. There was a bowl of chilli-covered nuts in front of me that I found myself reaching for repeatedly; the chewing seemed to help me think. I was so distracted I barely noticed Liam come in. He gave me a nod, took a beer from the fridge and opened it with a cigarette lighter that he took from his pocket.

'So,' he said. 'Poor old Stan. There's been a right old rate of attrition in Glendara this Christmas, hasn't there?

I sighed and took another nut. 'The sooner it's over the better as far as I'm concerned. I'm even looking forward to getting back to work.'

'Tough gig for the sergeant. I'd say he's under a bit of pressure to sort this all out.'

With a jolt I realised how true that was: murder, arson and a serious assault all within two weeks. It would reflect badly on Molloy if he was unable to bring the perpetrators in, and quickly, too, before people became really frightened.

'Why don't people talk to the guards, Liam?'

Liam perched on the stool beside me. 'You mean Molloy?

'Maybe.'

'Ach, people might find it hard to admit their mistakes to him. Maybe he could do with being a bit more approachable.'

I took a sip of my wine.

'But he's a good man,' Liam said. 'A good friend, loyal. That's not to be underestimated.'

'What do you mean?' I asked. Who would be Molloy's friends? I wondered. With a prickle of fear I thought of Laura Callan.

'Ach, just . . . maybe people need to trust him a bit more.'

Liam wasn't going to give me any specifics. He took a swig from his bottle of beer and changed the subject. 'The funeral was a tough one, wasn't it?'

'What did you make of George's eulogy?' I asked.

Liam shook his head. 'George has told me a few things in the last few days that I'm not too happy about.'

'Like what?'

He sighed. 'I'm not sure I should say.'

I felt a wave of exhaustion wash over me. I wasn't sure I even wanted to know any more. 'That's okay. I understand. You're friends.'

Liam shot me a smile. 'Ach, sure you and me are friends too. And I reckon you might have guessed anyway.'

'Go on.'

'Let's say he hasn't always been a good boy. Being a musician and all, I know the girls like him, but . . .'

I resisted asking for details. 'You never had your suspicions?'

Liam shook his head. 'He kept it to himself. I'd have told him what I thought of it if I'd known. With two wee ones at home, it's not right. Of course, there isn't much I can say to him now. I'm hardly going to kick him when he's down, am I?'

'I suppose not.'

Liam scratched his chin. 'The thing is, I think the guilt is getting to him. He wonders if maybe Carole was trying to pay him back and got herself in strife that way.'

'With a man she was having an affair with?' I wondered if George had any inkling yet that his wife was already married when he met her.

'Exactly.' Liam reached for a nut and tossed it into his mouth. He pulled a face. 'Jesus, what's in these?'

'Chilli.' I reached for another one myself. 'You were there

that night in the Oak. Was there anyone that wouldn't usually be there? Taking a bit more interest in Carole than normal?'

Liam shook his head sadly. 'I didn't notice, to be honest. I wish I had. I was only in for the one. But as I said, I thought she was on edge. Mind not really on the job. Maybe George is right – maybe she did know what he was up to.'

'Did she give any indication that she knew?' I asked.

Liam shook his head. 'He says no. But that doesn't mean she didn't.'

Liam had a point. It seemed to me that Carole and George had communicated very little, both with their suspicions about the other but neither articulating them.

Liam frowned. 'But he did say that this latest woman was causing problems. He wouldn't say who she was; just that she was putting him under pressure.'

When Liam left the kitchen, I poured myself another glass of wine. I knew I was being unsociable, but I didn't feel like going back into the living room, not yet, and the strains of 'Rocking Around the Christmas Tree' coming through the open door did nothing to change my mind. I missed Molloy but I wondered how comfortable everyone else would be having him here.

Phyllis appeared in the doorway. Seeing me alone, she belted out a chorus of 'You will always find me in the kitchen at parties' before resting her ample bosom on the island.

'You holding court in here? Should I make an appointment?'

I sighed. 'No, I'm just not feeling very sociable.'

'I don't blame you. Tony's doing his best, but it's all bit fakery-pokery out there to be honest. It's pretty clear that nobody really feels like being at a party but they all think they're putting on a brave face for everybody else.'

226

She glanced at the big silver clock over the window. 'You should come back in before midnight, though. I think we'll all probably head off then anyway.'

I looked at the clock. It was quarter to twelve. 'Okay, I'll come in now.'

'You can meet Susanne's new boy. That'll give you a bit of diversion.' She winked. 'Don't think Tony's too impressed. He's a bit slick. Older than her, too.'

I hauled myself off the stool and followed Phyllis into the living room with my glass of wine.

The room had filled up since I'd left it. It was warm and festive; the scent of Tony's mulled wine filled the air, and despite what Phyllis had said, on the surface at least people seemed up for a party. A typical New Year's Eve atmosphere. Ever the barman, Tony was opening bottles of champagne and lining up flutes at a sideboard in preparation for the big countdown.

Phyllis made her way over to Maeve and I followed her. On the way, Liam offered to refill my glass and I accepted. It was a night for a taxi, I decided.

A few minutes later, Phyllis moved in closer, her bulk preventing me from seeing who had joined our circle. Then I glimpsed something out of the corner of my eye that caused my chest to tighten as if the air had grown thinner. Logic told me I must be wrong. It was impossible. I was afraid to turn my head. Introductions were made, and I was next. I was aware of a scent that made it hard to breathe. I heard Phyllis say my name and I turned, moving in slow motion as her voice faded into the distance. Forcing myself to look into the smiling face, the cruel mouth, the cold blue eyes of Susanne Craig's new boyfriend.

Luke Kirby.

Chapter Twenty-Three

How I managed to get myself out of Tony's house and into the square to find a taxi, I'll never know. How I endured the chat on the journey back, found my keys and got myself into my house and bathroom before I threw up, I'll also never know. But I did. And when I had done all of that, I took three painkillers, locked the doors and windows and went to bed with Guinness sleeping at my feet.

Amazingly, I slept for a full nine hours. It was only when I awoke the following morning, New Year's Day, that I allowed myself to begin to absorb what had happened. My phone rang and I picked it up from my bedside locker. It was Maeve. She sounded worried.

'Are you okay? You ran out of Tony's last night like you'd heard a shot. I went after you but you'd disappeared.'

'I'm fine.'

'No you're not. You left before midnight, on New Year's Eve. What happened?'

I knew I would have to tell Maeve at some stage, but I wasn't ready; I hadn't yet processed it myself. And I certainly couldn't tell her over the phone.

'I'll tell you later. I just have to work out a few things first.'

'Okay,' she said reluctantly. 'But if you don't call me by tonight, I'm coming over.'

'I will, I promise.'

When I ended the call, Guinness, who had made his way to the top of the bed, rubbed his cheek against my hand and I scratched the little white patch on the top of his head. My own head was spinning. All the questions I'd blocked out the night before came flooding back in as if someone had opened a sluice gate. What the hell was Luke Kirby doing in Glendara, and what was he doing with Susanne Craig? Where had they met? Did she even know who he was?

The full implications of his presence began to hit. Inishowen was my sanctuary. It was where I had come to escape my past, to see if I could, over time, put the pieces of my life back together. If I could somehow forget, not my sister, but the awful way in which she had died and the man who had killed her. The man who I'd thought I loved, and who I now hated with all my being.

Was I now going to have to start seeing this man on the street? Accept him as a neighbour? Welcome him into the town I had come to consider my home? The town that had helped me recover from something I never thought I could? It had been bad enough last year when he had rung my office. Now I felt as if he had invaded my home and soiled everything that was important to me.

I knew I couldn't handle this on my own. I rang Molloy and got his voicemail. Instead of leaving a message, I called the Garda station and got McFadden. He told me that Molloy had gone to see Stan MacLochlainn, who had regained consciousness, and that he'd be back at the station in an hour.

When I climbed out of bed, I found I was shaking as if I

had a really bad hangover. I massaged the bones around my eyes, my skin feeling too tight for my skull. I decided to have a bath, threw in some lavender and soaked for about twenty minutes. I was almost asleep again when I heard a knock at the door downstairs. I sat up in shock, spilling water onto the mat. I began to shiver. Kirby wouldn't come here, would he? To my house? Last night he'd seemed happy to keep up the pretence that we'd never met. But it wouldn't be hard to find out where I lived, assuming he didn't know already.

I forced myself to throw on a pair of jeans and a shirt and make my way slowly down the stairs, legs trembling. At the door, I hesitated, wishing suddenly for a spyhole so I could see who was outside. I steeled myself, took a deep breath and opened the door to find Phyllis holding a basket of home-made mince pies and a pot of cream. I almost cried with relief.

'Okay, pet,' she said. 'I'm going to make us a big pot of tea, I'm going to heat these up and you're going to spill.'

I shook my head but was powerless to stop her marching past me and making her way to the kitchen, where she ignored my pleas while she filled the kettle and put it on to boil. Then she turned, her large rump pressed against the sink.

'Now,' she said gently, 'sit down and tell me exactly what's going on. You left Tony's last night as if you'd seen a ghost. I've never seen you like that. Tony and Maeve both followed you. What with everything that's been going on, they were worried sick. It was only when Tony spoke to one of the taxi drivers that we knew you'd got home safely and we decided to let you be.'

The taxi drivers in Glendara seemed to be awfully chatty this season, I thought.

'Tony saw what happened?'

Phyllis nodded. 'You raced out of there as soon as you were

introduced to Susanne's new boyfriend.' She looked worried. 'Don't you remember?'

Susanne's new boyfriend. I had a flashback of a hand outstretched, that arrogant smile. I sank into one of the kitchen chairs, my head pounding and muggy. I was beginning to think I might be developing flu along with everything else.

'I remember.'

How would Tony react if he knew that his daughter's new boyfriend was a convicted killer? I thought. The age difference was the least of his worries.

'You don't look well,' Phyllis said. 'Are you coming down with something?'

'Probably.'

'Okay, you just sit there quietly. I'll make this tea and then we can chat.'

She turned towards the sink and I watched her busying herself about my kitchen as if she'd spent all her life in it. I knew she wasn't going to take no for an answer. Not so long ago, a woman who had worked for her had been murdered, and she was still haunted by the fact that she had been unable to make the woman confide in her before she died. She wasn't going to allow me to fob her off now.

But the only people in Inishowen I had told about my sister's killing were Maeve and Molloy. I'd always thought that was the best policy. I'd come here to escape my past and start a new life. It would have completely defeated the purpose if I were to tell everyone and become the subject of town chatter. Now, though, without any notice, the rules seemed to have changed. Luke Kirby had changed them. With an unpleasant jolt, I realised there was no way he was here by accident. He knew this was where I lived. I had known that since he had

231

called me last year. And now he was throwing down the gauntlet and awaiting my response.

So when Phyllis had taken her seat at the table, poured me a cup of tea and handed me a mince pie with a huge dollop of cream, I told her. I told her everything, kept nothing back. I told her about my relationship with Luke, about how he had moved on to my younger sister, breaking my heart in the process, and how he had introduced her to cocaine. I told her how Faye had been found strangled in her own flat, and how Luke Kirby had eventually been convicted and sentenced for her manslaughter.

I avoided looking at Phyllis for most of the time I talked, the notion that the very man I was talking about was within ten miles of where we were sitting too much to bear. When I had finished, I looked up.

Phyllis was in tears. She had allowed her eyes to fill while I was talking, fearful maybe that if she moved she would cause me to lose my nerve. And so when I stopped, she rooted in the pocket of her dress for a large handkerchief, which she used to wipe her eyes and nose. It was the third time I had related the story of my sister's death and the first time I was the one with dry eyes.

'I remember it, you know,' she said. 'From the news. Your sister's name was . . .'

'Faye.'

'Yes. So that was you, the older sister. *This* is your story,' she said quietly.

I nodded.

'I always knew you had a sadness about you, but I never imagined it was something like this . . .' She trailed off, then suddenly stood up to envelop me in her huge arms.

I accepted her embrace gladly. There was a solid comfort and safety about her hug, as if I was being held by someone who could protect me. But it was then that the sickening realisation hit – if Luke Kirby really wanted to hurt me, there was very little anyone could do about it.

When Phyllis finally released me, she sat back down and helped herself to another mince pie. I joined her, feeling light-headed, and watched mesmerised as she added spoonful after spoonful of cream until the pie was an island in a pool of white.

'And he's a lawyer, like you?' she said, taking a spoonful of her mince pie soup.

'He was. We worked for the same firm. I don't think he's allowed to practise any more. At least I hope he isn't.'

'He probably advises all the other prisoners,' Phyllis said with a wry expression. 'That's what usually happens, isn't it?

'Probably. Although now that he's out, I don't know what he's doing for a living. And what the hell he's doing here . . .'

Phyllis widened her eyes in horror and I realised that I hadn't finished my story. 'Oh good God, that's why you ran out of Tony's last night. That's him, isn't it? Susanne's new boyfriend. He's the man who killed your sister.'

'Yes. Luke Kirby,' I said. I felt stupid. My reactions seemed dulled, as if everything I had had been poured into telling the story and there was nothing left. 'Isn't that what he's calling himself?'

'I don't know – he was just introduced to me as Luke, and you called him Kirby when you were telling your story. He might be using a different surname. If he isn't, Tony might recognise it even if Susanne doesn't.' Phyllis paused to think. 'Although he might not, since it was a good few years ago.'

'Ten. The trial was ten years ago.'

'Do you think Susanne's in danger?' Phyllis asked.

'I don't know, Phyllis. I only know that Luke Kirby killed my sister and he seemed absolutely certain that he would get away with it. He was utterly shocked when he was convicted.'

'A bit of a God complex,' Phyllis said. 'So what can we do about it? I mean, if he's served his sentence, I suppose that means he's entitled to live his life wherever he wants.'

'I suppose. I don't know,' I said.

'Have you talked to the sergeant?'

'Not yet.' I checked my watch. 'I'm going into Glendara now.'

'Should I tell Tony about this?' Phyllis asked.

'Maybe hold off until I speak to Molloy. It might be better to let him handle it.'

Driving into Glendara, I felt as if I'd let something out of the bag that I'd managed to keep contained for years. I wondered if it had been a mistake; I had no idea what the consequences would be. But then it hadn't been my choice, it had been Luke's; he was the one in control. I was afraid that nothing in Glendara would ever be the same again.

I parked in front of the Garda station, pausing to take a gulp from a bottle of water I'd left on the front seat. My throat felt scratchy and sore and my head was full, and as I walked the few steps to the door I noticed that my limbs were beginning to ache too. Flu was the last thing I needed. I reached for the door and it swung outwards, forcing me to stand back to let someone out. It was Kirby.

'Excuse me,' he said, without looking at my face.

He walked past me, leaving a trail of expensive scent in his wake, the one he'd always worn, the one I'd smelled the night before. I watched in stunned silence as he continued up the street. The door of the station swung shut. My hand trembled as I pushed it open again. Molloy was alone at the front desk; no sign of McFadden. He shook his head when he saw me. He looked appalled.

'No need to ask if you've seen him then?'

I nodded, unable to speak. He came around the front of the desk and took me in his arms, clasping my head to his front, the rough fabric of his uniform solid against my cheek.

'Are you okay?' he asked.

I nodded against his chest.

'He came to check in with us,' he said, when we pulled apart. 'He doesn't have to, it wasn't part of the terms of his release, but because he now knows you live around here, he said he thought he should do the right thing and let us know.'

'*Now* knows?'

'Claims he only realised when he saw you last night.'

My hackles rose. 'You know that's a complete lie. He's always known. Isn't there anything we can do?'

'Unfortunately, he's served his sentence,' Molloy said.

'Did he not get remission?' I asked.

'Only the bare minimum. He's subject to the usual requirement to keep the peace and be of good behaviour, but that's it. No obligation to stay away from anyone or out of any particular town. The only thing you could do to make him leave is make an application to the courts yourself. But he'd have to have done something to cause you to do that.'

Molloy was only telling me what I knew myself.

'I know it's no comfort, but I don't think he intends staying here long,' he said.

I put my head in my hands. 'I suppose it's better he's here than in Chapelizod, running into my parents.'

Molloy looked at me. 'You don't seem as shocked as I thought you'd be.'

'I met him last night at Tony's,' I said.

'So that's where he saw you. What was he doing there?'

'He's Susanne Craig's new boyfriend.'

Molloy's eyes widened. 'You're kidding. He said he had a relationship with someone here but he didn't give me a name.'

'I'm going to have to tell Tony.'

Molloy was quiet.

'What?' I demanded. 'You don't agree? I presume she doesn't know about his past.'

'He claims he told his girlfriend he's been in prison and she's fine with it. He says he has been completely open with her.'

I felt my remaining power drain away. All I wanted to do was sleep.

Chapter Twenty-Four

I was reeling when I left the Garda station. Was it actually possible that Kirby had told Susanne Craig the whole story, or at least his version of it? Could she really be happy to go out with a man who had killed his girlfriend? And should I tell Tony? I was sure *he* wouldn't be okay with it even if his daughter was. But doing so would involve revealing my own history. The fall-out would be considerable and I wasn't sure I was ready for that. People were bound to see me differently, and that would change Glendara for me forever. I didn't have any answers. But there was one thing I did know. I couldn't face the possibility of seeing Luke Kirby's face every day. If he didn't leave, then I would have to.

I stood on the street feeling lousy, but I didn't want to go home yet. I thought about tracking Maeve down, but I knew she would be working. I was about to go to the office – my last resort – with the intention of trying to get some work done when my phone rang. It was Stoop the newsagent, ringing to make an appointment to discuss administering his nephew's estate.

'I'm just around the corner as it happens,' I said. 'I was going to go into the office for a while, if you'd like to meet me there?

I can check the appointment book and we can have a chat about what I'll need you to bring in.'

'I can't leave the shop,' Stoop said. 'But you could come up? There's no one here at the moment.' Still, he lowered his voice. 'Although if someone comes in, you'll have to leave. I don't want the whole town knowing my business.'

I smiled to myself. 'Of course. I intended calling in to buy the newspapers anyway.'

'Come away on, so.'

As Stoop had said, the shop was deserted. When I remarked upon it, he gave a long, deep sigh.

'People just aren't coming out. They haven't been since poor Carole was found, and now Stan hasn't helped.' He made it sound as if Stan had beaten himself up just to cause trouble. 'And all this mithering about Dominic; it's as if they blame me for it. Soon there'll be no businesses open in the town at all.'

It occurred to me that he had a point; Stoop's was the third business in the town to be affected by recent events, after the Oak and the hairdresser's. It was beginning to feel as if someone were attacking the town itself.

'Although if it weren't for you, the fire in the Oak could have been a lot worse,' I said. 'It might have spread if you hadn't spotted it. People should be thanking you.'

'Oh I don't know about that. I'm just glad I saw it,' he said. 'Just happened to look out the window when I was up in the night and saw the flames.'

'That must have been pretty frightening.'

'It was. I won't deny it.' He shifted some newspapers around on the counter as if he needed something to do with his hands. 'It made me think of all those fires my nephew caused and the people who got hurt. And how many more might have been.'

'I suppose he thought he was doing the right thing for a cause he believed in,' I said.

He shook his head. 'As a wee boy he was all turned inwards. But something got into him when he was about sixteen and he changed. Got stormy, started giving cheek to the brother, fighting with him over the way he ran the farm. Pete didn't like it one bit. He was a terrible old tyrant. So when Dominic's mother died – wild sad that, she was only forty – the next thing we knew, Dominic was away to America and then to England. Not a word from him after that, even when his father died.'

'Would he have heard about it?'

'Oh aye. He was back in England at that time. We sent notices to the papers over there and all.'

I hesitated. 'Maybe he was in prison?'

Stoop gave me a contemptuous look. 'Aye, he was. But he was well able to contact me when he needed bailing out. If he needed money he'd call, no bother.'

'And did you give it to him?' I asked.

'I did. It was probably the wrong thing to do, but he was family. I couldn't see him stuck. And he never did get his inheritance from his father, never looked for it, never did anything about it. I always felt guilty about that, I suppose. I just let it sit.'

Which reminded me of the business at hand, the reason I was here. 'So you want me to administer his estate now?'

'Aye. I suppose you'll have to administer the brother's estate first, will you?'

'If the property is still in his name, yes.'

'Aye, it would be.' His eyes narrowed. 'I suppose it'll be very dear?'

'Let's see what's involved first before we commit to anything. I should be able to do you up an estimate. Have you any paperwork? Death certificates, title deeds, maps, that kind of thing?'

He nodded towards the ceiling. 'Aye, I have a load of that kind of stuff in a trunk upstairs.'

'Why don't you gather together anything you think might be useful and bring it to me on Monday morning? I don't think I've any appointments yet since it's the first day back after the Christmas holidays. Come in about ten, we'll go through what you have and I'll make you a list of anything else I need. Is that okay?'

'Aye that's grand.'

I left Stoop's with the *Irish Times* and the *Irish Independent* under my arm, glad to have something to occupy me for the afternoon and happy to discard my plan to go into the office. I was shivering despite my big coat, and I didn't relish the prospect of huddling over a radiator in the freezing-cold office while I worked my way through the holiday post. The whole lot could wait till Monday morning. I needed some time to recover on a number of fronts.

As I made my way back to the car, I heard a voice from across the road and looked up fearfully. It was Tony. I waved back, but when he called again I pretended I hadn't heard him, putting my phone against my ear as if I was answering a call. It was cowardly of me, I knew, but I didn't want to lie to him and I wasn't yet ready to tell him the truth.

On the way home, I slowed to a stop behind a group of five horses and riders hacking along the shore road. It was an attractive sight. They looked as if they'd come from the beach; there was a sheen on the horses' thick winter coats and their fetlocks were muddy with wet sand. As I slowly overtook them, one of the riders waved to me and I recognised Abby Grey. I pulled in and rolled down my window.

'What a nice way to spend a New Year's Day,' I said.

'Isn't it?' she smiled. 'Great that it's not snowing or raining or hailstoning for once. Have to take advantage of it.' Her smile grew broader. 'Have you met my son?'

I shook my head and she called to a young man in jeans and boots on a large black mare walking on ahead. He turned his mount around and approached the car, coming to a halt beside his mother, the two horses content to stand side by side.

Abby beamed with pride. 'This is Ronan. He came up on Christmas Eve.'

Ronan reached down to shake my hand through the window, not an easy manoeuvre for either of us. As he smiled and said hello, I realised he reminded me of someone. I thought it must be Ian at first – I could see he didn't look particularly like his mother. He was tall and long-legged, while she was petite with a small face and delicate features. But I couldn't see anything of Ian in him either. His eyes were distinctive, blue with a thin black outline around the iris, while Abby's and Ian's were both brown.

'Do you ride?' Abby asked me.

'Not for about twenty years. I learned as a child.'

Her eyed widened with interest. 'You should come out with us some day. We're planning on having stables up at Greysbridge.'

'That sounds lovely,' I said. 'I might take you up on it. I could definitely do with getting a bit more fresh air.'

'We've a big group going out tomorrow, if you're serious. Mostly beginners, but there'll be a few novices, so you can go at whatever pace suits you. As long as you have boots, we can lend you a hat. Wellies will do.'

'Maybe,' I said. 'I'll see how I feel. I think I might be coming down with something.'

'Excuses, excuses,' she said with a smile. 'Anyway, give me a call in the morning if you fancy it. Two o'clock. I know we have at least two horses free at this stage.'

She waved and I drove on.

As I headed towards Malin, I realised that it wasn't an adult Ronan Grey had reminded me of; it was a child. And it was the eyes, in particular the thin black line that ringed the iris. I racked my brains to come up with who the child was. It was a face I had seen only briefly. A sad, confused face, being pulled up into an adult's arms, comforted and taken away. A child who had given me a smile. I saw a plush sitting room in a crowded house, and my heart lurched. I pulled in by the side of the road to gather my thoughts, make sure I had it right. But I was sure. I knew who Abby and Ian's son reminded me of. It was two little boys, not one. Two little boys with the same eyes as Ronan Grey. Carole and George Harkin's sons.

By the time I got home, I was thoroughly rattled, my thought processes definitely not helped by the fact that all I really wanted to do was sleep. I couldn't allow myself to be sick at this point, two days before I had to reopen the office.

I managed to get through the afternoon by forcing myself to complete some domestic tasks that I had let slip over the past few days: long-overdue laundry, ironing and cleaning. I even managed to leave the house to buy some groceries. At seven o'clock, feeling utterly exhausted, I made tea and settled myself on the couch with a blanket. It didn't escape my notice that Guinness took himself over to the armchair, giving me a wide berth, as if he could tell I was infectious. At eight, I went to bed.

Saturday was a blur of Lemsip, paracetamol and sleep. In the evening, I tried to put my mind to work.

Could Ronan Grey be George's son? I wasn't imagining the likeness between the three boys; it was quite striking. Liam had implied that George had been less than faithful to Carole. Was it possible that Abby could have had an affair with him, eighteen years ago? It seemed unlikely given the age difference. But maybe it would explain the rows I'd witnessed between Ian and George. Or had Ian and Abby adopted Ronan? Was that the secret Ian had alluded to outside the pub after Carole's funeral?

And what the hell was Kirby's game? I had a horrible feeling that there was little I could do until he played his first card. But thinking about it made my head hurt. So I closed my eyes and listened to familiar sounds – cars whooshing by on the road outside, church bells ringing for Saturday-evening mass – and felt myself gradually drift off again.

Chapter Twenty-Five

On Sunday, I awoke suddenly. It was early morning and I was in bed with warm, heavy arms wrapped around me and soft breathing in my ear. I turned with some difficulty, waking Molloy as I moved.

He smiled. 'Morning.'

'How did you get in?' I asked.

'You let me in, of course.'

I had no memory of that. 'Did you . . . ?'

He grinned broadly, turning onto his back with his hands behind his head. 'Carry you up the stairs like in *An Officer and a Gentleman*? No. You came up yourself. Don't you remember?'

'Not really. It's all a bit hazy, to be honest. I still feel a little dizzy.'

'I'm not surprised. You staggered up here, fell into bed and were asleep in seconds.'

'I'm glad you stayed.' I yawned. 'Things aren't exactly easy at the moment.'

His smile disappeared. Avoiding my gaze, he climbed out of bed and pulled on a pair of jeans. I watched him move around the room while he searched for his shirt, dipping his head to avoid the low beam; he and Maeve both complained that my cottage had been built for small people. He looked good, strong shoulders, flat stomach; I tried to keep my thoughts on him rather than the other issues vying for my attention.

He pulled on his shirt and leaned over to kiss me. 'Stay put for a bit and see if you can have a snooze. I'll bring you up some tea.'

A snooze wasn't likely. Molloy had something to tell me and it didn't take a genius to work out that it wasn't of the good-news variety. I took two paracetamol from the blister pack on the bedside table and ten minutes later he returned with a pot of tea, two cups and some toast on a tray. He sat on the bed while I hauled myself up and put a pillow behind me. I felt marginally better than I had yesterday, but maybe it was just the painkillers taking effect. My nose was still blocked and my head felt like lead.

'So what's this in aid of?' I asked as he poured us both a cup of tea. 'I've never thought of you as the breakfast-in-bed kind of guy.'

'I need to talk to you about something.'

My stomach sank and I took a sip of tea to settle it. Inhaled the steam to clear my sinuses.

'I'm going to move in with you.'

The tea went down the wrong way and I choked, spluttering it all over the duvet. I don't know what I'd expected, but it certainly wasn't that.

When I had regained my composure and mopped up the mess on the bed, I said, 'Eh, why?'

'Not forever. Just for a while. Probably only a few days.'

'*Why?*' I said, more insistently this time.

Molloy looked down. 'I did some more digging yesterday after Kirby came into the station.'

'Okay,' I said slowly. I'd been right in the first place: this wasn't good news.

'I know that when he was released I advised you to move on, accept that he had served his sentence. But when I met him, there was something about him. I just couldn't take him at face value.' He paused. 'I know the assistant governor of the prison he was in, so I managed to get hold of his prison record.'

'Go on.'

He took a deep breath. 'Remember I told you that Dominic Stoop had just begun a new sentence in the UK when he died?'

I nodded.

'Well, before he was extradited to start that sentence, he was in prison here in Ireland. And guess who he shared a cell with?'

My head began to spin. 'Luke Kirby.'

Molloy nodded. 'It was shortly before Kirby was released, and it was only for a few months. It may mean absolutely nothing, but it's an unpleasant coincidence.'

'Jesus Christ.' I clutched at the duvet, struggling to make a connection that was just out of my reach. My brain was so clogged that I wanted to bang my head against the wall. 'So . . . ?'

Molloy handed it to me. 'The belt.'

Which was all I needed for my mind to race ahead at breakneck speed. 'The hairs on the belt. Dominic Stoop's DNA.'

Molloy nodded.

'If Kirby shared a cell with him, he'd easily have been able to get hold of a few hairs. He could have taken them from a comb or anything.'

'The shaft needs to be attached for them to extract DNA.'

'Kirby would know that. If necessary, he'd have yanked the guy's hair out while he was sleeping.' I shook my head, my voice growing louder. 'Kirby knows all about DNA; that was how he was caught for my sister's killing. Knowing him, he'll have a fucking PhD in genetics by now.'

Molloy remained calm, infuriatingly so, waiting for me to finish. 'Yes, he could have taken Stoop's DNA. That was the first thing that occurred to me. But *why* would he do it? What would be in it for him?'

'He wants something from me.' I pushed the tray aside and climbed out of bed, pacing across the room. 'He's not finished with me. He must have found out Dominic's connection to Glendara. He knew it was where I lived too; he knew from that call last year. He probably took Dominic's DNA thinking he could use it somehow.' I turned. 'How did Dominic Stoop die?'

'Heart attack. Same genetic problem as his mother.'

'So Kirby wouldn't have known Dominic was going to die.' My eyes widened as I worked things through. 'Maybe he didn't know Dominic was dead at all, since he died in prison in the UK. Maybe he thought he could blame Carole's death on him.'

Molloy crossed his arms. 'But why would Luke Kirby kill Carole?'

'Because he's a fucking psycho, that's why.'

Molloy shook his head. 'It can't be as simple as that. How did he even know her?'

'He's going out with Susanne Craig, isn't he? How the hell did he meet *her*? I mean, what's he doing? Working his way through all the females in Glendara until he gets back to me?'

Molloy was silent. I realised I was growing hysterical. Although it had cleared my sinuses. I took a deep breath and tried a more reasoned approach. 'Carole was married to Dominic Stoop. Maybe Dominic put them in touch with each other?'

'But *why*?' Molloy said again, frustrated.

'I don't know,' I said, collapsing back on the edge of the bed, exhausted.

I was moving too quickly, my thoughts disordered and panicked. I closed my eyes to relieve the pressure in my head, and when I opened them again, Molloy's expression had softened.

'I haven't worked out what all this means yet, but I'm not taking any chances. I'm going to stay here at night for a while. Or you can move into mine if you like.'

He reached for me but I pulled back. I was too wired. I stood up and walked towards the window, still dark enough for me to see my own reflection. I shook my head, tears pricking at my eyes. 'I'm not letting that bastard force me out. This is my *home* now. Glendara is *my* home. Inishowen is *my* home. Not Luke Kirby's.' And as I spoke, I realised the truth of what I was saying. I would not let Kirby win this time.

Molloy appeared behind me. 'I'm going to get McFadden to keep an eye on you while I can't.'

I turned to him and smiled through the tears. 'I don't need a bodyguard.'

But there was one thing I couldn't ignore. Molloy knew it too, though he hadn't mentioned it. My sister had been strangled, just like Carole Harkin.

Molloy left half an hour later. I pushed him out the door, determined to have some time to myself. It was good to have him looking out for me, but I wasn't sure how happy I was about being babysat by either him or McFadden. How would it even work? Was I about to see McFadden's red head peering around corners as I made my way to court, like some demented Inspector Clouseau?

But after he left, I felt uneasy. I found myself glancing into corners, closing doors I'd normally have left open. The notion of Luke Kirby and Dominic Stoop sharing a cell opened up all kind of possibilities, but more than anything, it made me convinced that he wasn't here by accident. I couldn't accept it was for Susanne. Luke was a charmer; he would have no difficulty in picking up a woman wherever he was. It was way too much of a coincidence that he just happened to meet someone from the town I lived in, having also shared a cell with someone from that town. It was far more likely that Susanne was easy prey, an easy mark, just as Faye had been.

But I kept coming back to the same question Molloy had asked: why? Luke Kirby was a calculating individual; his motives, even as a solicitor, had always been his own gain. It seemed highly possible that he was behind what had been happening in the town: Carole's death, the fire in the Oak. But why on earth would he risk his freedom to carry out such senseless acts?

I washed up the breakfast things and stood for a while looking out the window. It was grey and overcast, just as it had been the day before. But my plan to curl up by the fire and shift this cold didn't seem so attractive any more, not if I was going to be twitching at every little noise. Guinness had disappeared too, of course, just when I could have done with another heartbeat around the place.

Abby Grey had suggested I join them for a trek. Part of me wanted to go – it would be a distraction and I could see if I could find out anything more about Ronan – but the truth was, I didn't think I'd be capable of staying on a horse. Not today.

I checked my phone. There were two missed calls, both from Maeve, who I suddenly remembered I'd been supposed to call the day before. I rang her back but got her voicemail. She was working.

Then the phone buzzed in my hand. It was a text from Phyllis.

Come in if you fancy it. I'm not opening the shop today and I could do with some company.

I smiled. Phyllis was always perfectly happy in her own company, and with that treasure trove of books downstairs she was never truly alone. What she really meant was that she was worried about me and wanted to know if *I* needed company. I texted back.

I'm afraid I'm coming down with something. I might be infectious.

I'm immune to everything, she replied. *Too much padding for any infections to get through.*

Gratefully I grabbed my coat and headed out the door, leaving some food in the bowl for my wayward cat.

Phyllis had lit the fire in her cosy flat, and she made me tea with honey, lemon and chunks of raw ginger. I had to stop her from putting whiskey in it, since I was driving.

'That'll sort you out,' she said, sinking into an armchair with her own version of the drink that soothes: a hot chocolate with marshmallows and fresh cream. 'But make sure and have a hot whiskey when you get home.'

Fred padded into the room and flopped on the mat with a loud sigh while we sat in silence sipping our drinks, the warmth of the ginger tea soothing nerves I realised had been jangling for days now.

'They're gone, you know,' Phyllis said finally.

'Who?'

'Susanne and that man.'

'What do you mean, gone?'

'Dublin, I think. Too dull for Susanne around here, I expect.'

'Really?'

'There's some animal rights meeting tomorrow and they've gone down for it.'

'Animal rights? *Luke?*' I said. I remembered that my first doubts about Luke had arisen when he had shown no interest in my parents' dog – a sweet old mongrel called Belle, long since dead.

Phyllis fished one of the marshmallows from her drink and popped it into her mouth. 'Apparently that's what they have in common, he and Susanne. Or so Tony says. He was certainly talking the talk on New Year's Eve after you left. Like Susanne on Christmas Day.' She gave me a wry look. 'Maybe he's turned over a new leaf. Like finding God in prison.'

I wasn't convinced. I thought it far more likely that Kirby was spinning Susanne a line. It looked almost as if he were taking on Dominic Stoop's persona as some kind of eco-warrior. Maybe he'd told Susanne that that was why he'd been in prison. It would explain her attraction to him.

'They met in Spain, apparently,' Phyllis said. 'At some anti-bullfighting thing. Or maybe it was the running of the bulls in Pamplona. One of those.'

'When?'

'I'm not sure. Why?'

'Because it can't have been very long ago,' I said. 'Luke has only been out of prison a couple of months. He must have gone straight there. I thought he was in the UK.'

'Easy enough to get to Spain from the UK.' Phyllis shook her head. 'Still, at least it solves your problem, them both taking off. He's out of your hair.'

'True.'

She looked contemptuous. 'What a bastard, though. Fronting up to Tony's party knowing you were there.'

I looked up. 'How did he know I was there?'

'We were talking about you before you came out of the kitchen. If he'd had any decency about him, he'd have left then and there rather than putting on that bloody charade of pretending he didn't know you.'

'What was said about me in his presence? Can you remember?'

'I can't really . . . Just that someone should fetch you before midnight, I think.' Phyllis flushed suddenly. 'Oh, and *someone* may have said that you might be missing your sergeant.'

'Ah.'

Embarrassment coloured her neck and face. 'I hope I didn't say anything wrong.'

'It's okay. You didn't know who he was.'

'No,' Phyllis said, her voice hardening. 'I didn't. The man's entitled to live his life if he's served his time, but to my mind he should be required to stay at least fifty miles from you and your family.'

I smiled weakly. 'Thanks, Phyllis. I can't disagree with you.'

'Have you given any more thought to what we should tell Tony?' she asked. 'Do you think he has a right to know?'

'Oh Phyllis, I don't know.'

My head felt like lead again and I realised I didn't want to discuss Luke Kirby any longer. Maybe I should just be glad for small mercies and be grateful that he was gone. I looked around for a distraction. There was a book on the coffee table in front of me, a book about Irish sacred sites. I picked it up, as much to change the subject as anything else.

'Nice, isn't it?' Phyllis said, taking a sip of her chocolate. 'It's too good to put in the shop. I'm going to hang onto it, I think.'

'It's beautiful,' I said, running my hand across the cover. It was a luxurious glossy book with lovely illustrations. I opened it to the table of contents – there were sections on rag trees, fairy forts, stone circles, holy wells.

'The well at the top of Sliabh Sneacht is in it. Go on, have a look,' Phyllis urged.

I checked the index, found the page, and there it was: a clear colour photograph of the place Molloy and I had found on Christmas Day, before losing Fred and following him down the hill. Fred gazed up at me from his position on the hearth, as if reading my mind. I leaned down and rubbed his head. But as I did so, I had the same feeling I'd had before, that something didn't make sense, something just out of focus.

Phyllis looked at me curiously. 'You can borrow it if you like.'

Phyllis saw me to the door of the bookshop, where Fred lolled at her feet while we chatted on the step. Phyllis spent a lot of time standing in her doorway surveying the square, and she was doing that now.

'Emma,' she muttered under her breath. 'Well you've got what you wanted for Christmas, anyway.'

I followed her gaze and saw that she was watching Carole's sister across the street, struggling with two bulging shopping bags. I gazed at Phyllis wide-eyed and she caught my look, flushing suddenly when she realised what she had said.

'Oh God, no, I don't mean Carole's death.' She clapped her hands to her face. 'Lord, that really did come out wrong.'

'What *did* you mean?' I asked.

She looked embarrassed. 'Oh, I shouldn't have said it. I've always thought that Emma carried a bit of a torch for George. Not that she'd have done anything about it, I'm sure. Are you reopening the office tomorrow?' she asked, hastily changing the subject.

I nodded. 'I'd better go, actually, if I'm to get an early night.'

'Don't forget the hot whiskey!' she called after me as I turned to walk towards my car.

Chapter Twenty-Six

As good as his word, Molloy was over at my cottage by ten, just in time for Phyllis's suggested hot whiskey. Luke leaving Glendara hadn't changed his plans to spend the night with me, and I didn't object.

The following morning my sore throat and headache had turned into a ticklish cough. Less painful and debilitating but still annoying, especially for a day in the office. But we'd been closed for ten days and I needed to reopen. Molloy left at the same time I did, waving as he drove off. It felt oddly domesticated.

Leah was in the office before me, working her way through the post, sorting out which correspondence I needed to deal with and which bits were her responsibility. The fact that her pile was considerably larger than mine did give me pause for thought, although it didn't seem to bother her very much. There was an air of suppressed excitement about her that I couldn't avoid noticing. When I returned from hanging up my coat, I asked her what was up.

She beamed. 'We've decided to set a date for the wedding. It's going to be this summer. August probably.'

Leah had been engaged for a while, but until now, neither she nor her fiancé had seemed in any rush to take the next step.

'That's lovely news,' I said. 'We could do with something good to look forward to.'

'Well that's just it, to be honest. All this awful stuff happening over Christmas made us wonder why we were waiting.' She handed me a stack of opened post and screwed up the discarded envelopes to stuff into the recycling basket.

'That's great.' I flicked through what she'd given me to see if there was anything that I needed to panic about. There wasn't.

'Stoop the newsagent is coming in this morning at ten,' I said. 'Would you stick it in the book?'

But she hadn't heard me. Her mind was somewhere else; she was gazing at the wall at something I couldn't see. So I asked her again, she did as I asked, and in return I gave in to the inevitable.

'So, you have a wedding to plan, then?' I said, resting my elbows on the counter.

Leah rubbed her hands together. 'We do. And I was thinking about Greysbridge, Ian and Abby Grey's place. The setting really does look gorgeous. Do you think it would be ready by August?'

'I don't know. You could ring and ask him. I'm sure he'd be delighted to have his first booking before they've even moved in.'

She looked through the client list eagerly and picked up the phone while I took my stack of post and went upstairs. As soon as I was up there, I started to cough, so I came back down to get a glass of water.

'Did you reach him?' I asked.

'He says he's coming in anyway. Has something he wants you to sign. Is that okay?'

'Sure. I've only the one appointment yet, haven't I?'

She nodded. 'He said he'll talk to me about it then.'

At that moment, the door opened and I looked up to see Pat the Stoop bending to get through the narrow hall, finally living up to his name. As he reached reception, he glanced warily about him, and when he seemed satisfied there was no one else here, he wished us a good morning.

'Morning, Pat. Would you like to come up?' I asked.

'I will,' he said, as if granting me a royal favour.

He had a bag with him, concealed under his coat like contraband, and when he had settled himself, he pushed it across the desk towards me. 'That's all I have.'

It was a battered leather satchel with a strap and brass buckle and it was stuffed with papers of varying size and vintage. I leafed through the contents quickly: letters, maps, death certificates, copies of land certificates, old conveyances.

'It's going to take me a while to go through these,' I said. 'Can you leave them with me?'

He regarded me doubtfully.

'It should just be for a few hours,' I added. 'I'll try and get a look at them today.'

When he nodded, I took an attendance sheet from a drawer. 'I'll just take a few notes. Firstly, you're sure there was no will? Neither Dominic nor either of his parents left one?'

'No.'

'And you are sure that Dominic was legally married to Carole?'

'Yes. I think there's a marriage cert in there. He gave it to me, didn't want anyone else to come across it, especially the prison.'

'And they never divorced?'

He shook his head. 'They told no one about their marriage. I think they just chose to pretend it had never happened. Carole walked away and left Dominic to serve his sentence.' He looked down. 'She made the right decision. He spent the next two decades in and out of prison.'

'Did Dominic have any children?' I asked.

Stoop shook his head again.

'Because if he had, those children would be entitled to a share of his estate,' I added.

When Stoop left, Leah buzzed to say that Ian Grey had arrived, so I was surprised that he didn't appear for about ten minutes. When he did come into the room, his face was like chalk and he sank into the chair as if he'd just had a shock.

'Are you okay?' I asked.

'I'm fine.' He nodded.

'Leah said you had something for me to sign?' I asked.

'Oh yes. It's to do with a restoration grant,' he said distractedly. 'Look, do you mind if I ask your advice about something else entirely? I had no intention of discussing this with you, or with anyone to tell you the truth, despite what Abby might think. But now I think I should.'

'Of course.' I wondered if this had anything to do with the row I had witnessed in Culdaff.

Grey took a deep breath. 'It's about our son, Ronan. I've just met that newsagent man downstairs.' He shook his head. 'It's all going to come out now and it's far better coming from us than for him to hear it from someone else.'

He looked towards the window as if trying to convince himself of something. I coughed: not an 'ahem' type of cough; a cough because I needed to. It was enough to get his attention again.

'Sorry.' He gave me a weak smile. 'This isn't easy.'

'Not at all,' I said. 'There's no rush. I have no other appointments today.' I smiled back. 'Easing myself in.'

'Thank you. You're kind.' He seemed to steel himself. 'Look, it's this. Ronan is adopted. Not officially, unfortunately, but now that he's eighteen, that's of less significance than it was. We've ridden out the danger, so to speak.' He paused. 'We adopted him from a couple when we were in London, a married couple. A very young married couple whose relationship was breaking up.'

I knew who he was talking about before he said it. I'd finally figured out the connection.

'The couple were Carole Harkin and Dominic McLaughlin – that newsagent man's nephew. Carole was very young, a few years younger than Dominic. And Dominic was in prison, was going to be for a long time. They didn't know who was taking their son and they didn't want to know. Ronan was only a baby.' He looked down. 'Abby was the prison psychologist at the time – it was all done very unofficially.'

'You mean illegally.'

'Yes, if you like.' He leaned back defensively. 'Illegally. Abby and I couldn't have kids, and Carole was very young and completely on her own with Dominic in prison. I don't feel in the least bit guilty about it – we've given Ronan a good home – but he's grown up now, and I thought it might be good if they met: he and Carole. I knew she had come back here. And we were trying to buy back Greysbridge, so I thought, why don't we move up here to Glendara for a bit and see if we can live in Donegal, us city folk?'

'So that bit was true?' I said.

He gave me another weak smile. 'That bit was true. But I was killing two birds with the one stone.'

'And you didn't tell Abby.'

'Not at first, no. She didn't know that Carole lived here. And when she found out, she was livid, wanted to move back to Dublin straight away. But by that time, we had sold our house and were in negotiations to buy Greysbridge and there was no point in us moving again. I promised Abby that I'd say nothing to Carole. Anyway, Ronan was in school in Dublin; it wasn't as if he was around. He's only been up here twice since we came.'

'But you offered Carole a job at Greysbridge. Where Ronan was going to be working too.'

He looked uneasy. 'Yes, that I did. I still hoped they would meet. Although I fully intended to keep my promise not to say anything to Carole.'

'But you hoped she would guess when she met him?'

'Yes, I did. We'd changed his name but I hoped they would see something in each other. It seemed so unfair for Ronan not to know. We've told him he's adopted, and he's starting to ask questions. But it's getting harder and harder not to answer them. Especially when, unlike kids who are adopted through official channels, he has no route to follow if he wants to find his natural parents. But then when Carole was killed, I thought that was the end of it. It was awful, horrific, of course, but maybe for the best as far as Ronan was concerned. I know Abby thought that.'

'So why do you think it's going to come out now?' I asked.

'Because Stoop knows – that newsagent man.' He waved his hand towards the door. 'He's just made it pretty damn clear to me downstairs. I don't think he was expecting to see me here; we've succeeded in avoiding each other since we moved up.

He knew about the adoption, didn't approve but he knew. He remembered Abby's face from the prison and he's seen Ronan since he's been up. He put two and two together.' Grey looked at me across the desk. 'Ronan is the image of his father and getting more and more like him. You couldn't deny his parentage.'

I thought of the blurred pictures I'd seen on the website and realised that yes, there was a likeness. I had been so distracted by his resemblance to Carole's little boys that the other possibility hadn't occurred to me.

'Stoop asked me straight out down there and I couldn't lie.' He shook his head. 'Abby is going to be very unhappy with me.'

'But why would you think he's going to say something, if he hasn't up until now?'

'Because he says he's going to administer Dominic's estate, and Ronan is his only heir.'

So that was the real reason why Stoop wanted to administer his nephew's estate, I thought. It wasn't to expose Carole; it was so that Dominic's rightful heir would get it – the land would stay in the family. I assumed he would tell me about Ronan eventually, now that he had confirmed his identity. But Ian Grey was right. If Stoop went ahead, it would all come out in the wash: the illegal adoption, the bigamous marriage – the lot. How would George Harkin feel about that? I wondered.

Ian was staring out of the window. 'Of course,' he said, as if reading my mind, 'the other thing is that Ronan has two half-siblings who are his only biological family now. Maybe he has a right to get to know them.'

'What was going on between those two?' Leah asked when I went downstairs.

'Why?' I asked.

'Well, when Stoop saw Ian Grey coming in, he marched him straight into the waiting room and closed the door. He must have spent five minutes talking to him, arms going everywhere.'

'Oh?'

'I couldn't hear what they were saying, but you wouldn't usually get that much chat out of Stoop. When he'd finished, he left without a word and Ian Grey came out looking as if he was about to keel over.' She rested her chin on her hands, looking completely fed up. 'I didn't even get a chance to speak to him about the wedding.'

While I'd been seeing Ian Grey, an idea had occurred that would kill two birds with the one stone. So when I went back up to my office, I opened his file, checked the number and dialled. I was put through immediately.

The south Dublin voice sounded apprehensive. 'I wasn't expecting to hear from you again. Everything okay with the Grey purchase?'

'All fine. You'll get deeds in a few weeks. That wasn't what I wanted to talk to you about. You used to work in probate, didn't you?'

An uneasy pause. 'You know I did.'

'I wanted to ask your advice about something. I have rather a knotty one.'

'Fire ahead.' His tone was relieved. 'I've been out of it for a while, though.'

'Husband dies. No will. Leaves a wife and son. But wait for it, the child has been adopted and the wife has bigamously remarried in the meantime. Who inherits?'

'Christ. Child legally adopted?' A phone rang in the background.

'No.'

262

A sigh. 'Of course not. Okay. If the subsequent bigamous marriage didn't preclude the wife from inheriting and the child had not been legally adopted, then his estate would be divided between his wife and his son two thirds, one third.' He stopped to think. 'Although if the second marriage was seen as desertion, the wife would be "unworthy to succeed" under section 120 of the Succession Act. So the son would inherit.'

'I see. There's another bit. The wife then dies, leaving new husband and two new children.'

'Bloody hell. Right, let me think . . . Unless the wife made a will, her estate, including anything she inherited from her first husband, would be divided between all three children. I would assume her second husband wouldn't be entitled to anything since their marriage wasn't valid, but I'd have to check that further. To be honest, I'm not sure what effect a bigamous marriage would have on the whole thing. Jesus, my head is beginning to hurt.'

'So's mine.'

'I'd get counsel's opinion on it, just to be safe.'

'I will.'

There was an uneasy pause. 'I meant to call you.'

'I didn't expect you to. You were always more Luke's friend than mine.'

'I visited him a few times in prison.'

I felt a chill. 'Oh.'

'Until he hit me.' There was a trace of humour. 'I suppose I should have seen it coming.'

'Hit you? In the prison?'

'Lost his temper with me in the visiting area when I said something he didn't like. Took a swing at me. I never visited him again.'

'I'm not surprised.'

'But Sarah, I told him where you'd moved to. I know I shouldn't have, but he asked. Said he was feeling bad about things and wanted to write to you. And stupidly, I believed him. I didn't give him an address or anything, but I suppose he could have figured it out easily enough once he had the area.' He paused. 'I've been feeling shit about it for years.'

Lunch seemed a long time in coming. It always did on the first day back, but today I was distracted. I finally knew how Kirby had found out where I was. I was strangely relieved. I'd had my suspicions since the Greys' closing in Dublin. The solicitor had avoided my eye that day, though I'd thought it was simply because of his old friendship with Luke. It wouldn't have occurred to me that he might have visited him in prison.

I was distracted too by what Ian Grey had told me. In the end, he hadn't asked me for advice, had just needed to share, as if he had kept the secret for too long. So, Phyllis had been right about Carole's secretiveness. She had been hiding a marriage to a man in prison, a son handed over in an illegal adoption, and a subsequent bigamous marriage. Who would have thought it – religious Carole? The last thing she'd have wanted would be her past coming out, especially if she thought her hold on George was tenuous. Was someone blackmailing her? The only people who knew her secrets were Stoop and the Greys. It was in the Greys' interests to keep it to themselves, and Stoop had seemed content to abide by Dominic's wishes until now. It was only his pride and a wish to silence the gossips that was driving him to reveal all.

But then – my stomach dropped at the thought – there was

someone else who could have known about Carole's secrets. Luke Kirby had shared a cell with Dominic, so it was possible *he* also knew about Dominic's marriage and son; and since Dominic knew about Carole's second marriage, he might have told Luke about that too. Luke would have been playing the lawyer card in prison; he may have been giving Dominic advice. Even if he hadn't, he was a man people trusted, usually to their cost.

At one o'clock, Leah and I headed over to the shop to buy a couple of sandwiches to bring back to the office, some kind of self-imposed January discipline stopping us from visiting the café for chips. On the way back, we ran into Maeve. I'd finally managed to speak to her on the phone the night before to tell her about Luke. She'd been shocked and then quickly relieved to hear that he'd left town. Today she looked as if she was bursting with news.

'What's up?' I asked.

'Stan's signed himself out of hospital.'

'Really? Is he well enough?'

'He obviously thinks so. But,' she leaned forward confidentially, 'he's blaming Tony for the assault on the beach.'

'You can't be serious. Tony?'

'Apparently. Says they had a row and Tony hit him over the head with a bar. Phyllis has just told me. Tony's in a right state apparently. Says your sergeant wants him to come in to the station.'

I let her away with the 'your sergeant' this time. Before I could ask her any more, my phone rang. I recognised the number – it was Tony. I moved away to take the call.

He sounded breathless, panicked. 'Ben, I need to speak to you.'

'I've just heard what happened. Where are you now?'

'At home. Can you come up? If you're not too busy?'

The front door was unlocked; I pushed it open and walked straight in. I called Tony's name and a voice answered from the living room, where the party had taken place. It sounded slurred. 'In here.'

Again the door was ajar. The atmosphere was one of gloom, the curtains closed, blocking all daylight out, the air musty. Tony was sitting in a recess to one side of the fireplace, his hair tousled as if he had been repeatedly running his hands through it, a glass in his hand that I quickly realised contained whiskey. I'd never known Tony to drink during the day; it was the kiss of death for a publican. A reading lamp beside him provided the only light.

'Stan's signed himself out of hospital,' he said. 'Told the sergeant it was me who hit him.'

'So I hear.' I paused. 'You know I have to ask?'

He shook his head. 'It wasn't me. I've done enough to him in this lifetime. I'm not about to cosh him over the head and nearly kill him.'

'Have you told the sergeant that it wasn't you?'

He took a sip from his glass and winced. 'Maybe I deserve to take the blame for it. Maybe I deserve to be punished.'

'For something you did three decades ago? When you were a teenager?'

He stared into his glass. The man looked broken. I wondered if there was something else, something he hadn't told me. 'You're going to have to give a statement if he's made an allegation against you. You know that, don't you?'

He nodded.

I sat on the chair nearest him and leaned towards him, clasping my hands in front of me. 'Why would Stan say it was you, do you think?'

He shrugged 'Maybe he wants to punish me.'

Which prompted me to ask the question I'd been meaning to for a while. 'Do you think it was Stan who burned down the Oak? Seems pretty excessive for something that happened thirty years ago, but he had the opportunity, living above it.'

Tony avoided my eye. 'I don't know. I don't know what's happening any more.'

For a brief second I wondered if the rumours were true, if Tony had burned the place down himself for insurance, but I dismissed it immediately. Then I realised why I found his look so disquieting.

'You know who did it, don't you? You know who burned down the pub.'

Tony stared into his glass. It was nearly empty, but he didn't seem motivated to refill it. His voice was flat. 'No. I don't.'

I didn't believe him. If he didn't know for sure, he certainly had his suspicions.

He sighed deeply and stood up, placing his glass unevenly on the table and leaning on the mantelpiece. 'The insurance company have agreed to pay out, the full amount of the claim. I just heard this morning. They've decided it was "arson by person or persons unknown", which is covered by the policy.' He gave a snort. 'Once the person isn't the owner, of course.'

'But that's good news, isn't it?'

He looked at me, his eyes swimming. 'How can I spend all that money rebuilding the Oak with everything that's happened? It's like blood money.'

I walked over to him. 'The town needs the Oak, Tony. It

needs something good to happen, something to look forward to. Having the Oak back would help the town to heal. It may not seem like it at the moment, but the guards *will* find out what happened to Carole and who is responsible. I'm sure of it.'

He looked at me with unseeing eyes, his expression unreadable.

'In the meantime, would you like me to come with you to the station when you make the statement about the attack on Stan?'

He slowly focused on me, then nodded weakly.

'Okay then. Sober yourself up and I'll give the sergeant a shout and tell him we'll call in first thing in the morning.'

Chapter Twenty-Seven

I left Tony and returned to the office, having arranged to meet him at the Garda station at nine the following morning; court began at half past ten, so I thought that should give us plenty of time. I called Molloy to let him know.

I had no appointments that afternoon, so I started on my preparation for court, but became distracted again very quickly. The fact that I kept having to break off from what I was doing to cough didn't help my progress. I needed another one of Phyllis's ginger teas.

I stood at the window gazing out onto the street. The weather was unpleasant: hard, icy rain forcing people to dash from cars to shops and making the old office windows rattle precariously. I wondered if I should speak to Stan. Strictly speaking, I knew I shouldn't, since Tony was my client. But I wondered if he was back at Róisín's house, if that was where he'd gone when he'd signed himself out of hospital. I told myself there was nothing wrong with my calling, on a purely personal basis, to see how he was. So I left the office early, using my cough as an excuse. It wasn't a complete ruse; my barking was getting worse by the hour and my head was beginning to hurt again too. I ran across to the chemist to pick up some cough syrup and more paracetamol before I got into the car.

The McCanns' family home was about a mile out of Glendara on the Derry road, with a view of Sliabh Sneacht in the distance. It was an old detached whitewashed farmhouse with a yard and a number of outhouses; a traditional farm, which seemed to be becoming less and less common. More and more I was seeing huge steel poultry or pig houses with automated feeding and ventilation systems. They gave me the shivers when I thought about the miserable lives of the creatures inside. The smell of manure hung in the icy air and a Fred-type Border collie ran out to greet me in the yard.

I found Róisín and Stan together in a room Róisín's mother described as 'the parlour': chintz-covered armchairs with embroidered covers, and multiple ornaments on a dark wooden sideboard. They were deep in conversation, huddled around an open fire. One of the windows was open, creating a draught. When he turned at the sound of the opening door, Stan looked pale and frightened. There was a plain white dressing on his forehead covering the wound.

Róisín's mother, a plumper, older version of Róisín, brought us tea and home-made brown scones, then disappeared without a word.

'I'm going to lose my figure if I stay here too long.' Stan tried his best to be his usual acid self, but it didn't ring true. The dark crescents under his eyes showed he had already lost weight in the past few days.

'How are you doing?' I asked.

'Ach, grand. A few more brain cells missing, but sure I have plenty of those to spare.' He rubbed at his grey tracksuit bottoms, as if embarrassed to be seen in them.

There was a knock on the door and Róisín's mother stuck her head in again. 'Your phone's just rung, Ro. I didn't answer it, but someone's left a message, I think.'

Róisín stood up and followed her mother out of the room.

'I've spoken to Tony,' I said, after the door had closed and I had taken a sip from my tea.

Stan turned to me, stony-faced, all humour dissipated. 'What has he said?'

'He told me that he knew you in school.'

'It's taken him a year and a half to remember that?' Stan laughed, a harsh, bitter laugh. 'What else did he tell you?'

'He said that you were bullied, that he told the head teacher and it only made things worse. He told me that you were locked in a cupboard, that your mother died while you were in there, that you never got to say goodbye.' I paused. 'I can't imagine how hard that would have been for you.'

Stan shook his head. 'I knew it. I knew he'd leave out the most important part.'

'What was that?

He closed his eyes. 'He's my brother . . . Tony Craig is my half-brother.'

'What?'

'We have the same father. At least biologically. He was never a father to *me*.'

'But I thought you met at boarding school?'

Stan opened his eyes again. 'We did. My mother had a relationship with Tony's father years before. He was married. To someone else, obviously.' His voice was dripping with contempt. 'Tony's mother. He never left them, but he paid for me to go to boarding school; the same one as his *proper* son. Never spoke to me, never acknowledged me, but paid my fees in that hellhole.'

ANDREA CARTER

Stan looked at his feet. He was wearing slippers that were far too small for him; Róisín's father's, I suspected. I tried to see some likeness between him and Tony, and failed.

'I used to see him dropping Tony to school in his big black Merc and wonder if he would ever speak to me. Sometimes I'd walk past, on purpose, to see if my own father would notice me.'

'And did he?'

Stan smiled bitterly. 'He called me over once. Asked me to fetch him some water for his car.'

I imagined a first-year Stan, trying even then to be noticed. 'But he knew who you were? Your father, I mean.'

'He knew. I could tell he knew. My mother was supposed to keep it a secret – that was the deal. But when she knew she was dying, she told me. Maybe she had some romantic notion that he would take me in when she was gone.'

'But that didn't happen?'

'What do you think?' Stan gave a hollow laugh. 'Do you see me on brotherly nights out with Tony Craig? Playing the doting uncle to his kids?' He shook his head. 'Tony's mother knew about me but refused to have anything to do with me. After my mother died, I went to stay with my aunt. My *father* continued to stump up some kind of payment until I left school, and then that was it. End of contact.'

'Did Tony know that you were his half-brother?'

'I don't know. What I do know is that because of him, I was locked in a cupboard, with the spiders and the dust and the dark, while my mother, the only person who ever cared about me, was dying.' There was a tremor in his voice.

And with that I realised why Stan always kept doors and windows open, even in the depths of winter. He had claustrophobia.

272

I was silent for a minute, as I looked at his fearful face and contemplated the long shadows cast by childhood trauma.

'Why wasn't there a huge search for you if your mother was so ill?' I asked quietly.

'According to Tony, the boys hadn't been told my mother was ill; the school just said I needed to be found. But I don't believe that.'

I thought it seemed possible. Schools were notoriously secretive in the information they disclosed to other pupils. They'd have been unlikely to allow the news that Stan's mother was dying to get out before he knew himself. But I understood why he chose not to believe it.

'They were all at my mother's funeral,' he said with disgust. 'A guard of honour from boys I hated.'

'Does Tony know who you are now?' I asked.

Stan shook his head. 'I can't believe he was never told. I think he chooses to pretend that I don't exist, just like his father did.' He looked away. 'I'm sure it would have been highly inconvenient to have an extra brother when dividing out his father's estate.'

I knew from the title deeds that Tony's father had owned the Oak before him. Had he really administered the estate and taken over the pub knowing that he had a half-brother who would have been entitled to a share?

'But why did you do nothing at that stage? If you knew you had inheritance rights?'

Stan's eyes flashed. 'Because I didn't want anything to do with him, with any of them.'

I hesitated. 'But you changed your mind, clearly, if you came here?'

Stan was silent for a minute, staring into the fire.

'Is that why you came here?' I asked. 'Did you want a relationship with him?'

Stan laughed, unable to keep the hurt from his voice. 'Relationship? I've been waiting a year for him to even acknowledge me.'

'Is that why you talked about going to see your mother? To see if he reacted?'

Stan slumped visibly, his shoulders rounded. 'Pathetic, isn't it? I wanted him to know who I was, but I didn't want to be the one to tell him.'

It seemed to me that the flame of Stan's anger was weaker than he wanted it to be. Maybe, as he'd grown older, he'd realised that Tony had been the only one to try to help him, even if that had failed. And when he moved to Glendara, he'd seen what kind of an adult Tony had become.

But I had to ask. 'Did you set fire to the Oak?'

He smiled, as if he'd been expecting it. 'Destroying my birthright? Sounds almost biblical, doesn't it? No, it wasn't me. But I can't pretend I'm sorry about it.'

I knew I shouldn't ask him about the attack on the beach, but after what he'd just told me, it was too hard not to. 'Why do you think Tony hit you?'

Stan avoided my eye and picked at a piece of fluff on his knee. 'I have absolutely no idea.'

I met Róisín in the hallway and she walked me out to the yard.

'Is everything all right with Stan?' she asked.

'I just wanted to see how he was doing,' I said non-committally.

'He's had a rough time, the poor old thing. But I think he's on the mend.'

'Hopefully.'

She gave a whistle, a long, distinctive sound with six short blasts, and within seconds the dog who had greeted me earlier came bounding through a gate, skidding to a halt when it reached her. 'Ah, there you are, Jessie.' She bent down to pat the animal's head

I turned the key in the door of the Mini, then on impulse asked her about her return to Glendara the night the Oak had burned down.

She seemed unsurprised. 'The sergeant asked me about that. I had a row with Eddie and decided to come back here. Susanne and I shared a taxi. It was easier to get dropped at the Oak – we both walked home from there.'

'Oh?'

She smiled. 'Eddie was being annoying. He'd had too much to drink and he was getting on my nerves. Anyway, we didn't see anything, Susanne and myself. The lights were off and the pub was closed up by then. We both assumed Carole had gone home.'

'But she hadn't.'

'No,' she agreed. She looked up at the sky. 'I think it's about to rain again.'

She was stalling for some reason, wrapping her long blue cardigan around herself protectively. If she was trying to work out how to tell me something, or get up the courage to say it, I was happy to wait.

I followed her eyes. 'It seems colder than that.'

'Hail maybe. I don't think I could face any more snow.'

'I know what you mean.'

Eventually she sighed. 'I didn't have a row with Eddie. I came back with Susanne because she was upset and needed some company.'

'Why was she upset?'

'She'd had a talk with George. Susanne had a thing with George when she was still in school. She was only seventeen. She's still very fucked up about it. I don't know what she expected when she saw him that night, but it didn't go the way she wanted it to.'

'I see.'

Her eyes were bright with fury. 'He's a fucker, that man. I know he doesn't deserve what's happened to him, but he treated Susanne like shit. Used her and threw her away like a piece of dirt. I don't think she's ever got over it.'

'Does Tony know?'

Róisín looked horrified. 'God, no. And you can't tell him. He'd kill George with his bare hands. I think he's finding it hard enough to cope with the age difference between her and Luke.'

I drove away, tears of hail streaming down my windscreen, afraid to stay longer in case I said something I'd regret.

After a night of coughing, I had an early start. At my insistence, Molloy didn't stay; the need for him to do so had passed, and I knew I'd only keep him awake. Despite my lousy night, I was at the Garda station at nine as arranged. I'd hoped to get to speak to Tony about Stan before he made his statement, but he was waiting for me in reception when I walked in.

I was relieved to see that he'd pulled himself together and looked almost like his old self, a small slip enough to bring him to his senses. He'd been carrying so much the past few weeks, it seemed he'd cracked as soon as he received his first piece of good news. There was a new determination about him this morning, as if he was ready to pick himself up and carry on, do what needed to be done.

His statement didn't take long. It was simple enough. *It wasn't me; I wasn't there; I was on my way back to Glendara.* It would be difficult to prove either way; the pub had been packed, with people coming and going all afternoon.

As soon as we came out onto the street, I told him what Stan had said. He put his head in his hands.

'Did you know he was your brother?' I asked.

He nodded. 'Aye, I did. At least, I discovered that the Stephen Stanley I was in school with was my half-brother. A few years back, I found some of my father's papers in the cellar of the pub, tucked behind some old barrels. He had dementia in his last few years and he used to keep things in strange places.'

'This was after he died?'

'Aye. A long time after.'

'And your mother didn't mention Stan – Stephen – to you?'

He shook his head. 'She was ill when my da died, and she died herself soon after. When I found out about Stephen, I tried to track him down. That's why I went to that school reunion I mentioned. But I was told he'd gone to Australia. No one seemed to have contact details for him. Even the school's address for him was out of date.' His shoulders slumped. 'I didn't know where to go next.'

'And you didn't recognise Stan as Stephen Stanley?'

'I swear I didn't.' He looked at me, his eyes red. 'How the hell could I not have recognised my own brother?'

'I suppose he *was* only thirteen when you saw him last.'

He straightened himself to his full height. 'I'm going to fix things with him now. I want you to know that.'

I saw Molloy pass, looked at my watch and realised I was late for court. I said a quick goodbye to Tony, then raced back to the office, where I grabbed the files from my desk, and made

ANDREA CARTER

my way quickly through the square. Why had Stan claimed that
Tony had attacked him? I wondered. Was it just another attempt
to get his half-brother's attention? Stan had been missing that
day, I remembered. I'd been looking for him myself. I'd wanted
to ask him about the man he had seen Carole with in Derry, but
I'd never had the chance. I rang his number before I went into
court, but got his voicemail.

Court was hectic. All the cases that hadn't been dealt with
before Christmas were listed, along with new public-order and
drink-driving charges that had accumulated over the holidays.
My bread and butter. When the judge rose for lunch, I grabbed
a sandwich from the shop and barrelled back to the office to eat
it.

Leah looked up as I walked through the door. 'Busy?'

'Insane.' I threw off my coat and headed into the kitchen at
the back to make myself an instant coffee. It would taste like
dishwater, but it was all I had time for.

Leah called after me. 'What did you decide about giving
Susanne Craig a job, by the way?'

I stopped dead, my hand on the kettle, heart beating faster
than it should have been.

'Why?' I tried to keep the tremor out of my voice.

'Because she was in here with the boyfriend while you were
at court. Tony must have told them to call in.'

I swallowed as I emerged from the kitchen. My sandwich
wasn't going to be eaten now.

'I thought they'd left.'

'They're back here for a while. Just a few weeks, I think.' Her
eyes narrowed. 'Are you okay? You look a bit pale.'

I shook my head. 'I'm fine. It's just this cold I can't get rid of.'

'Anyway, I told them to come back this afternoon about

five. I hope that's okay.' She grinned. 'The boyfriend's pretty handsome.'

I stumbled up the stairs, coffee and sandwich forgotten, needing some time to think, away from Leah's curious gaze. I'd never told her about Luke. I'd wanted to keep the office as some kind of refuge also, where I could be professional, unaffected by my past. But now he had tainted that too. Luke Kirby had been *here*, speaking to Leah as if this was all perfectly normal.

I felt ill and afraid. I knew Luke Kirby. None of this was by accident or coincidence.

Chapter Twenty-Eight

At two o'clock, I returned to court. I have no idea how I managed to get through that afternoon; I certainly wouldn't have won any awards for my advocacy skills, although I hoped that my persistent cough provided something of an excuse for my slow reactions and needless repetition. I must have said 'Sorry, Judge, could you repeat that?' at least ten times. I glanced over at Molloy, prosecuting cases for the state, desperate to speak to him, but there was no opportunity.

I walked back to the office at a quarter to five, Molloy still in court, my sense of dread increasing with each step. The supermarket, Liam's place and Phyllis's shop all seemed far more attractive options than my own office as I passed them by.

When I walked into reception, Susanne Craig was in the waiting room. Alone. I felt faint with relief when I saw her; I hadn't realised how afraid I was of having Luke Kirby in my space. She stood and smiled with a politeness I hadn't seen before, her usual brazen expression and defiant stance absent. She followed me into the front room.

She started to speak before I had closed the door. 'I know my dad has spoken to you . . .'

'Yes,' I replied, my voice surprisingly calm. 'He has. But I thought you'd changed your mind. I thought you weren't staying around?'

'We've decided to stay on for a few weeks.' She looked down. 'There's somewhere we need to be, but not yet.'

I couldn't help but notice the *we*. Was it my imagination, or did she seem to be under some sort of instruction, not entirely in control of her own destiny? Or was I seeing what I expected to see? I offered her a seat, which she took, perching on the edge of it as if ready to take flight.

'I wondered if there might still be some work,' she said. 'Just for a week or two. Part-time. I'll do anything really.'

I looked at her hollow cheeks and the dark patches under her eyes and saw a vulnerability I hadn't noticed before. I also saw another pair of eyes, as dark as Susanne's, with the same shadows beneath. I shook myself. Susanne wasn't Faye.

'The thing is,' I said, 'we're not as busy as we were before Christmas. I'm not sure—'

Abruptly she stood up and made to walk out. So she had Faye's recklessness too, a readiness to throw everything away on the slightest whim. But what would she be going to? I wondered as I watched her turn the handle and pull open the door. A life following Luke Kirby around in whatever new persona he had created for himself? Until he chose to discard her too.

I made a snap decision.

'You can come in tomorrow, if you don't mind clearing out an attic that hasn't been touched in about twenty years?'

She turned back and smiled gratefully. 'I don't mind.'

'Great. There's only work for a week or so, but it'll be a good start to the new year if we get it cleared.'

★ ★ ★

I watched through the blinds as she crossed the street and thought about what Róisín had told me – the relationship that George and Susanne had had when Susanne was only a girl, if you could call it a relationship. That was what had made her such an easy mark for Kirby, I thought, a man so much older and more sophisticated than she was.

I told myself I had a plan. I would have Susanne work for me, keep her close, get her to trust me, and then I would talk to her about Luke. I would find out what she knew and I would tell her everything. I knew that I couldn't tell Tony. He might never forgive me for that, but he had enough on his plate trying to rebuild the Oak in the wake of Carole's death, as well as his relationship with his brother. I told myself I had a plan, but what I was really doing was following my gut and trying to protect Susanne in the way I had been unable to protect my sister. I could not let Luke win. Not this time.

I went back into reception and Leah looked up from her computer.

'Well?'

'She's starting tomorrow. Just for a week or two. Can you put her to work in the attic? We can't have her doing anything that would give her access to files, so that's really all she can do.'

'I hope she doesn't have a fear of spiders!'

I smiled. 'She's an animal lover, remember?'

Leah leaned back in her chair. 'You know, I think she may have got that from Róisín. Sinéad was telling me that Róisín was a veggie in school. She sent an email around once, using the school's address, saying that meat was no longer allowed in lunch boxes.'

'You're kidding. After the burst pipes one, or before?'

282

'After. Suspension didn't scare her, apparently.' Leah grinned. 'Always the quiet ones!'

That night, I cooked for Molloy.

When I look back, I don't know what we were thinking, spending the evening together. I felt terrible and Molloy looked terrible. I could see he was under pressure; it had been twelve days since Carole's body had been found, more than two weeks since the fire and almost a week since Stan's assault, and there hadn't been a single arrest. It made no difference to the people of Glendara that the National Bureau of Criminal Investigation was involved and they had been unable to get to the bottom of it either. As far as they were concerned, it was the local sergeant who was supposed to protect them.

I was tempted to share what Liam had suggested on New Year's Eve, that perhaps Molloy should try to be more approachable, but he didn't seem to be in the mood. Instead I told him about Stan and Tony, and he reacted as I'd expected him to, frustrated that people chose not to confide in him but pleased that I had told him.

It was when we were sitting by the fire with a glass of wine after dinner that I told him about Luke and Susanne's return and my giving Susanne a job in the office.

He leaned forward, glass in hand, eyes wide. 'You're what?'

'I'm giving her some work in the office. Just for a week or so.'

'Are you insane?'

I flinched as if I'd been struck. 'No, I'm not. She'll be clearing out the attic. No confidential stuff.'

His tone was incredulous. 'Why on earth would you do that?'

I looked away. Part of me wondered if he was right. 'I don't know. There's a vulnerability about her. I want to keep her close for a while. I don't know if she knows the full story about Kirby.'

'And you're planning on being the one to tell her?'

'Yes. No. Probably. If I get the chance.' I put down my glass. 'She needs to get away from that man.'

'So do you. But by giving her a job, you're inviting him back into your life.'

'No I am not!'

Molloy put down his glass too. 'But you'll see him regularly. He'll be dropping her into work. Collecting her. Meeting her for lunch. You're playing into his hands, Ben. It's dangerous.'

'I just need to—'

He cut across me. 'Listen to me. A few days ago, you thought it was possible that Kirby had killed Carole Harkin. And now what? You've changed your mind?'

'No,' I said indignantly. 'But we don't know what happened to Carole, do we? We haven't got proof of a damn thing.'

Molloy looked hurt, and immediately I wanted to take it back.

'We'll get there, Ben. It's just taking some time. But the fact remains that there *are* links between Luke Kirby and this murder. There's the fact that he shared a cell with Dominic McLaughlin, who is the only one whose DNA was found, *and* that he has a prior conviction for killing a woman. By a similar method,' he added quietly.

I felt a stab. The fact that both Faye and Carole had been strangled hadn't escaped either of us, I knew, but it was the first time we had acknowledged it.

Molloy's voice softened. 'Those are facts we can't ignore, Ben. That *you* can't ignore.'

'Don't you think I know that? Why do you think I want to keep Susanne Craig close?'

He shook his head. 'You can't protect her on your own.'

'Well maybe if you arrested Kirby, I wouldn't need to.'

'You know we don't have enough to do that yet. He didn't leave any DNA; we have no witnesses. There is no direct connection that we can find between him and Carole.'

There was silence between us for a few minutes. Guinness seemed to sense something wrong and climbed onto my knee to nuzzle my hand, not something he did very often.

'It doesn't mean we're not keeping an eye on him, you know,' Molloy said. 'If it was him, at some point he's going to make a mistake. If he hasn't already.'

'I wouldn't bet on it. He doesn't seem overly concerned anyway, hanging around the town as if he owns the place.'

That was the final straw for Molloy. He stood up. 'Look, I'm going to leave you to it. I have work to do. I'll ring you later and I'll come back and stay.'

'There's no need. I'll be fine,' I snapped.

I didn't want him to leave, but I was furious with him. How could he not understand my need to try and protect Susanne after all that I had told him about Faye? As he walked towards the door, I remembered something.

I still don't know why I said it. I think I just wanted to take a potshot at him. 'Why did I see Laura Callan on the Malin road on Thursday?'

He stopped in his tracks. 'What?'

'Laura, the pathologist, your ex. I saw her the other day coming from Malin. Why was she still knocking around? She'd finished her post-mortem on Carole by then.'

He looked at me, astonished. 'She's from Malin Head. Her

285

parents still live there. I presume she went up to see them for a few days after she finished working in Letterkenny.'

'Is there a reason you never told me that she was from Inishowen?' My voice was icy.

'Not particularly. I thought you knew.'

'How would I know?' I tried to soften my tone and failed. 'What are you not telling me? I know there's something.'

Molloy shook his head. 'Look, I'm going to go. I think we both need some breathing space.'

'Agreed.'

I locked the door behind him, fuming. Badly needing a distraction, I slumped on the couch and turned on the television. Flicking angrily through the channels, I came across a film that I loved: John Huston's *The Dead* – his adaptation of the James Joyce short story. Guinness leapt onto my knee and I settled in to watch the final scene, where the couple Gabriel and Gretta are in their hotel room in Dublin after the party. Gretta is crying over a boy who loved her when she was young and who died, and Gabriel turns to the window for his final monologue, jealous that he has never loved in the same way.

I felt my anger subside and began to think about the shadows that past relationships could cast. A well of emotion that must be managed, kept in the background, so that you could move on. I thought about Carole and her secret marriage to Dominic; about Susanne and her affair with George while she was still a teenager. Both relationships long past but present nonetheless. I had picked a fight with Molloy about his ex, but I knew Laura Callan wasn't the real problem. I'd felt for a while that Molloy was hiding something from me. It was making me doubt myself, wonder if I had made a mistake in trusting him with so much.

The last man I thought I loved was Luke Kirby. That's how

good a judge of character *I* was. I had loved the man who killed my sister, was full of grief and jealousy when he left me for her and because of that ignored her call on the night she died. An appalling misjudgement that haunted me every day.

Chapter Twenty-Nine

Morning brought with it a tangle of emotions. Molloy had phoned later that night and offered to stay, but I told him I didn't want to see him. I regretted that now, but I wasn't yet ready to talk. Where had he been those evenings when he had cancelled at the last minute? And why was he so reluctant to go public with our relationship? Suddenly these things bothered me. He was hiding something, and with Luke in the shadows reminding me of how badly I'd got things wrong in the past, that was the last thing I needed.

Leah rang when I was on my way in to Glendara to ask me to pick up some milk. She had forgotten to get some herself; the phone was ringing off the hook and she didn't want to leave Susanne on her own. She sounded stressed. Molloy's 'Are you insane?' began running on a loop in my head.

I parked the car and ran up to the square, not wanting to leave Leah for too long. Town was busy. I noticed a man in a suit with a clipboard in front of the burned-out crater that was the Oak and wondered if he was a surveyor, if it meant that rebuilding would start soon. Phyllis was leaning against the door of her bookshop with a mug in her hand and Liam was opening up the estate agent's office. Things seemed to be getting back to normal. But things weren't normal. Nothing that had happened in the past few weeks had been normal, and nothing had been resolved.

And right now, Luke Kirby was walking towards me, down the main street of Glendara. Pins and needles ran up my shoulders and into my neck. I thought about ducking into a doorway or crossing the street but I knew I wouldn't be able to face myself if I did that. So I steeled myself and kept walking. He flashed me a smile. My breath quickened. It was the first time he had acknowledged me since our meeting in Dublin. He stopped, hands buried in the pockets of his long waxed coat.

'I've just dropped Susanne off. Good of you to give her a job in the circumstances.'

I felt panicked. Was Molloy right? Had I allowed him back in? Dropping her at work, taking her out for lunch, Molloy had said. It was happening already.

I refused to look at him. 'I didn't do it for you.'

He sighed, as if tired of my petulance. 'Look, Sarah, I know I'm the last person you wanted to see. But we're going to have to learn to tolerate each other. I'm not going anywhere.'

We're going to have to learn to tolerate each other? We're? I felt a sudden searing pain in my head. How could I ever have thought I had feelings for this man? When I forced myself to look at him now, his duplicity, his conceit, his utter coldness seemed written all over his face.

He moved to withdraw one of his hands from his pocket, and I stiffened. A voice called to me from across the square. Phyllis was waving from the doorway of her shop, summoning me. A wave of relief washed over me and I turned to go, but as I did so, Kirby touched my arm. The effect was like an electric shock. I bristled and pulled back.

He gave a bark of laughter. 'Relax, woman. I just wanted to give you this.'

I looked down. He had something in his hand. My wallet, the one that had been stolen in Derry.

'Where did you get that?' I demanded, but he was already walking away.

'Found it,' he called back. 'You're welcome, by the way.'

I made my way over to Phyllis, my legs like jelly. She glared at Kirby as he strode down the street, her eyes boring into his back.

'Thought you needed rescuing. What the hell is he doing back here?'

I managed to pull myself together, but when I spoke, my voice was shaking. 'He and Susanne are back for a few weeks.' I swallowed. 'I've given her a job in the office, clearing out the attic.'

Phyllis raised one eyebrow. It seemed I was alone in thinking that was one of my better ideas. I was beginning to wonder myself.

I checked my watch. 'I'd better get back, Phyllis. Leah is on her own with Susanne.'

She nudged me. 'You were being watched, by the way, while you were talking to that man. Not just by me.'

She nodded across the square. McFadden was standing in the doorway of the hardware shop. He glanced in my direction when Phyllis pointed, then looked away.

'I think Molloy might have asked him to keep an eye on me,' I said.

'Well that's a good thing, isn't it?' She smiled. 'We're all looking out for you.'

As I made my way back to the office, I hoped to God that I wasn't bringing trouble on the whole of Glendara.

★ ★ ★

Back at the office, I found Leah showing Susanne how to use the photocopier. I'd asked for copies of any documents she found in the attic, but clearly it wasn't going well. Leah raised her eyes to heaven above Susanne's head when I said good morning, while Susanne glanced up, returned my greeting and went back to pressing random buttons. I shot Leah a sympathetic look and went upstairs, wondering how someone could have reached the age of twenty-five without learning how to use a photocopier.

At my desk, I went through my wallet. Everything was there. How the hell had Luke managed to get hold of it? Had he been in Derry that day? Did he want me to know he had been there, watching me? I shivered. The sooner he was gone, the better. But how could I stop Susanne from going with him?

Ten minutes later, I went downstairs to get a coffee and Liam McLaughlin strode in, newspaper folded under his arm. 'Have you got a minute?'

'Sure. Come on up.'

Liam refused to sit, which I took to be a good sign; it meant he didn't intend staying very long. He came straight to the point. 'Stoop's just been on to me. He wants me to have a look at his brother's old cottage. Says he wants to sell it. Can he do that?'

I was a little taken aback. I had to think for a minute.

'He said to talk to you about it, that you were acting for him,' Liam added.

'Well he's rather jumping the gun, but in theory, yes, it can be sold. Whether Stoop is the one to do that is another thing. It depends on the beneficiaries. But I haven't checked all that out yet. He was only in with me on Monday.'

Liam grinned. 'So hold your horses is what you're telling me?'

'Something like that.'

291

'Fair enough.'

My eye was suddenly drawn to the newspaper he'd come in with, which he now had clasped to his chest. The headline read: *Thousands of euros of damage caused in arson attack at poultry farm in Co. Monaghan.*

'Can I have a look at that?' I asked, gesturing towards the paper.

He handed it to me and I found the article while he played with the coins in his pocket.

'No one was caught apparently,' he volunteered. 'They broke in, let the chickens out and set the place on fire. Lunatics. Those animal liberation people probably.'

I remembered the animaloutrage website Susanne had liked on her Facebook page. Industrial farming was one of their issues. Phyllis had said that Luke and Susanne had gone to Dublin for a meeting, but was this where they had really been? Was Luke so serious about playing this part? I scanned through the piece but learned nothing more than Liam had told me.

When I looked up, he was over by the window. I joined him, handing back the paper. The weather had turned nasty again, the street outside a mire. We watched as people dashed in and out of shops battling the icy rain. I saw McFadden running for his car, jacket pulled over his head, glad to see he drew the line at staking out the office.

Liam turned to me suddenly, interrupting my thoughts. 'Can I tell you something, in confidence?'

'Of course.'

'The problem is, I'm not sure it's mine to tell. But I'm afraid if I don't . . .'

I leaned back against my desk, arms crossed. 'I promise I'll keep it confidential, whatever it is.'

Liam nodded. 'It's McFadden. Andy. He came to me a few weeks ago, wanting to sell his house.'

'Okay,' I said slowly, unsure where this was going.

Liam took a deep breath. 'Andy has a gambling problem. A bad one. He's in serious debt.'

In a rush, I recalled McFadden's mood swings, his loss of weight, running into him on the street near that casino in Derry.

'I didn't do anything about it,' Liam continued. 'Selling the house. I had my suspicions and I didn't think he should have access to a lot of cash. There's no mortgage on his house; he inherited it from his uncle. So . . .' He paused. 'I went to the sergeant on the QT.'

'Right.' I found it hard to hide my surprise at this development.

'The thing is, the sergeant knew already. He's been dragging Andy out of casinos in and around Derry for the past few weeks. Trying to help him. He's even bailed him out, paid some of his debts. It was Andy who told me that, not the sergeant,' he added.

I felt a wave of shame as I remembered the tension I'd seen between Molloy and McFadden. Was this what Molloy had been doing those evenings he had cancelled on me?

'I told Andy what I'd done,' Liam continued. 'I thought he'd threaten to report me, but he didn't. He was grateful.' He shook his head sadly. 'He's broken so he is, that man. He needs help.'

I was lost for words. I picked up a pen from my desk and twisted it in my fingers as I tried to organise my thoughts.

'The thing is,' Liam said again, 'the sergeant is trying to set something up for him without him having to stop work and everyone knowing about it, but it's taking a while. And it occurred to me that Andy might come to you directly looking to sell.' He shook his head. 'He doesn't trust himself at the moment, so I suppose I shouldn't either. And there's no shortage of people who would be only too happy to take advantage of him. Pay him a fraction of what it's worth. So I thought if he did, maybe you could . . .' He left the sentence hanging.

'Discourage him?'

Liam looked relieved. 'Exactly. Just until he sorts himself out.'

'Of course.'

As soon as Liam left, I rang Molloy, feeling thoroughly ashamed of myself. I got his voicemail and left a message asking him to ring me back.

To stop myself from watching my phone, I began Stoop's paperwork. I opened the satchel and took out the contents, working through them as methodically as I could, setting aside the documents I would need. There were death certificates for Dominic's parents but not for Dominic himself – I made a note that one would be needed. There was a land certificate and a map of the cottage and land, which I unfolded to examine. The little copse of trees was there, so I traced the route that Molloy and I had taken on Christmas Day with my finger. When I looked again, I realised there was a second laneway to the cottage from the Derry road out of Glendara. The route must be overgrown now, since we hadn't noticed it – not surprising if the cottage had been empty for fifteen years. Could that have been the route that Carole had taken that Saturday night with whoever she was with? Had that even been considered? I made a mental note to mention it to Molloy. If he ever returned my call.

I went downstairs an hour later to make a coffee and the front door opened as I reached the bottom step. It was Eddie Kearney. I hadn't seen him since the funeral. I asked him how he was doing and he shrugged. 'Oh, you know.'

294

'What can I do for you?'

He started to reply as he followed me into reception, but stopped dead when he saw Susanne. If that was her effect on clients, it was just as well she was only here for a week or two, I thought.

I felt the need to explain her presence. 'Susanne is here to help us clear out the attic, God love her.'

'Aye, I see.'

'Do you want a chat?' I asked, nodding towards the stairs.

He nodded gratefully and followed me up to my office, where he sat in that wide-kneed pose I was so familiar with from before he went to Australia. He came straight to the point. 'My keys to the Oak are missing. I know they're not much use now, but I thought it might mean something.'

'You need to tell the sergeant,' I said. 'It might be important.'

'Aye,' he said, without conviction. 'I will.'

'Do you want me to do it?' I asked.

He looked up gratefully. 'Aye, would you?'

'When did you notice they were gone?'

He looked sheepish. 'Just these last few days. With everything that's happened I didn't check before now. They should still have been in the jeans I was wearing that night. They've never gone in the wash so I know my mother didn't take them.'

'You mean they're still lying in a heap on your floor.'

He gave me a furtive grin. I pitied his mother if she was still expected to do his washing two weeks after losing her daughter. Australia hadn't changed Eddie as much as I'd thought.

'Do you think someone took the keys or that you just lost them?'

He looked down. 'I don't know.'

Seconds passed.

'Is there anything else, Eddie?' If people were going to talk to me anyway, I decided, I might as well ask a few questions too. 'Anything that would be useful in finding out what happened to Carole?'

He gave a deep sigh. 'I think George is carrying on with my sister. My sister Emma,' he added quickly.

I wondered if that was why he'd been so taken aback when he'd seen Susanne downstairs. I presumed he had known about George's affair with her, since Róisín had known about it.

'I don't like it. It's too soon *and* she's married.'

'That's not easy,' I agreed.

He swallowed. 'The thing is, I'm wondering if it was going on before Carole died. If maybe that had something to do with it.'

'You mean George had something to do with her death?' I was surprised. It seemed that George had been serially unfaithful to Carole, but I didn't think he had killed her. Molloy had confirmed he'd received the texts he'd said he had, ostensibly from Carole.

Eddie shook his head vigorously. 'No, I meant that's why Carole needed money. If she was going to leave him.'

As soon as Eddie left, I rang Molloy and left a message about the keys, my second today. When I hung up, Leah came in. She closed the door behind her and lowered her voice.

'I have to run out to the post. I'd send Susanne but I want to go to the bank too and I don't trust her to do that.' She gave me a wry look. 'So would you mind . . .'

I finished her sentence. '. . . keeping an eye on her? Sure. I'll go down in a minute. Is she still upstairs?'

She nodded. 'I've diverted the phones up here, so you'll have to answer them.'

★ ★ ★

Susanne must have known I might come downstairs while Leah was gone, so I was taken aback to see her leafing through the diary at reception, examining each entry. She must have snuck down – I hadn't heard her pass my door, had assumed she was still in the attic. She had the grace to look embarrassed, but there was something about her reaction that made me think she was more afraid of something or someone else than she was of me. But maybe I was projecting again, seeing what I expected to see.

'Looking for something?' I asked.

'No, sorry. I was just checking the date.'

I closed over the book. 'Are you okay, Susanne? Is everything okay?'

'Aye. Why wouldn't it be?'

She was defensive, of course she was. I would be too. She made to go back upstairs. I decided to grab my opportunity. I didn't know when I'd get the chance to speak to her on my own again.

'How are things with Luke?'

She turned and gave me an odd look.

'Did you know that I know him?' I corrected myself. 'Knew him, a long time ago?'

She avoided my eye, but nodded. 'He told me. After Dad's party.'

I chose my words carefully. 'He went out with my sister. She died.' I paused. 'He served time for it.'

Something leached from her features. Self-assurance. She braved it out, stuck her chin out defiantly, pretending that she knew, but I could tell that the version I was giving her wasn't the one she had been told. Or certainly not as stark. She didn't

297

reply. Her expression closed, like Faye's used to when I tried to reach her. She moved towards the stairs again.

'Susanne?' I called after her. 'Are you really okay with that?'

She turned to me, her expression fixed. 'I knew he was in prison. He's never hidden that from me. He even went to the guards here to let them know. He's served his sentence.'

'Susanne,' I said, my tone insistent. 'Luke is dangerous. He can be very charming but there's something wrong with him. A darkness that he manages to hide when you get to know him first.'

Her eyes shone. 'He told me he dumped you for your sister and you've never forgiven him for it.'

With an effort, I kept my tone neutral. 'Does your father know about Luke's history?'

She rounded on me, her tone fierce. 'Why should he? It's none of his business. It's none of anyone's business.'

The front door opened with a creak. Leah was back. I let Susanne go. I had made my move too soon.

Chapter Thirty

I left the office at lunchtime to meet Maeve; we picked up sand-wiches and took them to her clinic. I felt a little guilty leaving Leah alone with Susanne, but I thought it was wisest after our earlier exchange. Also I had a bit of catching-up to do with Maeve. Though I had spoken to her on the phone, I hadn't seen her since New Year's Eve.

Being back in her clinic reminded me of Guinness's near escape and all the unpleasant things that had happened since then, not just major ones but the minor ones too. Was it pos-sible they could all be connected? While Maeve made coffee, having shooed the practice dogs outside so we could eat without soft reproachful eyes following our every bite, I told her about Luke's return and that I'd given Susanne a job. Her response was similar to Phyllis's.

'God, are you sure about that?' When I didn't respond, she gave me a half-smile. 'Is she any use?'

'Not much, judging by this morning.'

'And what about *him*?' She handed me a mug. 'Jesus, Ben, I know the man has to live somewhere, but really, does it have to be here?'

'I don't think they'll be around for very long. I *hope* they won't be around for very long,' I corrected myself, remembering Luke's words on the street.

Maeve perched on the counter, legs swinging, mug in hand. 'There's a right age difference between them, isn't there?'

I nodded. I was tempted to ask if Maeve had heard any rumours about Susanne and George, but didn't.

'How long have they been together?' she asked.

'It can't be very long. A few months at the most. Which is quick work even for a rake like Luke Kirby.'

She smiled. 'And what about your own relationship? How's it going with the handsome sergeant?'

I felt a pang. Despite the two messages, Molloy hadn't rung back. 'I'm not sure, to be honest. I don't think he's too happy about my giving Susanne a job, even though it's only for a week or two. He thinks I'm inviting Kirby back into my life.'

'He might have a point,' Maeve said seriously. 'I'm sure that's not your intention, but surely you're as well keeping as far away from him as possible.'

I decided not to share my plan to get Susanne away from Luke. I knew what Maeve's reaction would be – the same as Molloy's.

She raised her mug in a mock toast. 'Well, I hope it works out with Molloy. You deserve a bit of happiness.'

'Thanks, but I'm not sure that's going to happen until this whole mess is cleared up.'

'Carole and the Oak?'

'And Stan. It's all pressure.'

Maeve sighed. 'Poor Stan. I saw him earlier and he's looking very shaky on the old pins. That attack really took it out of him.'

I remembered Stan sitting by Róisín's fire, trying his best to be his usual arch self, and had a sudden flashback of driving to the McCanns' house with the snowy summit of Sliabh Sneacht in view.

'How would you have driven to Pete Stoop's place when you were his vet?' I asked.

Maeve thought about it for a second. 'Up the Derry road and turn right – it's overgrown now, but that's the way I'd have gone back then. It wasn't great, but you could get through it with a jeep. I doubt you could do that now. It only leads up to the cottage, so no one else would be using it.'

I realised that must be the route I'd seen marked on Pat the Stoop's map. Maeve picked up her sandwich and undid the cellophane with an odd expression on her face.

'What?' I asked.

'I've just remembered, I saw Carole heading up there once.'

My eyes widened and she quickly added, 'Not recently. Years ago, when you could still walk up that way.'

'After Dominic was gone?'

'Oh aye, years after. She was back from England. I think she was even married to George. The cottage would have been empty. It's a bit creepy, though, the idea of her heading up there on her own when you think what happened to her years later.'

I couldn't disagree. 'I wonder what she was doing?'

'Maybe she was curious to see where Dominic had grown up?'

'But she was with George at that point.'

Maeve smiled. 'I know, but people can be funny about their exes, can't they? Maybe there were times when she wondered if she'd made the wrong choice.'

The afternoon was long and tedious. Leah and Susanne left together at five, with Susanne studiously avoiding my eye, although she looked suitably dusty so at least she'd spent the afternoon where she was supposed to be, in the attic. I left at six, avoided the temptation to call into the Garda station and drove back to Malin.

Dinner was a tin of soup, bread and cheese and a big glass of wine with a cat on my knee. There was no response from Molloy all evening. I couldn't blame him. I suspected he'd seen a side of me he didn't like very much. I wondered what the future held for us.

The book on holy sites that Phyllis had loaned me was on the coffee table, and when I'd cleared away the remains of my food, I poured myself another glass of wine and picked it up. The photographs of the Well of the Eyes made me think back to Christmas morning before we found Carole's body. It sounds maudlin, but it felt to me now like the last time I'd been happy. I took out my phone to have a look at the photographs I had taken that morning and scrolled through. There were images of the cairn at the top, the holy well, Fred. None of Molloy, I noticed. Maybe that was prophetic.

I discovered that one of the pictures was actually a video. I must have been trying to take a photograph of the holy well and pressed video by mistake. I played it. It was short, about thirty seconds long, the camera fixed on the well throughout. But there was sound: wind, laughter from Molloy when I stepped in the wet, all before Fred disappeared. Then something else. I tried to make it out. It was so faint that I wondered if I was mistaken, so I turned the sound up and replayed it. There it was again: a whistle, way in the distance, long and low, with six short blasts.

When I arrived at the office the following morning, Leah was alone.

'Where is your able assistant this morning?' I asked, dumping my bag on the reception desk.

Leah looked at her watch. 'No sign of her. Day two and she's late. Doesn't exactly bode well, does it?'

I wondered if our chat the day before was the reason for her absence. I could have kicked myself for weighing in too soon. The last thing I'd wanted was to scare her away.

'Maybe she's decided all that dust wasn't for her,' Leah grinned.

I climbed the stairs and opened a file, but couldn't concentrate on work. Where the hell was Susanne? My stomach lurched when I realised she had probably told Luke what I'd said. But why shouldn't I have said what I did? Luke claimed he had been honest with her, so I shouldn't have been telling her anything she didn't already know.

I needed some fresh air.

'I'll be back in ten,' I called to Leah as I headed out the door.

The morning was grey, overcast and cold. Unwisely I'd gone out without a coat and was hunched over crossing the street when I ran into Stan. He was standing outside his salon watching Róisín climb into a car with her mother in the passenger seat.

'Are you back to work?' I asked in surprise.

'One foot in, one foot out. Short-staffed.' He looked pale and spoke softly, not like him. And he didn't seem to want to chat. Before I could ask him anything more, he turned to go back inside.

I called after him. 'Stan. Are you okay?'

He turned reluctantly, his face pinched, eyes wary.

'You still don't look well. Are you sure you should be back at work? Are you sure you should even be out of hospital?'

He looked down. 'I'm fine.'

With a jolt I realised that he was afraid. I don't know why I was so surprised; the man had recently been attacked. I knew I should let him go back into the safety of his salon, but I had an uneasy feeling that I might not get the chance to ask him again.

'Stan, the man Carole was with in Derry, that night before the fire. Are you sure you didn't recognise him?'

His eyes widened and he looked around him fearfully. Róisín and her mother drove by; he gave them a small wave, then suddenly his expression changed. He clenched his fists and seemed to come to a decision. 'It was Susanne Craig's new boyfriend.'

A chill ran down my spine.

Stan avoided my gaze. 'It was true that I didn't recognise him at the time, but I've seen him since. I didn't say anything because I realised it was nothing to worry about. I assumed they'd met through Tony or Susanne.'

The final two sentences sounded rehearsed. Stan didn't believe there was nothing to worry about any more than I did. The reason he hadn't said anything was because he was afraid. But why was he telling me now? Before I could ask him, he turned to go. I pulled on his sleeve as he walked away, but he refused to say anything more.

Blood pounding in my ears, I raced back to the office to ring Molloy. Luke had been with Carole the night before the fire, probably the night before she was killed. They knew each other. This was the connection he had been looking for.

Leah was on the phone when I arrived in. She was chalk white. She put her hand over the receiver. 'It's Susanne,' she whispered. 'She sounds very strange.'

I took the phone from her. 'Susanne, is everything okay?'

The voice on the other end sounded slurred. 'Don't switch on the kettle.'

'What?'

'Don't switch on the kettle. There's a device in the socket . . . switching on the kettle will activate it.'

I felt my heart rate speed up. 'A device? What do you mean, a device?'

A note of urgency entered her voice. 'This wasn't my idea . . . I swear to God, I didn't know. Those explosives were for—'

The phone was snatched away from her and the line was cut. I put down the handset.

'We need to leave,' I said, as calmly as I could.

'What?' Leah said, her eyes wide with fear, a tear welling in the corner of one of them.

'Now,' I shouted. 'There's some kind of device. Explosives. I don't know. Come on!'

I ran upstairs to grab my keys, and we raced out onto the street, startling a couple of schoolkids on their way to the dentist and ordering them to come with us. I called Molloy as I ran.

An hour later, we stood on the footpath of the Malin road on the outskirts of town. The entire square had been evacuated within minutes of Susanne's call, and Molloy had immediately contacted the Defence Forces. The decision had been made to treat the threat as real because of the trace of explosives discovered in the pub, but so far nothing had been found. Temporary barricades had been set up at various points along the road and people stood about in groups of twos and threes, some talking, others just staring at the building on the other side. Our building. Our office. Over the time we had been standing there, shock had faded to boredom, frustration and cold. It was raining, stinging, icy rain. And the army's bomb disposal experts remained in our office.

I used the time, shivering by the roadside, to tell Leah about Luke, the whole story from beginning to end. When I had finished, she was trembling with cold and shock.

'He went to the bathroom,' she said quietly.

'What?' I asked.

'Susanne's boyfriend. When he was here earlier in the week, he went to the bathroom. He must have planted something then. We were there all day yesterday with something in the office that could have blown us up.' She wrung her hands. 'I turned on that kettle umpteen times.'

I touched her arm. 'I really think it must be a hoax. They'd have found whatever it was by now.'

She glared at me.

'But you're right,' I said hurriedly. 'It doesn't change the fact that I should have told you who Luke Kirby was as soon as he appeared in the office.'

'Yes, you should have,' she said, and turned away.

I felt a twist in my gut as I realised that Leah had every reason to be annoyed with me. Whether or not this was a hoax, I had put her and everyone who came into the office at risk by not disclosing what I knew.

Molloy emerged from the crowd, looking drawn. 'They haven't found anything yet. Tell me about that call again. Exactly what was said, word for word.'

I did. 'It's Kirby. I know it is. He's got Susanne somewhere, against her will. We need to find her.'

He frowned. 'Are you sure they're not in this together?'

I shook my head. 'She was frightened. I could hear it in her voice. Where could he have taken her?'

'That house in Derry,' Molloy said urgently. He ran towards the squad car, calling back to me. 'I'll contact the PSNI on the way. Stay here and I'll let you know what happens.'

I watched him leave, shifting from one foot to the other. It was freezing and we had come out without coats. Leah wasn't speaking to me and I didn't feel like speaking to anyone else, despite the fact that I knew most of the people in the crowd. I felt as if I had brought all of this down on my friends and neighbours. I felt useless and responsible, a lousy combination.

My phone buzzed in the pocket of my suit. I jumped, thinking it was Molloy.

Drive out the Derry road. I'll let her live if you come.

The words swam in front of my eyes. Luke, I thought. How had he got my number? It must have been written somewhere in my wallet. I tapped Leah on the shoulder and showed her the text.

She looked horrified. 'You're not thinking of responding, are you?'

'I have to. What if he has Susanne hostage and there's something I can do? I'd never forgive myself if . . .'

'Ben . . .'

I typed a response, hands trembling: *Okay.*

Avoiding the blocked-off square, I took a route through a network of muddy back roads before ending up on the Derry road just as it began to rain again. The Mini's wipers screeched like nails on a blackboard and the road was a mire, strewn with branches and mulch, Sliabh Sneacht in the distance, a brooding presence against the stormy sky. My head was spinning. I tried to figure out what I would do once I found Luke. I knew it was a trap. But I couldn't let what had happened to Faye happen to someone else.

A figure stood at the side of the road just ahead. I swallowed. Luke, I thought. But when the windscreen cleared briefly, I saw that it was a woman; a slight woman in a long waterproof coat. She was standing under a tree outside the McCanns' farm. It was Róisín, hitching a lift. Things were beginning to make a sickening sort of sense. She waved me to a stop. I pulled in and rolled down the window. The collie I had seen when I had called to the house was crouched at her feet, as soaked as she was.

She pushed back her hood. 'Are you heading to Derry?'

I struggled to come up with an excuse and failed.

'Can I have a lift? Please. I'm a bit stuck. Eddie was meant to drive me, but—'

'Go on. Get in.' I bowed to the inevitable.

She took a bag from beneath the tree and climbed into the car, pushing the bag through the gap between the front seats. Before she closed the door, she sent the dog back into the yard. 'Go on, Jessie. Stay inside in the dry.'

Jessie. Of course.

As I pulled away, my phone buzzed on the dashboard. I picked it up. A text from Molloy, two words: *Flat empty.*

'Is everything okay?' Róisín asked.

'You heard what happened in town?'

She nodded. 'I presume it's a hoax?'

'We don't know yet.' I turned onto the shore road towards Derry. 'Where do you want to go?'

'Culdaff.'

'I thought you were going to Derry?' I felt something cold on the back of my neck.

'I've changed my mind. Now turn the car around and head back towards Culdaff.'

With horror, I realised that the object at my neck was a gun. I stopped to turn and a tractor approached, puffing out smoke, with a line of cars behind. I waited, heart racing, for the traffic to pass, the sea beyond a muddy brown, the sky grey and threatening. Part of me wished for a collision, anything to stop what was about to happen. But when Róisín took my phone from the dashboard, switched it off and put it in the pocket of her coat, I knew I could no longer be traced.

Chapter Thirty-One

Róisín lowered the gun out of view and kept it trained on my waist while I drove back towards Culdaff, knuckles white on the steering wheel. I tried to calm myself down by asking questions.

'What's going on, Róisín? What's in Culdaff?'

She didn't reply.

'What have you got to lose by telling me? There's not much I can do with a gun pointed at me, is there? Do you know where Susanne is?'

My questions belied my fear. But I was appealing to the Róisín I'd known before, the sweet girl who was anxious to please. This one was stony-faced, impenetrable.

'You're involved with that animal rights organisation, aren't you? The email address is your dog's name. Did you have something to do with what happened in the office?'

She snorted. 'Nothing happened in your office.'

'I don't think you can say planting an explosive device is nothing.'

'There is no explosive device.' She nodded towards the back. 'Those are explosives. So it might be a good idea to just shut the fuck up and drive.'

I did. I shut the fuck up and drove, glancing fearfully at the bag stuffed so carelessly into the back seat, just behind where Róisín was sitting. She remained silent for the rest of the journey, eyes and gun trained on me, while I tried to get my brain to function, to piece things together. I knew she'd been the one who'd whistled for Fred on Christmas morning; I knew now that she'd run the animaloutrage site. I knew that she'd left Australia to go travelling. Had she gone to Spain? Was that where she'd met Luke? I caught sight of her expression. It was cold as steel, all trace of softness gone. Her wet hair hung in rat tails about her face, and there was an intensity about her that reminded me of Dominic Stoop.

Before we reached Culdaff, she ordered me to turn left, and I did so, passing a petrol station and some housing estates. I saw a client on the road, a woman in a motorised wheelchair who recognised my car. I tried to wave but Róisín slapped my hand down painfully. It was stupid of me. About a mile later, she told me to turn right. We were heading towards the pier.

'Is it a boat?' I asked. 'Are you leaving on a boat? Is that why we're going to Bunagee?'

Again I was met with silence. Before we reached the pier, she directed me to drive up a laneway to a small boatshed surrounded by scrubby bushes.

'Drive around the back.'

I did what she said and parked the Mini at the rear of the building, behind a stack of old crates and fish boxes, wind and icy rain battering the little car. Róisín took the keys from me and forced me out with the gun. I stumbled towards the shed in the driving rain, trying my best to get my bearings. The laneway we'd driven up snaked ahead along the coast, but there wasn't a creature to be seen, human or beast. She took a key from her pocket and used it to unlock an old rusted padlock, then pulled open the door and pushed me roughly inside. A stale, salty odour with something rotten underneath greeted us. The shed must have been used to store fishing equipment, but all that remained now were a few torn nets and buoys piled up in the corner. There was no light and Róisín made no attempt to switch one on.

Something moved in the corner by the nets, and I started, thinking it was a rat. When my eyes adjusted, I saw that it was a person, shunting from a lying position to a sitting one against the wall. In the gloom I made out a face. Susanne Craig. She was tied at her feet, with her hands behind her back and her mouth gagged. She looked at me with wide eyes, her cheeks dirty and tear-stained.

Róisín pushed me over to her and tied me up in the same way, gagging me with a stinking rag that made me want to retch. Then she left us without a word, slamming the door behind her and turning the key in the lock. I shivered in my damp clothes, my skin starting to sting. I looked at Susanne in an attempt to convey something – I wasn't sure what; it wasn't as if I had anything comforting to say – but she avoided my eye.

The gag was digging painfully into my cheek when the door opened again. Luke Kirby strode in, wearing a long waterproof coat with a hood, which he pushed back as he approached, and carrying a small stool and bag. I felt my whole body contract when he placed them on the floor beside us and flinched as he untied my gag. Despite the removal of the stinking rag, it was his expensive scent that turned my stomach.

'What about Susanne?' I asked, when I could speak.

'No point. Susie rarely has anything interesting to say.' He

312

sat on the stool, his long legs stretched out in front of him, and cocked his head to one side. 'Has other talents, though. Just like your sister.'

I bit back a response and tried to keep my voice calm. 'What are you doing? Why are you even *here* in Donegal?'

'I told you I wanted to come up and see you, didn't I?'

I had a flashback of his phone call to the office. *It's been too long.*

'But—'

Kirby raised his hand to stop me speaking, then looked at me for a minute without saying a word, regaining control. I held his gaze, my heart beating wildly.

Eventually he bowed his head. 'Since you ask, an opportunity fell into my lap. Thanks to you, I'm not a high-earning lawyer any more, so I needed another occupation. That's the thing with these organisations. You can start again from scratch: new identity, safe passage. Especially if you're carrying something they need.'

'Explosives.' I ignored the warped thinking that allowed him to blame me for the loss of his career.

'I made some interesting contacts in prison.' He smirked. 'Can pretty much get anything these days. Still a whizz at striking deals.'

Still an arrogant, slimy bastard, I thought. 'Dominic McLaughlin,' I said.

He nodded assent. 'Dominic, my old cellmate from your neck of the woods. He thought a legal brain could be useful to "the cause", so I told him I wanted to do something I believed in for a change. Fucking obsessives, Sarah, you know what they're like. They'll believe any old shit once it accords with their own twisted view of the world. And of course,' he reached out to run his finger slowly down Susanne's cheek, 'I met the beautiful Susie when I went to join my new tribe in Spain.'

She pulled back, her eyes wild and panicked.

My mind raced ahead, trying to make connections. 'But what about Carole? What did she have to do with it?'

Kirby picked up a piece of loose timber from the ground and started to tap the floor with it. 'Dominic was surprisingly chatty – prison can get pretty fucking dull, you know; told me all about his marriage and son, how his wife had conveniently forgotten both and moved on to a new family.'

'You blackmailed her.'

'If you want to call it that. When Dominic went back to prison in the UK, I contacted her pretending I was him.'

'How?'

'How do you think? Do you know how easy it is to get a mobile phone in prison? I texted her, dropping hints about our son, saying that I wanted to find him, to get to know him again.' He shrugged. 'When I got out, I asked for money. And she paid it, on the condition I left him alone.'

The money she'd earned from taking on extra work, I thought, and what she'd taken from Eddie.

'And you made her hide explosives for you.'

'I told her we needed somewhere to keep some equipment for the cause. She came to Dublin to collect them, said she'd store them in the cellar of the pub. At that stage I told her I was a colleague of Dominic's.'

That was why she'd taken the bus back from Dublin rather than the plane, I thought. And why she needed the suitcase. The noise Stan had heard was probably Carole panicking in the days beforehand, moving things about, trying to find somewhere to hide the explosives.

'Why the hell would Carole help you?'

'You're a lawyer, Sarah. You know that secrets are power. I made it clear what I knew and I think she'd have done anything to keep me quiet.' He grinned. 'If she'd been more of a looker, I might even have been tempted. Although she was a bit fucking stupid. Lord knows what Dominic saw in her – he was a lunatic, but no fool. I mean, who thinks Christmas is a good time to hide anything in a pub cellar?'

'You made her bring you to the cottage.'

He dropped the wood and sat back with his arms crossed. 'Clever girl. I told her to come up with somewhere remote to move the explosives to. She took me there when she'd finished work. Nice pub that, shame it had to burn down.' He winked at Susanne and she whimpered, her eyes wide and hurt.

I pictured Carole in her final hours walking up to that creepy cottage with Luke Kirby and I felt a wave of nausea wash over me. 'But there was no trace of explosives in the cottage.'

'That's because they never got there. Róisín sorted that out – moved them to her parents' cowshed.' Kirby gave a bark of laughter. 'Explosives in a fucking cowshed – it's like something out of the IRA.' He leaned forward, so close I could feel his breath on my face. 'Don't you miss the bright lights?'

I pulled away, and was surprised to feel a slight slackening of the ties on my wrists. They weren't as tight as I'd thought they were. Had Róisín tied them loosely on purpose? I began to work them, rotating my wrists back and forth behind my back, hoping Kirby wouldn't notice in the half-light.

'You killed her,' I said.

'What do you say, Susie? Did I kill the barmaid?' Susanne withdrew deeper into the corner. 'Did you know Susanne didn't

315

like Carole very much? Ever since she had a thing with randy old George when she was a youngster?'

Susanne looked towards the wall, her eyes wet with tears.

'Anyway, she's been useful, haven't you, Susie? She remembered this shed where she used to meet George. And she got him to organise a trawler. There's another man with secrets he doesn't want getting out. Of course, you did think you were coming with us, didn't you, Susie?'

It still didn't add up. 'But *why* would you *kill* her? Why would you plant Dominic's DNA?'

He laughed. 'I expect that caused PC Plod to do a bit of head-scratching. Dead man's DNA. Unfortunately that was a bit of a fucking cock-up, since I didn't know he was going to die when I took it. But I thought I'd plant it anyway, stir things up a bit.'

'Carole turned you down, didn't she? That's why you killed her,' I spat.

Kirby's smile faded. 'I've never had to force myself on a woman, you should know that, sweetheart. That barmaid had one more thing to do for me. If she'd done it she wouldn't be where she is today. It's her own fucking fault she's dead.'

I looked away. I had a sudden horrible feeling he would say the same thing about Faye.

There was a pause before he leaned over me again. 'Don't you want to know what I wanted her to do?'

I snatched my head back and hit it painfully against the rough wall behind me. I felt a wetness – I was bleeding. But the ties on my wrists were getting looser. I kept rubbing them together, terrified that he would notice the movement.

Kirby hissed into my face. 'I wanted her to get you to the cottage. I told her Dominic wanted to give it to her. That it could have been a nest egg for her if she ever wanted to leave

George. I knew Susie's story at that stage, so I thought it was a possibility. Said she should ask you to have a look. You're so fucking nosy, I knew you'd come. And I'd have been waiting for you.'

Suddenly the door creaked open and Róisín appeared, a slight figure silhouetted against the white-grey sky. She tapped her watch and beckoned. Luke tensed, as I'd seen him do in the past when someone pulled rank, his expression danger-ous. Unintimidated, she glared at him, clicked her fingers and left. He stood up, reached into the bag he'd brought and with-drew something, flipped a switch and threw it into the corner. Susanne shuffled away from it in panic, like a crab. A car engine started up outside.

Kirby nodded. 'That will go off in a couple of minutes. Don't worry. It'll be clean. No missing limbs or anything.' He spat into the corner. 'You can join your sister, if you believe in that sort of thing.'

He turned to go. My heart pounded in my chest and waves of terror washed over me, but I couldn't let him leave, couldn't let him get away with it again. If we were going to die, he was coming with us.

'Why are you so interested in me?' I shouted. 'Why didn't you just go and join your new tribe? Why even bother with me?'

He turned. Luke Kirby could never resist having the last word.

'Maybe you never got over me,' I taunted. 'Is that what it is?'

A vein pumped in his forehead. 'I'm not interested in you in the slightest.'

'You killed Carole because of me. You wanted me to know about it. And now you've just told me everything like some tod-dler showing his shit to his mother.'

Temper flashed in his eyes but he suppressed it. 'Unfinished business. Nothing more.'

'What unfinished business?'

'You lied about me in court. You said Faye was afraid of me.'

I tried to keep the tremor out of my voice, but it was impossible. 'Faye *was* afraid of you.'

His face took on an ugly sneer. 'Faye wasn't afraid of anything. Without your evidence, the jury would have accepted that what happened was an accident. Your sister liked a good time. Which was more than could be said for you, you boring bitch.'

A noise from outside interrupted him; unmistakably a car driving away, the same engine I'd heard starting up earlier. Róisín was leaving without him. His eyes darted towards the door, flaring with anger. One more rub and my ties would be loose enough to extract one hand. Kirby froze, his head turned. My ankles were still tied, but I had to try. How long would it be before that detonator went off?

'Sounds as if you're not as important as you think you are,' I said.

He turned. I pushed my knees to one side, twisted my body and lunged at him, screaming, grabbing at his legs with all the strength I could muster. 'You fucking coward, you killed my sister. You left her to die.'

I knew I hadn't a hope; I was no match for him. But it was enough for him to snap. He dived at me in fury and put his hands around my neck, his thumbs pressing into my throat. I tried to swallow and couldn't, felt myself panic. I clawed at his hands, tried to pull them from my throat, but it was no use.

'You bitch.'

I struggled for air, felt myself getting dizzy. I was going to lose consciousness, and soon.

Then a series of noises: a loud cracking noise as Kirby fell away from me and slumped to the floor; Susanne whimpering beside me; the low, insistent beep of the detonator. I coughed and gasped as I tried to get my breath back, realising that Molloy and for some reason Stan MacLochlainn were in the shed with us. Molloy's eyes were dark with anger. He shouted at Stan to stay back.

His face was above me, concerned. 'Are you okay?'

I managed to nod towards the corner. 'There's an explosive device . . .'

Molloy untied my feet and I stood up, my legs giving way immediately. He placed my arms around his neck and picked me up. Stan began to untie Susanne, but Molloy barked at him not to, that there wasn't time. In desperation they half carried, half dragged the two of us outside.

About twenty yards from the shed, we threw ourselves onto the grass. Almost immediately I felt Molloy get to his feet again, and I twisted around on my hands as he ran back towards the shed. I called after him, mind numb with panic. Before he reached it, it exploded, the blast forcing us to flatten ourselves again, Stan covering Susanne protectively. We lay there, face down, noise, heat and stench filling the air, until we heard the sound of sirens and saw flashing red lights.

Chapter Thirty-Two

By the time we reached the pier, it was in chaos and swarming with guards. Two black dogs bounded about, getting under everyone's feet, and there was a shout for someone to control them. The battered old Punto I'd seen at Sliabh Sneacht the day I'd met Róisín and Susanne had been dumped carelessly at the top of the stone steps leading down to the water, and was now being examined by the same men in protective clothing who'd been in our office earlier. For some reason, I had a flashback to the sleek black Lexus that Luke had driven when I had known him first.

'Where has she gone, do you think?' I asked.

Molloy and I stood gazing impotently at the rough grey sea, the land on the other side cloaked in mist. I could just make out Culdaff beach, where Stan had been hurt on New Year's Eve. He'd saved Susanne's life, just as Molloy had saved mine. We hadn't talked about what had happened at the boatshed. Molloy didn't seem ready; his face was strained, a blackened mask of shock. Being closer to the explosion than the rest of us, he could easily have been killed, but the main force of the blast had been in the other direction, towards the sea, saving him. The ambulance had wanted to check him out, but he'd refused, insistent on following Róisín's trail while the fire brigade battled the blaze. I'd insisted on coming too. I didn't know what I was feeling yet – relief, disbelief, anger – but I knew I wanted to be with him. I was shaken and sore, knowing that in some strange way I'd experienced what Faye had, and that the shock of that would set in later.

'Scotland probably,' Molloy replied. His voice sounded odd. My ears were still ringing after the blast, but I knew it wasn't just that. 'At first, anyway. All coastguards have been alerted. Hopefully we'll get her.'

I'd realised that that was why Susanne had been meeting George – she was blackmailing him to arrange a boat. She really had been under Luke's thumb, using her contacts to get what he wanted, thinking all the time that she would be going with him. Or maybe she'd done it for Róisín, her old school friend? I pictured Susanne's pale, stunned face as she'd climbed into the ambulance with Stan. I hoped the loose ties were design rather than accident. I wanted to believe that Róisín had wished for our escape.

'How come Stan was with you?' I asked. I didn't mention Luke, but I knew Molloy was thinking about him – it was written all over his face.

'He rang me while I was in Derry. You were right, by the way. Kirby *was* staying there. Registered in the UK, but Northern Ireland rather than England as we assumed. One of the flats in the house was registered to a Dominic McLaughlin – Kirby was using his name.'

I nodded. Somehow I'd known that Luke had been in the vicinity the past few weeks, even before I'd met him at Tony's party. I suspected he was behind the small, taunting things that had been happening too.

'It was Kirby who hit Stan,' Molloy said. 'Róisín told him Kirby wanted to kill him and that she was the only one stopping him.'

I pictured the two of them sitting at the fire, the look of fear on Stan's face. 'I thought Róisín was protecting him, but instead she was the one who was threatening him. Stan saw Luke with Carole in Derry. He had to be persuaded to stay quiet about that.'

Molloy nodded. 'Róisín made him go to the beach. She told him Tony wanted to meet him to talk. And then she persuaded him to put the blame for the assault on Tony rather than Luke.'

'And all Stan wanted was a relationship with his brother. What made him decide to tell, finally?'

'Exactly what you've just said. Family. He made up with Tony earlier today, once he thought Róisín and Kirby were out of the picture. Tony told him that he had decided to divide the pub with him and acknowledge him as his brother. Stan hadn't expected that.'

'So he decided to save Susanne, his niece?'

Molloy nodded. 'He didn't want Tony to know what was going on, that he'd been aware Susanne was at risk. Stan knew about the boat and the boatshed, having overheard Róisín and Susanne on the phone. Unfortunately for Susanne, she was only aware of part of the plan.'

'Stan kept quiet because he felt isolated,' I said. 'He thought Róisín was his only friend.'

Molloy was silent. One of the dogs appeared at my feet and I bent down to rub its head; there was something comforting about the brown eyes and untroubled face that gazed up at me.

'You were right about a lot of things,' Molloy said at last. 'I'm sorry. Kirby *was* after you.'

I shook my head. 'Getting back at me was just a bonus. He wanted a new life, a new mask. It was all an act. Luke Kirby would have used that organisation for his own ends, whatever those happened to be. Although he underestimated Róisín.'

'He couldn't have had his own agenda with an organisation like that,' Molloy said. 'Once Róisín had the explosives, she was fully prepared to ditch him; she'd realised he might be a liability.' His jaw tightened. 'Susanne thinks he killed Carole in a fit of temper. She said there were times when she thought he was going to hit *her*, but he never actually did.'

I'd seen Molloy speak to Susanne at the door of the ambulance but hadn't heard what had been said. The truth was that I had no idea what she had been through these past few weeks.

'That's probably because she always did what he wanted,' I said. 'That was always Luke's problem. If someone didn't do as they were told, he'd lose it. I think that must have been what happened to Faye.' My voice broke and I swallowed back the tears, knowing that if they came, they wouldn't stop.

Molloy put his arms around me.

'Kirby is dead,' I whispered. The words didn't seem real.

I felt Molloy tense as he gazed out to sea. 'I lost it when I saw him with his hands . . .' He trailed off. 'I've never killed anyone before.'

I pulled away. 'You didn't kill him. Luke Kirby was killed by his own bomb.'

He didn't look at me. His face was grey beneath the black. 'If I hadn't left him unconscious, he'd still be alive. He'd have been able to escape the blast.'

'But you saved my life.'

Chapter Thirty-Three

It seemed to have been raining for days. St Brigid's Day, 1 February, is the first day of spring in Ireland, but usually a day when it appears as if the weather is having a laugh at the very idea of it. Today, though, the sun was shining. My office was a latticework of light and shade, and I found myself gazing at patterns on the wall cast by the blinds. I'd been distracted, unable to work all morning.

I stood up and walked over to the window, pulled the blinds aside and looked out. The street was silent, empty like a ghost town, although I knew it wouldn't be for long. The phone rang and I returned to my desk to answer it: a client making an appointment for next week. I took a note. Leah had diverted the phones for the hour or so she'd be gone. She'd forgiven me; the events at the boatshed had washed away all upset in a flood of sympathy and concern. Also, she'd moved into full wedding-planning mode, which had helped to take her mind off things.

I heard them coming. Footsteps, marching. Chanting. *Hands off our Garda station. Hands off our Garda station.* I returned to the window. This time the street was full, the crowd stretching from footpath to footpath. Townspeople with placards, punching their fists in the air. Familiar faces – Phyllis, Maeve, Liam, Leah. A protest march.

I heard the door open downstairs, then footsteps taking the stairs two at a time. A voice behind me, a Cork accent. 'It's not going to do any good.'

I turned. Molloy was standing in the doorway, dressed in jeans and a grey sweater; it matched his eyes, didn't match the dark crescents underneath.

'The decision is made. The station is closing in a month, no matter what happens – it's a question of numbers, population.' He looked down. 'I've known it's been coming for a while.'

'I figured that. Although I wish you'd told me instead of making me think you were having second thoughts.'

His face softened. 'About us? Is that what you thought?'

'Among other things.'

'I didn't want you to take all the flak for going out with the local sergeant only for me to be moved.' His expression darkened. 'I was also afraid I wouldn't be able to protect you if you needed it.'

'Where will they send you? I suppose there's no chance it will be Letterkenny?' I smiled weakly.

I felt a pinprick of fear when he didn't reply. Instead he came over to join me at the window, and we stood in silence looking down at the march. I spotted Susanne Craig, still pale, shaken, holding onto her father's arm for support. But she was also holding onto Stan.

'So, Stan finally gets his family,' I said.

'Tony's going to need the support,' Molloy said. 'Susanne's been charged with arson.'

His voice was tense. He still looked drawn. I'd thought things would improve in the weeks since the explosion, but they hadn't. He'd stayed with me a couple of nights, but his sleep had been so disrupted by nightmares that he'd left at six each morning. I was worried about him, worried that I was part of the problem. When the shock of Luke's death had eased, I'd felt a rush, a release of something I'd been holding onto for years, but I knew Molloy was feeling the opposite.

'Any news on Róisín?' I asked.

I'd caught sight of her parents below, a couple who seemed to have shrunk visibly in the past few weeks. I was pleased to see them taking part.

'Arrested at an anti-whaling protest in Russia. She was part of the protest but there was no evidence against her for anything criminal, so she was released without charge. They didn't know we were after her until it was too late.'

I'd been to see Róisín's mother the week before. She told me that Róisín had been a vegan since she was old enough to work out what meat was; that she'd wanted to become involved politically but they had discouraged her. They'd had no idea how deeply she'd been involved online, or that she had used her trip to Australia to travel to meet other activists, returning via Spain, where she met Luke. She'd shown me a picture that had made her cry. It showed Susanne and Róisín standing in a square in their school uniforms. They were surrounded by pigeons; each girl had one on her head and two or three feeding from each hand. Susanne was beaming, Róisín unsmiling, intense.

I crossed my arms. 'They thought when she came back from Australia that she'd stay, especially as she was going out with Eddie. But she only came back to say goodbye; she'd made the decision to devote her life to what she believed in. Poor Eddie was just a beard. She'll do this for the rest of her days now, won't she? Until it kills her. She's another Dominic Stoop.'

Molloy nodded, shielding his eyes against the sun. 'So it seems. Susanne was a liability. She says she only became involved in the first place because of Róisín; went to Spain to meet her. They met Luke there. He could organise explosives, which, together with Dominic's introduction, made him accepted. The corporate lawyer turned eco-warrior. But you were right, he did have his own agenda.'

'Luke always had his own agenda,' I said quietly. It still felt strange to use his name in the past tense.

'After he killed Carole that night, he rang Susanne,' Molloy said. 'She and Róisín had come back from Culdaff to move the explosives from the pub cellar to Róisín's parents' farm. When Susanne got to the cottage, Luke was there with Carole's body. Luke terrified her, hinting that her presence would make her a suspect, especially since she'd had an affair with George. Susanne was drunk and scared and agreed to keep it quiet. They left Carole strangled in a chair.'

I shuddered. The image was grim.

'As you said, Kirby was careful about DNA,' Molloy continued. 'He'd been burned once. He left to go back to Derry, didn't seem too concerned. But Susanne panicked. She went back to the Oak with Eddie's keys and started to drink on her own. The drunker she got, the more she convinced herself that if she set the pub on fire, then everyone would think that Carole had done it and that was why she had run off. She also had Carole's phone.'

'So she sent those texts to George over the next few days to reinforce that?'

Molloy nodded. 'I suspect she may have gleaned some satisfaction from taunting him. She said that Luke knew how hurt she'd been when George didn't leave Carole for her.'

'Never a good idea to confide in Luke Kirby.'

'Or Róisín. Susanne told Róisín everything a few days later when she overheard you talking about going up to Sliabh Sneacht on Christmas Day. She panicked again, thinking the body would be found. She says that Róisín thought the body *should* be found, that she persuaded Susanne they should move it and Róisín would give her an alibi. So that's what they did, on Christmas Eve, using the overgrown laneway from Róisín's house. Susanne even put petrol on Carole's hands in an attempt to exonerate herself.'

'So Róisín had *some* feeling for Eddie's family then.'

'Looks like it.'

'And that's why they put the socks by the body,' I said. 'As a kind of flag. And to make doubly sure, Róisín went up there on Christmas morning and whistled to Fred, the whistle I captured on my phone. What about the belt?'

'Susanne says she found it in her bag. She thinks Kirby left it there to scare her. She and Róisín took it up to Sliabh Sneacht and left it there, thinking it would have Kirby's DNA on it.'

Molloy turned to me. 'The tests on the sandwich are back, by the way – it was clear. Guinness must have picked up the antifreeze somewhere else, if that's what it was.'

'Really? So a case of paranoia on my part, then.'

Molloy gave me a wry look. 'Except it wasn't, was it?'

'No, I suppose not.' I wrinkled my nose against the sun. 'How is Andy?'

Molloy looked at me in surprise. 'He's good. He's getting some help.'

I looked down. 'I owe you an apology . . .'

'Ben, there's something I need to tell you.' Molloy pushed the blinds aside and looked down at the crowd again, as if it were easier not to meet my eye. I felt a crushing sensation in my chest. Whatever it was, I was pretty sure I didn't want to hear it.

'I've been placed on leave pending an investigation into Kirby's death.'

I spun around. 'What?'

'There's to be an inquest. And they'll probably be looking into my relationship with you.'

'I don't believe you. How can you be so calm about it?'

He turned to me and smiled. 'It's fine. It's what should happen. It's perfectly possible that our relationship clouded my judgement.'

'How long?

'A few months.' He looked down. 'Maybe six.'

'Are you staying here?' I asked, but I knew the answer before the words left my mouth.

He shook his head.

'You're going back to Cork?'

He nodded. 'I think it's better. Just for a while.'

I reached for his hand, and he pulled me close.

Acknowledgements

Those who are familiar with Inishowen will know that whilst the town of Glendara is fictitious, many of the locations I use in my books are real. So, I hope I will be forgiven for some of the liberties I have taken with the landscape and topography in this one. Sliabh Sneacht is a much longer climb than I have portrayed here, and while there may be derelict houses in the area, the cottage portrayed in this book is fictitious.

Culdaff has some great pubs but the Bunagee Bar is not one of them. And while the pier exists, the boat shed does not (or at least not the one in the book!). Thankfully, Lagg, or Five Fingers Strand, exists in all its majesty but it is not a safe place to swim. The Barclay Arms and the Hampton Beach Casino in Derry are also works of fiction. The Dublin-Derry flight no longer exists, I believe, but there are hopes it may be re-instated.

Thank you to the Tyrone Guthrie Centre at Annaghmakerrig, to Maria McManus and her husband Martin, Lily McGonagle, Henrietta McKervey, Natalie Ryan, Jo Spain, Joe Butler, Mark Tottenham, Fidelma Tonry and Una ní Dhubhghaill. All provided advice and support which was invaluable. All errors are of course entirely my own.

Thank you to all my friends and family who continue to support me and say nice things about my books even when they don't have to. And to my fellow crime writers both here and across the water – I've discovered they're a cracking bunch. As are the booksellers.

Thank you to my publishers, Constable/Little, Brown, to Hachette Ireland and to my fantastic agent, Kerry Glencorse.

And finally, love and thanks as always to my family and to Geoff.